MW01047236

As A Roaring Lion

Jack Welles has had a varied working life from seeing action as a professional soldier through flying helicopters commercially to his own practise as an attorney. He now writes full time and is currently based in a small village on False Bay, near Cape Town, South Africa, and is married with one son.

Also by Jack Welles

A Shadow On The Sea
pied_piper.com
The Holy Father Deal

AS A ROARING LION

Jack Welles

Pertech Publishers

A Pertech Book

AS A ROARING LION

By Jack Welles.

First published by Pertech Publishers 2013

ISBN 978-0-620-65605-4

Pertech Publishers, a division of
Madison Financing (Pty) Ltd
Bordage House
St Peter Port
Guernsey
Channel Islands

Pertech Publishers, a division of
Madison Financing (Pty) Ltd
P O Box 15824
Panorama
7506, South Africa

.

Be sober, be vigilant; because your adversary the devil, as a roaring lion, walketh about, seeking whom he may devour.

The First Epistle General of Peter v 8

PART ONE
18 April – 18 May
1985

Mary-Ann Webber stopped halfway along the passage.

Did she look worthy of what she'd been offered?

She shook her head, pulled a face: always the trouble, you generally don't give a damn, suddenly when it mattered, panic attack!

Glanced up: gold lettering, *Professor John H Prins, Dean, Faculty of Wildlife Management,* a statement over brown varnished wood.

She smoothed back her hair: pointless – a tightly tied pony-tail already held it flat back over the top of her head. She hitched up her baggy jeans: meaningless – lived in, faded, nothing was going to improve their appearance.

Mary-Ann sighed, gave up, opened the door, squared her shoulders, stuck out her chin, breezed in.

"Mornin', Susan," she sang out: Deep South modulated by flat vowels, marinated by years in Africa, sun-browned face, even teeth a happy white slash.

A quick look as response, then down, studious opening of a file, tight lips, hunched shoulders.

"Wow! What a way to head into the weekend, with tomorrow being Friday an' all!" Mary-Ann bubbled. "This has gotta be one of my best days ever." Neat bum familiarly perched on the desk corner. "It's my twenty-eighth birthday in just three weeks and I can't imagine a better present."

The Professor's secretary looked up, raised an eyebrow. "Good morning, Doctor." Face carved from the hard wood of a camel thorn tree.

"What's with the 'doctor' stuff?" Mary-Ann laughed out aloud. "I know sitting through one dry old convention speech after another isn't everyone's idea of fun. And I'm not even a participant, just an observer ..." she hesitated, paused for a time, needed to share, bounce off a friend.

"I'm sure most people wouldn't understand, but it's like a reward," Mary-Ann said finally, sunrise across cheeks.

"Recognition for all those years studying." Head shaking, pursed lips. "I don't even have a boyfriend. I've *never* had a *real* boyfriend."

Susan shrugged, flung a white A4-sized envelope across the desk.

"Everything you need is in there, including a return ticket. You're travelling business class with the Professor himself. Because it's an international conference and you have an American passport, you won't need a visa for Argentina. The Professor will be meeting any incidental expenses himself, like taxis and that sort of thing. I don't think there's anything else you'll need from me ... Doctor."

"Susan! What's wrong?"

Mary-Ann grimaced: okay they weren't the biggest buddies in the world but this was like really weird. She knew that being from the States her ways and ideas could be very different to those of the local women, especially the Afrikaners. But she was always careful to keep her more potentially controversial opinions to herself, it couldn't be anything she had said.

Maybe it had to do with Susan herself. Maybe she had a problem. Mary-Ann suddenly realised she had been selfishly running off at the mouth about how wonderful things were for her, maybe Susan had an issue of her own.

"You did go to the concert last night?"

"Yes," Susan said.

Eyes down, hand on papers, head turned away, straight-edged piles on the desk.

Mary-Ann eyed her for a moment, stepped away.

"This is bullshit! I've obviously done something to offend you and I want to know what it is."

*

In the United Kingdom – it being a few weeks into April, and thus on British Summer Time, which is one hour behind Southern Africa, which uses Central Africa Time – Roger Denton, in Wales, could be said to have started drinking early when at 11.35 am, local time, he took a modest – for him – sip of whisky.

His younger brother, Patrick, seemed to swell with importance. Then, standing tall with chest pushed forward, aggressively upright at the fireplace, Patrick deliberately threw down a gauntlet.

Roger's wife, Michelle, poised gracefully on the edge of a chaise lounge, groomed, like always ready for a *Vogue* cover shoot, slowly turned her head in Patrick's direction and, with a barely discernible narrowing of the eyes, willingly accepted the challenge.

Roger slumped lower in his armchair, one leg slung over the arm, cocked his head slightly to one side. It should have been no contest: a foot race and Patrick would have been disqualified at the off with Michelle away to a clean start.

No, Roger thought, not a footrace, it was more like a high stakes boxing match, extremely high stakes, and Patrick, as befitted a London banker, was a cautious soul. So why the challenge? Why now? What was his secret weapon? There had to be something Patrick knew that they didn't.

Roger sank half the remaining whisky in his glass: an engaging contest, two worthy contestants, both happily deploy the most brutal of weapons, no quarter asked or given.

But he wasn't prepared to play referee ...

"You'll have to do without the Queensbury Rules."

But that shouldn't bother either of them, he thought, it hadn't in the past.

Two elegantly coiffured heads swung in his direction, eyebrows rising in unison, two pairs of eyes, cold, peered down, dismissing as irrelevant. He slumped deeper in his chair.

A chilly day in Powys, the fire crackled, spat against the fireguard.

A short silence.

"What *are* you mumbling about?" Michelle demanded, back rigid.

First, Roger thought, by dint of marital practice.

Patrick half-turned to face Roger squarely. "You've been awfully quiet. You must agree it would be for the best. After all, you're half American," he made it sound like an unpleasant social disease.

"Papa!" Michelle exclaimed suddenly. "Should you be up?"

Dayfydd Denton, sagged against the door-frame, propped up by a hawthorn walking-stick: spare frame, bones and hollows, clothes, despite obvious quality, shapeless rags on a beggar. Every bone prominent, cranium to jawline: a skull for demonstration purposes in a medical school.

Roger sprang up and hurried across the drawing room. "Michelle's right. You ought to be in bed."

Dayfydd: fifty-nine, going on seventy-nine. Roger still horrified: unwelcome news, unacceptable, that day heard for the first time. The call to come down from London on a Thursday was unusual, especially in the tail end of winter before spring had made its presence felt, but that was not by itself alarming, so he'd had no premonition of what now faced them all.

He helped his father into the nearest chair, gently, a basket of fresh eggs.

Back in his own chair, leaning forward, elbows on knees, manufactured a grin, hoped it looked better than it felt: "In good British tradition we were talking about the weather and how it should soon be bringing the garden alive."

Patrick, lounging against the mantelpiece, raised his eyebrows in Michelle's direction. "If you don't mind, my dear. A little private family business. It will be of short duration." Looking down his nose, "I'm sure you understand."

*

In South Africa Mary-Ann stared at Susan, determined, there had to be a reason. Stood there, demand unspoken, waiting, stubborn when needed.

Slowly pressure built up. Mary-Ann was damned if she would crack first.

Susan suddenly burst out, "You must be careful, Mary-Ann! That's if you only know the Professor academically. Then you'd ... on the other hand if ..." a long pause, "no, it's none of my business ... but I admire you so much, I brag to all my friends about knowing you and ... no, never mind, better leave it."

Mary-Ann waited a beat, and then a bit longer, when sure Susan was going to say no more, waved her hands in the air. "And? And better leave *what*?"

"I can't afford to upset anyone. My husband's in politics and in politics you have to be careful. He's right. I should keep my nose out of other peoples' business."

"But I'm *inviting* you in. I want to know what the hell you're talking about!"

"No!" Susan gestured at the envelope which lay on the desk between them. "You have everything you need. Your flight leaves tomorrow night. It's all in there. I'm sure you have a lot of packing to do."

Susan refused to say another word, responded only in monosyllables. Eventually Mary-Ann shrugged, left.

*

In Wales, Roger tried once more. "Now isn't the right time," he drawled, more mildly than he felt.

"I support Father on this," Patrick replied. "We chatted yesterday. He has concerns." He turned around, raised his eyebrows, "Michelle, if you please?"

Roger had difficulty hiding his frustration, but better to keep his feelings from escalating any tensions already there. So Patrick's sucker punch *was* the old man. And yesterday! The little bastard had come down early, he had being priming Dayfydd. Make it all seem like their father's idea.

Cunning – as usual.

Michelle looked helplessly around the room: outflanked, hadn't even tested the defences with so much as a tentative glove. She stood, drew herself up, regrouping as best she could.

She sniffed. "Well, I hadn't intended staying through to the weekend."

Roger suddenly sympathised. "I remember. You said. I'll stay for a while, follow on tomorrow. The breakfast train."

Michelle tossed the black curls of her expensively casual hairstyle, nodded to no-one in particular, hesitated, and with no civilized alternative, swayed out of the room.

"Father," Patrick said, "you'll recall our conversation."

Roger stirred in his chair, tried for nonchalant. "We can sort it out later."

Dayfydd shook his head, looked down at the walking-stick, still clutched in both hands, upright between his knees, as though he needed the additional support even when sitting.

The old man spoke at last, digging deep, hauled up words, one by one. "Patrick's right ... to be worried about the family name. I respect that. I've tried to do the right thing by it all my life. He shares my values."

Roger grimaced inwardly: like hell he does. But no one could tell the old man that – especially not now.

"You're the oldest ... of course, the title, and everything that goes with it, normally yours," the old man paused to cough, his body jerking, "but I'm worried ... Patrick's right ... waited a long time ... and time ..." he fell silent again.

Dayfydd stooped, shoulders bent, weight of a world with changed rules. Defeated eyes peered out from under bushy eyebrows, prepared to surrender the dark caves at the slightest suggestion of an attack.

Roger's lips tightened. Damn Patrick! It was wrong to put the old man under this sort of pressure. Patrick stirred restlessly alongside the fireplace, made as though to speak, caught the expression on Roger's face, kept quiet.

"I'm sorry, my boy," Dayfydd said, a little too loudly. "There just isn't any other way of dealing with it. It's all tied up together by the old Entail."

The old man coughed, lungs convulsing: the leukaemia he had told them about that day wreaking havoc. The doctors thought Dayfydd could live for another year or even, maybe, two. But as a high-risk patient it depended on the extent to which the chemotherapy, and radiation therapy to the head, if necessary, and the blood transfusions, kept the condition under control.

"It's all or nothing," Dayfydd added. "That's the way it is. But you know all this. Was relying on you, being the oldest. Even though your mother and I ... well ..." he broke off to cough into his handkerchief and was quiet for a while.

"All right, Dad," Roger said at last. "What is it you really want?"

*

The next day, Friday, was going to be busy making sure her desk was clear for the time she would be in South America. So at her flat Mary-Ann had a suitcase open on her bed, with arms half-folded, chin propped on a fist, standing in front of the half-open wardrobe, wondering where to start.

Her indecisiveness bugged her: where was Ms 'Super Efficiency' now?

Normally packing was not a problem. But that was for the bush. And, except for her basic schooling, she hadn't been off African soil since her father had brought her over as a young girl. And what she remembered of their previous home – in the Louisiana Everglades – could be engraved on a pinhead with room to spare.

"Damn it," Mary-Ann muttered aloud.

But she wasn't fooled: the indecision was not about what to pack but what had happened earlier that day. Susan's attitude had her more uptight than she could remember being for ages: it was like waiting for exam results.

And it was unfair! This was one of the most exciting developments in her life: it was taking her career to a new stage. Doors were beginning to open that would take her from the narrow confines of academia out into the real world: where she could even dare to begin imagining that her ideas – ideas from when she was a little girl – could end up influencing conservation thinking, not just on the local level, but on an international scale.

"Damn it," she said again, addressing her image in the tall mirror on the cupboard door.

She grunted: tension, just one quick answer, her sport could be more than a competitive outlet and a means of keeping fit.

She shrugged, trying to loosen the tension in her shoulders before she started, uncomfortable, clothes too tight. Deliberately, steady breathing, mind closed to confusion, focus on emptiness, strip down to bra and pants.

Slowly she sunk, knees bent, arms flexed, into the cat stance, always the start of her taekwondo *hyung*: pose held for a short while, longer than a beat, feeling the surface tension drain away. And then, soon afterwards, the stillness sinking into her inner, centred self.

At peace, mind clear, she went through her favourite formal *hyung* in slow-motion – a sequence of carefully controlled and balanced movements – ended in the back stance, held it for a moment, felt poised, balanced and calm all at the same time.

"Yiah!" she yelled.

Spinning around, launched a round-house kick at the open cupboard door, heel of her foot extended. At the last split-second, a micro-millimetre away from the target, holding back, using just enough energy, a door moving gently to the closed position, a faint click of the latch signalling it had gone exactly the right distance.

She grinned, and then laughed out aloud.

"You go, girl!" she exclaimed.

Feeling calmer now, she slowly began to assemble items of personal clothing on the bed. But the gentle warmth from the *hyung* faded, tempered by the remembrance of Susan's strange, out-of-character behaviour.

*

Roger had sat quietly still, patiently, ignoring the uproar inside his head, not in his hands now. All he could do was wait and hear his father out.

"Patrick has always done well," Dayfydd said. "A born leader. President of Pop at Eton and a Sixth Form Select. All firsts at Cambridge. Now doing damned well in the City. At the old bank, too, where you should have stayed ... it all belongs together, you know. Not allowed to have it all over the place. Got to rely on Patrick. No one else now. That's why the old title should ... he's right about that ..." and his voice faded away as he again coughed into his hand. His face carried the grey pallor of the small clouds that scurry ahead of really bad storms. "I'm sorry, old son. Don't want to pull the rug out from under you. No choice really."

Roger was motionless. The family had never understood, maybe never believed, he didn't give a rat's ass about the title: more like his Republican American mother than his Conservative Welsh father. And it was certainly way beyond anything Patrick could imagine. But the title and family name meant so much to Dayfydd to stress that now would be a slap in the face for the old man, that's for sure!

Respect, belief, trust, understanding, worthiness – okay, unearned maybe, all right, if he's being honest here, definitely unearned – but still basically worthy of the title, but not the title itself. Definitely not the title – damn the bloody title! But to ask him to give it up, in effect take it away from him – that was saying that he was no damned good and never would be. Put together with Patrick going even further and effectively trying to hijack the damned thing and Roger felt – perversely – like putting up a fight.

Bugger the little prick!

A thought suddenly occurred: born out of the time frame in which the old man had phrased his request – a possible reprieve – temporary maybe, but still a reprieve. He sighed to himself: Michelle was going to be a problem. He didn't give a damn about Patrick. But how the hell was he going to juggle things to keep both Dayfydd and Michelle happy at the same time? He knew how much this meant to her – maybe even too much?

"Tell you what," Roger suggested at last, "when the time comes –"

Out of the corner of his eye, on the edge of his peripheral vision, he could see Patrick lean forward as though craning to hear someone else's whispered conversation, the knuckles of the clasped hands white.

"– and may that be a hell of a long time from now, if I haven't got an honourable purpose for the title, I'll give it up and Patrick can have it."

Patrick straightened, frowning, half-shook his head. He turned to his father, made as though to speak, but when Roger waved him down and simultaneously nodded in Dayfydd's direction, Patrick hesitated. But he was still rigid, still leaning forward, still tense and still kept his eyes fixed on the old man.

Roger smiled blandly, just for once he should prove them wrong. And when they had seen the light he would give it up anyway. He suddenly grinned: what a pity Patrick wasn't a more deserving recipient of such a possible future generosity.

His father stared gravely at him. "On your word of honour?"

Roger went blank. Christ! Wasn't his saying it enough?

He inclined his head slightly. "Yessir," he said. "On my word of honour."

"That's good enough for me," declared his father, nodding his head in relief, as though he had just managed to extricate himself from a nasty bramble bush.

"But Roger can't ..." Patrick spoke softly, more like thinking aloud. He quickly glanced at Roger, clearly embarrassed and annoyed with himself simultaneously.

"*Can't* ..." Roger repeated the word quietly, added tersely, "What were you about to say?"

"Am tired ..." Dayffydd obviously missed the low-voiced comments, deflected the muted exchange, "... need to lie down now ... can't keep going the way I used to."

"Sure," Roger nodded, "need a hand up the stairs?"

Dayfydd smiled at him, shook his head. "Not that far gone yet. Can still do it meself." Then suddenly bobbed his head, "Dammit yes – I'd 'preciate that."

Roger gave Patrick a quick glance. "I'll be back in a minute."

But when Roger returned to the drawing room Patrick was no longer there, and on checking discovered that his younger brother had already left to return to London.

Well, Roger would also be in London the next day.

He stared out of the window at the long shadows, as they almost imperceptibly grew during the extended twilight; the sun, faintly visible through the clouds, slowly disappearing behind the Cambrian Mountains, purple in the distance.

He walked over to the liquor cabinet and poured himself a tumbler full of whisky.

*

Waiting in the queue to pass through immigration, checked boarding card and passport. A dream come true and nothing must be allowed to spoil that. Lost in her thoughts, belatedly realising the voice from behind was intended for her ears.

"Mary-Ann Webber! I thought it was you."

A glance back over her shoulder, recognised bushy eyebrows. "Hi, Dr Fourse. I'd heard you were leading the delegation. Congratulations."

He inclined his head graciously.

"Have you seen your father recently?" Fourse was a bulky grey-haired man in his late fifties, wearing an open-necked white shirt under a brown checked sports coat. "Is he still the same?"

"I phoned yesterday, to tell him about this trip. He hasn't changed. Never says much." Mary-Ann shrugged. "He may have left the States after burying my mom but he's never forgotten. Still blames himself. Silly stuff about scientists being meant to prevent these things."

Fourse nodded. "It's a horrible disease. My grandmother had it. It's terrible to watch. At the end she was in so much pain. She'd look so much better with a transfusion and almost immediately start to weaken again." He paused, then asked, "Where you off to?"

A grin, broad and happy. "Same place as you."

"The CITES conference?" Eyes widening, eyebrows rising, inflection noted. "In what capacity?"

"Only as an observer." Reply cheerful, innocent, a smile. "Don't worry, your position as conservation spokesman isn't in any danger."

He returned the smile. "Maybe not now. But I'm not so sure about the future. We're all *very* well aware of your abilities."

A healthy warmth spreading from neck to cheeks.

"Mmmm," she mumbled.

He nodded, eyes wrinkling. "I was pleased to hear you'd left private practice. Conservation needs people like you."

Embarrassed, new subject, quickly. "I couldn't handle making sure the nails of pampered poodles were properly cut."

The real reason hidden, a private obsession, the underlying theme of a doctoral thesis, not yet disclosed. Even her promoter, Professor Prins, hadn't yet realised what actually drove her research. He would have to know, but only when she was able finally to substantiate her idea scientifically.

"It had to be conservation," added lightly, "it's the family business."

He nodded. "I remember. Your father once told me *his* father was US Fish and Wildlife. But how come you're going to the conference? When I was a postgrad I couldn't afford trips to South America."

Laughing out aloud. "Nothing's changed. I'm still as poor as a church mouse. Prof organised the whole thing."

"Prins?" Fourse's mouth turned down, he frowned. "Through some sort of grant or student aid fund?"

Puzzling tone, strange attitude, a bad vibe, little understood.

Shrug of slender shoulders. "I haven't had time to think about it. Only found out yesterday, haven't seen Prof for a week. I'm just so excited to be going over."

"That's odd." Words heavy, corners of a mouth pulling down the ends of a grey moustache. "These things have to be planned well in advance. You can't be certain of a seat."

Another shrug. "Maybe a cancellation. And Prof has those political connections. I don't know." She waved her hands in the air. "Does it matter?"

"Well ... maybe not ..." his voice trailed away.

"What's the problem?"

"Nothing. It's none of my business ... I can't afford trouble."

First Susan and now Fourse: a bad taste, expectation dragged down by undercurrents. Why spoil her trip? She wished she knew the man better, could demand an explanation.

"Passport and boarding card, please." The young man in the white shirt and blue trousers, about her own age, looked up, did a double take, raised his eyebrows in appreciation, smiled fawningly.

Typically, Mary-Ann didn't notice his reaction, still wondering what lay behind Fourse's attitude. On being handed back her boarding card and passport, duly stamped, she deliberately waited on the other side of the barrier.

A few seconds later Fourse also cleared immigration. Before she could resume the conversation, he quickly excused himself, saying he wanted to look around the duty-free shop, hurried off without a goodbye. Mary-Ann took the escalator downstairs to join the queue waiting to go through the security checkpoint.

As the queue shuffled forward she reviewed the week's events. Was it just her? She knew she was quite simply no good with people. Being raised in the bush hadn't helped. Her single-minded approach to study and research had exacerbated the situation. It left her little time for a social life, which she didn't want anyway. What she wanted was to be taken seriously on conservation issues.

Being invited to attend the CITES – the Convention on International Trade in Endangered Species of Wild Fauna and Flora – at COP 5 – the fifth meeting of the Conference of the Parties – even just as an observer, was the first small step to being recognised as an intelligent conservationist, someone serious, who did dedicated and valuable scientific work, someone with a worthwhile contribution to make.

*

Patrick's secretary at the bank had already left to go home at the normal close of business. So it was his personal assistant who beckoned to Roger, giving him a half-apologetic grimace.

"You can go through now," the PA said, not meeting Roger's eyes.

Roger again glanced at his watch. His train had arrived in London at ten in the morning and he had made his way straight to the bank, keen to have things out with his brother. It was already well past six on the Friday afternoon.

Now he stormed through, slammed the door closed behind him, marched up to Patrick's desk, leaned across it, on his fists.

"Did you really think I'd give up and go away?"

"I have been in meetings. Some of us spend more time working than drinking."

Roger eyed Patrick for a moment. "Let's talk about yesterday. You *have* been a busy little fellow, haven't you?"

When Patrick didn't respond, Roger hooked a chair across and sat down.

Patrick fidgeted, rose to his feet, walked over to the big bay window behind his desk, stood looking down at the street below. His back was to Roger, who was hard put to stifle his irritation.

Patrick cleared his throat. "I don't have to listen to this. And certainly not from you."

"But you want the title, and what goes with it, so badly you can't afford to have me thrown out, can you? And I'm the oldest. So I have to give it up for you to get it. You can't buck the Entail, can you?" After a pause Roger added, "And if you hadn't selfishly stuffed that sick old man around I might have been more obliging."

"If you think I had anything to do with causing Father to be concerned, you're dead wrong! He approached me on the subject. He asked to see me early. To see how I felt about things. He's worried about what happens when he ... you know."

Roger grimaced: always on the back foot, always feeling guilty, there had to be something he could do. Damn it! Was it as simple as a change of attitude? Like giving up smoking ...

"I can come back to the bank if necessary."

"You haven't managed a decent day's work since you were asked to leave the navy." Patrick sniffed. "You certainly didn't overwork yourself while you were here." And after a beat he added, "And you drink too much."

"It was my choice, I resigned my commission."

It felt as though he spent his whole life making excuses. Suddenly, desperately, he wished things were different. For both the old man and himself.

"And I *have* worked. You know damned well I've commentated sports for ITV."

Patrick turned around to face Roger. He leaned back to half-sit on the window-sill. "I'm impressed," he said flatly, his face in shadow with the light of the window behind him, but despite that clearly smiling. "What was it again – a dinghy race on the Thames?" His eyebrows went up like two black cockroaches on his forehead. "Or maybe I have that wrong? Maybe it was two dinghy races."

"You're a pain in the ass, you know that, don't you? Come to think of it, you always ... ah, forget it. It's crazy the two of us arguing like this. It doesn't prove a thing. And it certainly doesn't help Dad."

"The solution is in your hands. You could put father's mind at rest with a simple phone call. Why don't you? He's seriously concerned about the estate, and the title is part of that, and a major say in this bank is part of it, too. If my side of the family was next in line it would alleviate his concerns." Patrick paused a beat. "And you know it."

Roger squirmed slightly, projected a different role for himself in the future: what would it be like to have Patrick confide in him, discuss developments, ask his opinion? Better still, he wondered what it would be like to have his father phone him to ask him to come down a day early when important family matters were to be discussed.

For a moment, and not for the first time, he really wanted to be part of the British side of his family: a useful part. His mother had gone on to a new life in the States with a new husband and a new young family: there was no place for him there. Having spent much of his teen years growing up in America after his parents were divorced hadn't helped the feeling of being outside the inner family circle in the UK. But he wanted to be someone the others looked up to, whose opinion they respected. Perhaps if he gave up the title now they would think more of him, maybe even involve him in the family business.

Then he caught the expression on Patrick's face. This was exactly the deal the little bastard was trying to sell him. Respect him, involve him in family decision-making –

would they hell! Patrick was trying his damndest to squeeze him out even further than he was already. Then they would have even less reason to deal with him. Then he really would be on the outside looking in!

"I made my promise." And after a beat added defiantly, "I might surprise you all one of these days."

"I can hardly imagine how. You're just an ex-sportsman – a has-been!" Patrick sneered. "And you drink," he now paused a beat, almost mockingly, and added deliberately, "too much."

"Unless I change my mind about the promise, maybe when Michelle and I have an heir –"

"But you can't have any children!" Patrick interrupted triumphantly, and, with a hand to his mouth, it was clear he instantly regretted having spoken.

Patrick swung away to stare blankly out the window once more.

Roger was on his feet. "So that's what you started to say yesterday. How do you know?"

Patrick shrugged again. "I just do."

Roger took three long strides forward, put his hand on Patrick's shoulder and spun him around. Patrick tried to shrug him off. Roger grabbed his brother by the lapels of his double-breasted jacket, jammed him up against the wall next to the bay window, held him high so that he was up on his toes. "There's no such thing as 'just know', you sleazy little shit."

When Patrick made no reply Roger slammed him backwards and Patrick grunted involuntarily as his back hit the wall. "Come on, how do you know?"

Patrick shrugged, trying for casual, clearly intimidated. "I hired someone ... to check up. You know ... a private person. It was some sort of sporting accident. We wondered why you had no children .... Why shouldn't we?" He demanded defiantly. "The title's at stake. What happens if you don't give it up *and* you never have children?"

"You know damn well. You, or your little Peter, get it when I die."

"But it doesn't mean anything to you. And in the meantime, control of the estate would mean so much to me. Everything is in limbo the way things are now. Your giving it up would assure me of the chair on the Bank's board. The City has a proper regard for that sort of thing – even if you don't."

Patrick jerked himself free from Roger's hands, brushed himself off and carefully rearranged his lapels, regaining his composure as he did so.

"Aren't you anticipating a little. Surely the old man's got to die first. It could still take a year or two."

"Of course ... but if you publicly announce it now everyone would know my side would be next in line ... that would be enough."

"It *was* you that stirred the old man up, wasn't it? I didn't think he'd come up with it by himself. And you're telling him it's the family honour you're worried about –"

"We have to worry about that, too," Patrick interrupted hastily

"– instead of which you just want it for yourself."

"All you've done is a bit of sailing, some power boating and that sports broadcasting. With Michelle's income from her father you're set up. It doesn't matter you're not really good at anything."

"I did all right at sailing –"

"When you did it!" Patrick interjected, as he scurried behind the safety of his desk.

Suddenly – more than anything else he had ever wanted – Roger wanted to prove his brother wrong, wanted Dayfydd's unqualified approval and Michelle's respect.

*

She was unaccustomed to travelling long-distances by air so even Mary-Ann's excitement could not provide a foil for jet lag. She took strain from the effects of the long flight from Johannesburg to Heathrow and then the connecting

flight to Buenos Aires and, as a result, what was left of
Saturday passed by without her leaving her hotel room and
without her really noticing it.

In any event there wasn't anyone she knew for company
as the official members of the delegation were not so lucky.
They tried to ignore the weariness by indulging in desultory
strategy-planning sessions with delegations from other
countries on the African sub-continent.

But Mary-Ann did use the Sunday to explore Buenos
Aires, although in a limited fashion because of the dire
warnings by, amongst others, the Hyatt Hotel concierge,
about the scourge of pickpockets and the chance of being
mugged, apparently in broad daylight if you went about on
foot. But she did want to get out as a way of thinking about
something other than the lingering unease generated by
Susan and Fourse.

Mary-Ann, who had spent most of her life in Africa, a
dusty, dry and mostly brown environment, was overawed
by the strong colours and scents of Buenos Aires, the
Argentinean capital. She thought that the city had an
exuberant and beautiful buzz and the wide boulevards,
green parks and French-inspired architecture were awe-
inspiring.

But, on foot outside of a taxi, and still conscious of the
warnings, she stuck to the Recoleta neighbourhood, which
she was told had the city's most exclusive shops, not that
she was into shopping. The area had many cafes too, but
when lunchtime came around, true to type, all she did was
make do with a quick hamberguesa from a street side
kiosko, while hugging her bag close in to her side.

A big moment for her was a visit to the Recoleta
Cemetery where Eva Peron had been buried. Mary-Ann
wasn't particularly interested in all the other notables
buried there, of which there were many, but Maria Eva
Duarte de Peron, as Mary-Ann always thought of her, had
for so long been one of her heroes as a woman ahead of her
time in standing up for women's rights and for her passion

and combativeness in fighting for what she believed in, that the cemetery was a must visit.

But the surrounding mausoleums, despite their intricate architecture, instead of impressing her, soon intruded and somehow got her back to thinking about Susan and Fourse so she hurried away from there and returned to the hotel.

In the hotel dining room for the evening meal Mary-Ann was once again on her own. And again Prins and Fourse shared a table with the other two delegates. She was not invited to join them. She had hardly sat down when a young man she hadn't seen before asked if he could sit at her table for the meal.

"It's pretty full," he said, waving a hand at the dining-room.

Mary-Ann looked around, smiled to herself, a few tables were still empty, but she could do with the company. "Go ahead."

She sneaked a peek at him from under lowered eyelids: not bad looking, about her own age, maybe a few years younger. And by his accent clearly American.

After exchanging pleasantries and when she told him she was with the South African delegation as an observer, he suddenly leaned forward, intense, putting both hands on the table.

"They want to trade in elephant products."

"Yes," she replied cautiously: he sounded surprisingly vehement.

"Doesn't it make you sick – people actually wanting to kill animals?"

"Not really," she said coldly. "They have scientific reasons for their stand."

"Did you see the demo outside? I helped organise that. Didn't you get the message? Threatened species have to be protected."

"It seemed a little over the top."

"I wanted real blood on the hotel steps."

Mary-Ann felt the heat in her cheeks, banged her fist down on the table hard, drew one or two glances from surrounding diners, didn't notice. "Using hysterically emotional tactics while professing to support the principle of protecting threatened species doesn't impress."

"What specific principle do you support?"

"To ensure the sustainable utilisation of species – such as elephant – which support thousands in rural communities as well as major industries."

People at nearby tables now openly stared at her.

"It looks," he said triumphantly, "like your lot aren't going to get their way."

"Sure," she replied, sitting up straight. "It's countries who have no elephant, know nothing about elephant and probably don't give a damn about elephant who are going to make the final decision. Like the South Americans here doing little political deals on the side, to avoid being punished internationally for the continued rape of their forests."

"But that doesn't justify the killing of animals. That's the principle that counts."

Mary-Ann stared at the young American. Clearly he hadn't heard a word she had said.

"Do you want to save the elephants from extinction or stop the killing? They're two different things."

"Animals have rights, too," he said stiffly, as he stood up, "and it's about time murderers, with blood on their hands, are forced to respect those rights."

Mary-Ann watched him thread his way through the tables, heading for the door. She sighed to herself –

that went well.

So much for her social graces – and for the company.

*

Late on the Sunday evening, in the sitting-room of their London townhouse, Roger sat slumped in his favourite armchair, waiting for Michelle. He could no longer put off dealing with her, as he had been doing, since his conversation with Patrick. What was she going to make of his promise to Dayfydd? He took a serious swig of whisky, stared gloomily at the glass in his hand: bloody stuff wasn't doing its usual job.

He squinted up at the oil painting which hung above the fireplace. Artfully placed lamps highlighted Roger's paternal grandfather, resplendent in his admiral's uniform. No other lights were on in the room making the portrait even more conspicuous than usual. His illustrious ancestor frowned down at him.

He saluted the painting with his glass, took another deep draught.

He became aware of being watched from the doorway, looked across.

"Michelle," he nodded warily, by way of greeting. "I couldn't find you."

"I had to go out." She dismissed the subject with an elegant wave of her hand.

He nodded. Everything had to be elegant, as elegant as she was beautiful.

"I phoned Dayfydd earlier."

"You what? The old man's sick!"

"I'm your wife. I'm entitled to know what happened after I left. To make sure you hadn't done something irrevocably stupid!"

Roger was at a loss for words. Jesus! They were all so goddamned selfish!

"He told me about your promise," she said, "at least *he* seems pleased with you."

She stared at him with *that* expression on her face – an entomologist studying a bug stuck on the end of a pin.

"You did really well once I left, didn't you?" she remarked, her tone mild. Then she shook her head, smiling. "Without me ..."

Roger shrugged, as usual, once again on the back foot, at a loss for words.

"No killer instinct. That's why you were such a really, really great sporting success. No backbone."

He stirred uncomfortably.

"It seemed a fair compromise at the time. It defused the situation. Father's ill, seriously ill," he added pointedly.

"Your coach once told me you were one of the few football players he'd ever come across who could've played in any position. And it wasn't just football. You were good enough for pro baseball, too ..." she paused for a moment.

He closed his eyes for a fraction of a second: did she enjoy these conversations?

"You tried out for the NFL while still in high school. You were one of the most promising rookies they'd ever seen. But it ended right there. You could've done so much, gone so far. And then – of course – there's the drinking ..."

Normally he would just wait for the storm to pass, it was easier that way. Was that the problem: always taking the easy way out? And then – for some reason which was to him unclear – he suddenly decided he wasn't ducking situations anymore.

"If I'm so useless why hang on to me? Genuine question. Why don't we just part company now? You've got all the money. I won't want alimony." Roger added with a quirky smile, "I'll give you that in writing."

Momentarily Michelle seemed taken aback, then nodded to herself. "Hmmm – clearly you've been drinking." She raised her eyebrows. "I suppose it must be love."

She smiled – a cat watching a cornered mouse.

He hated to admit it, but Michelle was right. He had a quick eye, reliable hands that turned the worst-passed ball into a good one. And it wasn't just ball games. He also had the feel for the wind in a sail. He was – *had been* – a natural when it came to sport. So where had it all gone wrong?

"You lack killer instinct."

Was something lacking? He had also dropped out of Cambridge after a few years of engineering. Perhaps he had just never needed to put himself out, always being content with things the way they were, just gone with the flow. He sat up straight. Now there was Patrick's attitude, Dayfydd's leukaemia, his approaching thirtieth birthday, the look on Michelle's face ...

He felt a sudden need. Why not make something happen? All he required was the right project ....

"Even the proposal that never happened. I had to do that for you."

And a 'yes' had seemed easier than a 'no'. He sighed, probably not the best reason to get married ...

"You're not going to let your family pressure you into doing something stupid, are you?"

He studied Michelle for a while. If she thought so little of him – what was in it for her? Did the social status mean that much? A hugely respected title in the offing ...

A sudden insight: maybe she needed him to be the way he was – *had been?* Maybe feeding off his inadequacies kept her going, made her feel strong. He squirmed, it was like playing host to a blood-sucker.

"Well," she demanded, "are you going to be stupid about this?" she stamped her foot, impatient at his lack of a response.

"About what?" he asked tiredly.

"Giving up the title, of course. What else could we be talking about?"

He hesitated, considered denying the importance of what he had promised his father, just doing the usual, taking the easy way out.

She stared at him. "Well, what are you going to do?"

He avoided her large olive-shaped eyes by studying the portrait of the Admiral above the fireplace, splendid in his formal uniform, chest awash with medals.

An idea suddenly occurred, inspired by his maritime ancestor. A damned good idea. And it could work. He had the contacts, through Cambridge and family. For that reason – if no other – he stood a better chance than the average guy of putting the plan together. Dayfydd, for one, would love it.

Roger looked up at the portrait again. Had the Admiral stopped frowning? He certainly wasn't smiling. But maybe just a glint of approval in the old goat's eyes?

"Well?" demanded Michelle.

Roger wasn't a complex human being. He knew that. Subtlety wasn't his long suit. If he was going to run with a ball he would just go up the middle of the field. And simply do his best to run over, or through, any opponent who got in his way. So he was about to share his thoughts with Michelle when some atavistic understanding of their relationship stopped him. He dared not tell her about his embryonic idea. Let it grow a little. It was too vulnerable to be exposed to something like sarcasm or contempt – probably couldn't even handle being patronised.

"Yes?" she queried again, more loudly this time.

Hell! It could even get worse: if he was right about her really needing him to be a failure, wouldn't she be inclined to actually sabotage his efforts?

"I'll think of something," he mumbled, flapping a hand in the air.

He avoided her eyes, kept his gaze fixed on the portrait above the fireplace. Was the old goat showing minuscule signs of approval?

Fanciful?

Perhaps – but who cared?

Roger knew what he wanted to do, needed to do and he had what was left of the evening to get some sort of basic proposal on paper and he knew just where to go with that, too.

*

Breakfasting alone, Mary-Ann was happy. Waking up in Argentina – in South America! – and to know the bit of time she had spent exploring at least a small part of Buenos Aires hadn't been a dream, was already enough to make that Monday perfect. But with the CITES conference to come – it was all just incredible – unbelievable!

She saw three of the four South African delegates seated at another table but decided not to try and join them. They would want to discuss tactics. She would be in the way. She was just an observer.

Professor Prins stopped on his way past her table. "Don't make any arrangements for tonight."

"What?" Caught by surprise it took her moment to comprehend what he had said.

"Sure," she nodded finally, shrugged, smiling.

Some time later the delegates trooped out of the dining-room. Mary-Ann quickly signed the hotel chit for breakfast and hurried after them. Unsure of herself she hesitated after climbing aboard the bus. She didn't want to be a nuisance. Towards the back Prins was deep in conversation with Fourse. The two younger members of the team sat forward on their seats, in the row behind the two older men, listening over their shoulders.

As she hesitated, one of the younger men looked up, saw her and nudged his companion. The first one whispered something, talking close to the second one's ear. The second young man glanced up at her and laughed behind his hand.

She hadn't realised how much of an outsider, a stranger, she would feel: a leper. She sighed to herself. She was simply no good at social situations. So she kept to herself, near the front of the bus, well away from the four men.

Later that morning, in a corridor, she saw Fourse walking towards her. Having been on her own since they had arrived she was pleased at the idea of having someone to talk to. But he turned away when he saw her, presenting her with his back.

That evening, sitting on her bed, she answered a knock on the door. It was Prins. He invited her down to the cocktail lounge for a drink. She was more than happy to be out of her hotel room and to have someone to talk to.

Sitting in the lounge with a glass of white wine Mary-Ann felt emotionally drained by the day's events. "I never realised it would be so depressing."

"I have the perfect antidote. I'm taking you out to dinner. Just the two of us, and ..." he held up his hand like a policeman on point duty, "... it's absolutely *verboten* to talk shop. I'm going to concentrate on cheering up my favourite student."

Mary-Ann squirmed a little, feeling awkward. He had always been formal with her. And she was just so bad at social situations. So she shrugged off her misgivings: Prins clearly also felt good about being in South America. And Argentina was still exciting even if the CITES conference for the moment was proving to be less so.

"In that case," she said, half-rising to curtsy, "I'd be happy to join you for dinner."

During the meal the Professor continued to make personal comments. Too much so for Mary-Ann's liking. He kept ordering new bottles of wine – or so it seemed to her – insisted on refilling her glass after every sip. Soon she lost track of how much she'd had.

When she asked him to take it easy, he made her feel ungrateful for the trouble he had taken on her behalf. As a result she drank more than she usually did. By the end of the meal Mary-Ann was tired, had a headache and wanted to go to bed.

"I've had enough," she said finally. "It's been a long day. I really need to get back to the hotel."

He smiled slyly. "That suits me."

As they entered the hotel he suggested coffee in her room – an appropriate end to the evening. Mary-Ann hesitated. She had already decided there wouldn't be another evening out with Prins. The man was too pushy by half. Then she sighed to herself: what harm could a cup of coffee do?

"Okay," she agreed reluctantly.

She didn't want to appear ungrateful. After that she would be rid of him.

In her room, while waiting for room service to appear, Prins kept walking around and his nervous fiddling with things irritated her. She just wanted him gone. Suddenly he turned to face her.

"You're a beautiful young woman."

Mary-Ann wryly twisted her mouth. "Mmmm," she responded, feeling uncomfortable, adding quickly, "Please excuse me. I have to use the bathroom."

The rooms were en suite. She didn't really want to go, but felt increasingly claustrophobic.

"I hope you're changing into something more comfortable," he said lightly, his eyes unsmiling.

She closed the bathroom door behind her, puffed out her cheeks, blew the air out in a rush, sat on the side of the bath, relieved to be on her own. Prins seemed odd. Was he drunk? What the hell to do? She decided to stay in the bathroom until the coffee arrived.

After a few minutes she heard the outside door. She quickly stood up, tugged her skirt straight, went back into the bedroom. A waiter was placing a tray on the table. Prins dropped a coin into the waiter's palm, winked at him.

The coffee was hot, burnt her mouth, was gulped down anyway, determined, had to have him out of her hotel room as soon as possible, annoyed with herself for having allowing him in at all. Prins sipped at his cup, taking his time.

"I'm sorry," she said, not sounding sorry at all. "You'll have to go now." She put her empty cup down firmly on the tray.

Prins raised his eyebrows, made no move to leave. "I'm disappointed in you, Mary-Ann. You're not showing much gratitude."

"Don't be silly." Muscles worked in her cheeks. "Of course I'm grateful, but I'm tired. I want to go to bed."

"So do I." He winked at her.

Mary-Ann took a deep breath. "You! – Out! – Now!"

He stared at her for a while.

"Who do you think paid for your flight?" Prins asked at length. "Where do you think the money came from for all of this?" He waved a hand around the room.

"You'll get every cent back," she said quietly, not knowing how she was going to raise the money: it must have cost a fortune. But she would find it somewhere – that she was determined to do.

Now she'd really had enough so added, fiercely. "Now GO!"

He stared at her.

"If you insist – for the moment," he said at last and stalked out of the room.

With a sigh Mary-Ann sat down on the edge of her bed, stressed, capitulation had come too easily, too quickly, suspiciously so after his earlier attitude. And what had he meant by 'for the moment'? Or was she quite simply being paranoid?

She buried her face in her hands, it was hard to believe: Professor Prins was the leading wildlife conservation scientist on the African continent, much of the work her own father did in Kruger – for the Washington-based Wildlife Research Trust – was under Prins' aegis, he being their leading consultant. And what must the other South African delegates be thinking? Is this why the uncomfortable atmosphere she had sensed earlier?

Wearily, tired beyond words, she stood up, stripped naked, stretched, and stood there for a moment looking at herself in the tall mirror next to the dresser. She wondered if the Professor had meant what he had said about her being beautiful. Or was it just a line to get her into bed? Because it didn't seem that way to her. Sure, she had no great faults, except that her legs were a little too thin for the rest of her – and too long! She looked like some sort of antelope – perhaps the rare bongo. That gave her the giggles. Then the tears welled up – much to her annoyance. She dried her eyes, determined to not let it get her down. It was probably the booze. She wasn't used to it.

She went through into the bathroom and turned on the water in the bath, waiting for it to fill up before she got herself wet. About to step in she noticed the speaker on the wall. The bathroom was wired for sound.

"Excellent," she muttered aloud, "Classical music and a long hot soak."

Anticipation already had her feeling better. Mary-Ann made her way back into the main room. The radio and TV controls were built into the bed's headboard. She knelt on the bed and leaned forward. A scraping sound behind her. She jumped off the bed and spun around. Prins stood just inside her room, his back to the door, which he had already closed behind him, leaning on it with his shoulders. He stared at her. His being fully dressed made her feel all the more naked. She quickly grabbed the bedcover and held it in front of her.

"Are you mad? And how the hell did you get in?" she demanded. "Oh hell, I should've checked the door when you left. You probably didn't close it properly."

When he shrugged, she added, "I suppose it doesn't matter. Well, you can get the hell out of here exactly the same way you got in!"

He continued to stare. "I see you've got yourself ready for me."

"That's bullshit!" she said aggressively, but for the first time that evening more scared than angry. "You're an arrogant bastard! Just who do you think you are?"

He didn't blink, his eyes fixed on her. "I've been waiting a long time for this. Since you first joined my faculty." He started forward, moving deeper into the room, coming towards her. "I need you, Mary-Ann. Help me. I've waited as long as I can." The wheedling tone of a beggar.

"Any closer and I'll scream."

His face hardened and the wheedling tone was gone. "Maybe someone will hear you," he shrugged, "on the other hand maybe they won't. But I can tell you this – who's going to believe you would let a man of my age into your room, while you were naked, without being provocative? I'll say you were trying to bribe me because I wasn't happy with your research, and when I refused to accept ... what you were offering ... you threatened to shout rape. Either way you lose."

After a pause he added, "Why make this unpleasant? There's no avoiding the inevitable."

Her eyes narrowed. He took another step forward. A cold fury possessed her. She tried to control it, alcohol got in the way, she felt herself losing it.

"Go to hell!" she said, watching him carefully.

"Think of your father. He works for the Wildlife Research Trust."

"Go to hell!"

"You're asking for it," he said, breathing harder, abruptly lurched forward.

She calmly waited for the right moment, when it came she had all the time in the world. An arm's length between them and she allowed the bedcover to drop.

Prins stopped dead in his tracks, mouth open. Breathing raggedly he stared at her. "God, you're beautiful!" A constricted, cluttered voice.

She sunk into the back stance, carefully poised, perfectly balanced, inner centre calm, while her mind raged, egged on by alcohol.

"Yiah!"

A roundhouse kick launched, the heel of a foot crunching into the nose, cartilage crushed, nose bone fractured, bridge destroyed. Another yell, and a straight punch from the shoulder followed the kick, also to the nose, the carnage complete.

Prins gave a strangled scream, added a small mewing sound, clutched his face in both hands, staggered backwards.

Her scream of pain was almost as loud as his. She flopped backwards to sit on the edge of the bed, convinced she had broken her hand. The continuing effect on Prins was more dramatic: he slumped back ending up on his backside on the floor. Head hanging forward his hands covered the mask of his face.

Mary-Ann couldn't help herself. Prins looked ridiculous. She was ridiculous. The whole scene was ridiculous. Softly she began to giggle. She tried to stop – but couldn't.

The booze, she thought, it had to be the booze.

Slowly Prins stood up. He took his right hand away from his face and stared, it was covered in blood. Mary-Ann stopped giggling. His upper lip had split against his teeth and was also bleeding. But the main damage was to his nose, it had been crushed back into his face, flattened across under his right eye. The blood pumped out of the cavity as though it was the end of a hose.

Catching sight of himself in the mirror he desperately hauled out the front flaps of his shirt, quickly covered his face with that, tried to stop the red tide.

"Help me," words garbled, hardly intelligible.

Mary-Ann calmly bent forward to pick up the bedcover, she wrapped it around herself like a pale-lemon sari, tucked in one corner to make sure it stayed up, grabbed Prins by an ear, marched him toward the passageway door. She flung it open with the other hand, dragged him out into the corridor.

"Get out," she said, added, "don't you ever dare pull a stunt like that again."

A finger stuck out to point the way, imperious. She looked down the corridor, was horrified to see Fourse walking towards them. Adrenaline dissipating, embarrassment rushing in to take its place. She mustered as much dignity as she could, drew herself up to stand taller, stuck out her chin and with all the grace of a cheetah stalked back towards her hotel room.

Prins lurched a few steps down the passageway, unsteady on his legs, partially concussed. He stopped and looked back. The entire front of his shirt was now covered in blood.

"You'll be sorry for this," broken nose thickened the voice, split lip making him almost unintelligible. "And you have no idea how sorry!"

Mary-Ann hardly registered Prins' words, although she would have reason to remember them well enough later.

More important: how was she going to face the others in the morning?

*

Because of the solicitor's standing in the City and his terminally busy schedule Roger knew it wasn't going to be easy getting to see his long-time friend Hugo Morris, of Morris & Rosenberg. However because of their history together he was able to fix an appointment for late that Monday evening after seven pm. Roger suspected that it had been done specifically to accommodate him and felt that that was confirmed when he arrived at the solicitor's offices to find him alone, albeit still at his desk.

The solicitor's cherubic face lit up as he saw Roger appear outside his office door.

"Still going at this hour?" Hugo croaked with the habitual rasp in his throat. "By now the idle rich are supposed to be at play."

"Things to do, people to see," Roger responded, smiling warmly.

"Come in. Take a seat. I'll be back with coffee in a few minutes."

It wasn't long before Hugo reappeared carrying a tray. He placed it on the desk in front of Roger. "Help yourself." Slowly he worked his bulk around to his side of the desk.

They were opposites in almost every way imaginable and it had always been an unlikely friendship. Being very young when he finished A-levels Hugo had gone to an American college as a pre-university year before joining the Faculty of Law at the University of Cambridge. In America he had got off to a bad start because being short, fat and very clever and with a pronounced English accent he had become the target for unpleasant practical jokes by a bunch

of football jocks. Roger had stepped into the breach and put
an end to all of that after taking some stick himself for
doing so. Later they again met up when Roger became a
student at the Department of Engineering also at the
University of Cambridge. And the unlikely friendship had
flourished.

Hugo was methodical, always took his time, refused to
be rushed, but when he acted it was decisive – and usually
correct.

Now Roger was patient. It would be worth it. Hugo had a
reputation second to none in the City's financial
community. Roger couldn't think of anyone who could
make better use of the public school and Oxbridge old boy
network.

Having settled himself down on his high-backed leather
chair, Hugo leaned forward, smiled at Roger. "So, talk to
me. What's this about?"

"I need a place to operate from for a few days. There'll
be some typing, maybe a few messages. Most of all I need
you to steer me in the right direction," and Roger proceeded
to tell Hugo exactly what he hoped to achieve.

When Roger finished talking, Hugo nodded, sat back.

Elbows on the arms of his chair he steepled his fingers,
frowned. "Your best chance will be a company where you
have an ally on the inside. Someone who, for their own
reasons, needs the deal you're proposing."

Roger smiled to himself: Hugo's frown was a good sign,
his friend was interested. And Hugo hadn't asked why he
wanted to work away from home. He was glad about that.
He wouldn't like trying to explain something he didn't
really understand himself. He was operating on pure
instinct. This whole project had to be kept away from
Michelle, not to mention Patrick. This didn't sit
comfortably with him. Roger knew he was a
straightforward soul. Keeping things hidden and being
devious was a new experience.

"Have you tried your father-in-law?"

Roger glanced quickly in Hugo's direction. The tubby face was bland. Was there anything behind the question? Did Hugo know what Michelle's father, Basil Hawke, was really like? Perhaps not.

"I don't think his business could benefit," Roger responded awkwardly.

"Hmmm … just a thought. You know him better than I do."

After having glanced through the draft idea Roger had come up with on the weekend Hugo nodded. "A full proposal will take you ages to put together. I'll ask Sam to _"

"Sam?"

"My partner, Samantha Rosenberg, she's a phenomenon, could operate at the highest level if she was prepared to deal with clients directly. But generally she won't so mostly only I get to see how brilliant she really is. Her team will put some flesh on it." Then he smiled. "Don't worry, twenty-four hours and you'll have a complete and detailed proposal to work with."

"Perfect." Roger waved a hand in the air. "Thank you very much … for everything."

"Your ... er ... problem makes a refreshing change from endlessly reading contracts." Hugo hesitated, then said softly, "You always stuck up for me," he paused for a beat, "when I really needed it."

Surprised, at a loss for words, Roger shrugged self-consciously: this wasn't the sort of thing you normally talked about.

"We're friends," he said quietly.

Hugo nodded to himself, watching Roger's face. "You'll be okay on this? Intend giving it a full go?"

Roger guessed he meant goofing off and drinking. "Yes."

"I don't see why we can't make it happen." Hugo smiled. "Let's see what else we can do to help."

It soon became obvious to Roger as to how much of a selling job his idea was going to take. He had assumed the

advertising exposure would have had a number of
companies jumping at the chance. He was wrong. At first
that depressed him and made him feel thirsty. He resisted
the temptation and eventually the feeling went away. What
would have seemed a minor triumph to some pleased him
mightily.

On the Friday evening he again met with Hugo.

The tubby solicitor grinned. "Any joy yet?"

Roger shook his head despondently, eyed Hugo
suspiciously. "All right, tell me about it."

"I think we have the answer," rasped Hugo. "The name
of an old student acquaintance of ours has surfaced courtesy
of Sam, who, I might tell you, has become mightily
enthused about your project ..."

He paused. "Do you remember John Basingthwaite?"

"Smooth fellow. Fancied himself with the girls."

"That's the man. He's the marketing director for a
company that sells a designer line of clothing and
accessories worldwide. Got the job through contacts but, a
little bird told Sam, he hasn't being performing too
satisfactorily. It could just be he needs your idea as much as
you need him – if not more. She's come up with few other
prospects if Basingthwaite doesn't work out."

"His company's big enough?"

"Absolutely! One of the biggest in the business."

"I'll make contact right away," Roger said. "And
thanks."

*

On the Tuesday morning Mary-Ann hesitantly entered the
hotel dining-room. Without looking around she quickly
made her way across to sit at the table which she had begun
to think of as her own. And that amused her despite the
self-consciousness generated by the events of the previous
night. She had been there for a mere forty-eight hours and
had already staked out bits of territory as her own, like a
wild animal in the bush. Sometimes it amazed her as to how
close people still were to their atavistic roots.

She straightened up the knives and forks in front of her to form neat right-angles with the spoon and knife across the top.

She looked up, realised too late Fourse was passing, quickly put her swollen and bruised right hand under the table, but his eyebrows had already gone up. A few minutes later she saw him talking to the two younger members on the team. She grimaced as they all looked her way.

Defiantly she set her chin. She would simply ignore them. She had done nothing wrong and she was going to enjoy her breakfast. With her handkerchief she quickly dabbed at the corner of one eye. She was just fine and – like always, thank you very much – preferred being on her own. She didn't need anyone!

A while later, from under her eyebrows, she saw the three of them get up to leave. Fourse, however, made his way across to where she sat. She casually put down her cup of coffee, allowed her right hand to lie on her lap, hidden under the table. She looked up.

"You're attending the convention today." It wasn't a question.

Earlier that morning, when she had woken up, she had decided to stay away, but now her head went up and she stuck out her chin even further.

"Of course. Why not?"

"You'd better get your skates on. The bus leaves in a few minutes." He used his thumb to indicate the other two delegates. "We don't want you making the rest of us miss our transport."

"Yessir," she beamed, scrambling to her feet, breakfast forgotten.

Prins didn't put in an appearance at the CITES conference that day.

Mary-Ann ended up having dinner with the rest of the team. After the evening meal they excused themselves for a planning session involving delegations from all the Southern African countries. The vote had gone against them

on the elephant issue. Were they now going to register a
reservation? That would allow them, while remaining part
of the CITES process, to depart from the previous day's
resolution. It was an important issue.

Mary-Ann stayed behind at the dinner table to finish her
coffee.

"Say, Doctor, y'all mind if I join you?"

Blankly Mary-Ann looked up at the middle-aged man
with the polite smile. He wore a nondescript tie and a
brown sports jacket over black denim jeans. Where had she
seen him before? Ah yes – he was an accredited journalist
to the CITES convention.

This was all she needed. "There are plenty of other tables
free."

He nodded. "I know. I'd like to talk to you, ma'am. I
overheard you tear into one of the demonstrators on
Sunday." He had a flat-as-Kansas speaking style that
pinned him to the mid-west.

"And you still want to be seen with me?"

"Hell," he said, smiling. "I'm a reporter. We talk to all
kinds. It goes with the territory." He stood behind the chair
across the table from her. "With you it's really no hardship.
You surely got to be the downright purtiest doctor I ever
laid my sore old eyes on –"

Instantly she froze, like a leopard in a tree. Not again, not
after the previous night. "I'm not in the mood," she
growled.

"Hey, Doctor," he held up a hand, palm forward. "Don't
you misunderstand me. I'm lookin' for the background to
the story – and a cup of coffee. Nothing more, ma'am. I
promise."

"There's no point talking to me. I'm not an official
delegate."

He pointed across the dining-room. "The gentleman over
there suggested it. He was right complimentary."

Mary-Ann peered in that direction. Her eyebrows went
up. The journalist had indicated Prins. She couldn't believe

it. But she had to be fair. The Professor was probably trying to make amends, trying to let her know he'd had too much to drink the night before, that he had made a mistake. It was his way of apologising. She had to be big enough to accept.

She stared across at him, gave a small nod. The mask of his face was swathed in sticking plaster, holding his swollen nose in position. It seemed as though he gave her a small nod in return, but she couldn't be sure. Mary-Ann turned back and studied the journalist for a while.

"Okay," she said at last.

"The name's Pilsudski." He held up a hand, grinned. "My grandparents were from Poland. Everyone calls me Joe."

Mary-Ann inclined her head. "Mary-Ann."

Joe nodded happily. "I wasn't hitting on you when I said you were beautiful – you are. And it interests me, as a journalist," he added hastily when he saw her expression change, and then asked, "What are you a doctor of?"

"I'm a vet," she replied, unsure of herself, being interviewed was a new experience. But she could hear her dad's voice in her head –

1.   you just tell the truth, girl, and you'll be okay.

So it probably wasn't that complicated. What could go wrong?

"And that's all?" He pursed his lips. "There has to be more to your story than just that."

She smiled. "Not much. I qualified as a vet, didn't enjoy the work, and now I'm doing research into the optimum conditions for ensuring the survival of wildlife in the wild. Both physical and economic," she added as an afterthought.

"Wildlife in Africa?" he asked. "Don't I hear another accent in there somewhere."

"Yep," she nodded, then added, "but I've been in Africa like forever. Especially in the south where some of the most advanced work in Africa had been done on ensuring the survival of threatened species."

"You say that as though they – and by extension, you – are the only people who care. Isn't that what everyone wants?"

"I don't know." She frowned. "A decision taken by well-meaning people isn't automatically correct."

"So you think the decision to ban all African elephant trade is bad?"

"Yup, no question. Just like the American decision to support Leakey's proposal was a bad one."

"What do you think should've been done?"

She stared at him. "CITES decisions should be based on biological data and trade statistics. It's meant to regulate the trade in wildlife and wildlife products – in order to ensure the survival of endangered species. But in First World countries – like the States – where animal rightists hold sway, quite often politics becomes more important than the real issues at stake. The convention's being used as a weapon to further a different agenda – animal rights. It's got nothing to do with conservation."

"So everyone's out of step except you?"

She smiled suddenly, face lighting up, looked much younger than her twenty-eight years, could have been a teenager. "That's worried me, too. I've thought about it a lot. But I've studied the subject. And for many years, too! Most of the people I disagree with have only studied their navels – saying 'om' all the while."

"Effectively you're criticising the famous Dr Leakey. As head of the Kenyan delegation, he's the one who raised the issue of elephants being placed in Appendix A."

"Yeah, I suppose I am. But he's an archeo-palaeontologist – not a wildlife expert. The Kenyan Government presumably had no specialists available when they made him head of their conservation programme or they were playing politics. As far as Southern Africa is concerned it's a parochial move by countries that can't look after their own elephant."

"In what way?"

"All the countries in Southern Africa," she said fiercely, "have proper conservation programmes and they *don't* have high-placed government officials and politicians involved in the poaching of ivory. They've worked hard to protect their game reserves. Like Kruger, where they completely avoid a certain valley my father knows contains –" suddenly she broke off, almost clamped her hand over her mouth, stopped herself from doing that, carried her hand up to rub at her eye.

Damn, why *did* she talk so much?

"What is it?" Joe asked quickly. "What were you about to say?" He narrowed his eyes, smelling a secret, journalist's instincts working overtime.

"I think I've something in my eye. Please excuse me. I must go to the bathroom."

When she returned she changed the subject. Although Joe pressed the issue, he soon realised it was pointless.

The next day, as she was about to climb aboard the lunch-time bus back to the hotel, Fourse approached her. He frowned heavily, chewed at his lip.

"How could you talk to a reporter like that? The American papers have printed your comments as being official South African policy."

"But I told him I wasn't an official delegate! And I'm American, not South African."

"Well, that isn't how they've printed it. Not to mention your criticising Dr Leakey. Do you know what an international following the man has? What got into you?" He shook his head. "I'm sorry. You can't stay. You're an embarrassment now. We have to show you're not part of the official team. You'll have to go back early."

"But Prof Prins sent him –" abruptly she shut her mouth.

"I'm sorry," Fourse said again, and then added, "I don't like Prins, but he's right. You've embarrassed us, especially with the Kenyans and the Americans. Everyone's talking about it."

Four hours later, still stunned by the suddenness with which she was on her way home, Mary-Ann sat in the hotel lobby with her suitcases. At least she could dress comfortably again. She leaned back in the chair, stretched out her legs in faded jeans, crossed her boots at the ankle, closed her eyes, waited. The concierge was arranging a taxi to take her to the airport. She heard someone stop alongside her feet, looked up. Professor Prins loomed, staring down, radiating pure malice. Her eyes flew wide open. She quickly sat up straight, the better to defend herself.

"This is only the beginning," he said nasally through swollen lips, barely understandable, the sticking plaster pulled tight across his face. "I'll personally see to it that you and your family are forced out of conservation altogether. The name of Webber will stink like old carrion. This I promise you."

*

As soon as the slightest possibility existed that the company's offices were open on the Monday morning, Roger Denton dialled the telephone number Hugo had given him. John Basingthwaite was not then available, but an hour later returned Roger's call. Roger started to explain why he had called. But Hugo, and his partner, Samantha, had already thoroughly prepared the way.

"Dear boy," Basingthwaite interrupted. "Apparently you can help me. I've got to come up with a high-profile concept which will give us publicity around the world." He hardly paused for breath. "At the same time it must be able to form the core of a marketing campaign in every country."

Roger smiled into the telephone handset – *thank you, Hugo and Samantha!*

"When can we meet?" he asked.

"My dear chap, I'm desperate. Why not come through now?"

As soon as Roger was properly ensconced in John's office he, with some embarrassment because he was not used to doing this, launched into a sales pitch.

When Roger finished John said, "My Lord and Master is pretty keen on doing something in the next year or two. How much will this cost?"

"A million pounds."

"Good grief!"

"That includes nearly two years living expenses!" Roger said quickly. "As well as the hard costs involved."

"Won't your lovely lady help? I understood you haven't exactly been scratching for a living since you got married."

Roger studied his shoes for a while. Slowly the muscles tensed in his cheeks until they bulged, forming hard ridges under the skin. "I want to do this on my own."

"Okay, old son. Don't get your knickers in a knot."

"What's the likelihood your lot will bite?"

"I'm pretty sure it's the type of deal my Lord and Master will go for. It almost exactly fits the brief I've been given. There's just one thing ..."

It was John's turn to hesitate.

Roger raised his eyebrows.

"Well," John said at length. "You know how the chaps talk. I mean rumour, old son, has it that you ..." John shrugged, squeezing his eyes half-shut, "you know –"

"I don't bloody know, *old son*," Roger growled. "So why not spit it out?"

"Rumour has it you don't always follow through ..." John blurted, red in the face. "Something to do with rough nights and tardy mornings – it'll be my neck on the line, too," he added in a mumble.

Roger shook his head in frustration, jumped up, paced back and forth. How did you explain all that had been said and done? How do you explain how suddenly things could change? Jesus, and this looked such a strong possibility, too.

Unfortunately, John was right! – *No! Dammit!* – that thinking had been right, past tense. Now he *was* going to show everyone, including Patrick, and especially his father, and even Michelle, that he had changed.

That was one of the reasons he had chosen such a long-haul project in the first place. It met all his requirements. Making it through this one would leave no one doubting his staying power. Least of all himself. He swung back to face John, leaning forward with his hands on the back of the chair on which he had been sitting.

"John, what can I say? Other than – I'll do it!"

"It's important to you, isn't it?"

"More than you could ever know!"

John stared at him. "Hugo seemed pretty confident ..." he muttered under his breath. "He, and his partner Samantha, are both personally underwriting your performance ... between them they've got one hell of a reputation in the City."

Roger felt his heart thumping against his ribs. Hugo and Samantha had really gone out on a limb for him. His knuckles were like small round pieces of chalk with the way he gripped the chair.

"Okay, old son," John replied at length. "I believe you. I'll lay it before my Lord and Master. In the final analysis it's his decision. But Hugo's backing will be a big help – a very big plus in your favour. Can you put together a proposal? Some background, the numbers involved, your experience, what sort of exposure we'd get, when we'd get it – that sort of thing."

"It's all done!" Roger cried.

He walked around the chair to where he had left his briefcase. His legs felt weak as the tension seeped away. He opened the briefcase and withdrew a bulky ring-binder file. "Everything you asked for and more. It's all in here."

John bounced the file in his hand before dropping it on the desk in front of him. "Good man."

He flipped through the pages, stopped to read here and there, nodded to himself. "All my work has been done for me. Very professional. Hugo said it would be. I'll get back to you ASAP." He sounded quite excited.

John held up a hand just as Roger turned to leave.

"One thing, old son," he cleared his throat. "Do you mind if my Lord and Master gets the idea a goodly bit of this was my work?"

Roger stared at John, feeling the excitement in the pit of his stomach. What had Hugo said the other day?

You're going to stand your best chance of having a company go for this kind of deal when you have an ally, a champion, on the inside ...

"Tell you what," Roger murmured. "It's your idea and that proposal is all your work."

"Hmm, 'preciate that, old man."

Roger suddenly felt he was on the threshold of redemption – the possibility of screwing up didn't bear thinking about. He wouldn't get another chance – he simply *had* to make this work.

*

Mary-Ann could hardly believe that only ten days before she had stood in the same spot, outside the same door. So much seemed to have happened and here she was again, hovering beneath the sign marked *Professor John H Prins*. It was lifetime ago. Unsure of her reception she stood outside for a long while. Eventually she gathered together the remnants of her courage.

The Professor's secretary, Susan, looked up, rose to her feet and began to clap.

Red in the face, Mary-Ann waved her down. "Oh no! Please don't!"

Susan wore a luminous smile. "Mary-Ann, welcome back. It's good to see you again."

"It is? Do you mean that? And you're not still mad at me?"

"Of course not, silly. I was chuffed to hear what you did. The man's a pig." She started to laugh, hand to her mouth. "Is he really covered in bandages? Please tell me it's true. Is his nose really squashed all over his ugly face?"

"You've heard? Already?"

Susan almost ran around the desk. She wrapped Mary-Ann in her arms, hugged and then kissed her on both cheeks. "Give me your hand," she said, holding out hers. "The sore one."

Reluctantly Mary-Ann held out her right hand, which she had kept hidden.

"Someone said you'd hurt yourself." Susan grimaced as she looked at Mary-Ann's swollen knuckles. "It must be very painful."

"What did you hear?"

"That you beat the shit out of the bastard, broke his nose, that he was covered in blood. That at first he hid out claiming he was ill. The story's all over campus."

Mary-Ann pulled a face. "I'd hoped to keep it quiet. I just want the whole thing to go away."

"You're a superhero. It's already a campus legend." Susan shook her head, the corners of her mouth turning down. "Too late for that now."

"And when I was here last? What was that about?"

"I didn't know what to think. He tries his nonsense on with all the women that come near him. Especially if they're young and attractive, like you. He's my husband's *brother* and he tried putting his hand up *my* skirt."

Mary-Ann felt the melting away of a tension that she hadn't realised was there. Deep down she had begun to wonder if she hadn't somehow been at fault.

"Thanks for telling me."

"Even the youngest woman students aren't safe. We're all very proud of you. And I'm sorry about your hand. I hope nothing's broken."

"I've always admired his dedication to conservation."

"Can't argue with that. But he's still a pig."

She suddenly looked grim, eyes narrowed. "More importantly, Mary-Ann, you must stay away from him. He's a bad enemy. I'm glad you did what you did. He's being asking for it. But the story's all over campus. And he's not a man to forgive and forget."

Mary-Ann shrugged. "Maybe it'll teach him a lesson."

Susan shook her head. "It's not safe to let you loose amongst people. Stick to your animal friends. They're a lot more consistent."

Mary-Ann stuck out her chin. "That's not fair. People can change. There's every chance he'll now see the error of his ways."

"The best thing you can do is pack and go before he gets back."

"No one could be that mean. He was in the wrong."

"Watch your back for a long time to come. He's a vindictive bastard. Mark my words, he won't forget this – ever."

Mary-Ann shook her head. "I don't know what to think."

"Can I help you pack?"

"I'm not packing." Mary-Ann again stuck out her chin.

Susan shook her head in despair. "I'm warning you –"

"I don't want to hear it," Mary-Ann interrupted stubbornly. "And what would I do? I've already spent two years on my thesis. If I leave here I'll have to start all over again. And he's the best in Africa. And this place is the only University with a fully-fledged wildlife department."

Susan shook her head. "You're stubborn, you know that? Just don't say I didn't warn you."

"Everybody deserves a second chance." Mary-Ann shrugged. "Even Prins."

Susan said nothing more – but her eyes reflected her deep concern for Mary-Ann. It was as if she was saying Prins was family – she *knew* Prins!

*

A few weeks later, at 9.30 am on 18 May, Roger Denton replaced the telephone handset in its cradle as carefully as

though it were made of antique crystal glass. He stared
blindly at the instrument, scared now of the commitment he
had made. It wasn't just his neck on the line. Now he was
suddenly burdened with a responsibility for others – and not
just family members. And yet despite his concern, a smile
grew, he stood ready, filled with emotion.

Michelle strode through the doorway. On seeing him she
stopped, frowned. "What was that all about? Why are you
grinning like that? Who called?"

Caught off guard, he was about to tell her when the same
instinct that had served to keep him quiet about his project
in the first place choked off the words in the back of his
throat.

"Well?" She stamped her foot. "Don't just stand there
like an idiotic Cheshire cat. Answer me!"

"Just an old varsity chum," he said at last. "He's asked
me to lend him a hand on a project he's busy with. I said
yes. I hope you don't mind?"

"No," she said indulgently, relaxing, talking to a
loveable, but spoilt, child. "You go ahead and play with
your friends."

.

PART TWO
May – August 1986

.

She stared at him: short of breath, tongue-tied, but wet eyes suppressed giving him little satisfaction. She had never – ever! – in her entire life, failed anything. Throughout her school and University careers, anything less than seventy-five percent had constituted a major disaster.

Now this!

"Ms Webber, do I need to repeat myself?" Prins smiled.

When she didn't – couldn't – immediately respond he added, "As you will. It seems you didn't hear me properly the first time ..." he paused giving his words greater emphasis, "I'm afraid your thesis just isn't good enough." He still spoke like someone with a really bad head cold, the nasal bone structure never having recovered from being so devastatingly destroyed.

"But the monthly progress meetings. You've never made an adverse comment. I've been working on this for almost three years. I thought that –"

"It's too practical," he cut in, with relish, "not academic enough. It's just not up to the standard this University expects. A doctorate is after all the highest academic accolade it's possible to bestow on a student."

She stared at him. The pompous pig. She suddenly remembered Susan's warnings. She lifted her chin. There was no way she would beg for anything from this grinning ape.

"All right," she said, trying for a smile, holding herself still, control: wouldn't let him see the price he was making her pay. "What do I have to do in order for it to be acceptable?"

"It really isn't satisfactory at all," he said, smiling hugely now. "There's a problem with both subject matter and approach. The whole concept is insufficiently academic." He paused for long time, clearly enjoying himself. "It'll definitely take a complete rewrite."

"But that's impossible," Mary-Ann burst out. "I've been working on this for three years. Not once did you suggest there was anything remotely wrong with what I was doing."

"You're out of line, Ms Webber. As it happens, I can remember telling you all along I had doubts about the direction you were taking," he said blandly. "I think you'll find my private notes accurately reflect the true position."

Mary-Ann stared at him, open-mouthed, again mute.

"I hoped your final rewrite before formal submission would change the slant. I've now discussed this with my colleagues. I also told them I had warned you. Unfortunately, you've done the very opposite of what I asked. Your thesis as it stands is totally unacceptable."

"I'll appeal to the University Council."

His eyes became small black lumps of coal. "You can try, Ms Webber, of course you can try. I think when it comes down to your word against mine there'd be very little contest."

"But a total rewrite means at least two years work!"

He smiled at her again. "We have high standards. In fact I've wondered whether you're actually suited to conservation. Ms Webber, why don't you go back to being a vet in some little suburban practice somewhere?" he asked kindly. "I say this for your own good, of course! I think that would suit you just fine. It's certainly my recommendation."

Abruptly Mary-Ann stood up, the chair she had been sitting on rocked back dangerously, almost fell over. "Go to hell, Professor."

He smiled at her. "Two years, Ms Webber, two more years. And, of course, there's no guarantee you'd get it right then."

Mary-Ann stared at him. Without saying another word she turned on her heel and stalked towards the door.

"Oh, yes," she heard him say as her hand closed on the door handle, "you'll recall you can't submit a doctoral thesis rejected by one University to another University in the hopes it may be accepted there. You'll also no doubt recall that the titles and subject matter of all theses are registered when they're started. I'd get to hear of it if you tried."

Mary-Ann slammed the door behind her as she left his office. Outside she leaned back against it, unable to take another step, too numb to move.

Susan looked at her with wide eyes, her voice soft. "I'm sorry. He's such a vindictive bastard. The family often talk about it. In that way, he's insane."

"So you know?"

"He told me this morning when I reminded him of your appointment."

Tears starting from her eyes. "Surely he'll be satisfied now? Surely now he'll leave me alone?"

Susan shrugged. Clearly she didn't think so: she *knew* Prins – he would *never* be satisfied: he would hound Mary-Ann forever!

Thirty minutes later Mary-Ann wheeled her car out onto the highway that led to the Kruger National Park. She had to get away from the city. She had to get back to the bush, where everything was always so much simpler.

Just over five hours later she pulled up in Skukuza, the main Kruger camp. Responding to the sound of an engine being cut off, her father appeared suspiciously from his cottage like an antbear emerging from its tunnel, small goatee beard prominent.

She climbing stiffly from the car, realised she had automatically taken her keys out of the ignition, smiled wanly. She really had been in the city for too long. She leaned in to the car, pushed the key back into the ignition lock. She turned to her father. At least he was the same. Perhaps a little more bent at the shoulders, but otherwise unchanged, a rock.

He stopped nearby, nodded, smiled briefly, not saying anything.

She grew a small smile. That was her dad, Jakes Webber, the ultimate chatterbox.

"It's good to be back."

He nodded, smiling slightly, eyes bright.

She wondered if their relationship would have been different if she had been a boy. She laughed at herself. Old notions long discarded had the disconcerting habit of behaving like bad pennies. Did people ever outgrow their childhood fears?

The truth of it was Jakes didn't do much communicating verbally. He just sat on his porch, stared out between the bougainvillaea-covered pillars, down towards the river, watched the animals live out their lives, not saying a word from one hour to the next. She knew that a lot of the time he thought about her mom. It was as if he constantly expected her to stick her head through the doorway to call him in to dinner – over twenty years after she had died.

She grabbed her rucksack: the hell with it, he was stuck with her not being a boy.

"I want to stay awhile. I want to spend some time in the bush."

He peered out at her from under bushy eyebrows. "You okay?"

"Yes, of course," she said brightly. "What makes you ask?"

Jakes shrugged, just watching her.

"I just want to take some time off from academia. I've grown unbelievably stale. I need to get out into the field, to remind myself what it's really all about, to recharge my batteries."

He knew something had happened. She was sure of it. She knew her father well, knew his body language the way most children know their parents' voices. It was a natural reaction to his saying so little. As the child she had learned to read his moods from how he moved and not from what he said.

But he didn't pursue the matter and she was grateful for that.

In Kruger the hours drifted slowly by for her, running from one into the other, and she slowly synchronised with the natural world, so that eventually Mary-Ann had distanced herself emotionally from what Prins had done.

After a week, Jakes told her Kruger management wanted her to take up a temporary position as a wildlife vet, with a view to making it permanent later, when a suitable post became vacant.

"They're as proud as I am," he said gruffly, coughing into his hand, "to have a Professor Prins student here."

Mary-Ann's heart flopped. She had found it impossible to tell her father her thesis had been rejected, always putting off the moment, waiting for a better time. She felt really sick. She hadn't wanted to offload her problems onto his shoulders. Was it now too late? Would she ever be able to tell him?

Mary-Ann sat alongside her father on the stoep that evening, watching the sun go down, a smear of orange silhouetting the hardekool, knobthorn and marula trees. The deep cough of a big cat hunting drifted in with the cool night air.

Surely three years of her life covered the debt. Wouldn't Prins be satisfied now?

Watching the sunset, she remembered asking Susan a similar question. And the memory of the shrug that had proceeded Susan's response gave Mary-Ann little comfort.

Suddenly she shivered as the balmy summer evening in the bushveld quickly turned into night.

*

Sheets of paper lay spread out on the desk.

Wearily Monty Cohen tried to concentrate on his proof-reading. Eventually this would be a small book of poetry. All of which had been written by a Professor in the Department of English of the Witwatersrand University. It was, according to the good academic, the distillation of a lifetime's work. He had also told Monty it was going to be well worth the expense to see it in print, before he retired.

Monty had conceived, started, owned and managed Vestal Publishers from the same downtown premises for forty-five years now. It was a good business and it had always provided him, even in bad times, with a steady income. Enough even to ensure that his three children were properly prepared in order to survive the vicissitudes of modern life. As much as one can provide for these things. God forbid too much should go wrong.

His eldest son and only daughter were both doctors. A good business, medicine. The sick would always be with us. And when people were sick they ran to the nearest doctor as fast as their legs could carry them. They took their purses along, too. His youngest son was a lawyer. Another good business to be in. Never mind the jokes, on the other side of their faces they would laugh, when they needed a lawyer.

With a sigh Monty put all that out of his head and returned to his proof-reading. He didn't know from good poetry. So on that basis it would never be interesting to him. However, if only it could have been a little salacious, it would have helped him concentrate.

The telephone rang. Contrarily, he didn't welcome the interruption, the professor was in a hurry for his book of poetry. But business was always business and his hand automatically went out to pick up the handset.

"Monty Cohen, Vestal Publishers." He spoke into the mouthpiece with little enthusiasm. "Good morning, can we help you?"

"I'm Professor Prins of the University of Pretoria." It was an officious voice, with a strong nasal quality. "And I've a publishing project for you."

Monty was cautious. Very few of the calls he received were from people who fully understood his business. "Of course, publishing is our business. What do you have in mind?"

"A thesis was presented to me recently. Although not suitable for a degree, it's the right sort of material for a book."

Monty was as yet unable to figure the angle. "We're talking non-fiction here, right?"

"I can assure you it's well worth your looking at."

Monty grimaced. There was nothing here for him. Curiosity prompted one more question. "What particular field does the work cover?"

"Conservation in Africa through proper wildlife management and –"

He had heard enough. "Sorry to interrupt, Professor, before we go on, I need to ask you something."

From past experience Monty knew the conversation would probably end soon. "Do you have any idea of the sort of publishing I do?"

"You're a vanity publisher."

Monty winced. "Yes … well … we prefer to call it subsidy publishing. I try to help new authors establish a foothold in the writing business," he said coldly. "It's a very difficult business to break into without a history of being published. So we provide an invaluable service. Having said that – do you know what it means?"

"I wasn't born yesterday!" Professor Prins snapped irritably. "You only publish a work someone pays you to publish. You never take any financial risks yourself. And just in case you think I'm still missing the point – it also means that you don't give a damn whether the work is actually publishable or not. As long as you're paid, and certain of your profit, you'll publish anything. That's why I contacted you."

The publisher stiffened in his chair. "I give an honest opinion if I'm asked for it. I'll tell the author whether I think his work has commercial appeal or not."

"Don't be offended." The Professor didn't sound conciliatory at all. "I was trying to show I have no illusions about your business. Are you now prepared to listen to my proposition?"

This suited Monty. The man was businesslike. There could be business here. He would still be cautious, but in a different way and for a different reason. He still didn't understand the other man's angle and that would have a major effect on the price which would ultimately have to be negotiated.

"Go ahead," Monty said.

"A young lady student of mine submitted a thesis to me which I consider to be a work of such value I would like to see it published. And I'd like you to do the publishing."

Monty pulled a face, rocked his head from side to side. There had to be more to it than that. He would have to go fishing. "How strongly do you personally feel about this work being published?"

"Don't worry, Mr Cohen. I'll fully finance a … limited … edition."

Monty suddenly smiled. Ha! A young *lady* student, hey? He'd had a similar case before.

"Of course, sir. We should meet at the earliest possible opportunity." He suggested a time for the following day and it turned out to be acceptable to the Professor.

"One more thing," the Professor said. "No one is to know I'm sponsoring the publication of the young lady's work. I don't want to be accused of favouritism. Until I have your word on that I'm not prepared to divulge her name."

"Of course, sir. I understand. I can assure you of our utmost discretion. Will you be bringing the young lady with you tomorrow? I'll need to meet with her at some stage."

"Of course not. No one, and that includes the young lady, must know that I'm sponsoring the publication."

Monty's jaw fell open.

"But what's the point … then how will …" he broke off and took another tack, "Please explain exactly what it is you want?"

"I want *you* to approach her with the suggestion Vestal publishes her thesis as a textbook on the subject of wildlife management. We'll have a private agreement covering all costs. This contract between the two of us will include the condition that should it become known – by anyone other than the two of us – that we have such an agreement you'll be unable to claim the recovery of the costs involved in the venture from me."

Monty was at a loss for words. In forty-five years of publishing he thought he had heard it all and then along came this.

"I agree," he said at last. "I'll see you tomorrow. As arranged."

After returning the telephone handset to its cradle Monty sat there staring at the instrument as though it had mortally offended him. He still didn't know what the Professor's angle could be and that meant he would have to quote his lowest price to make sure he got the business. He shook his head sadly.

Sometimes it was hard to make that little bit extra which ensured a good living.

*

"This title business," Michelle Denton said. "It's not really a problem."

Roger shrugged. "It'll be resolved within the next few months anyway."

Michelle still didn't know about his project. He wasn't naturally devious and he had felt increasingly uncomfortable. It had been almost a year now. The strain was starting to tell, even though the first stage had been easy to conceal, with most of the work being done by others. He had merely acted as co-ordinator. But now all that was about to change – radically.

He was going to be away from home a lot more in the future, culminating in the moment when he would finally have proved himself. When he had gained recognition from Patrick and his father for what he had achieved, when he had vindicated Hugo's and Samantha's trust in him and earned Michelle's respect, he would give up the title with pleasure. He hadn't wanted the damn thing in the first place.

He was pleasantly surprised to discover he really did want to share with Michelle. Not just because he didn't like sneaking around. He was convinced she would be as excited about it as he was, and that, in turn, would make it even more exciting for him.

"I've a plan," he said, feeling shy. "All the basic work's been done and we're into the final leg ..." Roger paused.

No! He didn't just want to *tell* her, he wanted to *show* her. He wanted it to be as tantalisingly exciting for her as it was for him.

"I want you to come down to Portsmouth with me," he said, unable to keep a pleading note out of his voice.

Michelle's eyebrows went up. "Oh! I didn't realise you were still messing about with your friend's boat. I thought *you'd* have given that up by now."

"Let's go down to Portsmouth," he repeated eagerly. "It's important to me. I want you to see something for yourself."

"No, *thank you*," she replied, with a toss of the black curls on her head. "What on earth would I want to do in smelly old Portsmouth? Anyway as I was saying – before you so rudely interrupted – the title isn't a problem."

"I've always had the reverse impression."

"That isn't what I meant," she said impatiently. "And do stop interrupting."

Roger grunted.

"You get it anyway, don't you? No one can take it away from you," she cried triumphantly. "You're the oldest son. You get the title when your father dies. And you just keep it. There's nothing anyone can do about that."

"You really don't understand." Roger tried to keep the astonishment out of his voice. "I gave my word."

She shrugged again. "Just change your mind. Say you're doing it for me!"

Roger felt curiously empty – and he felt like having a drink, preferably whisky.

"Have it your own way," he said at last.

"I will," she said loudly, and with conviction.

"I'll be spending a lot more of my time down there," he said flatly. He hadn't had more than a few beers and the odd glass of wine with meals for over a year and was determined not to fall off the wagon.

"I'm sure the novelty will wear off soon."

Roger pulled a face. Like hell it will. He had been right the first time round. She had to be kept out of it. Only a few more months to go.

*

The grey-haired Renamo fighter wearing a camouflage uniform strolled across the clearing towards the only tent in the bush camp. He brushed past the sentry, stepped into the gloom and sensed the antagonism before his eyes had adjusted.

"Good evening, *senhors*," Joshua said politely, deliberately speaking Portuguese as a courtesy to the two white officers present.

They were both fluent in Shangaan, which they needed to command their fighters, but Joshua believed in old-fashioned virtues. Few of his brother officers present would have bothered. It also served to underline his age against the average age of the rest of the men in the tent.

"Greetings, General Manyoba, we see you," muttered someone at the table.

"We have a problem," stated Abel Gamellah baldly, one of the younger men in the tent, unceremoniously cutting across the exchange. "Now that we're *finally* all here, perhaps we can address it." Then in English, "Time waits for no man."

Joshua curtly nodded by way of greeting, courtesy deserting him as he looked at the scarred face across the

rickety table, never quite sure how to respond to the other
man's constant use of quotes in English, many of them
biblical.

"What is it this time?" Joshua asked finally. The tight
curls of grey hair stood out against the dark blue-black of
his skin. His slightly chubby body belied the lean face of an
ageing guerrilla, with the laugh lines radiating out from the
corners of his eyes even more incongruous still.

"We need for you to put upon us the armour of light,
now in the time of this mortal life." Gamellah responded,
and turned to the young man who sat alongside him. "Speak
or forever hold your peace."

The young lieutenant nodded delicately. He had a soft
lilting voice which ill-fitted the topic. "As anticipated,
although it took a while, the signing of the '84 Nkomati
Accord between the South Africans and Frelimo has finally
dried up the arms supply from South Africa. As you all
know, that was our primary source after Rhodesia became
Zimbabwe."

While the young man talked, Joshua watched Gamellah.
The latter, seldom seen without a willowy lad by his side,
was also known as the Butcher of Beira for what he had
done to innocents in that port after the Portuguese had
decamped from Mozambique. Even the Frelimo leadership,
hardened after years of guerrilla warfare, had found it
unacceptable. To stay alive Gamellah deserted from
Frelimo, went back to the bush and joined Renamo, which
is why he was there with them now.

"That it took two years," the lieutenant continued, "is a
testament to the covert support of those who remained our
friends. But they're also beginning to bow to the inevitable.
Just as it is bowing to the inevitable that had senior South
African business leaders going to London last year to hold
open talks with the ANC overseas, even if it was against the
wishes of the Apartheid Government. The whole region is
changing."

Joshua listened carefully. The briefing was professional: start from the known, summarise the facts, define the problem. Despite his personal proclivities, the lieutenant was a good soldier.

"We still capture arms regularly from government troops," interrupted Sishuba, another up-and-coming young general.

"Firmly believe and truly," Gamellah agreed, from where he lounged in a canvas camp chair. A scar glowed red where it diagonally crossed his face from the left temple across to the right hand side of his mouth. "But the supplies are erratic, we're not always able to match ammunition to weapons, and it doesn't help in planning attacks if you have to hope to supplement what you have along the way."

"Perhaps it's not that important anymore," Joshua said casually.

Instantly it was out in the open. The tension was immediately palpable. It had been inevitable from the beginning.

"Prepare a table before me against them that trouble me. Why should our ability to continue functioning properly suddenly be of less importance?"

Gamellah's question was voiced no less casually than Joshua's, but it was obvious to everyone in the tent that two prizefighters had squared up to one another.

Joshua stirred in his chair. He had always suspected it would one day come to this. He was sixty-two years old now. The Butcher had not yet reached forty. Joshua only started fighting when conditions in Mozambique had deteriorated under Frelimo's hardline authoritarian Marxist/Leninist rule and when, on top of that, they had banned any political activity which wasn't sycophantic. The Butcher had been in it from the beginning. He fought for the pleasure of killing. And he had recently become worse. More vicious, more reckless, as though he no longer cared at all. There was something in his yellowed eyes that spoke of the abandonment of all hope.

Joshua shrugged. "Because Frelimo seems more willing to consider holding multi-party elections, to start talking."

That brought Gamellah to his feet, chair crashing over backwards, all of them flinching, an uncertain temper, well-known to his contemporaries.

"And why are they talking," he shouted, scar vivid, seeming ready to bleed again. "Because *some* of us have shown we're a force to be reckoned with. Because *some* of us have gone out of our way to smite them hip and thigh."

"Perhaps the collapse of communism and the consequent changes in the Eastern European nations, who provided them with funds, had a lot to do with it," Joshua said mildly.

He looked around the table, wondering who would support him and who would support Gamellah if it came to a showdown. He sighed to himself as the eyes slid away – one by one. They were all so scared of the other man. No matter how strongly they might agree with Joshua, they would rather stand behind the Butcher. However, it wasn't just politics that demanded the art of the possible.

He also rose to his feet. "I propose that we go all out to find alternative sources of funding for further arms purchases, with the intention of keeping up the pressure on Frelimo." And then carefully added, "But that's specifically to ensure they continue talking to us about a ceasefire."

Gamellah eyed him coldly. "I'll go along with that."

He righted his chair, sat down again. Immediately a relieved murmur of agreement sounded from around the table, shoulders went down, taut backs slumped in chairs.

Joshua also sat down. At least continuing talks with Frelimo was still a goal.

"Okay then," he added, "please continue."

The young lieutenant nodded, soft brown eyes sparkling. "There's no one out there to help us with arms for political reasons. We're on our own. Now we have to buy them. In order to raise money we're going to have to sell something. Any ideas?"

After a long silence the lieutenant nodded. "I believe General Gamellah has a suggestion to make."

Joshua snorted quietly to himself – *surprise, surprise*.

Gamellah continued lounging in his canvas camp chair for a while, before abruptly, dramatically, sitting forward and pointing at Joshua. "*You* know of something we can sell and *I* know how we can go about selling it."

Joshua squinted, wished he knew what Gamellah was up to. "I do?"

"Coal!" Gamellah crowed triumphantly. "Easily available coal, that's what we have to sell!"

A murmur of surprise, leaning forward, eyebrows rising, everyone awake.

Hiding his feelings, Joshua casually waved away a particularly persistent fly. How had Gamellah found out? It had been a long time ago. Joshua had been the only survivor of that geophysical survey team. Everyone else had been killed in an ambush on the way back after having made the discovery. Only one possibility existed. They had gone through his personal papers while he was away. They had been thoroughly professional. He kept that stuff carefully locked away. He hadn't noticed anything suspicious.

"That'll only be of value when we've had an election," Joshua protested. "Without the government's involvement you can't export the coal."

"Where is it?" demanded Sishuba.

"The seam runs all along a valley in Abel's area," replied Joshua. "It extends to the west and east of our border with South Africa. It's on both sides. The other half is in the Kruger National Park. But the stuff is worthless if you can't export it. Frelimo controls the harbours."

"Ah, brother! But I know a way."

A few years earlier and Gamellah's finding out would have really been disastrous. Originally the secret knowledge of the coal's whereabouts had been Joshua's personal passport to the presidency of a new government in

Mozambique. Funny – now it was in the open he felt
relieved. He had grown old. The war had dragged on for so
long he had lost all political ambition. Now he just wanted
a quiet place to put up his feet and rest. Joshua relaxed. It
had been quite a burden, knowing he could leverage it into
a presidency he no longer wanted.

"What do you suggest?"

"We sell the whereabouts to the highest bidder who can
provide us with the arms we need."

"What's the point," Joshua persisted, "without Frelimo's
co-operation? How would it be moved out of the country?"

Gamellah laughed out aloud. "Because, for a suitable
price, Dos Santos, the current Minister of Mining and
Mineral Affairs, will ensure the purchaser would have
official permission to exploit the field and export the
product. We, of course, can guarantee access to the site."

Joshua leaned back in his chair, eyes closed. This was
clearly *very* important to Gamellah. Much of the Butcher's
power in Renamo had derived from his having a high level
source in the Frelimo government. Everyone knew his
contact stemmed from the old days. But he had kept the
name a carefully guarded secret. Until now.

So Joshua knew *how* important it was to Gamellah, but
still didn't know *why*. The Butcher's revealing his source
also served to confirm the pattern that had emerged of a
man who had nothing more to lose.

*

The tea swirled gently as it poured into the bone china cup.

"One sugar or two?" Michelle asked Colin, more of a
confidante now than her interior decorator, although that
was how she had met him.

"I'll use my little pills, thank you very much."

Michelle sat down on the couch, staring silently for a
while at her cup.

"I've never really been able to let myself go sexually ..."
she said suddenly and then paused to look anxiously at

Colin. "Are you sure I can talk to you ..." she flapped a hand, "... about this?"

"And why ever not, darling?" He looked at her from under dramatically lowered eyelids. "I'm hardly going to take advantage of you."

"I'm always scared Roger will look down on me ..."

"When you assume the position, that's exactly what he's meant to be doing."

"Oh, please don't make fun of me. I'm so unhappy. I've never had an ... you know, with anyone, I've always faked it. I'm sure he's thinking I'm dirty or something when we ... you know."

"That's ridiculous, my dear. You're must do something about that crashing inferiority complex."

"You're being ridiculous! Why should I feel inferior? I went to one of the best girls' schools in England. My father gives me plenty of money, more than most people have. I'm married to a handsome man, which also means I'll be the Countess of Watbridge one day. I go to all the right parties –"

"Enough! Are you listening to yourself?"

"I just hate it when he's so independent."

"I rest my case, darling."

"That conversation we had some time ago. He said he was helping out a friend of his. Working on some smelly old yacht or something, but now I don't know what to think. He's behaving so out of character."

"I'm having exactly the same sort of problem with my new one. And it makes one so terribly insecure."

"I so hate this. Why can't things be the way they were. We've been perfectly happy for years. And now he's always away. I just don't know what to do."

"Why don't you join him?"

"I don't like being out of London. Unless everyone's going, of course."

"Of course," Colin echoed, looking at the ceiling.

"I like London. Worst of all, he hasn't asked for any money for what seems like ages."

There was always enough for both of them, he hadn't been drawing on the account, he would never go to Patrick or Dayfydd, there had to be a new source.

"So where could it be coming from?" she asked.

"Maybe," Colin twinkled, "just maybe, he's found someone else richer – and slimmer and taller. A blonde."

She suddenly loathed her black gypsy eyes, high cheek-bones and dark Mediterranean skin tones. Michelle felt short and dark and dumpy. She would even have settled for horse-faced and angular, if only she could have been a classic English county type. Like most of the other girls at the school she had attended.

"You could be right," she said, wretched, voice spiralling an octave. "Although he did ask me to have a look. But I suppose that doesn't prove anything. It's all very well inviting me down to see the thing, but if there was another woman involved he'd make damn sure she wouldn't be around while I was there." She peered anxiously at Colin. "Do you really think he may have found someone else? He's never, but never, behaved like this before."

"There's only one answer, my dear. Hire a detective!"

"Do you really think so? Do you really think I should?"

"Absolutely! It's the only thing to do under the circumstances. And I know just the person. He's the most darling man, very discreet, very reliable, and the most lovely eyelashes!"

Michelle nodded to herself. "You're right," she murmured, more confident, stronger, determined. "And as soon as I've found out what he's up to I'll put a stop to it!"

"I wish my one cared as much."

"Care?" she echoed. "No way! I damned if he's going to get away with it, whatever it is. He'll be begging me for mercy by the time I'm finished with him!"

"How deliciously tough." Colin arched his eyebrows. "I just love the conflict …"

*

Blenching, forehead creased, wincing as she watched her father pacing up and down the length of the cottage's porch. Jakes shook his head as though to rid himself of an irritating tsetse fly.

Mary-Ann groaned inwardly.

"Is what's happened really so bad?" she asked, culpable, contrite. "Surely you'd retire in a few years anyway. Why not take it easy until then?"

He stopped pacing to stare out over the trees. "Don't want an old-age home – sitting there, all by myself. Anyway, I don't have … no … that's another problem."

Mary-Ann had never heard her father talk so much before.

"Have you ever had any trouble with the Trust?"

Did she really want him to say 'yes' just to assuage her own guilt?

He shrugged helplessly. "Never. Tried appealing. Always dealt with Prins. Now he won't talk to me." He swung around to face her. "You know what it's like for people like us – it's … it's …"

"The same way farmers feel about their farms," Mary-Ann finished for him.

Jakes nodded his head.

"I know. I've watched you fuss around your adopted patch like forever."

"Exactly! It's my … my … farm they're taking away. Yesterday those were my animals. Tomorrow they'll be someone else's. It's as though all trace of me will be wiped out with a stroke of a trustee's pen."

Not for the first time Mary-Ann wished she had told him about the problem she'd had with the Professor. Now with a month gone by it would be too little, too late. And what if his problem wasn't caused by Prins? Surely her father couldn't have expected the Trust to keep him on forever. There had to come a time when the trustees would want to get in new blood, youngsters, recently graduated, up on the latest techniques. She hadn't wanted to worry him unnecessarily. She still didn't.

"I don't care who they find to take over my work. I hate just walking away. It's as though I'm leaving nothing of myself behind!" He suddenly stopped his pacing, his eyes alight. "And if they don't renew the contract I'll do something about that."

"What are you talking about?"

"Nothing," he said abruptly, face expressionless. "An old man rabbiting on."

Mary-Ann sighed heavily. Looking back it might have been easier just to let that pig Prins have his lousy way with her. This latest disaster could so easily have been engineered by him.

*

Roger sat cross-legged on the aft deck of the yacht. He was two-weeks unshaven with hair blown around by the wind. Dried paint, old grease and cracked varnish covered his jeans. His hands were dirty and fingernails blackened. He whistled tunelessly as he sat there, happy, a stripped-down winch between his legs, smearing generous quantities of grease on various parts of its internal mechanism.

He became aware of being watched and looked up. The man on the quay gave a polite nod and continued to stand there staring.

Roger returned the man's nod, turned his attention back to the winch. Probably just another rubbernecker. A seemingly endless stream of dreamers wander around yacht marinas. Most of them with a faraway look in their eyes. Most of them unlikely to ever sail anywhere. But dreams are cheap.

"Nice boat!"

Roger looked up again. "Thanks." Now that he'd had a second look at this character he looked less like a dreamer than most.

"You going somewhere special? You seem to be working awfully hard."

Maybe he was a dreamer after all. Roger could use a break. He stood up, stretched widely, ambled over to the guardrail. He smiled down at the short tubby fellow in his brown polyester suit.

"Yeah. I'm getting ready for the BOC Challenge."

"That sounds exciting." The little man in the nondescript suit held up his camera. "Can I take a picture?"

"Hey, go for it," Roger said, grinning happily as the man on the quay snapped away.

"What's the BOC Challenge?"

"An around-the-world race for single-handed yachts."

"I'd like to hear more," said the little man in the brown suit. "Can I come aboard?"

Roger hesitated. What the hell? Why not?

"Sure, but take your shoes off before walking on the deck," he said. "Use the gangplank over there and I'll tell you all about it."

*

Jakes shook his head. "What did you expect?"

"I didn't expect Kruger's management to make such a fuss," Mary-Ann replied. "My book's really just one person's opinion."

"Explain it to her, Brian."

"You really know how to stir it, don't you?" Brian Lombard, an almost two-metre tall, broad-shouldered young man, grinned. "The problem isn't what you wrote. Nobody likes criticism, but they're scientists and can live with differing opinions. But your book has somehow caught the media's attention and *they're* now having a go at management."

Brian wore a khaki short-sleeved shirt, khaki mid-thigh shorts, khaki socks and well-worn PCT boots. The exposed parts of his limbs had turned a mahogany brown from constant exposure to the elements, winter and summer. The green epaulettes signalled his status as a fully-fledged Kruger ranger.

"Having Professor Prins on TV, drawing attention to your book by slamming it and criticising you for criticising the National Parks Board, doesn't help your case. He's the guru."

Brian had been a family friend from the time the Webbers had arrived from the United States. His father – later killed by a buffalo while on a foot patrol – had been a Kruger ranger, as had been his grandfather. Brian and Mary-Ann had grown up together, like brother and sister, being pretty much the same age. He was the closest thing to a relative she had other than Jakes.

Mary-Ann sighed wearily. "I didn't know about the TV thing. When did that happen?"

"As soon as Vestal released the book. Prins kicked off the whole media circus. He made it pretty clear *certain* conservationists shouldn't be in the business." He looked at her quizzically. "He came down pretty hard on you."

"Did you know I've been asked to appear on TV?" Mary-Ann asked. "Twice. A magazine program and a wildlife slot."

Brian laughed. "Management would love that."

"They know about it. The TV people talked to them."

"And the reaction?"

"A resounding 'no'." She also laughed, although not much feeling like it. "I was told employees can't run around criticising them in the media. They want a united front until it all blows over."

"It's a wonder they haven't asked you to resign. You're a troublemaker, Mary-Ann!" He sounded quite proud of her.

"The reverse happened," she said. "They say they can't afford to have me leave now. Then I'd be free to give interviews, whatever. Further fanning the media flames they want put out."

"What happens now?" Brian asked.

"I don't know," she replied. "Management will meet to decide my fate."

*

Basil Hawke, Michelle Denton's father, waddled towards the wood-panelled boardroom. Today he was making the giant leap from the minor to the major leagues of international finance. He stopped in the doorway, for a quick first impression.

"Good," he murmured, "nothing out of place."

The transplanted Lebanese financier rolled his rotund body down the length of the room. He placed his calfskin briefcase at the head of the polished wooden table, which was long and sturdy enough to have served as the dining-room table in a well-populated medieval castle.

The man who had been christened Bashir Harik had – on moving from Beirut to London via Australia – conveniently shed his name the way a growing snake sheds its skin. He was the portly product of a Shiite Muslim father and a – nominally – Roman Catholic mother. Neither of whom however, after one brief encounter, wanted anything more to do with each other – or him, nine months later.

Bashir Harik – alias Basil Hawke – had scratched and fought hard to be able, cautiously, to talk in millions of dollars. In fact he made that first, and most difficult, magical million taking a mining company in Kalgoorlie, Australia, to a listing on the Australian Stock Exchange. That the mine, which was the company's sole asset, turned out to be less – very much less – than the original listing prospectus for the company would have led any incautious investor to believe, could hardly, and certainly not legally, be laid at his door.

He wasn't the geologist – the extremely well-paid geologist – who had produced the mining reports. Equally Basil Hawke couldn't be blamed for the subsequent collapse of the company and the suspension of its shares by the same Australian Stock Exchange.

But this new deal wasn't like that one. He had already sunk nearly every cent of his personal fortune into this one. Which is why the meeting today. With the added wrinkle he had recently thought up, it wouldn't be long before he was talking in tens of millions of dollars – if not hundreds of millions.

This was the big time. He was about to arrive. As were his guests. He could hear Spanish being spoken outside. He quickly waddled back to the doorway. He paused there, hoping it would frame him, knowing his corpulent figure and lack of height made it more difficult to sell deals, to be taken seriously.

After the initial introductions were made Hawke got straight down to business. "Coal, gentlemen," he declared with a flourish. "Coal so close to the surface we'll have the cheapest mining costs of any coal company in the world. And a third world government in the palm of our hands."

The Colombian brothers, Raul and Simon de Rivera, unresponsive, seemed singularly unimpressed.

"We are not in the coal business, *Señor* Hawke," said Raul, clearly the older brother and boss.

"Nor do we want to be," added Simon.

"I understand, gentlemen," Hawke replied at once. "I also understand the problem you have with money in the USA that needs to be … er … changed from its original form. My proposal, gentlemen, will do just that for you."

Ever irresponsible, Simon laughed. "We call it laundering."

Which earned him a rebuking look from his brother, Raul.

Hawke coughed into his hand. "I know of valuable coal deposits we can get permits to exploit. I list a new coal-mining company on the London Stock Exchange. But first I sell cheap to the Darien Cartel, yourselves, shares in the company to be listed. They'll cost you virtually nothing. When the company's listed you sell your shares, make a capital profit, and the source of your funds will have been changed."

"Why will you sell us these shares cheap?"

Hawke smiled happily. "Because of a small bank in the States, which has recently been taken over by BCCI – the

Bank of Credit and Commerce International – which is more … entrepreneurial … than most banks. This small bank will accept your cash deposits, no questions asked. The deposit will be 100 million dollars, to be transferred to me when the new coal-mining company is listed. You get your money back by legally selling shares. The funds in the small bank will only then be moved out of the USA."

Raul rubbed his chin thoughtfully. "I've heard of BCCI, it started as a Pakistani bank now mostly owned from the UAE, but we've had no dealings with them. Are you prepared to personally guarantee their ability to perform?"

Hawke hesitated. He didn't think it wise to mention an arrangement he already had with BCCI. He would be drawing against the Colombians' deposits in the USA bank in order to grease all the palms that had to be greased. Most of his own funds had already disappeared like the early morning mist on a hot day in the Middle East. One shipment of arms delivered to Renamo on a deserted beach on the Mozambican coast had seen to that.

But he would be drawing not more than fifteen, maybe twenty, million dollars before the new mining company was launched. The Colombians would get their money back from the sale of shares on the London Stock Exchange. He would get their money as well as the shares he planned on keeping for himself. It was a deal he couldn't afford to miss. He would make it coming and going.

"Gentlemen," he said grandly. "This is a winner. I personally guarantee you'll get your money back."

"We don't like losing," Raul said softly.

Hawke didn't allow the ice dripping down his spine to alter his smile, although his jaw muscles twitched momentarily in sympathy with the feeling in his back.

After they had gone through the whole thing in detail Hawke felt both exhausted and exhilarated. He saw the de Rivera brothers to the lift and returned to his own office. As was his custom he meticulously made notes of everything that had been said, and by whom, right down to the

Colombians' veiled threat. He smiled – there was no danger
of anyone he knew in London understanding what he had
written.

Carefully he stacked the loose pages so that their edges
were properly squared off, one with the other. Neatly he
slid the squared-off pages into the file on the centre of his
desk. It was to be his main focus for many months to come
– if not years. That file represented the big time.

His smile grew broader. Now for the Minister of Mining
and Mineral Affairs in Mozambique. He pressed a button
on the intercom box on his desk. When a young lady
appeared in the doorway he said, "Tell Karl I want him and
keep yourself ready."

Within minutes his *Schwyzerdütsch*-speaking Swiss
assistant, Karl Hoeniger, a tall angular fellow from Basle,
around twenty-five years old, with fair hair that flopped
over his forehead, stood before his desk.

"Open an account with Credit Suisse in Zurich, as usual
making sure there's a back door. The initial deposit will be
two hundred and fifty thousand United States Dollars."

"Very good, *Herr* Hawke."

"When that's organised get the estimable Minister of
Mining and Mineral Affairs in Mozambique on the line. We
have good news for him." Basil Hawke rather liked using
the Mozambican's full title. For reasons he didn't
understand – and didn't really care about – it made him feel
a good few notches higher up the social totem pole.

"Very well, *Herr* Hawke."

Karl swung around as though on parade and marched out
of the office. Having a blonde Caucasian kowtowing also
always put Basil Hawke into a good mood and now he
looked towards the doorway.

The young lady who graced the second desk in the outer
office, and who never seemed to have any work, still stood
there, waiting, flaxen-hair hanging loose around a
pleasantly round, but vacant, face.

"Lydia, come here," he ordered finally, then, as she started forward, gestured abruptly. "No! No! Close the door first!"

Obediently she closed the door, but after turning around, stayed where she was. "It's the wrong time of the month," she winced. "I'm sorry –"

"Come here!"

She crossed the room to stand sulkily on his side of the mammoth desk, next to his chair.

"On your knees."

She leant on the desktop for support, obediently went to her knees. Out of his sight she pulled a face. Although a day like today invariably involved a bonus, it didn't mean she had to like it.

Basil Hawke rolled the chair on which he was seated a few inches further back from the desk. He slid his backside forward along the seat as he swivelled to face her, framing her neatly between his knees.

"Now!" he demanded, voice thick with anticipation – and not just for what was going to happen over the next few minutes.

*

The sunbeam slipped through the window and, like a stage spotlight, lit the brown envelope lying on the desk. Still unopened, it carried the Wildlife Research Trust's stylised elephant logo on the top right-hand corner.

Jakes sat hunched in his chair, staring blankly at it.

The Trustees had phoned from Washington to tell him the current five-year contract wouldn't be renewed. All four of them, on a conference call. Could they have changed their minds? Realised they were wrong about him. Realised he would never have done that stuff. No, the envelope had to be written confirmation of what they had said. Not that he could get himself to open it. Not yet. If it wasn't a reprieve the decision really would be final.

He winced. Despite the end still being a few years away he felt incredibly vulnerable *now*, as though he was going to be thrown out the very next day. And that was just the half of it. What he didn't dare tell Mary-Ann, besides the accusations they had made, was that he didn't have a pension. He had worked from contract to contract, with the vague understanding the Trust would eventually do something for his old age. In that phone call – and very unpleasant it had been, too – they had gone on and on about his dereliction of duty. They had spoken of his self-enrichment at the Trust's expense. His corruption. He'd had no idea what they were talking about. Being Jakes he had said less and less in his own defence as the accusations flowed. And that was how the call had ended – he was out when the contract was over and no pension.

There was nothing he could do about the pension. That had been a verbal agreement with a previous batch of Trustees, long gone. Under the circumstances the present Trustees accepted no further responsibility. So future financial arrangements were in the lap of the gods. But for the rest of it he had to do *something*, dammit. He had to make his own kind of statement. Something to do with his research. He wouldn't take it whimpering. He would leave something of himself behind. The African bush could be a silent witness to his work on the re-emergence of recessive genes in an interbreeding population. He couldn't just walk away. But what to do?

He stared down at the desk before him, as unseeing as a new-born pup.

Then he remembered the idea he'd had a few days earlier when talking to Mary-Ann. An idea flowing from a recent conversation with a farmer whose game ranch shared a common boundary with the game reserve. And why not? It would be perfect and he trusted implicitly the only other people who would have to be involved. Lungile and Kambala were old school. The three of them had spent nearly a quarter-of-a-century in the African bush together. They knew what loyalty meant.

With a start he realised the sunbeam had moved on to the wall opposite the window. His eyes returned to the envelope. He couldn't leave it forever. His right hand crept back along his belt. He dragged the knife from its sheath. Despite the defiance, there still lurked a faint hope the Trustees would have realised they were wrong, given him a reprieve. But every movement took a huge effort, like being neck deep in molasses. He picked up the envelope between two fingers, slid the tip of the blade under the flap and slit the envelope open along the top. He lay the knife down on the desk and in one hurried movement plucked out the single sheet of paper and spread it flat on the desk alongside the knife.

Involuntarily holding his breath he focused on the short sentence in the middle of the page. He slammed his open hand down onto the page. The crack sounded like a rifle-shot in the confines of his office.

"What's the problem?"

Jakes looked up. "Don't you ever knock." It wasn't a question, but there was no real rancour in his voice.

Brian Lombard smiled easily. "You'd be disappointed if you couldn't complain about that one."

Jakes remembered as if it was yesterday the young boy who was always ahead of the rest, except for Mary-Ann. He had never quite managed to catch her. Not that Brian had ever minded. He had been as proud of her achievements as he was of his own – perhaps even more so. He had done especially well for having lost his own father when only nine. Amongst the rest of the Park kids Brian and Mary-Ann had shone like polished diamonds in a heap of road-building gravel. Now Brian had a problem. He also wanted to study further, but had been unable to raise the money.

"I thought your hand was going right through that desk," Brian said.

In the absence of Brian's real father, Jakes had done a fair job of helping Brian's mother raise the youngster. He was a fine loose-limbed specimen, with his sun-lightened brown hair kept very short, something Jakes particularly approved of. Jakes waved a hand at the letter, indicating Brian should read it.

Brian picked up the letter, scanned it.

"But they don't say why. Are they short of funds? I wish I could help ..." his voice petered out.

Jakes nodded, tried to smile at the younger man.

Brian stood looking out of the window, the piece of paper hanging loosely by his side. He turned around. "Why don't you just go with the flow? Go fishing down at the coast, you've always enjoyed that."

Jakes looked at Brian with suddenly sleepy eyes. He knew just the valley. It was perfect. By unspoken agreement everyone in the game reserve had kept all development away from there after the scare in 1978. That was the year the then-government had announced coal-mining companies would be allowed to prospect in Kruger. A strong public outcry averted that threat. But since then Kruger personnel had quietly kept the public well clear of the place. The valley fell in Brian's area. It was a natural for Jakes' project. But Brian would strongly disapprove. All the Park people were committed to interfering as little as possible in natural selection.

"You're probably right," Jakes said at length, carefully keeping his face expressionless. "Maybe I'll just sit back and enjoy."

*

The short tubby man in the brown polyester suit smiled, happily conveying good news for a change.

Michelle just stared at him. "You're saying there's no other woman involved – at all?"

The private investigator chuckled. "Not unless you consider a yacht to be female. He abruptly stopped chuckling as Michelle stared blank-faced at him. Perhaps she didn't think it was good news. And she was the client.

"In case you need them I have photographs of him on the boat." He slid a large brown envelope across the restaurant table. "In here. There's really nothing more to it than that."

"But you're saying this boat … this yacht … is for his own use. He's not just helping a friend."

"Absolutely not! You should be very proud of him. He put the whole deal together himself."

Michelle stared at the envelope, left it lying there, felt anxious for no good reason, a nameless fear. "And this race – what is it? I mean, where is it? Here in Britain?"

He shook his head emphatically. "Oh no! This is the big one. The granddaddy of all yacht races. Hell, many consider it the toughest sporting event in the world. It's called the 'BOC Challenge' yacht race. And it's solo. Your husband's entered for the one that starts next month, in August, and finishes next year. It's something to –"

"But that's ridiculous! Are you saying it goes on for ages?"

"It actually can take up six months. They're wonderful. They go single-handed."

She shrugged that off. "And who's paying for all of this?"

The large brown envelope lay half-hidden by now-empty coffee cups on the table. The private investigator pointed. "It's all in there, but it's an international fashion-accessories company called Fashion Plc. Their biggest label is '*Joie de Vivre*'. They've committed a million to the project. It's a big company, I'm sure you've seen the name."

Numbly she nodded. "Of course. So it's actually French?"

"No, the head office is here in London. Their accessories are marketed around the world. It'll be terrific publicity for them. Millions in countries around the world follow the race."

Michelle sat there with the nameless fear growing, slowly taking shape. He had actually gone out and found a sponsor to pay for all of this. A million pounds! And he had been on it for more than a year. And the race took months to finish. And what about her? What was she supposed to be doing while he was away? December had some of the best parties in London. Otherwise it would be the south of France. All on her own. It was ridiculous. What would he do next?

"And if he wins?"

"He'd be on the yachting world map for life. Whatever happens you should be proud of him. This is only for sailing's best. This is the toughest sporting event in the world."

Michelle winced. On a lower level the shape of the nameless fear became clearer.

"And if he loses?"

"You mustn't worry about that. Just to take part is an honour. If he's in the starting line-up he'll be a well-paid professional yachtsman overnight – in a highly-regarded sport. He'll have dozens of sponsors ready to finance other races. He'll be guaranteed a high-profile sailing career. Even yachtsmen from smaller places like Australia, South Africa and New Zealand make a good living at it. Yachting is a rich man's sport. Some of the smartest, richest people in the world have an interest in sailing. Winning would just be a bonus. You don't have to worry. I promise."

"But he'd be totally independent!"

He gave her a curious look, but it wasn't a question, so he didn't reply.

Panic flushed through Michelle as she hurried into the Berkeley Square townhouse clutching the brown envelope. She had to put a stop to this. She would talk to her father. He would help. She knew that, even if theirs was a strange relationship. She had attended Roedean. Only one of the best schools would do for Basil Hawke's daughter. It had proved a mixed blessing. She had desperately wanted to belong, still did. Her classmates were mostly English born, although she had soon enough sounded as plummy as the best of them. And she did have English nationality courtesy of her mother, so that wasn't the problem. Her father had been the problem. She had dreaded his visits. He was so different to the other fathers. But he had always been generous to a fault, giving her everything she wanted, whenever she wanted it. Normally that meant money. This time she needed a different kind of help.

After closing the front door, she hurried across to the telephone, without even removing her coat. The nameless fear dominated her. It would be pointless trying to talk Roger out of the venture. This thing had to be stopped dead in its tracks and her father was just the man for the job.

*

Brian smiled encouragingly. "It could've been worse."

Mary-Ann shrugged. "From their point of view it would make the perfect answer. I work as a vet but I'll be far away from the media."

"I know you think it's a punishment. But I was there. They need you. And I'm all in favour of helping the Maputo Zoo. Those animals are in wretched condition. Wait until you get there. Some have already died of starvation. Because of the war in Mozambique the people running the place just don't have a clue. Saving the animals that are still alive, getting the zoo back on to a properly run scientific programme, can only be good."

"I suppose you're right. I just wish I was volunteering. Instead I feel as though I'm being dragooned into doing it."

"Think of it as doing some good while the media furore dies down. All your problems will be solved."

*

The telephone rang.

Juan Batero Dos Santos, the Mozambican Minister of Mining and Mineral Affairs, picked up the handset. A crackling signalled a long-distance call. He sat forward on the edge of his chair, breathing a little faster. When he heard the voice of Basil Hawke on the line he leaned back, closed his eyes, sighed quietly to himself. Abel Gamellah's plan was going to work. He had wondered about that.

"*Senhor* Hawke," Dos Santos said by way of greeting, then remembered that he had to switch to English, trying to keep the tremor out of his voice. A person in his position couldn't be too careful. There was too much at stake to let anyone know quite how important this deal was to him. "I hope you have good news for me."

Hawke's voice was slightly muffled but he said exactly what Dos Santos had been waiting to hear. The Mozambican listened attentively, making a careful note of the account number and code words.

"Now it's your turn," Hawke said.

Gamellah had pre-arranged this with Dos Santos, but the Minister had decided on a little judicious editing by himself. "*Senhor*, as promised everything is in hand. But I cannot move too quickly. The area for which you require mining permits is controlled by our sworn enemy, Renamo. There would a great deal of suspicion if licences were summarily issued. Proper groundwork will have to be laid with my fellow central committee members. But it will be done."

As soon as Hawke was off the line, and without replacing the handset, Dos Santos dialled the local code, international code and telephone number Hawke had just given him.

"Account number 3-254-337-912, password 'miner', balance available please," he said in English overlaid by his heavy Portuguese accent. The sweat pearled on his lip.

After a slight pause, but without further prompting, the German-accented voice on the other end of the line responded by saying, "Two hundred and fifty thousand United States dollars."

Dos Santos smiled. He had it made. Just one small adjustment. "Change the password from 'miner' to 'president'."

After putting down the phone, for one mad moment he was tempted to say to hell with it and catch the next plane out. But the money wasn't enough reason to leave. It was more useful as a slush fund. He would be untouchable. There were other good reasons to stay. Fence-sitting had already proved extremely profitable.

A long black Mercedes Benz slid through his mind's eye, at the front of the bonnet a small flag fluttered. He could see the people on the side of the road, craning forward to see –

Look! Watch! It is him! It is the President!

He craved power the way a heroin addict craves his drug. And it could happen at any time, it just took a little luck, that was all.

He suddenly wondered if Samora Machel, the present incumbent of the presidential suite, hadn't maybe manufactured his luck? Should Dos Santos manufacture some luck for himself? He could afford it now. He sat there, slumped in his chair, wondering for how long he could delay the issuing of Hawke's mining permits – despite the arrangement with Gamellah – while still having as a safety net all that money safely stashed away in a Swiss bank account.

Suddenly he shuddered: just so long as he didn't offend the Butcher, of course. That would be a terrible mistake.

*

The telephone rang persistently and Jakes picked up the handset.

It was a neighbouring game rancher on the line, a call for which he had been waiting. The two men, old friends, exchanged greetings, discussed for a few minutes the late start to the rainy season and the prospects for the year to come, before getting down to business.

"I have what you wanted. You can come across and fetch it any time."

"Excellent!" Jakes replied. "Give me a few hours."

Fifteen minutes later Jakes was bumping along the road in his diesel pickup truck with the stylised elephant logo on the door. Lungile and Kambala shared the front seat with him.

"I need your help, old friends," Jakes said in Shangaan. "I can't do what I want without you."

As always, Kambala responded. "You tell us what to do and we will do it."

Jakes smiled. One day when they stuck him in an old-age home – somewhere in the Midwest, no doubt – he would sit quietly on the porch, knowing that a small part of the African bush would never be quite the same just because Jakes Webber had passed that way. They wouldn't be able to take *that* away from him!

*

The valley seemed ageless.

It was as though it had been there since the birth of time itself. But like most things – it too had had a beginning. Three hundred million years ago it could be said to have really started taking shape.

It was a time when steaming swamps covered the land. Tall ferns and other tree-like plants with broad leaves grew in profusion, dense and sweating in the heat. And as they died, these lush tropical plants gradually formed a thick layer of vegetable matter on the swamp floor.

Over many millions of years this hardened into peat.

Much later still the peat was buried under sand and other minerals, part of which became sandstone and shale. For over two hundred million years the various rock layers slowly built up, growing heavier and heavier. This increasing weight on top of the peat compressed the thick layers into thinner layers of lignite – the youngest of coals.

The huge pressures continued to grow and the lignite was in turn compressed into much thinner layers – the harder sub-bituminous coal.

Eventually the gigantic grinding pressures of many millions of tons of rock, pressing down over many millions of years, created from that original vegetable matter bituminous coal – the second hardest of all coals.

Ten million years ago, intense seismic activity turned that part of the planet's surface upside down and forced it upwards to form a long plateau – deep inside of which was layered thick seams of coal.

Two million years later, earthquakes, generated by enormous pressures from deep within the bowels of the earth, strong enough to create continents, tore the rocky mountain plateau apart, down the length of it, forming two ridges, rich with exposed seams of coal – leaving a rocky valley between them.

As the years drifted by in their millions, the wind ceaselessly brushed away at those two mountain ridges, gradually softening their lines, turning rock into fine sand. The annual rains carried this as silt down the sides of the two mountain ridges into the valley. Initially, freshets and streams would meet at the bottom of the valley and become – for short periods of time – a raging river carving its way ever deeper into the narrow floor. Eventually the river in the floor of the valley also silted up, with a deep rich soil, levelled out by the waters to form a narrow plain. The wind dispersed dormant seed across the sand. When conditions were suitable these seeds, each containing a tiny embryo consisting of an immature root and stem, germinated. And grass covered the soil.

Over time the plain became dotted with groves of mopane and acacia trees.

As the grass and trees flourished, game moved in. Long-necked giraffe gently swayed amongst the trees like tall yellow-and-black rocking-horses. Spiral-horned kudu, stood quietly on dainty hooves, always half-hidden. Striped zebra faced outwards when threatened. Clownish blue wildebeest kicked up their heels. Troops of mischievous monkeys scampered through the trees keeping the earth-bound animals company. Along steep cliff faces baboon, silhouetted against the sky, squatted showing yellowed fangs, on careful watch for marauding leopards. Barked warnings scattered the clan, the sharp sounds echoing backwards and forwards across the valley.

Over time the run-off found other pathways down from the high ground and then across the countryside. Now, during the rainy seasons, a river raged across the western entrance of the valley making it impassable from that side. Halfway along the length of it – to the east – it had been closed off as part of Kruger's electrified border-fencing programme, meant to deter poachers from Mozambique.

And the valley was perfect for the living monument Jakes Webber intended leaving as a sign that he had passed that way.

*

The Attorney leaned forward, elbows on his desk, hands cupped like a priest at prayer.

"My advice, Dr Webber, is to leave things as they are. Firstly, South America is outside the jurisdiction of our courts, assuming we could prove anything: given that we don't have any witnesses to what happened in the room. Secondly, we'd have the devil of a job trying to prove the Professor was behind the trouble you and your father have had. Thirdly, taking legal steps against the Professor would just publicise your difficulties, thus jeopardising future opportunities in the field of conservation.

"I'd advise you," he continued, "to go to Maputo with the rest of the Kruger team. Do one hell of a job there. Make yourself indispensable. Make them change their opinion of you. With a bit of luck the worst of it will blow over in time."

Mary-Ann nodded reluctantly. It was what she had thought he would say, but it had been worth a try. Whatever happened – Professor or no Professor – she was going to stay in wildlife conservation. If Prins thought she would dry up and blow away like an old leaf, he was making a big mistake. She would outlast him – one way or another. And the lawyer could be right, maybe Prins would leave her alone now …

*

Roger pushed his way through the glass doors into the foyer of the office building. A man wearing a dark-blue uniform with silver-embroidered 'SECURITY' badges on the upper arms of his jacket sat behind a white console. He was reading a paperback. He looked up as Roger approached, put the book down.

"Good morning, sir." His cap was on the desk next to his elbow and the grey hair contradicted the twinkling pale blue eyes and red-cheeked cherub's grin.

"Morning!" Roger gave him a beaming smile as he made his way to the lifts.

The security man stood up and wandered across as Roger waited for a lift. "'Tis a lovely morning, isn't it?"

"Sure is," Roger said.

"Just two weeks to go. You must be all wound up, sir. Aren't you nervous?"

"You betcha, but also very excited."

"I told the missus I'd met you comin' in and out of 'ere. She was right jealous, I can tell you. She'll be recording everything they show about the race – then I sees it when I gets 'ome. It's a wonderful thing, sir. A big challenge, but we're an island nation, we're all sailors at 'eart." He hesitated. "Was in the Royal Navy meself. A nation of sailors, is what we are."

Roger nodded. Once the news had become public knowledge he had been overwhelmed by the response, from all kinds of people, from all walks of life – and most of all from his father. Hell, even Patrick had phoned to wish him luck and to tell him people had been talking about Roger's entry in the BOC. For Roger the project had generated a momentum of its own, consuming his every waking moment and most of his dreams as well. Now it was no longer just doing something to prove himself, it was very much more than that.

As the lift door slid open the security man added, "You just bring that trophy back to England, sir. Them foreigners 'ave 'ad it for long enough."

Touched more than he would care to admit, Roger just nodded, at a loss for words.

Roger barely made it to Basingthwaite's outer office at the appointed hour and was shown through with no delay. He was surprised – normally they kept him waiting for at least thirty minutes, not that he had ever complained, he was too grateful for the opportunity he had been given.

He waved a hand at his grubby jeans. "Sorry about the dress. Deep into last minute preparations. Your request came as a bit of a surprise. It's always me keeping you abreast of progress. Trying to give you value for money. We're days ahead of schedule –" and abruptly stopped speaking.

He had finally become aware of the atmosphere, a feeling he couldn't quite place. John's eyes slid away from his to focus on the desk. A giant vice squeezed Roger's innards, a throb beneath the ribs.

"You can't be unhappy with my performance. We're way ahead of schedule –"

"It's not that," John mumbled.

"– and we've come in well under budget –"

"I know, I know." John stirred uneasily in his chair.

"Jesus, I've been living on bread and water to make sure I kept within –"

John almost shouted, "I said it's not that."

Roger sat down in the chair opposite John, staring at the other man, willing it to be some small, easily solved problem. He suddenly realised he was gripping the arms of the chair so hard his forearms ached. Deliberately he relaxed them.

With Roger sitting John seemed slightly more comfortable. "Business is business, old son. One has to go with the flow and all that sort of thing."

"What are you trying to say?"

"Sorry, old son. Orders from the top, don't you know. Don't want to pull the rug out from under you. No choice really."

Where had heard those words before?

I am sorry, old son – don't want to pull the rug out from under you – no choice really – .

Of course, his father had used them when extracting the promise from Roger.

"Say it in words of one syllable, will you?"

"Of course, old son. Absolutely. Why not, eh?"

Roger leaned back in his chair. He sighed softly as he closed his eyes. With the bright window behind John the world beyond Roger's eyelids was red. An appropriate colour. He felt like leaning over the desk, grabbing John by his fashionably over-long hair and banging his face into the desk.

"We're taking you off the project."

Roger stared, he didn't understand. "Look, you've spent most of the money already," he said finally. "If you've a money problem I'll organise a co-sponsor. Hell, I'll even ask my wife if necessary."

"Money's not the issue, old son. My Lord and Master has found another chap. A Frenchman of vast experience, he tells me –"

Roger lunged across the desk and grabbed John by the lapels of his double-breasted jacket. "You can't do that! We have an agreement, dammit!"

He let go and John slumped back into his chair. John pointedly brushed off his jacket, rearranged the lapels and the sit of the jacket on his shoulders.

"Nothing in writing, don't you know," he stated, the words like chips of ice.

"You can't –"

"We can, old boy. And we have."

"C'mon John! We were at varsity together. Scrub this other fellow. Haven't I done well? Haven't I kept all my promises. Even better – I'm ahead on time and budget!"

Surely there had to be some way of convincing Basingthwaite ...

"I'm sorry ... we can't." John ran a finger around underneath his collar. "The truth is, old son. I don't have a choice. You don't have a choice. My Lord and Master has spoken. Most strongly I can tell you." After a pause he added, "And the other fellow insisted on a contract and we've signed. Can't back out on that one now – even if we wanted to. Just isn't possible."

"But why? What the hell did I do wrong?"

It couldn't end like this ...

"Don't look at me like that. It wasn't my fault. I told my Lord and Master we were very pleased with you. He was adamant. I don't think it had anything to do with wanting this other fellow in. It was you he wanted out."

For a while Roger stood there staring at John.

This wasn't possible ...

"Can I see him?" Roger asked at length. "Can I talk to him myself? There has to be a reason ... some kind of mistake ..."

"I can try to find out for you, old son. But it won't be soon, that I can tell you. My Lord and Master has gone away for a while. Look, as soon as I know something I'll give you a call. It's the best I can do, old boy."

Feeling numb, Roger left the office, mind blank, almost unable to muster the will to continue putting one foot in front of the other.

He walked out of the building, past the doorman, didn't see the forefinger raised in salute. He found himself halfway down Broadway, leaning against the low wall that marked the boundary of New Scotland Yard. He stared at the three-sided Scotland Yard sign slowly turning on its pedestal, endlessly going around, going nowhere, always ending up from where it had started.

Why do they bother? Why had he bothered?

He walked down the road, bumped into people, no apologies, not sure of the direction taken. At the first pub he came across he pushed through the door like an automaton and bellied up to the bar.

.

PART THREE
August - November 1987

Messages were always left on the telephone table in Jakes' cottage.

Having just arrived in Skukuza for a two-day break before returning to Maputo in Mozambique, Mary-Ann idly went through them. The only one for her was from Monty Cohen, the publisher. Warily she picked up the handset of the telephone, hoping her book hadn't caused more problems. During her time at the Maputo Zoo her life had returned to an even keel and she wanted it to stay that way.

Cohen answered the telephone and they exchanged greetings. Hesitantly she asked why he had called.

"Your book's doing unexpectedly well. From overseas I've had some interest. A London publisher. To negotiate those rights, I need your permission."

"That book has caused more than enough trouble already."

"This a wonderful opportunity – for both of us. A good deal I'll get you, I promise."

"I don't know if it's worth it."

Cohen's voice clearly reflected his anguish. "It's worth it, it's worth it. Please. What trouble could it cause?"

"I don't know –"

"The dream of a lifetime, help an old man achieve it. Please …"

Mary-Ann cast her eyes heavenward. She just didn't know. On the other hand England was so far away. It was difficult to imagine how anything happening there could constitute a problem for her or her father in Africa.

"All right," she said finally.

She replaced the handset. Had she made the right decision? She didn't want to rouse the sleeping dog Prins represented. She shook her head. This was ridiculous. She was becoming paranoid. It was highly unlikely anything would come of negotiations in the first place, and if something did happen Prins would never know about it. What could possibly go wrong?

She put the whole thing out of her mind.

*

The South African Deputy Minister of Foreign Affairs, Jan Barend 'Barrie' Louw, running to fat now in his early fifties, was a big man with cropped hair and the scarred ears of a rugby lock forward, which he had been in his younger years.

He shifted his bulk in his chair and looked across his desk at Professor Prins. "Your brother said you might have something for us."

Prins carefully stirred his cup of coffee, nodded. "It's common knowledge the trouble we're having with the anti-apartheid campaigns around the world. The economic effect it's having on the country."

Louw grimaced sourly. "It doesn't help that those traitors went to talk to the ANC in Dakar. Afrikaners, too, most of them. Just like you and me. I can't believe it."

"We need some good PR of our own." Prins smiled. "I have for you a young lady who would be perfect for one of your international good news schemes. She's a vet who's gone into conservation. A book she wrote is doing unexpectedly well ..."

A bitter tone, annoyed, even angry.

Louw looked at the other man quizzically. He started to say something but then let it lie when Prins himself seemed to shrug it off and carried on talking.

"There is one caveat though. It's important that I mustn't be seen as favouring one ex-student over another. My name must be kept out of this."

Louw waved a hand in the air. "That's no problem. How exactly do you propose we should use her?"

Smiling all the while, Prins spent the next hour spelling out exactly how he thought they could use Mary-Ann Webber to help counter the effects of the bad news that dominated the international media when the subject was Apartheid and the South African Government.

*

The patronising tone was unmistakable – and the last thing he needed to hear.

"You look really great this morning." Michelle Denton said again.

Roger groaned and rolled over to bury his head under a pillow. Bad enough a jackhammer at work in his skull and a taste in his mouth as though he had been used as a human trash compactor, throwing in that superior voice as well was expecting too much of a man.

"You have a visitor. He's downstairs in the drawing-room. Shall I also tell him to go away?"

Although a great deal of the past year had disappeared in an alcohol-induced blur they had still been the worst twelve months he had ever lived through, even if he had consistently avoided all mention – whether radio, TV or newspaper – of sailing generally and the 'BOC Challenge' race in particular.

It hadn't been easy.

When people had started to talk about it he would either change the subject or simply walk away. Dayfydd, Patrick and Hugo had come in for special treatment. He hadn't seen them at all and had flatly refused to talk to them when they telephoned or called around.

"I don't want to see anyone," he muttered from under the pillow.

"I'll tell him."

"Don't bother because this time I wouldn't listen anyway," rasped a hostile voice from the doorway.

Michelle spun around. "How dare you come up here without being invited? I'll thank you to leave this –"

"Oh, what the hell. You may as well come in, Hugo."

The rotund solicitor waddled into the room, pulled a chair away from the writing desk, turned it to face the bed and settled himself onto it.

"I'll be downstairs." Michelle flounced out of the room.

"You can't avoid me forever. You let us down. We deserve an explanation. We went on the line for you."

"I don't know what happened. I swear it's the truth. The project was under budget and easily on time. The whole thing just doesn't make sense."

"And if not for me then for Sam. My partner was caught up in your quest when she prepared your proposal and it was her idea to approach Fashion PLC, and she used her contacts behind the scenes that got you the meeting with Basingthwaite and her unequivocal support that got your acceptance by them."

"I didn't realise it was really all her doing."

Hugo shrugged. "It's the way she operates. Out of the limelight. So she went out on a limb for you, as did I. You owe both of us an explanation but especially her."

"We were under budget and easily on time. I don't know what happened."

"I don't know whether to believe you or not. And even if I did it's not good enough. I still think we deserve an explanation, don't you?"

Roger well knew he had made no effort. "Bloody Basingthwaite said he'd find out for me and never did."

"If it wasn't your fault, show us that."

Roger groaned. "What's the use? It's all gone to hell in a hand basket anyway."

"Are you saying we don't deserve an explanation?"

Roger stirred restlessly, looked around the bedroom as though searching for an escape hatch. Eventually he felt obliged to meet Hugo's accusing stare and the accompanying impression of hostility.

"I don't know … I suppose so … but how would I go about getting one? Where would I start?"

"We were very impressed with the way you tackled the project. You were a different person. For me that was the real you."

Roger grimaced. It was true. For fourteen months he hadn't taken a serious drink, had worked virtually day and night to make the race a reality and it had been the best and proudest time of his life. Hugo was right. The world had seen a different Roger and he, in turn, had learnt to see the world from a new perspective.

He missed that.

Hugo stood up. "Find out. Let us know whether you deserve to have us as friends."

"I learnt something about myself on that project." Roger said slowly. "And maybe I've learnt even more since then. Life isn't always just about right and wrong. A lot of the time it's simply about winning and losing – with each person having to be his or her own private army."

Hugo raised an eyebrow, managed to look a little less hostile, nodded. "You have to fight for what you want. Ask any of my tribe, they'll tell you – do for yourself or the world will do for you."

Roger spoke haltingly, exploring the idea as the words left his mouth, "If I accept what happened I'll always be the loser."

Hugo just stared at him.

"I enjoyed being a winner," Roger said with more certainty.

"And I have a meeting."

Roger looked at the portly figure framed in the doorway. "You didn't really come here just to hammer me for letting you down, did you?"

"Keep me informed. And in answer to your earlier question – when you want something, even just an explanation, you simply start at the beginning and carry on from there," Hugo said, and disappeared.

Roger stared at the empty doorway. Hugo was right. They did deserve an explanation. As did Roger's father. Because his time horizons were so much shorter, perhaps he deserved it most of all. And Roger did know how to go about getting one. He would start where it had all gone wrong and carry on from there, one step at a time. Just knowing he hadn't been at fault wasn't enough. He needed, deserved, an explanation.

They all did.

Basingthwaite had said he didn't know why his boss wanted Roger off the BOC project. So Roger had to talk to John's boss – and Basingthwaite was the person to organise that meeting.

Later that morning Roger set about telephoning Basingthwaite, but the calls were not taken and never returned. After a week of fruitlessly leaving messages, Roger finally accepted John was avoiding him – and he was more than just a little annoyed.

Roger took to hanging around the office block which housed the Fashion Plc headquarters. At 4.30 pm on the third day he eventually got lucky. Basingthwaite came out of the building, strode across Broadway, briefcase in hand, on his way to the St James' Park underground station. Roger hurried after him, caught up with him just outside the entrance to the underground. He put his right arm through John's arm, forcibly steered him away from the doorway and down Broadway.

"Hullo, *old son*. What a coincidence. Just the fellow I've been trying to get hold of these last few days."

John looked nervously over his shoulder. "I've nothing to say to you. I've a train to catch."

"But first we're going to catch up on some news. Aren't we, *old son*?"

"I don't have to talk to you."

"But, *old son*, that's where you're wrong. Why don't you look down at my overcoat." Roger kept his left hand in his coat pocket with his index finger stiff against the cloth. "I want to know what the fuck happened and why. You can start by telling me why you're so fucking scared."

"You're bluffing," Basingthwaite stammered, but he didn't sound as though he believed himself.

"Try me, you son-of-a-bitch!"

"I don't even want to be seen with you."

"Why not, *old son*?"

"Because you have very powerful, very nasty enemies in very high places. I almost lost my job through you. I have *never* seen my boss so angry and so disturbed. He was utterly and totally distraught. When I went back to him for an explanation – and, yes, I did go back to him, I felt I owed you that much – he made it very clear to me that if I ever even spoke to you or about you again it would mean my head. He gave me very clearly to understand that you were trouble – very big trouble – with a capital T."

"Shit and double shit! I've got to find out what's behind all of this! I deserve an explanation."

Some of Basingthwaite's jauntiness had returned. "Not through me, old son. If my Lord and Master is scared, then I'm scared – automatically."

"What's his name?"

"I told you, old son. You're *persona non grata* and –"

"Don't be a fucking egg, Basingthwaite. If I don't get it from you I'll get it from your company letterhead or the company records at the registry. It has to be somewhere – so you may as well give it to me."

"Osbourne-Kerr," Basingthwaite muttered. "Sir David Osbourne-Kerr."

"Cur sounds dog-like enough for me. Where does he live?"

"I'm not telling you. I've gone as far as I'm prepared to go. And it's spelt K – E – double R, and not C – U – R."

"Then I'll look it up in the telephone directory. One way or another this Kerr fellow is going to tell me what I need to know."

*

It had taken a while to work through the main agenda items but the Deputy-Minister of Foreign Affairs, Barrie Louw, was patient: his moment would come. It was an opportunity for him to make a contribution, to throw his hat in the ring towards a move up the party political ladder, maybe even to a Minister's portfolio. His boss, Roelof Frederik 'Pik' Botha, the Minister of Foreign Affairs, was overseas and less of a hawk than Louw.

Pik Botha, for instance, had been an early opponent of the information department effort designed to manipulate domestic and international public opinion by financing a pro-government English-language newspaper, *The Citizen*, and then against them trying to buy *The Washington Star* through intermediaries for the chance it represented to influence American opinion, while his deputy, Louw, had supported these initiatives.

Pik Botha had also, to Louw's frustration, and the State President's annoyance, made worldwide headlines earlier when, in response to a question by a German journalist, he had said it would be possible for South Africa to be ruled by a black president. This had earned him a public rebuke by the State President, PW Botha, which rebuke had also been accompanied by a strong reaffirmation of apartheid.

Louw believed that all of this had opened the door to his own possible advancement up the political ladder. Prins' plan involving Mary-Ann Webber was another chance to put his own stamp on his Deputy-Minister portfolio and to curry favour with the leadership.

Pieter Willem 'PW' Botha, the tall State President – no relation to Pik Botha, the Minister of Foreign Affairs, who PW had come to distrust – sat at the end of the boardroom table. A grey monk-like fringe encircled a mostly bald scalp, which wrinkled as he spoke. Neatly dressed in a dark blue suit with a breast pocket handkerchief matching his tie PW Botha now raised an eyebrow behind his plain-rimmed spectacles.

"Any other business?"

Louw sat forward. "We're not winning the international media battle."

PW Botha nodded. "It started a long time ago. Even our friends can no longer be trusted. Already Thatcher had the cheek to write to me privately asking that Mandela be released."

Louw shrugged. "Obviously we need to keep on with our current reform program at our own pace but the world sees it as too little too late. So we also need to show the world that we're at the forefront of changes in a field unrelated to politics. We have to keep on trying to change the trajectory of the international media dialogue on South Africa."

"Specific ideas?" asked PW Botha.

Louw nodded. "Conservation is a popular topic these days. We can show we're modern and forward thinking without it compromising any political decisions we make."

A third man further down the table said, "What do you suggest?"

"I propose we make use of a certain Dr Mary-Ann Webber."

"That American book girl, I've heard about her," said one of the other committee members. "Why should she co-operate with us?"

Louw shook his head. "I wouldn't expect her to co-operate."

PW Botha pursed his mouth. "Coercion? That could result in even more adverse media attention. If that gets out we'd be even worse off."

Louw smiled. "Not necessary. She won't know she's working for us."

"How do we get her co-operation then?"

"Persuasion, with our involvement hidden from view. She won't even know what's behind it," Louw said. "The special inducements on offer should ensure her ... er ... co-operation. I've given each of you a complete file."

The third man flipped open his file and gave a low whistle. "She's a damn sight better looking than most of the Miss South Africa's we've had in recent years."

Louw nodded. "She's also very bright and her book on conservation is doing well internationally."

"What's she doing now? Where is she?"

"She's a vet with the National Parks Board. On the Maputo Zoo project."

The third man cut in again. "The help-save-the-remaining-animals story? The one we've been using for political mileage internationally?"

Louw grinned. "It's fashionable to be green. And the field hasn't yet been politicised. We can still generate positive interest overseas. It all helps."

"Surely we've got plenty of conservation experts? Our *own* people. Afrikaners."

"But that's the point. She's not South African. Despite having lived here most of her life she's American. And she's author of a book which is receiving a lot of interest overseas. She's a natural for what I have planned."

He opened the briefcase in front of him and extracted a folder file identical to those he had earlier handed out. "It's all in here. Before we commit ourselves, however, you'll see on," he paused to flick open his file, "page 2," he paused again while the others obediently paged through their files, "I propose a small test to see how she performs. That way we also get to meet her anonymously."

The third man nodded his approval. "The fact that she works for the National Parks Board should make that easy to organise. We can work through Professor Prins."

"That's what I thought," Louw said happily.

*

The Rolls Royce eased away from the kerb to join the flow of traffic down Broadway in Westminster. Roger tucked his Rover in four car lengths behind. All of his previous attempts to make contact with Sir David Osbourne-Kerr had failed. Initially he had telephoned Fashion Plc and left messages, but the calls were never returned. He had received a similarly negative response on simply turning up at the company's offices and asking for a meeting. After a week it was obvious he would have to find some other way of confronting the man. He soon established that Sir David's private numbers were ex-directory. He then began monitoring staff movements outside the Fashion Plc building.

It finally paid off.

Roger now followed Sir David's chauffeur-driven Rolls Royce through London and on to the ring road. It led him straight to the Surrey village of Dorking, in the stockbroker belt, south-west of London. Outside the neat white Georgian house, Roger sat in his dark-blue Rover for a while, giving Sir David time to settle down and relax.

He watched the three children in the garden: two girls and a boy. The boy was very young, maybe five or six years of age. He sat seriously contemplating his shoes, as his sisters laughed and giggled, chasing each other through the shrubbery. When Roger finally opened the gate and walked up the pathway to the house, the girls stopped their game and all three gravely examined him. He felt tense about meeting Sir David, but managed a small smile. The girls happily returned it, clearly unafraid. They were pleasant children, who had grown up in a secure environment unaware of all the bad things that could happen in the world. Roger hoped the children's demeanour boded well for his meeting with what he reckoned must be their father.

Roger rung the doorbell. Sir David opened the door.

"Good evening," Roger started politely. "I hope you can spare me a few moments. We really need to talk."

Sir David had changed into a pair of corduroy trousers and an open-necked shirt under a tweed jacket. He was a slightly old-fashioned traditional British type, enjoying his evening at home. He was relaxed and politely returned Roger's smile.

"I'm Roger Denton. You'll remember your company agreed to sponsor my crack at the 'BOC' race last year. Well, John said that –"

Sir David's eyes bulged. "Good God! You! How in God's name did you find me?"

"All I'm asking is just five minutes. Hell, that's not too much. Please just tell me why –"

"Get away from here! Now! Don't you understand? I don't want you near me," Sir David screamed, verging on the hysterical.

Roger's jaw sagged. He quickly recovered. "It's desperately important. Please … I have find out what went wrong. It wasn't just a yacht race for me. I can't begin to tell you how much it meant."

Sir David took a deep breath, which seemed to steady him. "If you're not off my property in one minute I'm calling the police. And I mean it!"

A woman's voice called out from the interior of the house, "Who is it, darling? What do they want?"

Sir David looked back over his shoulder. "It's nothing, my dear. Just some wretched fellow – trying to cause trouble."

"But I'm not!"

Roger stared at Sir David. The man's hands shook like the branches of a tree in a storm.

"What are you scared of? What the hell's going –?"

"That's it! I've had enough of this. I'm calling the police!"

He slammed the door. Roger beat a hasty retreat.

He drove thoughtfully back to London. More than ever he had to find out why he had been dropped by Fashion PLC. He had to have something to take to his father and to Hugo and Samantha.

Despite the setbacks, first with Basingthwaite and now with Sir David, in a curious way Roger was enjoying this commitment to finding out the truth. It reminded him of how he had felt while on the 'BOC' project. And it wasn't just that it gave him something to do. He dimly understood there were other reasons why he wasn't prepared to give up. He felt tense and alert. Was it just a demand for the truth that moved him? He felt like a hunting dog with the scent of a quarry in his nostrils. Could it be the thrill of the challenge itself that excited him? Was this a new Roger Denton that had entered the lists?

Roger started a dossier on the Sir David. The man had to have an Achilles' heel. Ten days and he had a fairly complete picture. From Roger's point of view it was depressing. The man was a veritable pillar of the community. A lay leader in the Anglican Church. A senior member of the Conservative Party and chairman of the party's Fund-raising Committee. A highly regarded business figure in the City where, besides being the Executive Chairman of Fashion Plc, he was a director on the boards of at least five other companies.

Sir David was married with three children, two girls and a young boy, this last a relatively late arrival. He was even on the special advisory committee to Margaret Thatcher, the British Prime Minister, who had on a number of occasions publicly singled him out for special praise.

In lieu of a better plan Roger again took to following Sir David around. It had worked in locating the man's home in Sussex, he reasoned. And it kept Roger focused. He had stopped drinking and was totally dedicated to finding a chink in Sir David Osbourne-Kerr's not inconsiderable armour of respectability.

*

Basil Hawke settled himself down in his chair, made sure the tea tray was within arm's reach. He smiled to himself. Everything seemed easy. The result of meticulous planning?

"Herr Hawke?"

"Yes?" Hawke queried irritably.

Karl Hoeniger gestured in an apologetic fashion. "From a banking friend in Zurich. I'm sorry … it's bad news. Rumour has it that BCCI is under investigation for money-laundering. It's also under investigation for having gained illegal control of its American bank subsidiary."

Hawke stared at Hoeniger for a long while, then started, as though waking up from a nightmare. "What are you saying? My entire plan revolves around that bank."

Hoeniger pulled a face. "There's more …"

"More," shouted Hawke, "what do you mean – more?"

Hoeniger bobbed his head apologetically. "It's just rumours, in Swiss banking circles. Perhaps it doesn't mean anything."

Hawke stared at him. "What do you mean more?"

"They say BCCI was set up deliberately to avoid centralized regulatory review, and it operates extensively in bank secrecy jurisdictions. Its affairs are extraordinarily complex. Its officers are sophisticated international bankers whose apparent objective is to keep their affairs secret, to commit fraud on a massive scale, and to avoid detection …" he hesitated.

"Go on, go on," Hawke gestured impatiently.

Hoeniger continued in a rush as though to get out the rest of the news in one final go. "There might be problematic loans in its Hong Kong subsidiary. And apparently the major shareholder, the Sheikh of Abu Dhabi, Zayed bin Sultan Al Nahyan, has refused to provide funds to Hong Kong BCCI to cover those loans."

Oh Jesus Christ! It wasn't possible, was it? It couldn't be true, could it?

Numbly Hawke sat still then gestured to Hoeniger. "Put it all in writing."

Later when Hoeniger re-appeared with his notes on BCCI, meticulous as always, Hawke added the document to the file he kept on his desk, closed his eyes and lay back in his chair. So much for the Darien Cartel's 100 million dollars: how secure was the balance of that money now?

Numbly he wondered how long it would take before the telephone rang – if they bothered to use the telephone first.

*

On this particular Wednesday afternoon, Roger was on foot. He gave a satisfied smile. Sir David wasn't using the

Rolls, he was on the pavement trying to wave down a cab. Roger looked at his watch – six o'clock – definitely part of the pattern. Over time he had become better at anticipating Sir David's moves. So although his target had twice added a fortnightly variation which caught Roger off-guard, this time he was ready.

Roger was upstream and stopped a cab first.

"Ten pounds extra if you can follow that cab," he said, pointing to where Sir David entered a vehicle ahead of them.

The cabby looked in his mirror, caught Roger's eye, laughed. "Just loike in the movies, eh, guv?"

"I guess," Roger muttered, feeling silly.

Sir David's cab travelled back along Broadway, cut across to Green Park and then around the circle to travel down Piccadilly to Piccadilly Circus.

A search for the truth was no longer the only reason Roger stalked Sir David. The chase had developed its own rhythm. Also his obsessive single-mindedness was an act of faith, perhaps contained an element of desperation, although he did not like to admit that to himself. It posed the question: without this – what?

Now Sir David's cab swung around Piccadilly Circus and further along Coventry Street before stopping. Sir David climbed out, gave a hurried glance around, paid off the cabby. He didn't mess about. Long legs took him along a narrow side street. Roger hung well back. Sir David slowed suddenly, dived into a seedy-looking pub, like a rabbit down a hole. Roger loitered a few minutes, feeling furtive. Then cautiously he pushed through the same glass doors.

He allowed himself one swinging look. Towards the back, Sir David was in earnest discussion with a blonde boy seventeen, maybe eighteen, years of age. As they talked the boy pushed his longish hair back, arched his neck, watched himself in the mirror on the wall. Narcissus for rent. Both ears carried small gold rings. He wore a bright paisley shirt smoothly tucked into very tight black jeans. A short discussion, the two abruptly stood up, walked towards the entrance.

Roger barely had time to turn away. After they had passed he turned to watch them leave. Another young boy appeared at Roger's elbow.

"Don't worry, sexy. There's more of us where that one came from. Two for the price of one, if that's your fancy."

Roger swung around, looked at the slight figure next to him. He also had long hair and wore two earrings. The willowy youngster winked at him, sinuously swung slim hips from side to side: swaying to inner music for an audience of one. And Roger realised he had found Sir David's Achilles' heel.

"Er … no thanks," he said. "I'm in a hurry."

Roger ran out of the pub. He didn't want to lose his quarry. Outside he saw Sir David and the boy climb into a cab. Feverishly he paced up and down, finally managed to stop another cab. Sir David's cab disappeared from sight but they picked it up again as it rolled around Piccadilly Circus and came within five car lengths as it travelled along Piccadilly towards Knightsbridge.

Sir David's cab stopped just behind Harrods. Sir David and the boy climbed out. Sir David paid the cabby. About one-and-a-half blocks further on, Roger did the same with his cabby. Keeping well back, Roger followed the pair until he saw them go into a tall anonymous block of flats. He hurried along the road and into the foyer of the building. He saw numbers flashing on a screen above the lift doors, could hear the ancient lift creaking upwards. Desperately Roger ran up the stairs two at a time. Was he going to lose them now? Breathing like a stranded walrus he reached the third floor in time to see Sir David and his young companion enter a flat at the end of the corridor. Roger waited for the door to close and then walked down the corridor to confirm the number – 38.

Should he bang on the door, confront Sir David immediately? No, he might not answer and, if he did, Roger would need more leverage than a knock on the door could provide.

In the foyer Roger checked the board listing the tenants. Flat 38 was inhabited by a Mr Smith. He grimaced – very original.

The next morning, dressed in the old jeans and a work shirt he had used on the yacht, Roger studied the block of flats carefully. A fire escape had been built onto the outside of the building, around the back. That suited his half-formulated plan. He walked the three blocks to Harrods. He spent half an hour in the hardware department of that great store.

Roger, after checking the tenants' board in the foyer, banged on the door to flat number 3. A bent old man of about seventy opened the door.

"Yers?"

"Sir David," he said deliberately and then immediately – and very obviously – corrected himself, "Sorry! I mean Mr Smith, has asked me to see to a plumbing problem in the kitchen in thirty-eight. He said you'd have a key."

The ancient fellow looked at him knowingly from under bushy eyebrows and Roger knew the old man would go for it. They went upstairs together and the grizzled old bloke let him into the flat number 38.

"Thanks, mate." Roger smiled. "I'll let you know when I'm finished."

"I 'as to stay with you. It's the rules," the old caretaker replied, scratching the back of his head.

Taken by surprise, for a moment Roger was at a loss. Then he nodded. "No problem, mate. You can come through and give me a hand. Some of these pipes and things can be bloody heavy. You don't want to just sit in the living-room and do nothing, now do you?"

"I bloody well do," the old man said, very quickly and very firmly. "You does your bloody job and I'll do mine." He stuck out his jaw as he stared up at Roger.

Roger shrugged – thank God for the British workman.

"All right then, I'll bloody well do it alone."

In the kitchen Roger quickly removed the screws from the bolt on the back door. He gouged out the holes so that they were a bit larger than before, filled them with putty and replaced the screws by screwing them into the putty. The putty would soon dry. Unless someone actually yanked hard on the door no one would know it had been worked on.

Roger took the key out of the old-fashioned lock. As in so many households, a great deal of attention had been paid to fitting complex locks on the front door, leaving the back door secured by an uncomplicated mortise lock and the simple bolt he had already doctored. The number was stamped on the key – MH 32. It would be easy to get a copy. He cleaned up so that all seemed the way it had been before he arrived.

On returning to the living-room he discovered the caretaker deeply ensconced in an armchair half nodding off.

"Bloody fool," Roger said. "It was just a bit of paper stuck in the outflow pipe."

The next day Roger went shopping with his short – albeit carefully compiled – list. He only needed a few items.

*

Brian eyed the five men as they filed into the small conference room in Skukuza. He knew how important tourism people were to Kruger in attracting the holiday pound, dollar, yen, and every other currency under the sun, so that it could be used where most needed. But rather an infuriated elephant cow with calf at foot than this.

Where was the bloody woman? And why was she suddenly recalled from her banishment to Maputo? He thought they were trying to keep her away from the stage lights, not shove her in there. And now the presentation without the main speaker.

But managers spoke and minions ran. That was the natural order of things and Kruger rangers didn't believe in interfering in the natural order of things, did they? And presumably it also ran to human affairs, because he was about to get up on his hind legs and do what Mary-Ann was meant to be doing. Gritting his teeth, Brian braced himself as though against a great storm by leaning hard on the lectern. A weird wooden groaning. He hastily stood upright.

"Good evening, gentlemen," he started hesitantly. "My colleague Dr Mary-Ann Webber, who will be co-presenting this talk with me, should be joining us shortly. In the meantime I'd like to give you some background on the Kruger National Park. It sprawls across the north-eastern corner of South Africa, sharing its eastern boundary with Mozambique. While its northern boundary is Kipling's great grey-green, greasy Limpopo," he smiled – pleased with that line – but no one in the small audience returned the smile, so he quickly soldiered on, "shared with Zimbabwe. The border," and he paused for effect, knowing this was a goodie, "being in the middle."

Nothing happened. Not a smile. He could feel the sweat forming on his forehead.

How does the bloody woman do it? Hungry mouths happy to lift crumbs from her upturned palms. While he offered pearls and they countered with restless bums.

"Anyway," now he hurried as if fearing a rainstorm and seeking shelter. "Kruger is just under five million acres in area. About the size of Wales or a bit larger than Israel. It owes its existence to two very different personalities."

Was that a movement in the back of the hall? His eyes flashed. The payment would be meaningful. No! He was still on his own. Good God! Were they already falling asleep. He clenched his teeth, determined to keep the white flag furled.

"In 1898 President Kruger established a sizeable game reserve between the Sabie and Crocodile Rivers, despite the fact most people saw the area as a public hunting area. After the South African War of 1899 – 1902 the then-Major Stevenson-Hamilton was seconded from his regiment to become first warden, a 'temporary' position that lasted for nearly forty years."

The words tripped out now, faster and faster, like lemmings off a cliff.

"The Park is home to over 140 different species of animals. More than 1500 lion, 7500 elephant, 30,000 buffalo, 30,000 Burchell's zebra and 130,000 impala; large numbers of blue wildebeest; giraffe and hippo; growing populations of white and black rhino; antelope such as sable, roan, tsessebe and Lictenstein's hartebeest; predators such a leopard, cheetah, jackal, wild dog and spotted hyaenas have all found sanctuary here. Sanctuary from man, of course, but not from each other."

With a sigh of relief Brian saw Mary-Ann enter the lecture hall and, desperate to extract some sort of revenge, without further ado added, "Of course some people are never satisfied – so now I'll hand you over to my colleague, Dr Mary-Ann Webber, who believes 5,000,000 acres is not nearly enough!"

*

"This is what the big rush was about?" Mary-Ann whispered to Brian as she joined him on the podium. "Has management gone completely mad?"

He shrugged, casual, relaxed now. "Yours is not to reason why …"

"Gee, thanks," she murmured under her breath.

Mary-Ann took the lectern, looked at the small group of men, sitting stiffly, lost without ties and briefcases. Dozens of people were perfectly capable of giving lectures to visiting dignitaries – and since when did management think her ideas were good enough for public dissemination? Well, if they wanted her to talk publicly then that is what she would do. She smiled at her small audience. Almost immediately they all woke up, settled down, returned the smile, each as though she had smiled just for him.

"I'm proposing the creation of a giant transnational game reserve stretching from right here in Kruger, through Mozambique, through Tanzania and into Kenya and incorporating a large chunk of south-eastern Zimbabwe. We might even just throw in all of the Great Rift Valley for luck," she added with a smile.

One of the five men raised a hand. "What about the people who live there. Do they get thrown out?"

"No way. They must be part of the solution instead of being part of the problem. They must be well rewarded for the damage elephant may inflict on their crops. They must be well rewarded for allowing the wildlife around them to go unpoached."

"Where's the money coming from?" It was again the man who had first asked a question.

Brian ran a hand over his chin. Asleep they weren't. Their bug eyes made them look like bushbabies caught in a spotlight.

"If African wildlife is to survive it's going to have to pay its way. People who are hungry most of the time, generally aren't interested in keeping wild animals alive. They want to eat the damn things. That's dinner on the hoof out there. And it's even worse when those wild animals represent competition for grazing or, like elephant, come along and destroy crops hard grown in barren soil. I'm suggesting the wildlife situation has to be structured in such a way it supports itself – and has the support of local communities."

"But political realities don't look too promising. Mozambique and Zimbabwe, to name but two, would have to co-operate."

Mary-Ann threw up her hands. "Politics is not my purview. But the politicians have to figure out how to live together. My concern is conservation."

"Excuse us just for a moment, Doctor," said the same man.

Some kind of authority figure? The others deferring. Now a huddle. Heads bent forward. Gesticulations. Enthusiasm. Smiles. Approval. Nods all round. Unknown victories won.

She bent close to Brian's ear. "At least this lot's awake," she murmured.

He raised his eyebrows, rolled his eyes, but said nothing.

The five men settled down. She told them the longer it took the more difficult it would be. Different countries were developing different wildlife cultures. Time was important. People had to start talking. Only long after would animals be safe. Those that made it.

The same man raised his hand. "Is this your message to the world? We should start talking? Even if we don't agree politically."

Strange question. Funny man. Why didn't any of the others open their mouths?

"Yes," she said. "And I believe they will because the conservation of wildlife is crucial to all of them as much as it is to South Africa."

"And funding?"

"Take one idea. I'm sure you know the Pilanesberg Game Reserve near Sun City. They wanted to dart two rhinos. Instead of doing what they do here in Kruger...." Mary-Ann was forced to pause. Brian, scourge of the medical profession, was having a coughing fit. Subtlety was not his long suit. She looked at him, waiting. He shook his head at her.

"Instead of doing what they do here in Kruger," she reiterated, with the sweetest smile. "they 'sold' the darting to Americans. Those two city folk, craving a taste of 'real' Africa, paid eight thousand dollars apiece for the privilege of firing the darting rifle from a helicopter. Hell, one of them had a cast made of *his* rhino so that he could keep a full-scale model in his den. So there's part of the answer.

Pilanesberg carried out some necessary scientific research and earned themselves sixteen thousand dollars and they still have their two rhinos.

"Another example. To keep the elephant population at around seven thousand, which is all Kruger can sustain, we cull about three hundred every year. The rangers hate the job. Most of those elephant aren't suitable for trophy hunters, but there are a bunch of hunters who'd give their left ..." and glancing sideways she paused to laugh at Brian's expression, "... *arm* to participate in that program. And some of those elephant will be trophy animals. Then they'd get up to five thousand dollars apiece. That means this game reserve could be earning itself another seven-hundred-and-fifty thousand dollars a year for a job it's currently paying to do itself.

"Kruger has to cull about six hundred buffalo a year," she continued, "They could be sold off for a thousand dollars apiece. That's another six hundred thousand dollars. None of this takes into account the daily fees those hunters would pay or the rest of the money they'd spend here on trinkets and things."

The eyes of one of the men in the small audience lit up. "That's good foreign exchange. Besides the political aspect."

Interesting approach for a tourism person ...

Afterwards the men had many questions, probing, seeking more detail. By the time she had finished speaking Mary-Ann knew as little about what was happening as when she had started. After it was all over she turned to Brian.

"What was that all about? They didn't look like tourist boffins to me."

"I dunno," he replied, shrugging. "Managers speak and minions run.

                              *

It was almost another month before Roger could again begin to think he had his man. Either Sir David had skipped

a few of his fortnightly excursions or he had changed his
routine on those Wednesday nights in such a way he had
managed to lose Roger. So, it was only during the first
week in October, that Roger was once again on Sir David's
trail. He followed carefully.

Sir David headed into the depths of Soho, walking with
purpose.

Roger entered the pub, saw Sir David talking to a tall
willowy lad with long blonde hair, again not much more
than seventeen or eighteen years of age. The discussion
went on for some time. Sir David kept looking over his
shoulder or around the bar from under his eyebrows,
moving restlessly in his seat. The slender blonde boy shook
his head at regular intervals. Eventually he nodded.
Immediately, and without finishing his drink, Sir David
stood up and walked quickly out of the bar, the boy
following close behind. Sir David hailed a cab and within
fifteen minutes the two were entering the apartment block
Roger had earlier reconnoitred.

After twenty minutes Roger hurried around to the rear of
the apartment block. Quietly he climbed the fire-escape, his
soft-soled running shoes soundless on the steel treads. His
key fit the kitchen door lock perfectly. With a steady
pressure he pushed the door inwards and the screws holding
the bolt pulled easily, and quietly, out of the putty.

A few quick steps through the small kitchen and along
the passage. Roger paused outside the bedroom door. His
tongue stuck to the roof of his mouth and his heart thumped
painfully in his chest. He wiped his damp palms on the
sides of his jeans. Was he doing the right thing? Dammit!
He had a right to know why he had been thrown off the
BOC project.

Don't think, just act.

He slammed the bedroom door open. Started taking
photographs, flashlight blindingly bright in the dark room.
Five sunbursts of light before Roger even really looked. Sir
David naked on top of the naked blonde youth face down

on the bed. Two moons – round and astonished. Eyes wide and staring.

Sir David rolled off. "Shit! Shit! Shit!" he screamed in a high falsetto, tried covering himself with a sheet. Too late, he had been preserved in silver halide crystals.

"Don't you remember me?"

"Jesus Christ! Fucking Denton! I'll fucking kill you!" He jumped out of bed, pulling a corner of a sheet with him, stumbled towards Roger.

At a distance of a metre Roger held out the camera, triggered the flash-gun full in Sir David's face. The man reeled backwards as though he had been struck, screwed up his eyes against the blinding light. The blonde boy just lay there on the bed, naked, squinting up at the two men.

"Just tell me what I want to know. And I'll walk out of here. You'll never hear from me again. Why did you dump me?"

Sir David burst into tears. Roger didn't know where to look.

"For Christ's sake," Roger exploded finally, embarrassed and annoyed, and feeling more than a little guilty. "Just tell me what I want to know and I'll get the hell out of here!"

Sir David plumped himself down on the edge of the bed, buried his face in his hands. "But I'm damned if I do and I'm damned if I don't!"

"Why was I thrown off the project?"

After a long pause Sir David lifted his head. "And if I don't tell you?"

Roger waved the camera at him. "This'll be in the tabloids tomorrow. Bye-bye directorships. The Tories will disown you. The Church will publicly forgive you, it's their business after all, and six months later, bang goes the garbage can lid. Last, but not least, your wife and family. How will they take it?"

"That's exactly what the other man said!"

"What are you talking about?"

Sir David gave a long sigh. His voice was soft and lifeless. "A man phoned. Name's Hawke – some sort of bloody foreigner."

Roger stared at him in astonishment. For a long while he was speechless.

"You mean Basil Hawke?" he asked at length.

"He said he had photos. I wasn't aware of any being taken, but I couldn't take a chance – don't you see that? He said he'd publish them, give them to the newspapers, if I didn't drop you from our program. Now you've got your information, will you give me that film?"

Roger stared blankly at Sir David for a while. He had fully intended giving the man the film as soon as he had talked. Now all was quicksand. Why would Michelle's father have him thrown off the BOC project?

"No – not until I'm sure you won't tell Hawke."

"But I'm in the bloody middle, don't you understand? That's what Hawke said about you."

Angry and confused, Roger turned on his heel and stalked out of the bedroom.

"But what am I to do?" Sir David's distraught wail followed him down the corridor.

On his way home, Roger tried imposing order on chaos. On his own Hawke would have no reason to interfere. He could only have done it for Michelle. But Michelle was just scared. There were many ways to alleviate fear. Basil Hawke had chosen to swat Roger like a cockroach. Sir David was also a victim. Roger's stomach twisted, bile rose in the back of his throat: getting to the truth had been his mission, now, in an instant, Hawke became the target!

At home the next day, Roger still considering his options, heard the phone ring. His mind elsewhere, he picked it up, gave his name.

Basingthwaite didn't say hullo. "You dirty bastard, I know it was you. I can't prove it, but I know it was you. God! Was sailing in that bloody race so important?"

Roger grimaced. "Has Sir David been on to you?"

"Haven't you heard?"

"What are you talking about?" Roger asked tiredly.

Basingthwaite spoke heatedly, slammed down the phone.

*

Ms Mary Partridge squawked over the intercom. "There's a Mr Raul de Rivera on the line for you, sir."

For a wild moment Basil Hawke debated not taking the call. But surely worse things could happen than talking on the telephone? At least they hadn't turned up in person. Gingerly he picked up the handset, gripping it as though he knew it was a snake in disguise.

"Thees bank you suggested. Plenty of bad news. They closing their doors soon. What's happening?" Raul asked with his thick Spanish accent.

"A lot of rumours. I'm sure it'll be cleared up soon." A collar suddenly too tight, a pudgy finger running around inside, pressure not alleviated.

"That eesn't what we heard."

"Anyway, you're going to make your money from the shares, when we list the coal mining company. That hasn't changed."

"We have your personal guarantee," Raul said. The line went dead.

Hawke's hands trembled. Writing was difficult. Proper planning called for meticulous notes. But if he couldn't control a pen properly, what chance a listing? When finished he carefully slid the sheet of paper into the file, laid it neatly to one side on his desk.

The listing. The coal mining deal. A mythical bird rising from what was left of a bank. It had to be brought forward. It would be a lifesaver – his, anyway.

He wiped the back of a hand across his mouth. Again and again. He would take no chances – he must track down the geologist he had used in Australia. Afterwards make contact with Dos Santos in Mozambique. He reached out his hand to ring the buzzer for his secretary. The tremor had become a near palsy. He tried again.

Lydia appeared in the doorway. She looked at him with raised eyebrows.

"Did you want me?" she asked, showing small white teeth. "Shall I close the door?"

Who was this person? Why was she grinning at him? Why had she burst uninvited into his office when urgent work needed to be done? Was she mad?

"What?" he articulated at last.

"Do you want me now?"

He jerked as though his finger had inadvertently got stuck in an electrical wall socket. What else could cause such a convulsion?

"Get out!" he screamed at her. "Just get out of here!"

Lydia stared at him for a moment. His voice was abnormally high-pitched. A rat has a finely honed instinct for survival. Fear pervaded the air. Waters threatened to close overhead. She wondered if the time had not come to float quietly away.

*

Jakes sat on his porch. He didn't see the hardekool standing tall against the smeared orange light on the horizon. He didn't see the flamboyant red bougainvillaea framing the porch. He didn't hear the hadedas cry as they fled his front lawn. He was far away.

He hadn't worked on the Trust's research program for ages. But his personal project in the valley was on track. Almost a full cycle of seasons had past. The contract with the Wildlife Research Trust in Washington still had a way to run so he would be okay on that score. He'd had a reminder that he didn't really need.

But what if something went wrong? Who would make sure it would last? Someone's eye was needed. Making sure all worked well. Who would help? Who had he helped? Who was in a position to help?

"Morning," Brian called out cheerfully as he came around the corner, waving a hand at Jakes.

Eyes suddenly widened, Jakes raised a hand in response, jerked a thumb at the cane chair next to his. The valley was, after all, in Brian's area. Did he really want to tell Brian? So far it had been between Jakes, his two guys, and the African bush.

"My pickup gave trouble yesterday," Brian said. "I was about twenty k's to the east of that tall pointed hill. And my radio wasn't working. I had to walk to the main road to bum a lift."

Jakes had been lucky, he had always been able to live with nature's rhythms. Until now 'time' had provided no pressure. The only pressure he had ever felt was for a presence missing these twenty-plus years. Now the new sharpened the spurs of the old.

"Having to walk made me think of the early days. Like when you first arrived?" Brian cocked an eye in his direction.

A sardonic look at the younger man, a wave of the hands, an invitation declined.

Brian grinned, plainly amused his ploy had failed, comfortable with the surrogate father.

Jakes still looked inward. What if something went wrong? But daily the risks grew less. Soon nature would take its own course. And the rainy season lay ahead, that would help. Then a major concern would disappear. After that – Jakes shrugged.

He *would* tell Brian about his project – but not quite yet.
*

The blindingly bright orb in the sky settled its weight over the living, allowing no respite. Near to the valley's entrance a large mature lion – new to the area – sprawled disjoint in the shade of a mopane tree. Dun-coloured, even his proud mane was a dusty brown.

Further down the valley a restless lioness arched her back, driven by an inner heat. She nipped a young lion playfully on the flank. He was very dark, black to the casual eye, with his half-developed mane a deep coal-black. He swung a lazy head around, growled at her. Awareness, not anger, disturbed the air. Stiff-legged the lioness stalked away from the young male – then spun around – a short charge – she bit him on the shoulder.

He reared up. Swung a large dark paw at her nose.

She spun away.

The rough and tempting sounds bounced along the narrow plain: a lioness in oestrus with a male paying court. The clamour ricocheted off craggy rock-faces – caused nervous trembles for miles along the valley. Heads lifted. Flanks twitched. Small and large hooves alike danced in the dust. Yellow teeth bared on the crags. Tree branches quivered as small grey projectiles moved further from the ground.

A lash applied, the mature lion lurched to his feet, in the heat, a marionette controlled by a mad puppeteer. Sounds bounced along the valley. The whip again. He stood stiff-legged, nose raised. The lioness moaned. He started forward. He had no more choice than a shark fixated on a feeding frenzy.

The young male turned with the lioness, playfully bit her right shoulder. A mistake? Immaturity? She swung on him, growled. For a few moments this had little to do with a mating routine. She carried a deep and vicious scar that ran the length of her right side, starting from her shoulder all the way to her flank. Had his teeth closed a shade too hard on that? Was it an instinctive response provoked by a painful reminder of an attack on a young buffalo calf which had gone wrong?

The lioness had thought the four-month-old calf ripe for the taking once she had cut it out of the herd. She was right, but she was also wrong. She had taken the buffalo calf all right, landing on its back with one paw around the calf's muzzle, breaking its neck as they crashed to the ground, a flurry of dust. A few reflex kicks and it was over – almost.

The lioness had arisen from the small carcass too late to avoid the buffalo cow.

Why would this bovine-seeming beast be considered one of the five most dangerous animals to hunt? Over-large cattle standing around chewing grass. Quietly lowing to themselves. Occasionally, here and there, a head lifted to scent the breeze. And then a transformation. Wounded or aroused and it has the unstoppability of an express train. Buffalo can kill fully grown male lions.

This time the cow was not quite that successful. But she buried the tip of her right horn five centimetres into the lioness' shoulder. She swung that wide spread of horns the way a fighting bull hooks at a fluttering red cape. The full strike taken all along the right side – sliced with a surgeon's precision from shoulder to flank. A black snout diverted, nudging a felled calf, a dreadful lowing. The lioness dragged herself away. Many long months of healing, most of them hungry, living on carrion. The memory of that buffalo cow was buried deep in her instincts.

But a far greater tempest raged now than a bad memory from long ago. Her immediate anger was short-lived. The peak of the oestrus was a driving need taking precedence over all else. So she stiffened her back legs and arched her back as the young male drove at her, his teeth in her shoulder. Afterwards they lay idle in the shade, readying themselves for another bout. The eternal dance ensuring the survival of a species.

A half-an-hour away the large mature male walked slowly up wind, raised a scarred muzzle to scent the air. A faint smell drifted on the light breeze. His nostrils flared. He quickly changed to a swift ground-covering lope. A small fish on the end of fisherman's strong line has more choice than that old lion had. And the lioness, unaware it played angler, reeled him in with consummate ease.

The young male rolled over playfully, climbed slowly to his feet, stood hollowing his back, stretched against rigid back legs thrust out behind. The lioness raised her head. An unmistakable invitation, she rose to her feet. The young male nipped her flank. He drove at her again. And again they rested.

Then the young male again nipped at her flank. She swung around to respond, stopped frozen.

The dust-coloured lion, solid of shoulder, broke from the bushes – smashed his way into the clearing – blared his unmistakable challenge. At two-and-a-half years the young male was nowhere near full grown but he had been in the valley for close on twelvemonth. This was his territory. But inexperience showed. He swung to meet the challenge. He was too slow to start with.

The mature male's gouged yellow teeth, top and bottom, almost met in the young male's shoulder. Knocked off his feet, the dark lion writhed. A dust storm erupted. The young staked to the ground by the big. Survival over pain. The young male wrenched himself free. Shoulder muscle hung from the older lion's teeth, blood on his jaw. The young lion, stumbled to one side, avoided a fresh charge, bolted from the clearing, hopelessly outclassed by a seasoned veteran.

Escaping, his shoulder began to stiffen. The young lion hobbled. But on and on he stumbled, distance the goal. The older lion rampant. Then the young male stopped. It was as though a swarm of bees or of wasps or a red-hot poker burnt deep each time he moved his front right leg. Angry attempts to reach the shoulder were fruitless. The dark young lion entered the scrub, lay down on his side, in the shade of a false tamboti tree.

A deep wound played host to the foulness from a carnivore's teeth. He lay in the coolth with a quick shallow panting. The mythical master of beasts no match for microscopic bacteria. Fertile soil. They multiplied with astonishing speed, driving the poison deep in the flesh.

*

In Roger Denton's head the words rebounded time and again, back and forth.

Sir David has killed himself. And it's your bloody fault. God! Was sailing in that bloody race worth so much to you?

The evil men do and Hawke was the man. Wasn't guilt playing a part? If it did it certainly made matters worse. Was he just trying to transfer the hurt and the blame? No, dammit! Hawke was the problem, was behind everything that had gone wrong, so Hawke was the focus and he must pay. But how?

What was Hawke's *raison d'être*?

The simple answer – money.

How to make him pay? Hit him in his bank balance. How? A search of his premises, learn his business, ruin a deal, anything. It would be better than doing nothing at all.

The telephone rang. Roger answered it absentmindedly.

"Just so you know," Patrick said. "Father's very ill now. The doctors feel it's … it's close."

"Thanks for calling," was all Roger could manage.

After a lengthy pause, Patrick said goodbye and rang off. Words left unspoken, emotions suppressed. A bad time for all.

Roger timed his arrival at Hawke's offices just as they were closing.

"Sorry to bother you with this," Roger said.

Hawke was clearly annoyed by the imposition.

"Want to arrange a surprise for Michelle," Roger said. "I wondered if I might make a few calls from here. I want to do something special for her."

The magic name spoken, access soon followed. The rotund little man shrugged. "Go ahead. Just pull the main door closed when you leave, it'll automatically lock behind you."

"Thanks," Roger replied, smiling politely.

On his own Roger wandered around the offices, not sure where to begin, not sure what to look for. Hugo talking –

start at the beginning and carry on from there.

Hawke was the fountainhead of his immediate problems so the beginning had to be there. But where to start? But what if he returned? Roger nervously entered Hawke's office. With apprehension he sat at the great desk. A bulky file lay prominent. Roger carefully peeked under the cover. Good God! What was that? Arabic? Urdu? Some other language? To his Western eyes it was though a fly's feet had been dipped in ink and then the creature set down to wander over the piece of paper.

He kept giving quick and furtive glances at the door. He really wasn't made for this. Perched right on the edge of Hawke's rather grand chair, Roger ventured further. He got the impression the papers were filed in reverse order, the most recent date on top. He might be wrong. Either way he didn't understand a word of it.

Roger backtracked through the file. He found large-scale maps. These were in English. They showed coal deposits, somewhere in Africa. What information would be helpful and what a waste of time? Anything would be better than nothing. He made a note of the co-ordinates. He could later buy small-scale maps, see generally where they lay.

Roger returned to his task.

Ah ha! English officialise. This was better. A coal-mining company to be listed. Hawke was taking it to the LSE. He made notes as he read. The back of his neck felt exposed – enough was enough. He wanted out of there.

The next day Roger learnt a lot more about Sir David's suicide than he wanted to know. The man had returned to his family home, entered his study without speaking to anyone, stuck a shotgun in his mouth and blown the back of his head all over the wall. The two young girls Roger had seen in the garden had found the body. It was, apparently, a gruesome bloody mess. There would be no panacea powerful enough to repair those scarred souls. Two small faces accompanied him through long nights.

He groaned to himself: *thank you, Hawke!*

*

Barrie Louw, the South African Deputy Minister of Foreign Affairs, glanced around the table at his fellow committee members. His reputation as an up-and-coming politician rested partly on the successful implementation of plans like the one before them.

He leaned back in his chair, folding his hands over his generous stomach. "It's decision-making time. You've all read the file. You were there. You've met the subject. We need positive international attention to help counter political isolation and sanctions. Do we use her?"

The man with the bagged and tired eyes of a heavy drinker shrugged. "Every little bit helps."

The small man at the end of the table, turned his mouth down. "She makes a habit of being controversial."

Louw smiled. "All publicity can be good publicity."

The little man pulled a face. "It could also be bad. She could earn us negative publicity."

"Not if no one knows we're behind the whole thing. Anything positive will be good for us internationally. Anything bad happens and we wash our hands of her."

"Works for me," the heavy drinker declared. "And it's another reason why she mustn't know we're behind the project."

"Exactly," nodded Louw.

"Green is the in thing and it's not yet a politicised field," said the small man thoughtfully.

"We've largely exhausted this subject," Louw said. "Do we need a formal vote? Anyone not agree?"

Silence from around the table.

"For the record, we'll handle it through a dummy offshore company in the UK."

A murmur of assent.

"I'll give you one thing," said the heavy drinker, "she's easy on the eye."

General laughter clouded the room. And the curtain came down on the subject as they turned their attention to the next topic on the agenda.

*

"Well, my dear, you look *absolutely* dreadful," cooed Colin.

"Do I?" Michelle Denton quickly looked around the restaurant. "Do you think so really?"

"You're actually a positively gorgeous woman. I *absolutely* don't understand why you allow yourself to become quite so unravelled, quite so easily. What is the matter with you?"

Michelle sighed deeply. "The same old story I'm afraid. Roger!"

"I should've known. Although I thought we'd sorted that."

"So had I," she wailed. "But things aren't the way they used to be. I preferred it when he was drinking too much."

"I'm sure you did," murmured Colin.

Michelle looked sharply at him. "What did you say?"

His innocent blue eyes twinkled back at her. "Nothing, dear, nothing."

"It all started with that business of wanting to prove something. And that ridiculous idea of giving up the title. We were quite happy the way we were. There was absolutely no need for him to try that sailing thing."

"You should be glad it wasn't another woman. The sailing thing was easy to stop. Once they get *the other* itch …"

"I *want* to be the Countess. And things still aren't back to normal. And that's the way I want them."

Colin sighed deeply. "Tell me all."

"He still hasn't told me what he's going to do about the title. His father's near the end. The tension is driving me mad. And he's continuing to act peculiarly and I don't know what to do about that either."

"How exactly peculiar?"

"He's furtive and mysterious. And I don't know why."

"You're again trying to make decisions without having all the facts. Okay, we made a mistake the last time about another woman. But you still need to know what's going on. Have our little detective keep a close eye on Roger and then make your plans accordingly."

"I suppose you're right. But I do wish all of this wasn't necessary! It seems so sordid."

"Life is sordid, my dear! And now I must be off. But do take my advice. You can't possibly plan without having the facts. It always works for me."

"I'll think about it," sighed Michelle, waving him on his way.

After Colin had left, Michelle hurried home without finishing her cappuccino. Once there she opened her Filofax, peered at a number, picked up the handset and began to dial.

*

Brian smiled. "You look positively chirpy."

Mary-Ann waved a letter in the air. "Good news. It's a welcome change."

"Tell me about it."

"A British non-profit company, formed to support conservation projects worldwide, wants me for a speaking tour. Three months in the UK and Europe. To promote the views in my book."

Brian regarded her suspiciously. "Who's paying?"

"They are," she replied enthusiastically. "They're going to fund the entire thing. They've given me some ideas for an itinerary, but mostly they're even leaving that for me to organise. Oh Brian – it's all so exciting."

"So, effectively, it's your transnational park idea they want you to promote?"

"Yep," she replied happily. "They even go further. They're quite keen on seeing the south-east corner of Zimbabwe included in my plan. The Ghonarezou game park. They'd like me to stress that. They believe it's vitally important Zimbabwe gets involved with the project as soon as possible. As well as Mozambique, of course."

"Will management give you the time off?"

She laughed out aloud. "Even that's been organised. I'm sure they'll be glad to get rid of me for a while."

"Sometimes I do envy you. My plans never seem to work out."

Shadows chased each other across Mary-Ann's face. "Still no news on the bursary front?"

"Nope – nothing yet."

"I wish there was something I could do. If I gave a recommendation supporting your application it would be the kiss of death. Can you imagine Prins receiving that?"

Brian threw up his hands in mock horror. "Please don't help me! I'll do anything to avoid that. Absolutely anything."

                                *

The office was small and cluttered, a solitary desk in the centre.

There wasn't much bare wall to be seen. Posters covered everything. Some were old and some were new. A woman dragging behind her a fur coat which left a trail of blood on the floor. A mink hanging by one leg from a gin trap. Featherless chickens jammed in a coop so tightly they couldn't move. A rhinoceros with bloody holes where its horns should be. Bloodied baby seals with big brown eyes. Butchered elephant. Harpooned whales.

A theme.

The telephone in the centre of the crowded desk rang. Tony Burke picked it up, stuck it to his ear. A pigtail swung – dark, long hair tied tightly back – across the back of a slip-on Afro-shirt. It was collarless, dark-blue, smeared with bright yellow tribal markings, with borders of beadwork around the neckline and the ends of the wide sleeves. The shirt hung over patched blue-denim jeans. The face achingly without flesh, the bones starkly exposed.

A heavily nasal voice, abrupt, demanding, assaulted his ear.

"Do you have links with a publication in England with the same name as yours?"

The hair erect on the back of his neck. "This is the official Johannesburg address for five different publications," he replied stiffly. "Which one are you talking about?"

"Animal Rights Today."

Slowly, giving nothing away. "Why?"

"A Mary-Ann Webber is going to England soon on a lecture tour. She'll be promoting the culling and hunting of wild animals. Something should be done about it. Someone must stop her."

Still suspicion. "What, for instance?"

"Surely something could be arranged? Demonstrations, that sort of thing."

"Who are you?"

A long silence.

"A friend," came the reply at length.

A police trap. Not that he had ever been bothered by government agents, but you never knew in South Africa. Third-hand horror stories abounded amongst his friends. A shiver. Delicious. Perhaps a story of his own. Would they interrogate him?

"Why won't you tell me your name?"

"I can't afford to. I've a responsible position in conservation, but I sympathise with your views." Again an almost imperceptible hesitation. "One day I'll come out, reveal my true colours, you'll be the first to know." Again a momentary hesitation. "Will your people do something about Mary-Ann Webber?"

"I'll pass it on. But it will be up to them."

"Try your best. She has to be forced out of conservation –"

Burke frowned, cut in. "Forced out?"

Had he gone? The hum of an open line was still there.

"Ja, forced out," the heavily nasal voice said at last. "We need people in conservation who really care about the rights of animals. She doesn't!"

After replacing the handset Tony frowned for a moment. Discomfort. Why?

He shrugged, reached for the file in which he kept his telephone numbers.

*

Roger Denton turned another page of his newspaper. Stopped. What had it been on the previous page? An article. About what? What teased at the edge of his mind?

He turned back to page five, scanned it. Ah! Not an article. An advertisement.

CONSERVATION FOR THE NEW MILLENIUM
Dr Mary-Ann Webber is giving a series of public lectures throughout the United Kingdom and Europe. Her subject - the preservation of wildlife on the African sub-continent. How? - The creation of a giant game reserve stretching from South Africa to Kenya.

Then followed a list of venues and dates.

South Africa to Kenya? Surely that would cover Mozambique, where Hawke's coal fields lay? Prompted by curiosity Roger dug out an old atlas from a nearby bookshelf. Idly he flipped through to the section on Southern Africa.

Nights were not comfortable, young faces hovered. A cancelled stock exchange listing, a project abandoned, would serve Hawke right. Development costs lost, arrogance burnt.

He ran a finger across the page. No question. The proposed game reserve would have to include the area in Mozambique where Hawke intended opening a coal mine. Would they allow mining? Could a green outcry prevent the deal? Would this be the punishment? It could be worth attending a Dr Webber lecture.

After one of the lectures Roger left the lecture hall depressed: a waste of time.

A great deal of thought had been put into the cross-border concept. But the lecture given by – he glanced at the program in his hand – Dr Webber had been long on theory and how it could be funded, but short on how much progress the authorities had made towards implementing the concept. Without political co-operation between the countries involved there would be no progress. Without real on-the-ground progress it couldn't be used as a weapon to punish Hawke.

On the other hand, the way politics worked, if there had been discreet talks, there would be, at this stage, a serious reluctance on the part of other African countries to admit they were co-operating with South Africa. The anti-apartheid campaign was increasing momentum around the world. While he didn't for one moment believe that would influence the politicians one way or the other privately, publicly they would feel obliged to echo those sentiments. Wouldn't talks involving the setting up of transnational structures be of a sensitive nature? So, because it hadn't been mentioned in the lectures didn't mean it wasn't actually happening, did it?

He began to feel more cheerful. If that was so, then surely Dr Webber's crowd, whoever they may be, would like to know that a coal mining operation threatened their plans, forewarned being forearmed. They may even be in a position to prevent the mine from being established in the first place. And that would be a suitable punishment for what Hawke had done.

First problem – how to convey this information to the promoters of the reserve in such a way it was taken seriously? Second problem – how to ensure they actually used the information to prevent Hawke from starting to mine the coal fields?

Partial answer – attend the lectures, and certainly while they were being given in London, contrive to meet her, gain her confidence. Then she would be inclined to take him seriously.

A few lectures later and it seemed others were equally interested in what was going on and he idly wondered for what purpose. At every session he attended he saw the same group of young people – sloppily dressed, on purpose, of course, long skirts to the ground, beads, bandannas and more – also attended all her lectures.

He gave a mental shrug: not his problem, goals demanded focus, debts had to be collected on.

                                    *

The stocky young woman called Jenny stood up: broad-shouldered, firm, personal authority demanded attention, silence all around, expectant faces.

"All right, we've all had more than one chance to listen to the woman. You agree she's a legitimate target?"

"Yeah," a chimed agreement.

"Then why not tonight?" queried Jenny.

"Yeah," a chant – a mantra perhaps?

Brazen Jenny grinned. "I thought you'd say that." She placed a shopping bag on the table. She slowly drew a clear plastic bag out of the white plastic bag.

A dark-haired girl and a pimply youth, the two nearest the table, recoiled.

"Oh gross!" said the girl.

Pink-tendrilled testicles half-floating in what looked like diluted blood.

Jenny laughed at them. "We divide this into four separate bags so that we can be sure she'll be hit by at least one of them."

She opened the top of the clear bag to peer inside.

The dark-haired girl, who had earlier recoiled, moved further away. "Cor, Jenny, that stuff's really beginning to stink."

"Yeah, Jenny," cried the pimply-faced youth. "Thought you was gonna keep that lot in yer freezer?"

"But that's why I took it out," she declared sternly, winking at the other young woman nearby, tight t-shirt stretched over muscled arms, boot-camp marine short hair.

The marine put her arm around the waist of the dark-haired girl and moved her to one side. She stood braced alongside Jenny – elbows out, feet far apart, no shrinking violet. She picked up one of the empty plastic bags and held the mouth open, expressionless, giving nothing away.

"Thanks, Gabby. Here goes." Jenny tipped some of the contents of one bag into another bag.

"Cor, what a pong!" An unknown contributor from the back of the room.

The others suddenly caught on to what Jenny had earlier meant and bayed with laughter.

"Not keeping it in the freezer! Wow!" Someone screeched, and that set them all off again. "Jenny, you're a real card,"

"I doubt the bitch will see the funny side."

Jenny turned to the pimply callow youth. He was standing well away from the table – and the plastic bags and their grisly contents.

"Bert, you still have that list of numbers for the papers?"

He nodded. "I'll phone 'em in 'alf-a-mo. Hey, Jenny, this is gonna be great sport. I can hardly wait. The bitch is in for a big surprise."

*

Mary-Ann strode purposefully to the front of the old Scout Hall in Fulham Road. But it was virtually empty. The normal disappointing few. Two weeks of this. It was a waste of a good sponsor's money. She must tell them. It was beyond fair. It was a duty to be honest, to never tell a lie under any circumstances, not even by omission, and it was a duty she took very seriously. She took a quick glance around her meagre audience.

She recognised one particular face. A tall and upright man sat in the centre. He always sat there. What was in it for him? He was a … a beacon out there. She tugged at the waistband of her skirt, smoothed it down her thighs. Ran a hand over her hair. For the lectures she had been wearing a sober grey two-piece suit, hair tied tightly back in a severe bun and large owlish spectacles – instead of her usual contacts – a serious outfit, giving a serious look, befitting a serious subject.

Suddenly she wished she had worn something lighter, altogether more casual. More becoming, perhaps? And that was ridiculous. She straightened her notes. Why did he keep coming back? All her lectures were the same.

And then another distraction.

A group of fifteen or twenty youngsters, mostly in their late teens or early twenties, filed into the hall. Sitting close together, in an empty hall, a threatening bloc, massively silent. And that was how they stayed: no fidgeting, no talking, just staring, intent, waiting? Despite her experience she felt uneasy under the combined stare. Carefully planned jokes didn't move them. Sad little anecdotes flew past unnoticed.

Mary-Ann had given too many lectures to too many students to falter now. But experience speaks through instincts half-understood: something was wrong. The group disturbed her. Minutes before she was due to finish, they stood together, as one, a pre-planned move, an invisible signal understood by all, They filed out, still massively silent.

Leaving the hall, still despondent over another poor attendance, she discovered a surging crowd in a noisy semi-circle around the entrance. Many of them held posters.

The noise resolved itself into individual chants:

meat-eaters smell bad
animals have rights, too
murderer, murderer

Mary-Ann's first reaction was to duck back inside the hall where she could wait until the crowd had left. But she had never run away from anything and she was not about to start because a bunch of animal rights activists had targeted her for a demo.

She stuck out her chin, scanning the crowd. Besides animal rights' slogans some of the posters carried other messages: feminists, gay and lesbian liberationists and vegetarians had joined the fray.

She hesitated on the step.

The mob, although noisy and jostling around, still relatively passive.

Then the press arrived.

TV journalists, with cameramen dogging their footsteps, started circling the crowd. Press photographers exploded flashlights indiscriminately, holding cameras one-handed high above the crowd. Animation grew, a crowd transformed, a surging mass. Here and there individuals pushed and shoved towards Mary-Ann, the semi-circle drawing ever closer. She looked back. The mob closed the space, discretion trumped, retreat not an option, a bolt-hole neutralized, the circle complete. She stood tall and still, her chin high.

Neighbourhood rubberneckers arrived. The word soon spread. The crowd on the pavement grew rapidly and soon spilled over into Fulham Road, affecting the early evening traffic. Motorists hooted, cursed and jeered. Frustration grew. Numbers built quickly. The closest hurled abuse and screamed slogans, hot breath and spittle painted her face. A small group of four ploughed through the mob, a dedicated wedge.

The back of her neck prickled, she was a target.

Beware.

The stocky girl leading, bombed through the crowd, closely followed by three.

"Give it her now, Jenny! Go on, give it her now!" bayed a more distant chorus.

Without further ado, the four leapt forward and flung liquid grenades, uttering wild screams unintelligible in the welter of sound. But with the hurling came a hush, and the mass of people shrank back as though she was a leper and this the Middle Ages. The Press moved forward, flashlights exploded, like small bombs going off, blinding – and then even they backed away.

They all stood there like that, silently staring. The quarry at bay. No escape. What now? What would she do? Would she scream? Would she swoon? Oh God! To have been there to see.

Mary-Ann stood.

The mob stood.

She thought: why not a chant?

Like when someone is on a high ledge on a tall building. Jump! Jump! She wondered whether those sort of people ever felt embarrassed the next day? Why would people do that? What was in it for them?

She slowly looked around the hushed expectant faces. What did they want? For her to scream, perhaps puke. Well, no satisfaction here. She had seen dogs' testicles before. She was a vet. Hell, she had performed her last castration only a few weeks earlier in Maputo.

The tall man worked his way nearer, deliberately closer. He was but a few feet to her right. Their eyes met, his lopsided smile seemed sympathetic. She braced herself, ostentatiously winked at him, bent down, picked up one of the testicles, studied it carefully.

She wouldn't give in to these people. She lifted her chin.

"This vet did a good job." A lecturing voice, projected through the hush, reached the outermost edges. "A casual wielder of a scalpel often leaves small slashes on the testicle itself. This is a first class job. We could use people like that for wildlife work in Africa."

Mary-Ann turned deliberately to the stocky, young woman who had led the flying wedge. She looked her straight in the eye. "Didn't they call you Jenny? Well, Jenny, get the vet to contact me at –"

A keening sounded loud: a response too far, pushed back too hard, realised too late. Jenny barged forward, screaming like a hell-borne banshee, a mob reaction triggered, surging now, a low moaning all around.

Mary-Ann held her arms high, crossed them in front, a vulnerable shield against flailing fists, hating blows. A poster struck her left shoulder. She staggered sideways against the tall man.

She had to stay on her feet!

Nails gouged at her face, hands pulled at her hair, tore at her clothes. Legs kicked from behind, knees gave way, started to go down, the onslaught unstoppable. Then, a strong arm around her waist, support, she wasn't alone, she regained her balance.

Sirens sounded in the distance, pierced the din, the hard core scattered, took off down Fulham Road. No one tried to stop them. A suddenly quiet crowd melted away. Within seconds Mary-Ann was standing alone, except for the warm arm around her waist. The crowd kept backing away, the circle ever-widening, and soon it was large enough to easily accommodate the police when they arrived and pushed their way through.

They took a statement from Mary-Ann, but admitted it meant nothing. A formality. Under these circumstances there was little they could do. They couldn't catch them, they couldn't stop them. But the victim gets a warning. Now you're a target for every nutter in town. Go back to your hotel. Stay there, or better still go home, wherever that may be.

After the police had left, the tall man – who introduced himself as Roger – suggested coffee at a nearby bistro. Mary-Ann hesitated, but there was no good reason for her to be unduly wary – hadn't he just helped her?

Suddenly she was grateful for his calm presence, for the help he had given her, for the company.

"All right," she said, then pointed at the hall behind. "But you'll have to excuse me while I try to clean my coat."

*

"Of course," Roger said urbanely. "I'll be out here. Take as long as you like."

He waited outside. Had fate taken a hand? He wondered, what more could he have asked for? He had sensed it coming, had moved to her side, the opportunity to help, automatic trust. He grimaced: an internal warning? Wasn't this a mirror image of the attitude that led to Sir David's ....

No, why should it be? He had his own boat to row. Hawke was the debtor. Hawke had to pay. How could that harm this woman? He would get to know her better over coffee. Could Hawke's bailiff be a sun-kissed nymph?

The next day, in the evening, Roger watched her fork up another large mouthful of fettuccine and wondered at her ability to put food away – and retain her slim figure. Michelle and her friends pecked at haute cuisine meals as though they were made of the worst kind of prison swill, and still endlessly complained about weight problems.

A lot more fascinated him.

Only having met the previous day he had already grown to like this woman who chewed on her pasta with such fierce concentration. Momentarily he wished they could have met under different circumstances.

"Any second thoughts about last night? Are you going to cut your lecture tour short?"

"Absolutely not. Those people don't frighten me. And I know my ideas are right. This is a subject I've spent many hours studying, in theory and practice. In the real world animals don't stand a chance unless they have some commercial value. And there's no other practical way of giving them that value. I wish it was different, but it isn't and we just have to deal with it on that basis. I just have to convince people of that."

"The whole world? There's growing support for animal rights to be recognised. And, as a result, growing support for animal rights activists," he said mildly. "Are all these people wrong?"

Mary-Ann waved a fork in the air. "They're just zealots searching for new causes. People no longer believe in the class war. Apartheid is in the process of being dismantled, even if it doesn't always seem so at the moment, but inside the country you can see it happening. And that means they won't have South African racists to fight anymore. Where does that leave those people who see themselves as arbiters of what is morally and politically acceptable? What are they going to get excited about now?"

Roger could hardly contain his smile. "Hmmm, maybe …"

She waved her fork ever more enthusiastically as she got into her stride. Other diners were beginning to notice.

"They're a strange bunch collectively. At one end you have the pretty harmless moderates who simply want to be politically correct together with the squeamish bunny huggers. All the way across to a militant wing which includes the gay and lesbian activists, the radical feminists and the mystic greens, not to mention those maniacs that attacked me last night, the animal rights activists. I'll give you ten to one an anti-sexist will also abhor blood sports and a vegetarian will be feminist." Each point Mary-Ann made was well-punctuated with the fork.

Roger shrugged, he could not afford to be interested. A fixation is demanding. Hawke must be made to pay. Blocking his coal mine deal would do that. How to get through to the topic in which *he* was interested?

"I haven't really thought about it," he said.

But in a strange way Roger envied her: right or wrong, she knew exactly what she wanted. He thought about that, what it must be like: life with a single clear focus. A bright torch beam in a world of darkness. And then he remembered: he did know what it felt like. It was the way *he* had been when on the BOC project. But in the bigger scheme of things it had really been for such a short time. The bitterness rose in his gorge.

Aaah Hawke!

Then he shook his head. Time to change the subject. Wouldn't it be wiser for her to back off rather than risk another attack from the zealots about whom she was so scornful? Don't say that either ... it wasn't his problem. But were the plans to expand the Kruger National Park to the Mozambican side of the border in train? If so, how could he get her to pass on the information he had about Hawke's planned coal mine in such a way it was taken seriously and even stopped!

Despite his own agenda he heard himself saying, "As long as those animal rightists aren't even more violent the next time," and there was real concern in his voice.

She grinned happily at him. "I'll have to rely on another knight in shining white armour just happening to be on the scene."

Just happening to be on the scene.

Roger squirmed. To cover his discomfort he topped up the red wine in her glass and tackled his own plate of pasta. But he felt her eyes on him, looked up.

She was frowning, eyes very serious, small white teeth gleaming between slightly parted lips as red as the Bordeaux in her glass when held up to the light. "I left Africa with such high hopes. I just didn't realise how big the world is and how tied up everyone is with their own problems. There's millions of people here in London and I'm lucky if twenty or thirty turn up on a night to hear me speak. There's so little interest in conservation."

"Perhaps your project needs to be marketed in a different way. A good example of what can happen with a little publicity is the number of people who were there tonight. The hall was full."

"Because of the demonstration the day before, probably waiting to see if I'd get zapped again. Not 'cause they were interested in my lecture."

"You may have reached some of them. In this world you've got to take what you can get."

He watched her chew. She was dressed differently tonight and as a result looked much younger and even more attractive – if that was possible. Tonight she wore a pants suit of maroon cotton with a shantung silk blouse, a loose scarf thrown carelessly around her neck – and she had turned sophisticated London heads as they entered the Italian restaurant just off Piccadilly.

And he was happy in her company. Then he shook himself: it didn't matter, he thought, he couldn't allow it to matter.

The mission to make Hawke pay was all …

The world was full of attractive women. Michelle was a beautiful woman. He had to get Hawke where it would hurt him most – in his pocket. This young lady out of Africa was the best – the only! – bet he currently had. Blow this opportunity and he could be blowing his only chance of getting at Hawke.

Easy does it, he thought, *softly, softly, catchee monkey*.

He smiled pleasantly at her. "What is the single thing you'd most like to do in London tomorrow?"

*

Climbing out of the cab the next day Mary-Ann clearly heard a smile in Roger's voice. "There can't be many young ladies who'd have chosen a morning at the Natural History Museum."

The comment astonished her. "But it's a wonderful place. It's the most remarkable record of natural history in the whole world. It covers zoology, entomology, palaeontology and botany. Surely everyone wants to come here?"

"I'm not sure it's safe to let you out on your own," he muttered.

She studied the magnificent facade of the Museum building from across Cromwell Road. "I can hardly wait for this."

But wandering around the vast halls, Mary-Ann's mind was not altogether on the overwhelming bulk of great whales, the intricate delicacy of a humming-bird's feathers or a sea-shell's spiralling precision. Already two nights earlier, when drinking coffee at the bistro, she had known she would want to see Roger again. She remembered clearly how pleased she had been when he had eventually asked her to have dinner with him the following night. And again at the end of that evening, when he had actually suggested they spend time together during the day. His presence left her head in a whirl. And she remonstrated with herself sternly. It just stemmed from a need for company, after a few weeks on a lecture tour, so far from home. Obviously she hadn't realised quite how lonely she had been.

Later that day, as they left the Museum, Mary-Ann turned to Roger, her chin stuck out. "You're laughing at me."

Roger quickly extinguished his smile. "Not at all. But if the Natural History Museum was an odd choice, what does that make a visit to a gunmaker? Holland and Holland, wasn't it?"

"Yes," she replied firmly. "Holland and Holland."

"Frankly, I'm a little surprised. I mean you're supposed to be a conservationist."

"It's really for my dad. He's a big fan. And then I'll be able to tell him all about it when I see him again. Anyway hunting and conservation aren't mutually exclusive. Conservation must pay for itself. I don't understand either the bunny-huggers, who don't seem to know what they're talking about, or the animal rights activists, who don't seem to have the survival of species high on their agenda."

"Here we go again," he said mildly.

"Neither of them are prepared to pay what it would really cost to save the South American rain forests or African wildlife. And I mean pay by actually putting in money. I believe in scientific conservation and the industry having to pay for itself, because only then will the animals be truly safe."

He listened and watched in awe. A magnificent obsession. It made her eyes sparkle. It lit up London. It made his heart sing.

But it must not be allowed to get in the way of his primary mission.

"And what makes it worse," she continued. "Is that in Africa every cent the continent can find should be used to educate and house the underprivileged. The continent needs to create work for its people. There are millions who want land. If conservationists can't show that land can make money for the people – and especially those people who live on the borders of reserves – then those selfsame people are going to graze their cattle on that –" abruptly she cut herself off to glare accusingly at Roger. "You're laughing at me again."

"Are you always this fierce?"

A smear of bright warmth in both cheeks, a lowering of eyes.

*

Later that same day, leaving Harrods in Knightsbridge, an elderly man, with bright eyes and a cherub's cheeks, raised a finger as he passed them. "G'day, Sir Roger."

Mary-Ann pulled on Roger's arm. "What was that?"

Roger shrugged. "He's a security guard in Westminster. I used to visit the building a lot. We became friendly, in a casual sort of way."

"Come on," she stamped her foot. "That's not what I meant and you know it. Why *Sir* Roger?"

"My father's an Earl," he shrugged. "If I want I can use a minor title."

"But that's so romantic," she exclaimed excitedly.

"Do you really think so?" Roger's eyes were bituminous hard.

"Of course it's romantic. Anyway it seems so to me. There aren't Lords and Ladies like that in Africa or the States."

"And if I told you I'm the oldest son and would one day be the Earl?"

"I dunno. Depends on what it means, I guess."

He eyed her for a moment. "Hmm! Maybe I owe you an apology …" then he suddenly added, "A hypothetical question – what would you recommend under the following circumstances?" And he told her about the promise he had made to his father and why, then finished with, "it's been suggested the person just doesn't do anything. Just hangs on to it when the time comes." He watched her closely. "What do you think?"

"It must be a trick question," she burst out.

"Why?"

"The answer's too obvious. The person wouldn't have a choice. He'd have to keep his promise. There's no way he could go back on his word."

"I definitely owe you an apology." For some inexplicable reason he felt relieved. It felt as though a hurdle had been overcome. And that was wrong because it had nothing to do with his primary mission.

He sounded sad as he looked at her and said: "I should've realised you'd say that."

"I wouldn't care if the person's brother turned out to be the biggest crook in the whole world – never mind just having tricked his father into getting worried about the title. He absolutely cannot go back on his word. You must never lie, there can be no excuse."

She tilted her head. "Are you sure this is a hypothetical question …"

"I wish everyone thought the way you –" he cut the sentence short.

Did everyone include himself? And then realised that that was a question he really didn't want to answer.

In the evening after her lecture Roger asked for a signed copy of her book.

Mary-Ann turned pink. "Don't be ridiculous."

"You've no idea how much I admire you. And envy you. You know exactly what you want."

And you can talk about it, he thought.

*

She urgently wished she didn't blush quite so readily. She was nearly thirty, surely she shouldn't be reacting like a schoolgirl meeting a rock star.

As the days went Mary-Ann gained the impression Roger was holding back in some way. So she asked about it.

"Let's not get serious here. Lets enjoy a few days before the real world intrudes." He sounded quite bitter, so she dropped the subject.

They talked about the American heritage they shared. To her it was an omen. She told him a part of her Louisiana family, on her mom's side, was supposed to be from France.

"I had an idea last night," he exclaimed excitedly one day. "You've got a one week break in your schedule. Let's cross the channel. Then you can see where your family came from."

"Can we really? My mother always wanted to do that but never got the opportunity. My dad said that right up until she died there was always talk about visiting the past in Europe." Suddenly she paused, all confusion and blushes. "But ... can ... don't you ..."

"Don't I what?"

A question unasked often remains unanswered. Better that – than the truth you don't want to hear?

"Well, can you ... get away?" And then all in a rush. "But aren't you married?" And she reddened all the more furiously. And then quickly, "Don't you have to work? I don't even know what work you do."

Roger hesitated, a moment of decision, a question of precedence, one small step, a pebble in a millpond, ripples travelling outward – where might they find themselves?

"No," he said finally. "I'm not married and I have a private income. But what happened to your mother?"

"She died of leukaemia," Mary-Ann said, returning to that subject with sad relief.

He stared at her, startled.

"Remember my hypothetical question the other day that you understood wasn't hypothetical at all? When I told you about my father being ill and the promise I'd made him? Well, that's what my father has – leukaemia."

They stared at each other: a bridge across a moat, a connection, the fear of dying, the worse fear of being left behind. Every so often people are given second chances. He remained silent.

"It's a terrible illness," she said sympathetically. "My mom died a long time ago," and then added, "and my dad's always been so lonely …"

Children grow and leave home, couples grow old together, lean on each other, share a common history, a touch here, a look there – enough.

"… and I could never help with that."

The next day they stood shoulder to shoulder at the rail of the P&O Dover to Calais cross-channel ferry. The wind was up, slightly, and the damp spray found their faces, stinging with a nascent excitement. Ostensibly they watched the cold grey-green water slide past. Mary-Ann, however, was – surreptitiously out of the corner of one eye – studying Roger in profile. At last she understood. Her fellow female students had raved about it. Everything she had ever wanted, ever dreamt of, had, in a matter of weeks, become subordinated. This was unreal: so many years wasted. There's nothing quite like it: the promise.

She felt the light pressure of his arm against hers as they swayed slightly with the movement of the ferry. That touch. Oh yes – *that* touch. An explosive current coursed through her veins, burning already with sweet sorrow. How to get closer? Was a praying mantis right? Mate and then eat your mate. The ultimate proximity.

Aah! Just to mate, the delighted anticipation, and then the dread – would he find out? He mustn't know – could she hide it?

And that time came after a particularly high-spirited evening at a Parisian eatery, a red-roses ramble along the

Seine, brushed with moonlight. Arm in arm, tucked in close together, very close – no space for secrets …

They took a roundabout way back to their hotel. A stroll across the sixteenth century *Pont Neuf*, which connects the *Île de la Cité* with both banks of the river. Then they stopped at a small sidewalk cafe for a cognac. The laughter had dried up by then. A different kind of tension invaded the air, forced itself on them. A feeling of inevitability made it hard to breathe. Along the *rue des Archives*. Into the *Hôtel Bretagne*. The foyer was empty. Roger gently turned Mary-Ann around, placed his hands on her shoulders.

"Are you coming to my room tonight?"

"I don't know," she said miserably, unable to meet his eyes. "Please don't be angry with me."

Roger frowned sternly. "Haven't I been patient with you?"

"Well, yes …"

Oh, the games people play …

"Just kidding," he smiled. "Whatever suits you, suits me."

"I know. You've been patient with me. I'm sorry …"

"That's all right," he said. "I don't think I've ever been so happy … you're a breath of fresh air, Dr Webber."

"I *will* come to your room tonight," she said abruptly.

Roger, still holding her at arm's length, nodded. "I'd like that."

Finally she knocked on his door. It opened immediately. Had a hand been poised?

"I was beginning to wonder if you'd changed your mind."

She longed for it. She dreaded it. Roger entered her. An involuntary cry.

He quickly took his weight off, lay on one side, propped up on one elbow. "Are you okay?" he murmured, sensing her cheek with his lips.

"I'm sorry," she whispered. He must have felt, her cheeks were wet.

"Don't tell me you're … that you've never …" A curious melange of surprise, horror and awe split apart and were heard, one after the other, in quick succession.

"Don't be ridiculous …"

"Don't avoid the question. A simple yes or no will suffice."

"Of course not," she hesitated and then suddenly added shyly, "But only once before. And not really properly. It was a University party, I didn't want to feel left out, drank a bit too much, allowed a boy I didn't like very much … it was in the back of a car. He wasn't very good. It was awful. I don't think we did it properly." She started to giggle. "It all sounds very silly for a twenty-eight year old, doesn't it?" She could feel the heat in her cheeks.

Roger just lay there, shaking his head. But of words there were none.

Mary-Ann snuggled up close. She whispered. Her breath singed his ear. "But with you I really do want to make love. Just be gentle with me, please."

And he was gentle with her. And she knew she could very much get to like making love with someone she loved.

Their return to England seemed to signal a change in their relationship – or so it seemed to Mary-Ann. Roger disappeared. A few days went by. She realised she didn't know how to make contact, that she actually knew nothing about him. How could she care so much when she knew so little? And if she knew where to contact him – would she? It didn't seem right somehow.

When he turned up he didn't offer an explanation and she didn't ask. Couldn't, new emotions, little understood.

Sunday afternoon. Sitting on a bench, overlooking the Serpentine in Hyde Park, Roger casually hauled out of his pocket a map of the Kruger National Park. "I'd like to know more about where you spent so much time."

Mary-Ann giggled. "That is *so* sweet."

She showed him where her father lived, had spent twenty years on his research. She explained how well he had got to know the area. How she had, during school holidays, driven around with him.

Roger pointed to one particular area, a valley. "Do you know it?"

Mary-Ann frowned: what on earth could have possessed him to choose that particular valley? Stalling for time, she pulled a face. "The map's scale is too small. Why do you ask?"

Roger shrugged. "No particular reason. There just seems to be very little development around there."

"The Park personnel have always fought hard to protect the Park," she said, seemingly apropos of nothing. "To keep alive an environment in which many species as possible are guaranteed survival," she paused. "But over the years there have been threats. The worst year was 1978. With oil sanctions the government looked everywhere for alternative sources of energy."

"Isn't the situation controlled by an act of parliament?"

Small silence, surprise – how would he know about that? It must have been in the papers. Does love *prefer* not to know?

"Yes, it is," she replied at length, still feeling uncomfortable. "The Government threatened to change the National Parks Act to allow prospecting and mining in national parks generally. And they started to talk specifically about mining coal in Kruger. You can imagine the panic. They actually authorised geologists to drill there at one stage."

"But obviously it didn't happen."

She nodded. "Anyway that's why some areas of the park are never opened. They know what's there. It's not an organised thing. But each in his or her own way keeps certain areas off-limits." Suddenly she grinned. "But they are open to the animals. So from a conservation point of view it works just fine."

Afterwards, the whole conversation left a bad taste in Mary-Ann's mouth. She was becoming increasingly uncomfortable with the relationship. All the flows went in one direction only. Where did Roger stay? What did he do when he wasn't with her? Why didn't he talk about himself any more?

"It's hard to believe you're wandering around totally unattached," she commented one evening. "I know you said you weren't married, but don't you even have one or two girlfriends you occasionally date?"

"No," Roger said, looking down at the table. "I have no involvements at all."

*

The narrow little three-storey building on Westbourne Grove in Notting Hill was particularly unkempt, grubby and perfectly in keeping with the area generally. Michelle Denton breached the entrance with a pinched look on her face, as though she was trying not to breathe. But she did it without hesitating. Nothing was going to keep her away. She had to know what was going on. Perhaps it was the book on conservation she had seen lying around – signed by the author, a woman – that had started it, but Michelle's every instinct told her something was drastically wrong.

The ratty-haired secretary never stopped sniffing, dabbing away with her handkerchief at a red-pointed nose, gestured at a chair. Michelle looked at it, rejected the offer. She chose to stand.

When the private detective finally invited her into his office she became even more uneasy – the horrible little man knew something. She could tell. She was equally determined not to let him know how nervous she felt. "Your report's ready?"

"Sorry about being late, ma'am. My secretary says you've been waiting for more than ten minutes."

"That's okay," she said, jerked her head like an irritated horse twitching at its bridle.

"I'm glad you came here." He added, waving a hand, "I own the building."

"Good for you. You have something for me. You said it was important."

"This time it's got some meat. Not bare bones like last time, eh? This time I earned my fee, I can tell you."

Michelle wanted to shriek, but held herself in, forced herself to be still. After a few long seconds he slowly, almost reluctantly, slid an envelope across the desk. Did he enjoy his clients' discomfiture? His moment of power. Michelle didn't touch the envelope, said nothing. She was learning how to handle the man, how to keep him in his place.

"Your husband is seeing another woman."

Michelle stared at him. If it wasn't so serious it would have been funny. She had previously suspected Roger of being involved with another woman and it turned out to be a yacht. Now when she thought he had found another yacht it turned out to be a woman. The world was incomprehensible.

"It's all in there," the detective said defensively, as though her silence was a sign of disbelief. He nodded towards the envelope that lay between them on the desk. "Chapter and verse. Pictures and story. Irrefutable. You've got him cold, I can tell you."

Is that what she wanted? Did she want Roger *cold*?

Of course not. She wanted everything to be the way it had been in the early years. But she couldn't avoid reality. So she needed to know everything. Ironic. A few seconds earlier she had wanted to scream at the private investigator to say no more. To not tell her anything. Now she needed to know every last sordid detail. She nodded for him to go ahead, not trusting herself to speak.

The detective told her everything, obviously enjoying himself. Michelle felt herself growing hard inside. She wasn't going to give up that easily.

"All right," she said, standing up when he had finished talking. "You keep on watching my husband. And let me know immediately if anything unusual happens."

Standing on Westbourne Grove, she waited for a cab. So now the book on conservation made sense. Now she knew a lot more, but she still didn't know everything. She still didn't know how serious the affair had become and what she could do about ending it – soon and permanently.

*

The pickup truck headed for the western end of the valley, wheels hammering at the dirt and rocks. Dust furled away from under the chassis to shade the still hot air. Slowly, long after the vehicle had passed, almost imperceptibly, it drifted down. The head-high shrubs and occasional tree, which stood scattered on either side of the bumpy track, earned another fine crusting on their brittle brown leaves.

The dust cloud lessened and then ceased altogether as the pickup stopped. In front of the battered bull bars the vague, almost indiscernible, track suddenly descended steeply down to a sandy storm-cut waterway.

Jakes, a small wiry man, face charred by the sun, climbed out into dry heat. He stepped lithely to the front of the vehicle, stood wide-spread on bow-legs looking down. This would be his gate-keeper. His contract didn't have that long to run now. Soon he and the two Shangaans wouldn't be there. Nature would have to find its own way.

He pulled a smooth shiny pipe out of his faded sweat-stained khaki shirt, packed it with coarse dark brown tobacco. When it was full he slowly rubbed the bowl of the pipe against the short clipped grey hairs of his goatee beard before clamping his teeth on the pipe-stem, but he didn't light it. It would be good when the rains came again. Then the river would flow and *then* it would form a proper barrier for the rainy season. It would provide any extra time his project needed.

He stepped forward, the toes of his boots over the crumbling edge, looked down. The silted-sand lay undisturbed except for game spoor. No one else had come that way. That was what he had needed to know.

He carefully studied the bush on the far bank, looking beyond where debris from previous floods had lodged high in trees, piled up against bushes in thick grey-brown dried-out drifts. He could see no sign of the other two, not that he had expected to. They had been with him from the beginning. If they didn't want to be seen, he would stake his life on it they wouldn't be.

He could return to Skukuza now. The two men had supplies for another week. He would see them when he came to replenish their stores. He had just wanted to make sure. But no one else had come that way. The whole project was so close to having its own momentum now. And once the rains came …

*

Mary-Ann stared at the other woman as though she had just descended from a Martian spaceship. The very worst nightmare. An abyss opened before her feet. She teetered on the edge, footing insecure. Was she going to pass-out? How could she go so easily from being covered by a warm blanketing glow to having stilettos of ice plunged into her chest?

"Your name is … er … Michelle Denton? Are you … Roger's sister? He's never mentioned a sister." But she already knew the answer.

Oh God, she knew it wasn't, but pleaded that He make it so.

There was no mirth in Michelle's grin. "I'm his wife."

"I … I don't believe you."

Michelle threw something on the table. Mary-Ann looked down. It was her book. "I know all about you two – all of it. I want you out of my husband's life – as of now."

There had been small incidents, some really rather petty, which had worried her. She had ignored them. Love doesn't always want to hear, want to understand.

"Do you understand? Did you hear me? You're to stay away from my husband."

Mary-Ann didn't trust herself to speak, she was going to throw up, she nodded.

Michelle hesitated, turned, stormed out of the hotel room, slammed the door.

Mary-Ann lurched through to the bathroom, knelt by the toilet, throat scraped raw, sour smell all around. Head hanging forward, white ceramic cold on the cheek, fierce pepper-burn deep in the eyes. Couldn't she just go? Back to the African bush. Back to the rhythms of nature. She forced her arm up to where she could see the time – 3.20 pm.

What an effort!

Roger was due to fetch her at four.

Not enough time. She didn't have the strength to move now, so decided to stay right where she was until Roger appeared – if he appeared.

*

The young male lion limped through the shadows, always taking the path of least resistance, his shoulder stiff and sore and just beginning to smell. The burning gape, black-edged, was awkwardly placed. He had tried on a number of occasions to lick it, to work on it with the rough rasp of his tongue, perhaps to clean it out, but had been unsuccessful. Despite that, every now and then he still stopped, tried to reach the wound, but each such effort was of shorter duration than the time before.

But the spreading septicaemia wasn't his most pressing problem.

Much more serious was the lack of strength. He could still hunt. Although he wasn't as good as he once was and it was beginning to show. He was still getting food, but not nearly enough. Hip- and shoulder-bones thrust up under the skin, undulating hillocks of skeleton-stretched black fur rising and falling with each movement. His hide lacked lustre. The mange mite parasite had found a susceptible host. Clotted clumps matted the juvenile mane.

The young male looked ill, but worse was the listlessness, the strength-sapping torpor that enveloped him like a cloak. A suicidal lethargy warred with the deep-rooted instinct to survive. The more his shoulder swelled and burnt, spreading its angry heat through his once-rangy body, the closer the apathy, the feeling of weakness, came to defeating the need to eat, the need to survive.

Slowly the young lion continued to limp through the bush, making his way down to the river because it was easier than walking uphill. The push to survive forced him to keep on moving, barely holding off the desire to lie down and just let the weariness wash over him.

As he approached the ford in the river he crouched lower despite the pain in his shoulder, blended deeper into the shadows. He smelled the waterhole ahead. Every fibre quivered in anticipation of nightfall and the buck that would respond to their own need to drink before the hours of darkness.

He froze, muscles rigid beneath the skin as though he was sculpted in dark stone. His nostrils lifted, a deep warning burr rasped in the back of his throat, more a vibration than a sound. A strong man-smell tainted the air. After a few seconds the lion slid forward low through the grass, instinct holding him low while curiosity reeled him in like a kitten chasing a ball of wool. Now he was close. The man-smell bordered on being overwhelming. His nostrils spasmed in fear, but it could also mean something to eat, something slower moving than a buck and therefore easier to catch – albeit in other ways a lot more frightening.

The lion crept through the darker patches of bush. A faint wisp of smoke accompanied the man-smell. The combination resurrected an atavistic instinct that was overpowering. This he couldn't withstand. He turned away from the ford, quickly limped away, heading in an easterly direction, following the faintest of zephyrs wafting down the valley.

A few minutes later he heard a faint sound from behind: the merest whisper. He stopped, turned his head, scented carefully. Hyaenas followed, back there beyond the mopane scrub, just out of sight. They weren't far away, but still far enough to be out of his reach, still too scared of him to get closer than that. But hyaenas' instincts also run deep. They could smell his shoulder.

They knew what that meant.

Now the young lion's instincts pushed at him fiercely, applied a lash, drove him harder. Now the instinct for survival easily held sway. To keep some distance between himself and the hyaenas he limped his way uphill, but still in a natural funnel, working hard up a slope he could easily have taken at a run a month earlier. Two hundred metres further up and he came across a crevice cut deep into the rock, an ancient crack that spanned the width of the southern mountain. The crevice widened at the base where, over the centuries, water had washed it away, until it formed a cave-like hollow leading into the depths of the range.

The young lion limped into the cave.

He immediately flopped to the floor, facing outwards. His eyes, once yellow, now red with a bacteria-driven burn, stared blankly out from the cave mouth. His jaw agape, he panted quickly for breath.

A few minutes of respite.

He lifted his head, the thin sound of coarse hair sliding over rock, a ghastly cackle, like that of a demented witch, sounded from the grove of trees twenty metres down the slope. The lion ignored the laugh born in a cauldron, remained focused on the soft slithering just off to his right, a liquid movement, fast and fluent, the lion was up and bounding forward. A roundhouse swipe with a clawed paw broke the hyaenas' neck and it was dead before it hit the ground three metres away.

For a short while the young male lion peered balefully down. The carcass of the brown spotted hyaena lay motionless. The deep-rooted instinct for survival still had the upper hand. The lion picked up the body of the hyaena in his jaws, car the seventy-five kilograms with difficulty, slowly limped back to the cave.

He stopped in the entrance, faced the hysterical cackling, laboriously started to feed.

*

"But I asked you! That's what I don't understand. I actually asked you. And you said no."

Mary-Ann's face, Roger winced. A scene remembered: he was twelve, lost his temper with Patrick, who had used his mother's skirts to keep out of reach, a hugely frustrated Roger kicking the six-week old puppy the family had acquired a few days earlier. Roger had loved that puppy from the first moment he had seen it. When struck, the puppy had collapsed back onto its haunches and wailed – a thin and piercing sound.

He hardened his heart. "I had to. Don't you understand?"

"No! No! I don't understand!"

That look: he had just crawled out from under a particularly slimy rock. But what about Hawke? One thing at a time. If she truly loved him she should understand. She had herself said promises had to be kept at all costs. Hadn't she?

"So I lied. I admit it. Are you satisfied now. But let's not forget the important thing here. I want you to understand why it was necessary. Hawke has to be stopped. He has to be made to pay. It's as a result of what he did. You'll understand when I've explained it."

"I'm not sure I want to listen to any explanations," she said reluctantly, slowly. Does love want to be convinced? Do beaten women go back to their abusers? Why?

Roger talked. He told her everything, from the beginning, talked to her as he had never talked to anyone before. "I was scared," he concluded desperately. "I didn't know whether you'd be interested in helping me. I didn't … didn't … know you then. Hawke killed Osbourne-Kerr. His body was found by his daughters. Can you imagine that? Hawke has to pay."

"You did exactly the same thing to that poor man. You're no better than Hawke. Whatever punishment Hawke deserves, should be yours as well. You're transferring your own feelings of guilt to Hawke."

"I was scared you wouldn't want to help."

"You aren't listening."

"It's been my focus for so long."

She stared at him for a while. Was this a hopeless cause? When does common sense prevail?

"And you compounded the error," she continued at length. "by allowing – no, causing – me to .... Oh, just get the hell outta here. I don't want to hear anymore. And I don't want to see you again."

"I understand you're upset and want nothing more to do with me personally. But at least help me nail Hawke. How far have your people got in political discussions with the Mozambicans? We can pool our resources, prevent Hawke from getting his coal mine. We both want the same thing, it's just for different reasons."

"You're not even listening to yourself."

"Please, you must –"

"Jesus! What will it take? Fuck off! Do you hear me? Just fuck off!"

He stood and stared at her stupidly, not moving.

With both hands extended she pushed at him, towards the door of the room. He resisted, stood his ground, batted her hands to one side.

Mary-Ann stepped back, gave herself room, sunk into the cat stance, buried a small fist, diverted at the last minute, into his solar plexus. He mewed like a kitten, bent over double. Docile now, he stumbled backwards as she drove him from the room with a flurry of punches. He didn't know it, but he was lucky. She held back on them all, inflicted no damage.

He was in the corridor.

He stared at the closed door. Frustration welled. No one understood. Who else could he turn to? Who else would want to help stop Hawke's mining coal in a game reserve area? No-one seemed to care.

He had a sudden thought. That wasn't true. There were other people out there who cared very much – and they would be easy to find, too.

Roger walked determinedly down the corridor. But a face kept intruding.

"To hell with it," he muttered under his breath, but he was almost running by the time he reached the street.

*

Jakes again stopped the pickup truck at the crossing, climbed out to check the track. He ran his tongue around the inside of his mouth. It was so dry he couldn't spit. He turned back to the pickup, leaned through the window to extract a white plastic bottle from next to the driver's seat. He unscrewed the cap and took a warm mouthful, rolled it around his mouth before spitting it out again.

He cocked an eye upwards to contemplate a pure blue bowl.

The rains were late. Just when he needed them most. For all practical purposes a running river would close the door, a lion trapped, specially imported, in the valley for at least another full season. There were, of course, other places a lion could cross if he wanted, desperately needed, to leave. But the valley squeezed tight here and the other routes were few, and dangerously tricky, and the need to get out of the valley had to be high, very high, abnormally so. Lions are lazy creatures. Given an abundance of easily caught game for food, plenty of water, and no territorial problems, lions would always stay.

So his lion would be trapped for the summer, as long the rains were good. Then no one could stop what he had begun. His spoor, living in the genes of a species, the African bush marked forever.

Jakes raised the plastic bottle to his mouth. He tilted his head back again and drank long and deep. The water was warm, but wet. He watched as a tree-height dust devil swirled once, twice, spun a few metres along the dry river bed and collapsed.

Jakes climbed back into his pickup and eased it down the steep slope. He gunned the engine at the bottom, revved hard in low gear, kept the wheels spinning all the way across the soft sand in the bed of the river. On the other side he drove slowly through the bush until, a few metres further on, he saw a dark-skinned man in a khaki overall.

Jakes stepped down from the pickup. He nodded to the man, who squatted on his haunches beneath the spreading branches of an umbrella tree. "*Sakubona*, Lungile. *Kanjani wena?* How are you?"

"*Muhle, Mandevu.*" "Fine, Bearded one."

Jakes grinned, here was a man of fewer words than himself. Lungile remained squatting in the shadow of the thorn tree, his face screwed up as he twisted his head to look up at Jakes. Twenty years ago, when they had first started traipsing the African bush together, those eyes had flashed white in the dark face. Now his eyeballs were a dark yellow, almost brown, with age and the sparse tightly-curled hair had long turned grey.

Jakes supposed when the Trust finally got rid of him they would get rid of Lungile, too. But at least the members of his team would have pensions. Headquartered in Washington DC the Trustees would never dare not give a tribal African, after a lifetime of service, some sort of monthly stipend no matter how pissed off they were with Jakes. Politically they would be crucified and quite rightly so.

"Where's Kambala?"

Lungile pointed to a temporary shelter built out of the dead branches from an acacia tree. The roof consisted of riverbank reeds laid carelessly next to each other. It probably just about kept the dew off in the morning. The other man emerged from the shelter. He was even older than Lungile. Time had hunched his shoulders and he moved slowly.

"*Kambala ena kona,*" he said. "Kambala is here."

Jakes stepped forward to take Kambala's outstretched hand. Without thinking he went through the handshake Africans habitually use – with its three different holds in sequence.

Kambala's exclamation rang out. "Ow! Lungile, come see Mandevu's knife."

The two men nodded in admiration as Jakes slid his new hunting knife out of its sheath, the ivory handle smooth under his fingers.

"Did Mandevu also make this knife?" asked Kambala.

"Yep, just like others."

"It would be such a great honour to carry a knife made by Mandevu." Kambala grinned, knowing Jakes would see through his ploy.

Lungile silently and solemnly nodded his agreement, eyes fixed on the fine broad blade.

Jakes waved a hand in the direction of the valley beyond. "Is my lion still here?"

"Four week's ago I saw spoor along the fence," Kambala said, then added, "What would such a knife cost?"

All the planning, the manoeuvring, the organising without anyone on the Kruger staff knowing. They still thinking he had been beavering away at the Trust's research. That was all he needed now: refugees, even worse, armed poachers from Mozambique.

"The border fence?" Jakes asked quickly. "Did he stay there?"

Kambala shook his head. "He went up towards the mountains of smoke …"

"North," muttered Jakes. "And still no females with him?"

"I saw tracks of others, a lioness and another older male, a stranger to the valley. I don't think he was following them. But there might be a problem. He may be injured. He's dragging his front right paw."

"Are you *sure* it was him?"

Kambala grimaced. "Doesn't Mandevu want it to be his lion?" he asked softly.

"Are you absolutely sure it was him?"

The old man shrugged, said nothing, his eyes fixed firmly on the ground in front of his toes.

Jakes nodded. It would take patience. Once the rains came and the lion was definitely in the valley for the rest of the season there was time enough for him to find lionesses, to form his own pride, to carry on his very unusual – almost unique – bloodline. The addition to the local gene pool that would be Jakes' living monument ...

"The knife, Mandevu," Kambala reminded him gently. "What would be the price of such a knife?"

Jakes put a hand on the haft, long lonely workshop nights, a stream of sparks, companionship against the dark, concentration a shield against memories.

"You'll both get a knife," he said. "When that lion has lionesses to carry his cubs. A knife like this. One for each of you – I'll make them myself," he said. "Or you can choose whichever one you want from those I've already made."

*

The day after Mary-Ann's confrontation – with first Michelle and then Roger – was busy, exceptionally tiring, lectures afternoon and evening, uninspired, dragged over both.

Back at the hotel late evening the receptionist handed her a message with the room key. Brian had phoned, urgent she return his call. A welcome beckoning from far away, heart lifting a little. Already late in Africa she got straight through to Brian who was at home in Skukuza. The sound of his voice lifted her spirits even more.

"Wow, am I glad to hear you. I couldn't think of anything better for a lonely soul a long away from Africa. Oh Brian, I've been so unhappy."

"And you're not the only one. You've managed to make us pretty unhappy, too. I haven't talked to Jakes yet but he won't be any too pleased."

A slap in the face from a helping hand, shock, all that was needed.

"What the hell are you talking about? I'm really not in the mood for parlour games."

"I'm talking about your fancy lecturing tour of the UK."

Mary-Ann's voice hardened. "This call's costing a fortune. If you've got something to say, spit it out! Or say goodbye!"

"Are you saying you didn't know the South African Government was funding your trip overseas? That it's a political marketing exercise. It's in all the papers. Your little government-financed jaunt has even made the TV news headlines. They're calling it Conservationgate."

"Jesus, I don't believe this."

"That's what they all say when they get caught. How could you, of all people, play politics?"

"I'm not lying to you. I was told there was a company in the UK who was interested in promoting conservation and in particular my idea of a giant reserve. And they're supposed to be behind the whole thing."

She listened to the long silence over the air. It was important to her that Brian knew the truth, believed the truth.

"Okay," he said finally. "I was just so damned disappointed."

"How did the story break?"

"An anonymous caller phoned one of the papers. Said he was a concerned citizen. He said steps should be taken against people like yourself, for the misuse of public funds."

She stared blankly at the wall. Who would say a thing like that? Of course: Prins. Would it never end?

"I've been set up."

Mary-Ann swivelled around to study her image in the dresser mirror. Her eyes were sunken with bags under them. Her hair was lank. Her skin had no tone – and she hadn't seen a really tall sky for … for – what did her dad say all the time? – a coon's age. Old habits die hard. And then suddenly she wondered if that couldn't be construed as racist even though she had always been told it derived from something to do with raccoons. Well, best not to get in the habit of using it aloud, just in case.

She nodded at her reflection decisively. She was cutting the lecture tour short. She was on the wrong continent, doing the wrong thing, with the wrong people, and – even though she hadn't been aware of it – for the wrong reasons, too. She'd had enough. It was time to return to Africa.

*

The dingy terrace house to which he had been directed over the telephone was halfway along Nutbrook Street. With the number 12 mostly obscured by half-dead ivy, it took some finding. The small yard was concrete, barren, unswept.

He wasn't at all sure of himself. After a moment's hesitation Roger rung the doorbell. A fat girl, around twenty years of age, opened the door, scowled at him, hostile.

"What do you want?"

"I'm to see Jenny Barnes. I phoned."

She looked him up and down, pulled a face, seemed surprised. "Through 'ere." She pointed to a door that led off the hallway. He hesitated.

"Well, go on then."

Roger nodded, opened the door, paused on the threshold, entered the small, crowded room.

It hadn't taken long to track down the contact number of the animal rights' organisation which had demonstrated against Mary-Ann, just a few hours. He had then telephoned and was told to meet with a Jenny Barnes, and some others belonging to the group, in Peckham, South-East London. They represented his last chance of ruining Hawke's plans for a coal mine in Mozambique. After Mary-Ann's reaction Roger was determined to be even more cautious about gaining credibility before introducing his own agenda.

He passed through the doorway and the light fell on his face.

A pimply-faced youth elbowed his neighbour. "That's the guy who helped that hunting bitch the other night. In Fulham." His penetrating whisper effectively silenced the chatter.

Everyone turned to stare.

Roger made his way further into the room. He held up a hand. "He's right, but it was a mistake. I talked to her afterwards and I didn't like her ideas. I'd like to do something for animal rights. My name's Roger Denton. Is there a Jenny Barnes here? I'm supposed to meet her."

The pimply-faced youth turned to look at a stocky girl who leaned against the wall in the corner of the room. Roger followed his eyes and recognised her as the leader of the attack on Mary-Ann. Simultaneously he saw the flash of recognition in her eyes.

"Don't believe him, Jenny. What's an old guy like that want with us?"

The muscular young woman perched on the arm of the only proper armchair in the room, nodded her agreement. "Bert's right. His kind never support us." She half-leaned on the shoulder of a pretty dark-haired teenage girl who was sitting on the armchair proper.

Jenny gave the muscular young woman a quick calculating glance from under her eyebrows. "Gabby, since when have we been so quick to judge?" She nodded to Roger. "I'm Jenny Barnes."

"Just give me a chance." Roger added quickly, "You'll see."

The dark-haired girl sitting on the chair made a face. "Maybe Jenny's right ... give him a break, huh?" she added tentatively, drawing a scornful glance from Gabby who sat more upright, no longer leaning on her shoulder. Jenny suddenly had a tight grin on her face.

Bert took a step forward. "How do we know he isn't trying to infiltrate us, like? Maybe he's a cop."

"Yeah," Gabby nodded agreement. "He's a suit. You can tell."

"Maybe," Jenny replied. "But when they did try their people were our age and dressed like us." She pointed at Roger. "They'd be daft pushing in someone what looks like him."

Gabby set her jaw. "Maybe that's what they want us to think. It's a double bluff, like."

A murmur of agreement sounded around the room.

Jenny scowled at Gabby. Authority usurped. "So we'll test him. Then we'll know."

Gabby sneered. "Yeah right! Ask him a bunch of questions. He'll give all the right answers. And it won't prove nuthin."

"Do I get a chance to say something?" Roger asked.

"I've got a better idea," Jenny said. "We take old Roger here along with us tomorrow morning. We'll soon know."

"That's crazy," burst out Bert. "We don't know the guy. He could be a cop or anyone. When we get there they'll be waiting."

Jenny shrugged stubbornly. "First off, he doesn't have to know *what* we're planning or *where*, he just goes along. Then if he wants to make trouble it'll be his word against a dozen."

Bert shrugged. "Have it your own way."

"All right," Gabby said. "But it ain't a good idea. We should know people a lot better before we take them on missions."

Jenny turned to Roger. "You can prove yourself tomorrow."

Roger nodded. "That's fine by me. When and where do we meet?"

Jenny laughed. "It's not that easy, sweetheart. Now you stay. We're taking no chances. And we start out tonight, so we'll be ready early."

"Way to go, Jenny," exclaimed Bert, giving her the thumbs up.

"And who's going to sit on him until tomorrow?" Gabby asked sarcastically.

Jenny laughed out aloud, but Roger noticed she was watching Gabby's face all the while. "Don't worry. I'll make him my personal responsibility." She arched her eyebrows coyly at Roger. "Are you in?"

Roger paused. She didn't fancy him. The undercurrent was between Jenny and Gabby personally. But if he was going to earn their confidence, Jenny was the only ally he seemed to have in the room. So he would have to go along with her – whatever her private agenda.

Roger nodded. "I'm in."

"Good." Jenny held out her hand to him. "You just trail around behind me, like a good boy, for the rest of tonight."

Roger noticed that Jenny's eyes were still fixed on Gabby but he stepped forward to take the outstretched hand anyway. "At your service, ma'am."

*

Near the southern tip of Africa, a South African Air Force officer, Colonel Brett Wallender, sat stiffly behind his desk in his office at the Ysterplaat Military Airfield just outside Cape Town. As he studied the document that lay before him on the desk his mouth turned down at the edges. He gave the distinct impression he had been sucking a very bitter lemon indeed.

He looked up at the sound of a respectful knock on the door. "Come in," he growled in an ominously quiet way.

An MP opened the door, ushered in two young men in uniform who, to Colonel Wallender's jaundiced eye, didn't seem the least bit taken aback by what was happening although they did stand respectfully to attention in front of his desk.

He eyed them silently for a beat and then for a little longer but there was still no reaction.

"I don't want you two to say a word. First, I'm going to tell you what we know and then I'm going to tell you what we're going to do. Understood?"

"Yessir!" chorused the pair.

"We have it on record that you two had a night flight training exercise out in the general flying area on for last night. You signed out the Alo at 9.15 pm, refuelled and took off shortly thereafter."

He studied the pair for a while.

"Then, separately, we've been advised by ATC for the Cape Town Airport control zone that they had four helicopters operating in their area last night at about the same time. All were at a low level over the urban part of the city. One was a Sikorsky returning to base at the Waterfront. Two others were being used for medical emergency work, one for a road traffic accident and the other to move a very ill patient from a small clinic to a better equipped facility at Groote Schuur Hospital.

"The fourth helicopter appears to be more mysterious and they cannot give us any feedback on who was involved or what it may have been.

He paused for a while. "Then we also have a report from a security guard at Newlands Rugby Ground, which may or may not be reliable.

"He says that he saw a machine, which we will assume to be a helicopter because the gates were locked and there was no other way onto the rugby field other than by air, on the rugby field and two men and two women running up and down the field throwing a rugby ball around. According –

"Sir –" Captain Paul "Hammie" Hammond was immediately cut off by the Colonel.

"I said 'no speak' Hammond, not until I've finished and then all you will say is 'yes sir'. Now if I may continue …

He glared at the two men.

"In his report the security guard said he saw that the two men were enthusiastically tackling the two women at every available opportunity. I need to add here that he says that the two men and the two women were naked. Unfortunately he doesn't know what time he saw these goings-on and indeed wondered if he was not hallucinating but decided anyway to report it this morning. You returned to base in the Alo you had earlier taken off in at approximately 1.45 am.

Slowly the Colonel shook his head. "I would dearly like to break you both down to the rank of private. If the poor long-suffering taxpayers of this country hadn't spent over a million to date on your training I'd do just that." He glared at them.

"But we know no more than I have set out here and we cannot, one way or the other, prove anything against anyone. So this is what is going to happen.

"I am going to send you to the remotest field, on the remotest part of the border, in the remotest part of the Kalahari Desert that I can find. And you're bloody well going to stay there until you're old and grey. Now you are allowed to speak but," and he held up his hand, "all you are allowed to say is yes sir."

"Yessir," they chorused.

"Now get out of my sight."

As the two men shuffled out the Colonel stared thoughtfully at the closed door through which they had just disappeared. Suddenly he chuckled. He could still clearly remember when he was a young helicopter pilot. And how he would have loved to see an Alo flying into one of the most sacred rugby grounds in the country.

And with two –

The photograph on his desk, of a rather stern-looking woman, caught his eye, interrupted his train of thought, so he coughed, stood up. It was time to go home.

*

It was 9.35 pm when Jenny announced it was time to go.

Roger had long ago found himself a corner of the room and half-dozed off, uncomfortable, bored.

Outside the house Jenny waved a still sleepy Roger around to the front of an old rusty Ford Transit van with darkened windows at the back. "I'm driving. You sit up front with me."

Gabby, the muscular female with the marine haircut, was already at the passenger door. She scowled then climbed into the back of the Ford Transit with the others. Roger reckoned there were ten people, maybe eleven, altogether.

It took Jenny thirty minutes to work her way through the streets of Peckham onto the South Circular Road and onto the M3, heading south-west. About two hours later, and without warning, Jenny swung off the motorway. They drove along ever narrowing country roads that wound along between hedgerows, dark in the van's headlights. Eventually Jenny slowed, turned off the tar road to stop before a gate leading to a field.

"Open it," she said curtly.

Roger shrugged, climbed out of the van and swung open the wooden gate. He tried to peer into the field but there was little he could see. There were no lights visible. Vaguely, perhaps a hundred metres away, a large building was silhouetted against the faintly lighter skyline. Jenny stopped the van alongside him.

"When you've closed it come across to the old hangar."

Roger nodded, closed the gate, ambled across to the hangar, which looked to be a relic from World War ll. He took his time, enjoying the clean night air out in the country. Mary-Ann had been right about that. It was a different world away from the city. He wondered how much more different it must be in Africa. Deliberately he pushed those thoughts from his mind. Once he had nailed Hawke, he would reassess everything.

By the time Roger arrived at the hangar the others had unloaded the sleeping-bags, piling them in the centre of the floor. The place was half full of hay and was obviously used by a farmer as additional storage space.

Jenny beckoned to him, patted the floor next to her. "Come sit with me."

They all squatted down, arranged themselves in a loose circle around the sleeping-bags. Four of them started to roll cigarettes. Jenny lit hers, took three deep draws, holding her breath as long as possible each time. She held out the hand-rolled cigarette to Roger. A sickly-sweet smell permeated the air.

"Not for me, thanks," he shook his head. "I don't smoke."

"C'mon, this isn't tobacco, this is dope, you dope – good stuff, too."

Roger hesitated, wondered if he had a choice. Nobody else had refused. A number of them watched him surreptitiously. Reluctantly he accepted the joint. He raised it to his lips determined to fake smoking, but Jenny watched him closely and he had no option but to copy her actions. It clawed at his throat. With a great deal of difficulty he managed to suppress a cough. Copying the others he passed the cigarette over to the person on his right. Roger was surprised. He felt no different. He had assumed an instant effect.

The cigarettes did the rounds until they were tiny ends. Some of the activists then smoked them to extinction by holding them stuck on pins, the way scientists impale butterflies in their laboratories. Roger began to giggle at the thought of what would happen if the scientists came to work one day only to find that all their little butterflies had turned into marijuana stubs. Scientists like Mary-Ann – he immediately felt incredibly, deeply sad. Tears rolled freely down his cheeks.

Someone tugged at his shoulder. He looked around. Jenny lay alongside him on a sleeping-bag. He had no recollection of when she had left his side to collect it from the pile in the centre of the hangar. For the first time Roger became aware of the extent to which the marijuana had affected him.

Jenny smiled up at him dreamily. "Don't be shy." She held up her arms. "Come to Jenny."

"There's an awful lot of people here." But he didn't really care.

"It doesn't seem to be worrying them."

Roger looked around. Two of the pairs were already coupling inside their zipped together sleeping-bags, there was no mistaking the way those bags moved. Gabby was passionately kissing the pretty dark-haired girl.

"Well," Jenny demanded.

Roger lay down and put his arms around her. He didn't know whether it was the marijuana or not but he didn't give a damn that they weren't alone. He began to kiss her. Her response surprised him. She breathed heavily, gasped and moaned. Soon she pulled him over so that he was on top of her. Almost immediately her hands had undone his trousers and were inside his shorts, working at him with her short stubby fingers.

Roger was equally surprised by the degree to which he was turned on. The marijuana had created a surreal reality in his mind with a weird juxtapositioning of images and feelings. As he grew hard Jenny's hands left his shorts and he felt her squirming beneath him as she wriggled her backside out of her black denim jeans. She took a quick look across at Gabby and the dark-haired girl, then turned back to Roger.

"Do it to me," she gasped loudly, squirming under him.

Roger felt himself slide into her almost involuntarily and he began to make love to her as though his life depended on it. Jenny gasped and moaned in an exaggerated fashion, to the extent it even filtered through to Roger's marijuana influenced brain that something was not quite right.

He had just about worked this out when he felt a hard toe prodding him in the side. He stopped to look up. He felt very stupid and very vulnerable lying there. Gabby stood with her black leather jacket pushed back and arms akimbo.

"What's wrong? Don't stop," muttered Jenny, her voice muffled from under his chest somewhere.

Gabby grimaced. "All right, you win."

"I do?" Roger asked stupidly, confused.

Jenny opened her eyes and moved her head to one side so she could see past his shoulder.

"I'm not talking to you, idiot!" Gabby growled. "Well," she said, looking at Jenny. "You win, now are you going to get that … that … male idiot off you or not?"

Roger rolled off Jenny of his own accord.

Gabby squatted down cross-legged next to Jenny, tears running down her cheeks. "I promise not to do it again."

Jenny turned to look at him, in her eyes an understanding for his embarrassment. She also seemed mildly amused.

"Go and keep Merle company." She jerked a thumb in the direction of the pretty black-haired girl Gabby had earlier been kissing.

"Maybe we'd better just leave it," Roger responded.

"It's up to you," she said casually. Too casually?

A number of eyes were fixed on him. Especially those of the callow Bert and the muscular Gabby. A sudden realisation. He was still on probation. He was going to have to participate in all their games if he was ever going to win the group's confidence.

Roger took a deep breath and stood up. He felt momentarily giddy, realised he was still very much under the influence of the marijuana. Somehow that knowledge cured him of all shyness as though it provided a ready-made excuse for outlandish behaviour. Naked from the waist down he walked across the hangar to where Merle sat watching him with sleepy marijuana-swollen eyes.

Her nakedness didn't seem to bother her. Roger sat down beside her. He noticed her quick glance across the hangar and Jenny's small nod. Merle shrugged and lay back on the straw with her arms by her side and her legs apart.

The situation still seemed bizarre. The private act of sex overlaid with the public scrutiny of the others made it so. He found it weirdly exciting. Roger stood up again and took off his shirt so that he was completely naked. He hardly noticed the goosebumps on his arms and legs from the chill in the late night air.

He knelt beside Merle. She lay there like a doll, unmoving. She was no more than seventeen years old. Roger knelt between her legs and took a quick look around. Bert had lost interest and had gone back to kissing his girl, but both Jenny and Gabby were watching him, as were two of the other couples.

Roger felt giddy with power, as though the conquering of his public embarrassment through the use of marijuana made him want to do things he had never have considered doing under normal circumstances. Without a word he lay down on top of Merle. She lifted her hips slightly as he penetrated her. He knew he was being watched and he deliberately didn't pull the spread-out, zipped-together sleeping-bags around the two of them. Responding to some exhibitionist element of his character he hadn't known existed, he reached a strange high making love to a motionless Merle in front of so many eyes.

Merle in turn showed as much interest in the proceedings as a hooker grown old in the oldest profession. It may have been the drugs, the audience, the atmosphere in that old hangar or a combination of all three, but he climaxed having climbed one of the highest peaks he had ever attempted.

At the last moment Merle also made a small sound, maybe a climax, although he couldn't be sure, it was such a small gasp. Maybe she was just glad he was finished. He pulled the sleeping-bags around them and zipped them up from the bottom. Merle now showed some affection. She put her arms around him, huddled into his chest.

It was exactly what Mary-Ann had done the first night they had made love – and Roger felt nauseous. He felt as though he had betrayed everything she stood for. Everything that was clean and honest and decent. He felt the tears on his cheeks and wondered whether what he had done to her could be – in some way – undone. And he knew that that wasn't possible.

"Merle," he whispered softly into the black hair that nestled underneath his chin.

"Yes," she responded from around his chest.

"What's the target for tomorrow?"

"We're not supposed to tell."

"What do you think I'm going to do with the information now. If you're worried about the others whisper it in my ear."

She shook her head. "Wait 'til morning …"

He went to sleep soon after that, but thinking about Mary-Ann.

*

At 8.40 am on the Saturday morning, Carol Eastridge excitedly sat forward to lean on the dashboard. Her father turned the old grey Volvo, pulling a double horsebox trailer, through the gate. Theirs was one of the last cars to arrive. At least fourteen or fifteen horseboxes were already parked haphazardly in the farmyard.

This was Carol's big morning. She absolutely couldn't wait. It was to be her first proper ride on Stargazer, a 15.2 hands bay with a Roman nose and the disposition of an angel. Stargazer was Carol's thirteenth birthday present and her 'best ever' as she called it. Before Stargazer she had only had ponies, of course, and hadn't been allowed to hunt with her father.

Although she was quick to say she still loved each of the three ponies on which she had learned to ride, it had never ever been like the instant love affair she'd had with Stargazer. To ride out beside her father, the owner and manager of a local village supermarket, had been a dream of hers for so long she couldn't actually remember a time when it hadn't been there. And to do it on her ever-so handsome bay – who would ever have believed it possible just a few short months ago!

Peering out of the car window she remembered back to her birthday three months earlier. She was only supposed to get the horse if she did really, really well at school. But at the end of the year she had only managed three A's, two B's and a C and that wasn't good enough. On her birthday morning she found the big bay standing placidly outside, plucking with his fine strong white teeth at the green grass on the verge of the road. She had been over the moon to discover that this wonderful, darling, beautiful, strong, handsome horse was hers. And she knew why she had got it anyway, even though her marks were not anywhere good enough, although she hadn't yet revealed her secret to anyone.

Now her father braked the old Volvo in the farmyard and Carol jumped out before it had properly come to a stop. She ran around to the back of the horsebox to open up and lower the ramp. She first led Stargazer out, and then her father's big 17 hands black, leading them across to where they could drink water, before she ran over to greet her friend.

"I've been practising for three months and can handle most of the jumps now," she told her 'best ever' friend, June, who was actually a bit older than she was and had ridden to hounds the year before. "Dad said that was the absolute minimum."

June clapped her hands. "Oh Carol, I'm so glad you're riding with us today. It'll be such fun."

"My dad did say I was to stick close to him."

"Oh, that's all right. I'm sure he'll let us ride back together."

Carol nodded, hesitated, but June was her best-ever friend. "God gave me Stargazer," she finally confided her secret. "I really didn't do well enough in the exams to deserve him. But I prayed anyway and God gave me Stargazer. God loves horses," she added very seriously.

"He's a lovely horse," her friend said. "I really, really understand why you love him so much."

Carol loved the atmosphere of the hunt. She also felt so much more part of it in her new jacket of unfaded black, instead of having to wear her old check ratcatcher. The new one was just like her father's although his had already seen good service. And she was wearing new britches, specially bought for the occasion.

Today the hunt seemed different: the air was crisper, the grass greener, the early-morning smiles sweeter and even the horses hooves on the cobblestones sounded clearer. She could hardly wait for that strident call to issue forth from the horn of Nick, the angular, weather-beaten huntsman.

*

The animal rights activists were practised in their preparations. Roger glanced at his watch - 9.05 am. He stood with his back against the hangar door watching the others. He felt really depressed about the night before. The incredible thing was the extent to which he had enjoyed himself – until Merle cuddled into his chest reminding him of Mary-Ann …

Jenny came over to him, pulling a woollen garment out of the haversack she carried in one hand. She held it out to him.

"Wear this. And make sure you've no light coloured spots showing. Bert has some army camo cream you can use."

Roger nodded as he unfolded the item. He was going to feel a proper twit running around in a Balaclava, with his hands and neck painted brown like a mock terrorist.

Within ten minutes they were organised. The group left the hangar in a single file. Clearly the rest of them had been very carefully briefed. Talking was kept the minimum. The sun hadn't yet had an effect and the early morning air was bracing. They soon fell into a lope, led by Bert, the pimply youth.

Jenny indicated Roger was to tag along behind her, Gabby and Merle. When they reached a gate in the hedgerow on the far side of the field they broke up into three groups of four each. The two other groups silently split off left and right and disappeared from sight.

"It's a hunt we're after," Jenny whispered, her voice driven down by the tension that coursed through them all. "There are three possible routes the riders can take as they leave the yard. We've split up into three groups with each group posted on one of the three routes. That way we'll be sure to make contact."

The four of them climbed the gate into the next field. Jenny, who was leading, didn't cross this field direct. Instead she set off along the hedgerows until they had reached a wood on the far side of the field. Roger had no idea of where they were and trudged along in Jenny's footsteps almost bumping into her when she abruptly stopped near a gate.

"Keep down," Jenny whispered, pointing through the rails of the gate.

Through the wooden rails, in the distance, a Georgian manor-house stood square and white reflecting the morning light.

Jenny beckoned him closer. "Here's where we stop. The wood on either side is too dense to ride through. If they come this way they'll have to use the gate. And the gate isn't that high, so most of 'em will try to jump it."

Roger nodded. The rough wool of the Balaclava was coarse against his skin, but he was grateful for the warmth of it, a decided chill pervaded the air.

Jenny knelt, slipped the haversack off her back and opened it. She pulled out a coiled length of thin nylon rope.

Roger's eyes involuntarily went wide. He quickly knelt down beside her. He kept his voice low so that neither of the other two would hear. "That could kill someone."

"What do you think they're going to do to the fox?" She handed the coiled nylon rope to Gabby who had quietly come up behind him. Roger looked up. Seeing his discomfiture, she grinned at him.

Jenny and Gabby strung the rope across the gate opening, but in such a way that it lay hidden behind the top bar of the wooden gate and out of sight of anyone coming from the other side. They tied it tightly on the one side. On the other side they used a slip-knot which could quickly be pulled taut one way, but which wouldn't slip if pulled on the other way.

The four concealed themselves by lying down further back into the wood behind some low scrub. Jenny and Gabby were on the side from which they had approached the gate. Merle and Roger were sent to the opposite side: where the rope had been permanently fastened. It was clear that they didn't trust either Roger or Merle to put tension on the rope, but still wanted them there, just in case it came loose – or so Jenny said.

Roger lay on the matted carpet of dead leaves, with the warm coffee smell of bracken strong in his nostrils. They were right not to trust him. He was horrified at the thought of what could happen to a rider in full flight. Should he put an end to the farce by standing up and drawing the hunt's attention? But he had to get Hawke. And these people, as little as he liked them, were his only hope. Perhaps the hunt would veer away in some other direction and he would be off the hook.

Something Mary-Ann had said came to mind –

Hate can just as easily destroy you as the person you hate. Revenge will ultimately harm you more than it will your target.

He forced the thought out of his mind. The simple truth was that he couldn't both warn the riders and have the activists learn to trust him. He had to make Hawke pay.

So he did nothing except wait there in the wood.

*

Nick Jones, the huntsman, resplendent in his red jacket, looked inquiringly across to the Master of the Hunt, Sir

Richard Giles, who nodded. Nick released the hounds which had been milling around and jumping up and down in excitement. They bayed and barked their way out of the yard, jostling each other in their enthusiasm.

Seated on top of the big bay Carol Eastridge felt both excited and nervous at the same time. The drinking of the stirrup cup – although she had only taken the tiniest of sips – had left her teeth on edge with the rich port after-taste. She shivered: it was just the most wonderfully romantically fantastic 'best ever' ever.

Not too long after the hounds were out of the yard, the riders clattered their way over the cobbles and out through the gate of the farmyard onto the road and then into the field beyond. Carol's 'best ever' friend turned to wave as she rode through the gateway. Carol returned the salute but hung back, obedient to her father's instructions. With the reins tight Stargazer danced sideways skittishly until he bumped into her father's big black.

Her father winked, wagged a finger at her. "Now, remember, young lady, no heroics." He spoke sternly, but he was smiling.

A few moments later he nodded. "All right, Kitten, now it's our turn."

Bridles jingling they trotted along in the wake of the rest, far behind the huntsman. Carol shivered again. Stargazer blew steam out of his nostrils and shook his head making the bit rattle. Carol felt the rhythm of the horse's deep even breaths between her thighs. Her whole body tingled.

Suddenly across the field – a great deal of howling.

The hounds took off as though just released in a dog race. They had picked up a scent. Off they went, streaming downhill towards the rivulet. The riders wasted no time. The more reckless starting galloping before they were properly off the hard ground and onto the grass.

Carol felt the heady pull of the hunt for the first time. It was a bewitching cocktail. A combination of the dynamic movement of the horse beneath the saddle, his breath streaming back from his nostrils, the sound of excited hounds and young life coursing through her veins. Her excitement communicated itself to Stargazer and even he, normally so placid, stirred restlessly and twisted sideways, before she managed to bring him under control again.

Then her father was gone and she after him. It was all so quick she was caught by surprise. Stargazer hit his stride and she easily pulled up alongside her father.

"Caught you," she cried, not sure whether he could hear her.

He nodded, smiling, but continued to hold the reins of his black tightly against its head. From somewhere far ahead Carol could hear the increased yapping of the hounds as the scent in their nostrils grew stronger. She hoped her father knew where to go.

Together father and daughter thundered across the field. Carol rode with Stargazer's nose a half-a-head in front, and she was utterly convinced her 'best ever' bay had the beating of her father's bigger black.

*

The fox skipped nimbly across the stones in the stream and stopped on the far bank. His proud brush stuck out behind him and his red coat had already thickened for winter.

Off to his right leaves stirred and then were still. Instantly he crouched. He remained immobile, unmoving as though carved from a piece of red cedar. Only the bright eyes flickered against the black of the mask across his face. After more than a minute the soft scratching started up again. The fox gradually went down until his belly scraped the ground, slowly he moved forward, absolutely silent. He moved with the scratching sounds, when that stopped, he stopped.

Finally out into the open hopped a pink and white rabbit. It sat up, rubbed its fluffy paws on either side of its nose. The poised fox sprang, but just too late, the split second he moved the rabbit dived to one side and vanished into the ground. The fox trotted forward, passing where the rabbit had disappeared, hardly giving the burrow a second glance. It was too small for him to even try to get in.

Abruptly he froze into immobility. He held his head up, nose high. His ears twitched from side to side, half-swivelling like miniature radar scanners. From far in the distance the baying of hounds reached him. The fox started forward as though someone had scored him with a cattle prod. He broke into a trot, keeping his head high.

The hounds grew steadily closer and the fox stretched his legs, twisting and ducking as he wove his way threw the bushes bordering the stream. The baying grew louder, hard in his radar-scanner ears and the fox's heart began to pump for all it was worth, thumping in his chest, extended to capacity. His legs were at full stretch on every stride and he could go no faster. The blood pounded in his ears and panic spurred him on, driving him along, thin branches whipping across his mask like miniature cats-o'-nine-tails.

The fox veered, running up the bank, away from the stream, towards the copse of trees where he had his lair. The sound of the hounds was so loud now it drowned out even the beating of his heart in his ears. The wild song of a hunting horn backed up the baying of the hounds.

The fox started up the bank, but almost immediately instinct told him he wasn't going to make it. The hounds would be between him and safety. At full stretch on every stride, his red coat gleaming with the wet of the dew on the grass, the fox turned back downhill, heading for the stream.

*

At first Roger thought he wouldn't have to make a decision. He could hear the hounds coursing wide around where the four of them lay hidden in the wood. The riders closest to the hounds had followed them around to cut through the field next to the one in which Roger's group lay hidden. The sounds swung down and away towards a far stream at the bottom of the next field.

Roger rolled over onto his back, breathed a sigh of relief. It wasn't his decision to make after all. He stared upwards at the canopy of trees through which the morning light softly filtered. Somewhere in the copse he could hear a robin singing and a magpie swooped by low overhead closely followed by its lifelong mate.

Roger heard the sound of horses' hooves. Too late he realised they were coming down the bridle-path towards the gate. Their sudden proximity caught him by surprise. He half rolled over and sat up to peer through the undergrowth. Two riders came down the path, the horses, a black and a bay. He groaned to himself. They must have fallen behind and were taking a short cut in order to catch up.

Roger felt powerless, having no time to act and yet it all seemed to happen as though in slow motion. The man on the big black slowed. Roger thought he was going to come to a complete stop, so that the girl on the bay could open the gate for the two of them.

Roger was wrong.

The male rider on the black waved the girl on the bay through. He gave her a clear run at the gate. As Roger opened his mouth to shout a warning, it was already too late. The horse was in the air, front legs bent and reaching for height, back legs tucked up underneath to clear the obstacle. The rope sprang up in front of the bay catching it across the knees. Horse and rider smashed over the gate, crumpling like discarded Christmas wrapping paper.

Roger started to get up, but Merle grabbed his arm and hung on, holding him down. Across the bridle-path he saw Jenny and Gabby, bent double, disappearing along the hedgerow which led away from the gate and back towards the hangar. Roger and Merle stayed where they were. They had to cross the bridle-path in order to make good their escape. Had Jenny set them up?

"We've got to help that girl," he said. "There's blood all over her face."

"Don't be a fool," Merle said huskily as though she had a very bad cold. "They'll throw you in jail for what's happened today. The magistrates are all on their side." She pushed herself up so that she was also kneeling and could see what was happening. "That man's with her."

Roger nodded. She was right. Breaking cover now wouldn't help the girl. The other riders appearing on the scene would handle the whole thing better than he could.

"Keep down," he whispered, "there's more of them coming."

They stayed low in the undergrowth and the voices by the bridle-path carried easily to where they lay.

"Carol's okay," someone called out, "It's just a small cut on the forehead, but the bay's leg is broken."

The girl called Carol screamed. "No! No! You're lying! You're all lying!"

After a while she quietened somewhat and her soft sobbing was almost indistinguishable from the other noises: the jingling of bits and the soft sound of horses blowing out through their nostrils, chopping the earth with their hooves. The older man had ridden away towards the farmhouse as soon as the first of the other riders arrived.

Roger risked another peek. The young girl sat in the mud cradling the bay's head on her lap.

"What are they going to do?" she asked, over and over again, but no one there would look at her and no one answered.

Five minutes later the older man who had been riding with the girl returned in a dark green Land Rover which Roger assumed belonged to the farm. Another man, with a beard, drove the vehicle. The bearded man climbed out. He wore old brown corduroy trousers tucked into green Wellington boots and in his right hand he carried a double-barrelled shotgun over one arm, broken at the breach.

"No! No!" screamed the little girl.

The older man picked her up, holding her in his arms, pulling her away from the bay. He put her down a few metres away from where the horse lay on its side, blowing hard through its nostrils. Holding her hand he forced her to walk with him back along the bridle-path and through the gate, away from where the horse lay blowing into the soil. Roger could see the blood was beginning to dry on her face, turning a much darker red – almost a black-maroon – colour.

A single shot rang out in the woods. The girl jerked like a puppet on a string. She suddenly stopped crying altogether. As the older man and the girl slowly walked on, Roger heard her say, "Stargazer's going to be all right, Daddy. I'll pray for him. God loves horses so He will make him better."

She started to cry again. "But my nice new coat is dirty. I'm sorry, Daddy. My nice new coat is dirty."

Her face was wet with tears as she pointed to her sleeve, where the black cloth was stained brown with what was probably the horse's blood.

The man looked down at her and quickly looked away again, biting his lip. "I'm sorry about Stargazer. I should've taken the gate first. I had no idea that thing was there. Oh, those dirty bastards!"

The girl stared straight ahead, expressionless, no longer crying, hugging her arms to her chest as though she was desperately cold. "My coat is dirty, Daddy. Didn't you hear me? My coat is dirty," and then they passed out of earshot.

The other riders discovered the rope. Roger and Merle quickly squirmed backwards, deeper into the undergrowth, as two of the riders traced it back to where it was tied to a tree on their side of the bridle-path.

One of them turned to the other. "The bastards must have been on the other side. Geoffrey said it's tied with some kind of slip knot over there. It was on that side they pulled it taught as Carol and her Dad came along. The lousy shits!"

The Master of the Hunt, Sir Richard Giles, a distinguished grey-haired gentleman, and a large landowner in the area, galloped up to the group standing around holding their snorting horses by their bridles. "That's it for the day, folks. We're packing it in. The fox crossed the stream and Nick's already called in the hounds."

"Aren't we going to try and find them?" Someone in the group called out. It was a man's voice, crackling with anger, involuntarily going to a higher note.

"There's no point," Sir Richard replied, sitting tall in the saddle, jerking his horse's head around with a hard pull on the reins. "The cowards are always quick to disappear after doing their dirty work."

After that it went very quiet in the wood. The riders swung up onto their horses and slowly walked them back to the manor-house. The Land Rover bounced down the bridle-path in the same direction.

As soon as it was clear, Roger and Merle scrambled across the path, staying close to the hedgerow which led them back the way they had come. They easily retraced their route and ten minutes later were back at the hangar. The others had almost completed loading the Ford Transit. Roger wondered if they would have waited if they had finished before he and Merle had returned. An air of tension hung over the group. This time Gabby drove with Jenny sitting up front next to her. Roger was the last into the back of the van.

As the van pulled away from the gate, back on to the winding tar road, narrow between the hedges, the tension broke. Suddenly they were all talking at once. A babble of triumphant voices. All of them grinning at each other. It was not long and they were back on the M3 and slowly the noise subsided as the van ate up the miles between them and London. A soft drizzle drifted down and the tyres sang on the damp tarmac.

Having climbed in last, Roger was sitting near the doors. He kept his eyes fixed on the small square windows in the back of the Ford Transit, ostensibly watching the road reeling out behind them. But he saw nothing. He was trying to make sense of it all.

"Now you've seen what we can do!" Jenny sang out from the front of the van.

Roger started as a sharp elbow hit him painfully in the ribs. It was the callow youth, Bert. "'ere, Jenny's talking to you!"

"My mind was elsewhere. What was that?"

"Well, what do you think?" called out Jenny.

Roger shrugged. He didn't yet know what to think, but he had begun to feel claustrophobic in the back of the van. None of them had bathed since leaving London the day before. He became increasingly aware of the proximity of hot bodies. The picture of the little girl cradling the bay's head and shouting 'No!' at the people around her stayed before his eyes and suddenly he was angry.

"I thought you believed in animal rights?" he called out loudly.

The van became still. "What do you mean?" Jenny asked from the front.

"I know you don't care about that girl and what could've happened to her. But the horse is dead. What about its rights?"

"But we saved the fox, that balances the horse," Jenny said. "And we stopped their hunt. Some of them will give it up altogether once they've had a few lessons. It won't be worth it anymore."

"Yeah," said Bert, from so close Roger could smell his tart breath. It was all he could to do to avoid recoiling. "They don't like it when they're the targets. They're all bloody cowards, chasing after a poor little fox, with thirty, maybe forty hounds after it, and all of those people on horses. That ain't clever!"

"Which means," Jenny continued, "that it was a victory for animal rights."

"So you don't care about the horse?" Roger persisted.

Bert stared at him. He flung over his shoulder at Jenny, "I bloody told you about 'im, didn't I?" He faced Roger again. "That horse was a soldier lost in the battle for animal rights."

The whole situation was almost comical with heads turning, as though at a tennis match, when first someone at the front and then someone at the back spoke.

"At times the animals themselves have to pay the highest price in the fight for their rights," Jenny added.

"If man doesn't have a use for animals they won't keep them, won't look after them. Animals are more likely to survive if man has a commercial reason to keep them around." For a moment he wondered where that had come from, then he remembered.

"He's a meat-eater," declared Gabby, speaking for the first time. "I knew he was a meat-eater."

What had Mary-Ann said about these sort of people?

Where does that leave those people who see themselves as arbiters of what is morally and politically acceptable? ... one of their new targets upon which to visit their zeal is animal rights ...

"You're all crazy. Zealots with no real challenges left, nothing of substance to get excited about, to lecture the rest of us about."

A stunned silence fell over the van. Gabby swerved onto the shoulder of the M3.

"Get out!" she screamed.

"Yeah," Bert shouted in his ear. "Get out of 'ere!"

"My pleasure," Roger said, but he did not get the chance to exit the van with any dignity as a boot in his back propelled him out onto the verge where he ended up on his knees being unable to catch his balance in time.

Roger stood up in the soaking drizzle as the Ford Transit's wheels spun gravel against his legs.

"What the hell do I do now?" he muttered to himself and he wasn't thinking about how to get back to London.

*

The hunger and the fever weakened the lion.

It had been three weeks since he had eaten the hyaena and he hadn't had another chance at one of those. Deeper in the cave he had found a black-backed jackal's lair and in it a litter of five almost-weaned pups. A week back a large porcupine had strayed into his path – he still had a broken-off quill stuck in his cheek – but he had fed well on that. He had also eaten of the tsamma melons and gemsbok cucumbers growing outside the cave entrance.

So he had kept alive, but his condition was poor and the wound in his shoulder was openly septic, flies clustered around the seeping hole. He couldn't catch prey easily because his leg hampered him, slowed him down. The lion's right shoulder had grown very stiff. His wound was hard and black around the edges, with flies having laid eggs deep in his flesh. The stiffness and numbness in his shoulder had spread further, penetrating deep into his chest. That impaired his muscle control and his front leg shook each time he moved it forward. What should have been easy was now impossible.

He stepped out of the cave, unexpectedly came across a dassie – rock hyrax – sunning itself in a sheltered spot. It was trapped there and the lion soon made short work of the small animal, which at up to 5 kilograms in weight has the elephant, at up to over 5 tonnes in weight, as its closest living relative.

He dragged himself back to the cave entrance. His quests for food were short-lived and virtually useless. He had to do something. Within two or three days he had to find something substantial to eat because of the drain on his reserves.

The area in front of the cave was clear again. The hyaenas had left in search of easier prey, but they would be back. The lion lay down, rolling onto his side in such a way that he could still see out of the cave. He lay there like that, on his side, in the sun, looking out over the valley, eyelids drooping as he stared flatly ahead at nothing.

Down at the river crossing the man-smell had been very strong, he felt the need for a kill pushing at him to return to that place – but the man-smell was also terrifying – and he was not yet desperate enough to try them for food – not yet …

*

Her direct superior, Adrian Windermere, shrugged. "All I can do is pass on the message as instructed. You're being asked to resign your temporary appointment. There's never going to be a permanent place for you. It's this Conservationgate thing."

"Can I stay here with my father until I find something else?"

She could see the relief in the man's eyes when he quickly looked up. "Of course! We're not unreasonable. This whole thing mustn't be taken out of context."

She joined her father in his small office. He read her expression and understood something disastrous had occurred. He gestured to the empty chair on the other side of his desk. "You want to talk?"

So she told him she was unemployed, but made no mention of Professor Prins. That was still her problem to solve.

"Now I'm at a loose end. Can I stay a while?"

He nodded, giving her one of his rare fleeting smiles.

She smiled thinly at him, then forced it a little wider. "We can start off by my taking charge of your kitchen. How would you like a few grilled lamb chops, still pink inside, with that mushroom and garlic sauce from Mom's recipe book. We'll bake a potato or two, share a bottle of good red wine, get quite maudlin and tell each other lies about what we're going to do with all our tomorrows."

"That's a date." Again that tiny smile, sometimes of such short duration it left her wondering whether it had been there at all.

As she trudged across to the cottage she now finally understood there would be no end to the vicious vindictiveness of Professor Prins. She also understood that she had no idea of how to combat the evil.

*

The helicopter pilot, Captain Paul Hammond, lifted his second leg up to the scarred wooden table and crossed his flying boots neatly at the ankle. "My good friend and colleague, read that." With a flick of his wrist he threw the signal from SAAF GHQ in Pretoria across the table.

His flight engineer, Sergeant Walter 'Marty' Martins, leaned forward to pick it up, suspicion writ large upon his open features.

He scanned the sheet of paper. "Jesus! That's great. I wonder what decided the boss to let us off like this."

"Ah-hem," Paul cleared his throat meaningfully, checked the fingernails of his extended right hand, polished them on his flying overalls and again inspected them. During this process he rode his chair back dangerously on two legs, to the very limits of his balance, teetering there happily as he studied his fingernails.

Marty rasped a hand across his unshaven chin, studied Paul under peaked eyebrows. "Okay, out with it. How the hell did you manage it?"

"It works as follows. When a flying team has a married man in its midst and he puts in for a posting home in order to have time with his family over Christmas and he's already spent more than a month in a designated border area he must be granted said leave as a matter of urgency."

Paul paused, wagged a finger in the air. "Are we clear so far?"

"You still have the floor."

"If the normal CO is away on a Staff Officers' training course and certain punishments were in-house no one else would know about them. So the acting CO would have to grant the request. It goes without saying the whole team will have to go because there's no point in having a helicopter without a flight engineer around to stuff things up, now would it?"

"Go to hell," Marty said mildly. "And I never put in for no posting. Not to mention the fact that I'm in the process of getting a divorce and have no children. You know very well I haven't lived with that woman for years."

"Oh, but you forget – mainly because you're an ill-mannered, undisciplined lout – that you're an enlisted man and I'm your immediate superior officer and I put in a request for you as soon as I heard the boss was going to be away." He smiled proudly. "And they agreed. What would you do without me?"

Marty shook his head mournfully. "The old man's going to kill us when he gets back –"

"By which time we'll have had Christmas in a place a little more congenial than this."

"Hammie," Marty jumped to his feet. He bowed from the waist. "You're a genius."

"I know, I know." Paul acknowledged with a royal wave of his hand.

*

By Tuesday morning Roger had had three days to think about his excursion with the activists. He had sunk to a new low. At least they sincerely believed in what they were doing. And, to be fair, for him, the whole idea of a fox being torn to shreds by a pack of hounds was beyond imagining. But what had he been thinking? And sex with Merle – it was as though he had cheated on Mary-Ann, without his own wife even coming in to the equation.

And *that* was truly ridiculous.

About Mary-Ann, he had to be as logical as possible. He had acted stupidly enough for ten idiots. He had probably alienated her forever – understandably so. It was something he was going to have to accept – it was right.

But there was more …

Mary-Ann:

… *hate can just as easily destroy you as it can the person you hate.*

How far would he go to punish Hawke? Did Hawke really deserve it that badly?

Mary-Ann:

… transferring your feelings of guilt for what happened to Sir David.

Was he wrong? Was she right?

Was it time to let go, start again, find a new direction – as simple as that?

Suddenly Roger felt a great sense of relief. It *was* time to leave Hawke alone – to think about the future and not the past. Nothing he did now could bring back Sir David. Both he and Hawke had behaved abominably.

To make amends – do something for Mary-Ann – do something for the planet. Was that so bizarre?

And he *could* make a contribution – he had an idea.

It also had other spin-offs. The more he thought about it, the more he liked it. Not only would it do her a favour, it would also resolve the impasse that currently existed between him and his family – both father and brother. But to implement it he had to talk to Mary-Ann … and they didn't have much time … not if Dayfydd was near the end.

Having a plan, pushed for time, Roger called directory enquiries and was given the telephone number of the Kruger National Park in South Africa. When the Park exchange answered, he asked to speak to Dr Mary-Ann Webber.

"Sorry, she no longer works here," said a female voice, hollow over the long-distance line.

His eyes went wide. Mary-Ann was gone and he would never see her again. The whole world went a little darker. He was astonished by the strength of his feelings.

"What's it about. I'll put you through to the right person."

"It's a personal call … do you have a forwarding address?"

"That's easy," the telephonist responded. "She's staying with her father. I'll give you his direct line number," and read it out to him.

A little short of air, breathing hard, Roger dialled the number he had just been given. Wonderfully, heart-stoppingly, he heard the familiar voice over the line.

"Hi … it's Roger."

A very long silence ensued – and then – an unmistakable click as the handset on the other end was summarily replaced in its cradle.

Roger hit the redial button. It rang for a long time before it was answered and again he heard Mary-Ann say hullo.

"Please – just one moment. I know you're angry and you have every right to be. I want to apologise. You were right about everything. But I have an idea I need to discuss with you. It's not personal. But we don't have much time because of my Dad. It's a good idea. You'll like it. I promise."

Mary-Ann's voice came from the Antarctic. "I listened to you before. More fool me. There's no circumstance that justifies telling a lie."

"At least let me explain my idea. Before you put the telephone down I just want –"

The line went dead in his ear.

When he heard the dial tone he again hit the redial button. All he got now was an engaged signal. He tried a dozen times – each time an engaged signal.

Roger left it until late that night and tried again. This time a male voice answered. He asked to speak to Mary-Ann and was told she wasn't available. He tried again later for the same response. Frustrated and worried he finally gave up trying to talk to her on the phone.

With the pressure of time weighing on him, he dug out an atlas and turned to a map of Southern Africa. He found a small-scale section that showed the Kruger National Park. He stared at the tiny dot marked – Skukuza. So that's where she was. It didn't seem that far away. It was readily identifiable on an ordinary map. Skukuza was south of the centre of the Park from a north-south, and more towards the west from an east-west perspective.

He scratched through his Hawke notes. The co-ordinates for the coal deposits placed the point some way north of Skukuza and on the Mozambican side of the border. Looking at the map of the giant game reserve, Roger felt close to Mary-Ann. It seemed odd to think she was there, at that small black dot marked 'Skukuza'.

The next day – unable to leave it alone, worried about Dayfydd – he took his Hawke notes to the British Museum and Library. There he found a large-scale topographical map of the game reserve, showing the ground features in great detail. Having organised himself a table in the high-ceilinged reading room he again used the co-ordinates from his Hawke notes to pinpoint the coal deposits.

In a way the geo-political location of the valley made a mockery of the European colonialist-inspired arbitrary positioning of borders. And also – in its own small way – supported Mary-Ann's concept of a giant transnational game reserve. And it was another reminder of why he so desperately needed to talk to her.

He was more than ever sure she would respond positively to his idea – if he was ever given the chance of putting it to her – if she could only move beyond the way she felt about him personally. That he wasn't being given a chance made it increasingly frustrating. A letter would no doubt suffer the same fate as his telephone calls and would in any event take too long. The personal antagonism seemed an impassable barrier at a distance. If left too long to fester, nothing he said would get through to her.

By Thursday it occurred to Roger, as he again studied his atlas, if he could explain his idea personally she would want to go along with it.

And why not face to face?

An electric current of excitement surged through him –
why not, indeed – it certainly wasn't as though he had
anything else to keep him busy.

He took a taxi through to Shepherd's Travel Agency in
Regent Street, where the Dentons had a convenient
arrangement. All travel costs were added to an account
which was paid automatically via direct transfers from
Michelle's current account at the bank.

Mr Shapiro, the owner-manager, waddled out of his
office to attend to Roger personally, offering him a warm
welcome. The Dentons were amongst his very best
customers. They travelled a lot and payment was never a
problem. As soon as he heard Roger's request though he
had to apologise.

"I'm sorry. That game reserve is always booked out
ahead of time. Certainly with regard to normal
accommodation in the main camps such as Skukuza."

Roger hadn't considered the possibility that he might not
be able to get in. "Absolutely nothing? I'll stay in a tent if I
have to."

"The only accommodation available on short notice is
the kind of block bookings corporations use for seminars,
employee workshops, visiting firemen – that sort of thing.
But even that isn't directly available on short notice.
Specialist agencies pre-book that space. They then make it
available at short notice to companies and other groups. At
a rather large premium, of course."

"Can you find out if anything's available?"

"Of course. Give me a few minutes." The travel agent
turned to his telephone.

Roger nodded and wandered off to look at the brochures
on the rack. His eye was immediately drawn to the section
on Africa. He grimaced; when would he stop thinking of
her in that way?

About thirty minutes later the tubby Mr Shapiro called
him over.

"If it's just yourself there really isn't anything suitable."

"Are you saying there's nothing at all?"

"Well … no … there's a small camp that sleeps eight about a hundred kilometres north-east of Skukuza. It's called N'wanetsi … but the place has to be taken as a block booking … with a premium … and that's not cheap."

"I don't give a stuff what it costs. Book the place as soon as possible."

Mr Shapiro shrugged. "Of course, Mr Denton. And you'll be by yourself?" Eyebrows raised.

Roger nodded. "Can you confirm that now? And organise the appropriate flights?"

The stout travel agent nodded. After some time spent on the telephone and computer – with a side trip to a printer – he came back with his printout and confirmed the bookings.

"You're on British Airways flight BA 057. You spend the night in Johannesburg – the Sandton Sun Hotel. On Sunday you go through to Skukuza where they'll put you up for one or two nights in transit accommodation –"

"Why can't I have that then," Roger interrupted, "so that I can stay in Skukuza?"

"That's kept available for special circumstances. It isn't open for normal bookings. You'll then go through to N'wanetsi the next day if it's ready or the day after. You'll drive yourself there, having picked up a hired car en route," he hesitated, "is this still a single booking?"

"Absolutely," replied Roger.

He fought to hold down an excitement that had the blood coursing through his veins – in less than a week he would be seeing Mary-Ann. Whoa! He had to keep the personal side out of it – the idea was all. She would surely listen to him if he turned up on her doorstep?

*

Basil Hawke rolled into his offices on the Friday morning – late even by his standards – it was 11.43 am. His middle-aged secretary, Mary Partridge, eyes big behind large spectacles, followed him into his office, discreetly closing the door behind her. She clutched a notepad in one hand.

He got the distinct impression she had been standing there waiting for him all morning.

She shuffled her feet. "A message yesterday … it seems really important … I didn't want to leave it on your desk –"

"Give it to me." He held out a pudgy hand, palm up.

"Of course," she responded quickly, tearing off the top sheet from her notepad and handing it over to him. She just stood there.

Hawke looked at her, frowning. "Well?"

"He … sounded awfully angry … and strange. I really thought you ought to know," she finished in a rush.

Hawke waved her away. "That'll be all, Miss Partridge."

Standing there he glanced down at the message. A sudden pain in his chest. Was this what a heart attack felt like?

He returned to the message. The Colombians were starting to apply pressure – a lot of pressure. He leaned on his desk for support, stumbled around to the other side and when he finally made it to his chair, simply slumped down like a sack of old potatoes. The feeling of being suffocated, of not being able to breathe, slowly passed and he considered his options.

They were few.

Over the past few months he had talked to Dos Santos, the Mining Minister in Mozambique, a number of times – although it had become increasingly difficult to get hold of the man – and each time had been told all the necessary permits and licences were being processed.

Hawke hadn't wanted to push too hard. He needed the man too much. But now he had to make something happen. The Colombians wanted action, their threats no longer all that veiled. His own resources, having been cut off from the funds in BCCI, were overextended. The time had come to implement the next stage of his plan, even if he had to force the issue.

Hawke buzzed Ms Partridge on the intercom, asking her to get him a Maputo number.

Soon the telephone on his desk rang. When he picked it up he heard Ms Partridge say, "Your party's on the line, Mr Hawke."

"Is that Mr Dos Santos' office?"

A woman with a strong Portuguese accent answered. "Yes, *Senhor*. Who is calling, pliss?"

Hawke gave his name and a few moments later the same woman told him *Senhor* Dos Santos was not available. On pressing her for more details – on the grounds his call was one of the utmost urgency – she again put him on hold. Shortly she came back on the line. The message was unequivocal.

"*Senhor* Dos Santos is away. We do not know when he will be back."

Hawke took a large and colourful handkerchief out of his jacket pocket. He mopped his brow, wiped his face. Dos Santos was there, he was sure of it. Hawke's options were growing fewer with each second that ticked by.

He pressed the button on the intercom. "Miss Partridge, send in Karl."

He had barely finished speaking and the door to his office opened. His blond assistant, Karl Hoeniger, appeared. "*Herr* Hawke?"

"Come in. Close the door. We've got urgent work to do. You must go to Mozambique. Take the first available flight. Talk to Dos Santos personally. I want the documentation he promised us. And take Fitzsimmons, the Australian geologist, with you. We need a fresh evaluation of the coal mining site. Make contact with the Renamo people. The Maputo contact numbers are in the file. They must organise an escort to get you out there."

"Of course, *Herr* Hawke … but I thought you'd seen the original geological survey reports –"

"Of course I have, you idiot. Do you think for one moment I would've gone this far without them? And I had them authenticated. We now need a recently-dated geological report for our company prospectus in order to meet the listing requirements of the London Stock Exchange. That drunken fool Fitzsimmons needs to actually see the place. If there have been any geological changes in the last few years he can include them in his report. All we need is for some smart-ass to have recent satellite information showing our information to be dated. The whole listing would be jeopardised."

"I'm sorry, *Herr* Hawke."

"Just get hold of Shapiro and have him make the travel arrangements. Make sure Fitzsimmons keeps himself available. Report back to me when everything is in order."

Within fifty minutes Karl was again standing in front of Hawke's desk.

"It's all done, *Herr* Hawke."

Hawke glanced at his watch. He hoped Karl would be able to use the same Swiss efficiency sorting out matters in Mozambique. "Prepare Dos Santos for your arrival. Give him all the necessary information so that he has no excuses." He pressed the button on his intercom. "Miss Partridge, the same number in Maputo."

When the telephone rang Hawke handed the handset over to Karl without saying a word.

Karl took the handset and exchanged greetings with the person on the other side. "This is an urgent message for Mister Dos Santos. Please tell him Karl Hoeniger, from Mr Hawke's office in London, will be arriving in Maputo on Tuesday afternoon – that's this Tuesday coming, the fifth of November." After a pause he added, "I'll be staying at the Polana Hotel in Maputo – room 126. Could you please repeat the message?" After a further pause, he added, "Please make absolutely sure Mister Dos Santos gets the message. It's of vital importance that I meet with him as soon as possible."

Hawke stared soberly at the lanky blonde Swiss. "It's up to you now, Karl. There's nothing more I can do from this end. And don't forget about your share options. You stand to make a million ... in pounds ... when the mining company's listed."

Karl nodded. "I haven't forgotten."

*

The telephone rang in the Denton's Berkeley Square town house and Michelle answered it.

"Oh, it's you," she said. Instinctively she looked around the hallway, but Roger was out. "Go ahead."

The private investigator sounded as snide as ever. Michelle realised she actually detested the little man. She suddenly wondered why Colin had recommended him so highly. It would explain his attitude. Then she felt guilty – no one could say she was anti-gay – wasn't Colin one of her very best friends?

She could clearly hear the rustling of papers over the line. "Your husband spent most of yesterday afternoon in a Regent Street travel agency called Shepherds. Do you want me to find out what he's planning?"

Michelle snorted. It would be easier for her. She paid the bills. She cut the investigator short. "I'll do it myself."

Twenty-five minutes later a taxi deposited her on the doorstep of Shepherds. Five minutes after that she was in Lionel Shapiro's glass-enclosed office at the back of the travel agency. She told him what she wanted to know. "You don't have a problem with that, do you? You do know who pays around here?"

Shapiro told her everything she wanted to know. "Please don't tell your husband where you got the information. Can you say you got it from another source?"

"Whatever." Michelle smiled at him, and in great detail proceeded to tell him exactly what she wanted him to do. "Do you understand all that?"

Lionel Shapiro inclined his head. "Yes, ma'am. Everything will be exactly as you've requested. You and your father are highly valued clients. Please be assured that we'll always do everything we can to give you the very best of service."

"Good," Michelle smiled. "I'm glad we understand each other so well."

That evening she made no mention to Roger that she too had spent time at Shepherd's Travel Agency. Nor over the following few days did she say anything about it. But on the following Thursday – the day before his British Airways flight was scheduled to leave from Heathrow – she casually told him she knew where he was going, and that she was accompanying him on the trip. "As a dutiful wife should, of course," she murmured.

Roger shook his head firmly. "I don't think so."

Michelle smiled at him quite gently. "But *I* think so and that's much more important. And if you don't believe me – ask our little travel agent."

Roger stormed over to the telephone in the hallway, flipped open the address-finder and dialled the travel agent's number. After a few minutes he had Shapiro himself on the line. Roger glanced across at where Michelle placidly stood with one foot elegantly placed slightly behind the other.

She smiled at him. "Our tickets are linked, darling. Ask the man. He'll explain."

Her posture told him he was on a treadmill going nowhere. But he had to make sure.

"Will you unlink those bookings?"

"I can't do that. I'm sorry, Mr Denton … but your wife … um … her bank … she pays the account. I have to do what she says."

"I take it you won't release my bookings to another travel agent?"

"No sir. My instructions are clear."

Roger put down the telephone and turned to face Michelle. "What do you want?"

"To go along on this African jaunt."

Roger studied her face for a while. She calmly accepted the scrutiny.

"I can go to another travel agent," he said at last. "It'll all just happen at a later date."

"Of course," Michelle nodded, "but you'll have to find the money somewhere. This sort of thing is really quite expensive."

Roger took a deep breath and let it out all at once. "All right, you win. Phone and tell him you'll be going along."

"Oh, that won't be necessary. It's all arranged. The same bookings, the same flights, in fact we're booked to sit alongside each other on the plane. But that's right, isn't it? I mean we are married, aren't we?"

And Roger knew their marriage was over. And they had to discuss it. But only later – first he had to make sure he got to Africa.

.

PART FOUR
14 - 22 November 1987

.

On Thursday, 14 November, at midday, Karl Hoeniger, from his room at the Polana Hotel in Maputo, Mozambique, finally made telephonic contact with Basil Hawke at his London offices.

Karl's voice had an echoing quality over the line. "I've being trying to get hold of Dos Santos since I got here Tuesday. He's deliberately avoiding me."

Hawke stared off into the middle distance for a while. Strident alarm bells rang in his head. He was liking this less and less all the time.

"*Herr* Hawke, are you still there?"

"This is what you must do. Make contact with our other friends. You have to get Fitzsimmons out to the mine site so he can start work. Tell them about our problems with Dos Santos. They brought him in. I'll try to put pressure on him from here, but I'm not hopeful. It's really up to you and our other friends."

"Very well, *Herr* Hawke. I've already made initial contact with the other people. And I'll try again to see Dos Santos when I get back to Maputo."

"And make sure those people give Fitzsimmons as much time as he needs to do his work. Don't let them rush him."

"It will be as you say, *Herr* Hawke."

After Karl had rung off Hawke used his private line to dial the Zurich number he had originally given Dos Santos. It was Hawke's custom to keep careful track of amounts drawn down by other people, as a kind of insurance. That's why he always used two passwords, a form of back door. His clients invariably changed the one they were given, trying to cut him out of the loop.

When he heard the *Schwyzerdütsch* he simply gave the other code word associated with the Dos Santos account — and the account number he had given Dos Santos. Within seconds he was advised the balance was still USD250,000. That worried him. If it had been drawn against, he would have owned the man. What was Dos Santos up to?

Hawke hoisted himself to his feet, waddled over to a safe concealed behind a picture on the office wall. He took a bunch of keys out of his trouser pocket and unlocked it. He swung open the steel door, extracted a plastic pouch, of the kind travel agents give to their clients in which to keep their travel documents. Lifting the flap on the pouch he slid out one of the passports inside it and weighed the small green book in his hand.

It was good to know it was still there, reassuring.

Did Dos Santos have a hidden agenda? Hawke decided to freshen up his other arrangements – it was the least a prudent soul could do, like an atheist repenting on his deathbed, just in case.

                              *

Roger made his way upstairs. He sourly watched from the dressing room doorway as Michelle packed another suitcase.

"Why so much? We're going to a game reserve, for Christ's sake."

"You never know who you're going to meet," she replied, smiling.

The telephone rang.

"I'll take that," she said brightly, stepping across the dressing-room to an extension telephone. Almost immediately she held it out to him. "It's your stepmother."

The news wasn't good.

We've just had the specialist in," she said. "Your father's taken a turn for the worse and the ambulance has just left. Doctor Margolis isn't sure how much longer he'll live. The chemo isn't working nor the radiotherapy. They're going to try another blood transfusion. The doctor's not sure it'll work. And if it doesn't … then … then … the end is very near. I'm sorry, Roger. I know how much you loved your father – and he you. I'm truly sorry. I'll keep you informed."

"We have to go overseas tonight. I'll give you the itinerary – in case you need to make contact."

After he replaced the handset, Michelle looked at him with wide-eyed innocence.

"Perhaps we should postpone this trip,"

Roger shook his head morosely. "Nope."

"You selfish bastard," Michelle yelled at him, ran into the bathroom, slammed the door.

Roger scrubbed a hand across his face. It was now even more urgent he should get to Africa quickly. If Mary-Ann was positive about his idea, he would be able to give the old man the greatest gift it was in Roger's power to give.

*

The knock on the hotel room door was loud. Fitzsimmons gave a start.

Karl quickly opened the door. "Yes?"

A swarthy man in a sober business suit nodded. "*Senhor* Karl? It is as arranged. I am from Joshua."

Karl swung the door wide to let the man into the room and then quickly closed it behind him. As he re-entered the room Karl scowled at the Australian. The nervousness was contagious. Before he could say anything Fitzsimmons cut in.

"I'm going down for a drink, mate. I don't like this cloak-and-dagger shit."

Karl turned to the newcomer, shrugged. "Our highly-esteemed geologist, Carter Fitzsimmons. I don't know your name. I can't introduce you."

The swarthy man waved a hand at him, shrugged. "You may call me Luis."

Fitzsimmons laughed croakily at that. "Nobody gives a toss, mate. I surely don't want to know it, now do I? If anyone wants me, I'll be in the bar." He slammed out of the hotel room.

Karl waved a hand at the door. "I'm sorry. Fitzsimmons can be very –"

"Please, *Senhor*. We have very little time. You have a message for Joshua."

"Fitzsimmons and me, we must get to the coal-mining site as soon as possible. Will you arrange that?"

"Not me personally, *Senhor*. But you'll have an answer within three hours." He looked at his watch. "I should be back by two. Sooner if possible. Please do not leave the hotel."

Karl nodded. What he had so far seen of Maputo so offended his Swiss sense of orderliness and cleanliness he had absolutely no desire to leave the hotel, which was itself hardly to be recommended.

"I'll be here."

After Luis had left Karl lay down on one of the two beds. He didn't feel hungry. Perhaps later he would be hungry enough to eat in such a dirty place. For now he would just wait. He fell asleep.

It seemed as though, in an instant, he was woken by a loud knocking. When he opened the door Luis quickly squeezed past him without waiting for an invitation. Karl checked his watch. He was pleasantly surprised to discover Luis had returned thirty minutes before his self-imposed deadline. He hadn't anticipated punctuality, not from these third-world brown types.

"The arrangements are as follows. Someone else will fetch the two of you at ten tonight. Please be ready. Do not pack too much clothing. You'll have to carry it yourself. But make sure you have some warm things, the bush can be cold at night."

"Will we be going directly to the site?" Karl asked. "If you're not going, who's travelling with us?"

"You and *Senhor* Fitzsimmons rendezvous with Joshua tonight. Abel will have some of his men there before dawn. It's his job to see you safely to your destination." He paused, shrugged. "I saw *Senhor* Fitzsimmons in the bar. Please see that he is fit to travel. Any questions?"

Karl shook his head.

"No? Good! Then I leave you. I doubt we meet again. I hope you have good trip."

Karl saw Luis out. He gave the Mozambican a few minutes to get clear before he went in search of Fitzsimmons.

*

Dos Santos switched off the tape recorder.

After Hoeniger and Fitzsimmons had been seen leaving the hotel in the company of an unidentified local, his people had exchanged the tapes from both the telephone and room recorders in the foreigners' Hotel Polana room.

The important question was – what did he do now?

He paced up and down his living room. Dos Santos was convinced the ceasefire currently being negotiated between Renamo and Frelimo would hold once the details were settled. He was having to seriously reconsider his personal strategies for the future. There could be no more sitting on the fence. The time had come to make decisions.

If there were free and fair elections, he was confident he would be re-elected. Then, compared to how much he could make as an elected politician, USD250,000 was the equivalent of dust on the bottom of his shoes. He would be re-elected because he had always kept his public nose clean. No one could associate him with the excesses perpetrated in one form or another on the people of Mozambique since they had been granted independence from Portugal.

Except … except for one particular area – there he was exposed – no, not just exposed. It was the time for big decisions. So it was the time to be honest with himself. He was horribly vulnerable in that he had been playing financially-profitable games with Abel Gamellah, the Butcher of Beira. If that collaboration became known, he was dead – literally. No sane man could allow that sort of information to become public knowledge.

So a new strategy had to be adopted. All links with the Butcher had to be severed immediately. But that wasn't enough. The Butcher was not one to let the pressure he could put on a Minister go to waste. In other words, Dos Santos would still be no better than the maniac's puppet.

So now the answer to the problem was even simpler – Gamellah had to die. And Dos Santos knew, from the tape recordings made in Hoeniger's hotel room, something of the Butcher's movements over the next few days.

Surely that information should be enough to get rid of his albatross?

Dos Santos made a telephone call and settled down to wait. The person he had invited over would not take long to arrive. He had also managed to find himself a house in the most exclusive area of Maputo, so they were virtually neighbours. Being a Saturday had made it even easier, the man was at home.

The fearsome Manuel de Oliviera da Silva, the Minister of Defence, or MoD, half Shangaan and half Portuguese, and frighteningly unpredictable, was there within ten minutes. He had wasted no time.

"If there's a chance of us getting the Butcher we must go for it. So I've called on our most reliable field commanding officer. Who has his own reasons for hating the Butcher."

"What are they?" Dos Santos asked.

A motor car pull up outside and the engine shut off. The MoD strode to the window, tweaked the curtains to one side. "It's the Colonel."

Quickly, and in a low voice, the MoD answered the question. The details of what the Butcher had done horrified even Dos Santos. The Colonel was definitely the right man for the job.

Dos Santos started the meeting by telling the two military men he didn't know where the Renamo group's starting point would be, except that it was probably within three or four hours travel of Maputo. What he did know was *when* they were leaving and their *destination*.

Colonel Adalberto Domingo was excited. The MoD was immediately suspicious.

"From where," he demanded, "does this information originate?"

Dos Santos was not without clout himself. He was second in authority in the Political Bureau of the Central Committee of Frelimo, which was a hard-line authoritarian/socialist party at the time. He was just behind only the new President, Joaquim Chissano, who had recently taken over the reins after the previous incumbent, Samora Machel, who had, a month before, died in a mysteriously unexplained aeroplane accident. For a moment dos Santos wondered to what extent Chissano had manufactured *his* 'luck' then brushed the thought away. It was irrelevant.

Chissano was out of the country at this time cementing relationships with a neighbouring African country. So Dos Santos was the senior man in the country on the Central Committee, if only temporarily.

So Dos Santos drew himself up. "I'm not at liberty to reveal my sources," he said blandly. "But the information was so vitally important I thought we should act on it immediately. Don't you agree, Comrade Minister? Or do you think we shouldn't make too much fuss about trying to get rid of the Butcher forever?"

The MoD was caught off guard. "Of course, Comrade Minister. Of course. We must make every attempt to get him."

"Good. Then we can continue making the appropriate plans."

"How sure are we of this information?" asked the MoD, still fishing, albeit now in restricted waters.

"Comrade, please believe me when I say this information is of the very best." Now Dos Santos smiled at the MoD. "We cannot take a chance of the Butcher escaping once again. May I suggest to your colleague that he doesn't bother taking any prisoners?"

"Of course, Comrade Minister, my thoughts exactly." He turned to the Colonel. "I think your objective and orders are clear. Get on with it."

The Colonel snapped to attention. "Yes sir. Knowing his destination means we can trap the Butcher against the border fence. We'll annihilate him once and for all."

*

On the Saturday night, spent in Johannesburg, South Africa, it was as though Roger and Michelle had formally declared a truce. They dined at *Ma Cuisine*, a fashionably cosy restaurant in the suburb of Parktown North. The food was too nouvelle for him, but Michelle enjoyed it. They both carefully avoided the most obvious topic – why specifically he had wanted to come to Africa.

The evening drifted by with both of them being restrained, polite and civilised. Their taxi stopped outside their hotel, the Sandton Sun. They climbed out into the warm African night air.

Michelle turned to Roger. "Why don't we compromise. I understand why you feel you can't keep the title. Let it go to Patrick. You tried to prove yourself. It wasn't your fault it didn't work out. You are what you are."

Roger didn't reply, couldn't, he just listened. Compromise? Michelle was beginning to sound desperate. She didn't want someone strong. Her soggy self-image couldn't take the strain of having someone around who was really independent. Clearly he, at some stage, had to tell her the marriage was over. But it also seemed to him that she understood that and was trying for a rearguard action. However the time had not yet come to bring it all out into the open. Now he just shrugged.

Roger asked at reception for their room keys and was also handed a message by the pleasantly smiling desk clerk. He opened it.

"What is it? Are you okay?" Michelle asked.

Wordlessly he handed over the note and she read it aloud, "Father passed away in his sleep last night. Urgent you contact me immediately. Patrick."

"I *am* sorry, Roger."

She clearly meant it. He nodded but didn't say anything.

Michelle slipped her arm through his. "You've all expected this for such a long time and it was in his sleep. It means he went peacefully."

Roger shrugged, not trusting himself to speak. Of course she was right. In a way it was a relief. The old man would no longer have to suffer such terrible agony. In another way Roger was bitterly disappointed. He wasn't going to get the chance to show Dayfydd that the main family title – the Earldom, and everything that went with it – would be in good hands.

And there was another problem. Now he really had very little time. His breathing space would last as long as he was incommunicado, but that wouldn't be forever. He wouldn't respond to Patrick's message just yet. First he had to talk to Mary-Ann. He had to get her to listen, to understand that his idea had nothing to do with his personal feelings and she should also not allow her personal feelings to get in the way either.

But he had to discuss this with Mary-Ann face to face. She was the only one who was guaranteed to make it work. Would she listen though?

*

Yuri Petrov was a minor trade official with the Soviet's Mozambican trade mission in Maputo. Like most of his ilk around the world he knew, by that Sunday, 17 November, there wasn't as much urgency as there used to be in carrying out his secondary function of gathering information.

One result of President Mikhail Gorbachov taking over the reins in the Soviet Union from Leonid Brezhnev, and Gorbachov's policies of glasnost and perestroika, was his rapprochement with President Ronald Reagan of the United

States. That in turn led to the start of co-operation between the Soviet and United States intelligence agencies. The unthinkable had happened and the end of the Cold War was in sight.

So Petrov was in no hurry to meet with his most important Mozambican informant, a junior clerical officer attached to the Frelimo military headquarters in Maputo. He took his time ambling along the sun-drenched, palm-lined promenade which parallels the sea front just outside Maputo.

They finally met at 10.33 am local time. There was little to disturb Petrov's equanimity. All he received was a vaguely interesting morsel about a government army contingent which had the previous day headed off in a westerly direction on an otherwise secret mission. Later that morning would be perfectly adequate in passing it on to the real Committee for State Security – or KGB – officer.

The KGB man however, despite everything, was still proud of his punctuality. The information concerning a secret military mission went out on the air, from the offices of the Soviet trade mission in Maputo, at exactly midday, local time.

*

The lion had been living in the cave for over a month now. Most of the time he just lay in the cave mouth on his side, ribs heaving as he panted. He was barely surviving on lizards and the occasional small dassie. His hollow flanks were covered in dust. He was thin and gaunt with hip bones tenting out what looked like a badly-tanned, moth-eaten skin which had lain on a floor somewhere in front of a fireplace for far too long.

What the immature klipspringer, a very small antelope – even when fully grown only topping out at around eighteen kilograms in weight – was doing was anybody's guess. Perhaps he had been frightened by a prowling hyaena or he may simply have been too young to be keenly aware of danger. The result was fatal. The klipspringer scrambled into the cave mouth, bounced on the tips of its hooves – which have the consistency of a sturdy tractor tyre – and blundered straight into the lion.

Generally lions do not need to drink water. They can get their fluid requirements from their prey. Which is why they can survive in deserts. But if water is available they will drink, especially after eating. The young ten kilogram klipspringer teased the lion's appetite not just for water but also for more food. It also gave him enough energy to drag himself to where he could get both.

The lion hesitated in the cave mouth, tested the air. Slowly he shambled out into the blistering afternoon sunshine and limped downhill towards water and the man-smell near the river crossing. The man-smell represented food which couldn't move as fast as an impala, which couldn't hear like a kudu and which couldn't fight back like a buffalo.

*

As a result of the one hour time difference between Maputo and Moscow it was at 1.06 pm local time on Sunday, 17 November, that the information about the Mozambican military mission reached KGB headquarters, located in a large building at 2 Dzerzhinsky Square, at the top end of Karl Marx Prospekt in Moscow.

Troop movements – even if in relatively unimportant parts of the world – were always accorded a higher priority than, say, agricultural, industrial or general scientific information, which could be analysed at leisure before being slotted into the bigger picture for the decision-makers to consider.

So at 1.36 pm local time the cipher clerk personally placed the message on the desk of Vassili Vishnayev. This very junior information analyst was doing weekend duty in his position as an employee of the 2nd Directorate, the KGB arm which dealt with foreign intelligence.

Vishnayev, not terribly excited about the information, wandered off two hours later in search of a superior to whom he could pass the responsibility of deciding what to do with it. Being Sunday, and without a full staff complement present, he eventually decided to take it straight to his commanding officer.

Colonel Dmitri Kukushkin, a campaigner grown old and wise in the service, understood full well all the implications of the recent public utterances of the politburo members. At the same time it went against a grain – sandpapered in by twenty-three years of active hostility towards the Americans – to make them privy to information of any real substance. So the information handed to him by Vishnayev was perfect. It was unimportant enough to leave him feeling easy about having passed it on. At the same time it made it possible for him to show his superiors he was as enthusiastic about the new policies as they were.

He initialled the corner, looked up at Vishnayev. "Have this sent to the Americans at Langley."

Vishnayev, happy to get out of the Colonel's office in the same condition as he had gone in, wandered off in the general direction of the Communications Directorate.

The information went out on the air from Moscow, Russia, at 6.24 pm local time.

*

Lieutenant Marcos Barrios da Gama hesitated, decided to speak, "Surely with scouts sweeping in front of our advance party we'll make slow progress? Can't we use aircraft to locate him?"

The hard-bitten Colonel Domingo, a professional soldier all his life, liked the youngster, who reminded him of himself at that age. He was not like the low-life types that made up the bulk of the Frelimo – and therefore the Government – army.

Everyone had grown tired of the war. With the collapse of communism world-wide came the realisation socialism had destroyed the Mozambican economy. Civil war hadn't helped but could probably have been averted if there had been a multi-party democracy in the first place. The people realised this and young men were simply not doing their military service.

The situation was chaotic.

The government used press gangs to round up conscripts. Without them the bulk of the military would have melted away. Just a hard core of professional soldiers, like himself and the Lieutenant and , indeed – thank God! – most of his own men, would have been left.

"It's a good thought," Colonel Domingo replied at length, "but not against the Butcher. As soon as he knows we're looking for him he'll give us the slip. This is the first time we've known his destination as opposed to being told where he was last seen. That's going to make all the difference."

Ten minutes later they heard running footsteps. The sweating scout stopped panting before the Colonel, executed a sketchy salute.

"We've found sign. About thirty men. Maybe one or two civilians."

Colonel Domingo grinned at the Lieutenant. "So our information is good." He turned to the scout. "Take us to this spoor."

The two officers followed the scout through the scrub to where another three scouts stood waiting. Wordlessly the man they were following pointed out the tracks.

"You said some might be civilians?"

The scout pointed out a series of footprints. "These are the tracks of ordinary shoes. Sometimes Renamo wears civilian shoes, but not often."

"Could they be prisoners?"

The scout walked quickly along the spoor which he read as easily as the Colonel would read a book. "I don't think so. You can see that here and here they were moving around without boots following, like someone guarding them. They go willingly."

"But they could be Renamo in ordinary shoes?"

The scout shook his head. "These two sets of tracks walk lighter. The rest of the group are carrying loads."

"How long ago did they go through?"

The scout broke off a thin stick from nearby bush and pointed. "See the dew on the spoor and the wind this morning has rounded the edges – they came through early. But here they walked over the spoor of a porcupine which would have been out last night." He shrugged. "It was between two and four this morning."

The Colonel waved for the Lieutenant to follow. "Let's go back to our maps."

The Colonel pored over the map of the area for a while. The Lieutenant shifted his weight repeatedly from one foot to the other, eager to get going. After a while the Colonel drew a curving line from the place where the tracks were found to the co-ordinates he had been given as the Butcher's destination.

"This is the route I think they'll follow."

The Lieutenant frowned. "And now we follow them?"

The Colonel shook his head. "The Butcher always keeps just as good a lookout backwards as he does forwards. He has to take a devious route. We can go straight. We have time to get ahead and prepare a reception committee. Look here at the map – at this area here." He pointed with one finger, indicating the co-ordinates of the mine site.

"See how the contour lines run in parallel lines. The Butcher's destination is in a valley. See how close together the lines are. The sides are steep. We let him get deep into that valley. He won't escape easily to the sides, north or south. To leave at any speed they'll have to go either east or west.

"We'll go ahead and wait, to the north-east of them. We'll let them get past us and a bit deeper into the valley. Then we come down and in behind them. We'll trap them against the electrified border fence with South Africa. It lies to the west of where we'll first make contact," he paused.

The Colonel stared at the western horizon with unseeing eyes. "And then, Abel, it will be my turn. At long last it will be my turn."

*

The information about the Mozambican troop movements, which had originated from Maputo, Mozambique, and had so far travelled via Moscow, Russia, finally arrived at the information receipt and dispersal centre of the CIA headquarters in Langley, West Virginia. There was an eight hour difference in time zones. It was 10.24 am local time, on Sunday, 17 November.

Not being of much significance, Walt Kendrick only got around to thinking about it an hour later. After reading it twice and reflecting on the strangeness of a world that, seemingly overnight, had the Soviet KGB openly feeding the CIA with information, albeit most of it with no real substance, he decided to talk to someone with current experience of the African situation.

Then it would be quick to get rid of one way or the other. He had a pile of paper growing on his desk like a monster cabbage in a horror movie. He walked quickly through the outer room, the rubber sole on his left shoe squeaking slightly. He entered Larry Jackson's glass-enclosed office without knocking. Jackson was the Regional Deputy-Controller of Operations.

"Jesus H!" Jackson leaned back in his swivel chair. "Walt, you gotta do something about that shoe."

"Oh yeah, then how the hell would anyone know I was coming?"

Jackson's eyebrows climbed towards his hairline. "Who the hell wants to know anyhow?"

Kendrick leaned across the desk, beckoned Jackson closer. "That new blonde in the typing pool for one," he whispered.

Jackson slammed back in his chair but the abrupt movement didn't quite hide the speculative look which appeared in his eyes.

"Bullshit!" he growled. "And I still think that's exactly how you've built your reputation."

Kendrick held one finger alongside his nose and pushed it lightly to one side. "My lips are sealed."

"Bullshit! You're doing it again! Now what is it you wanted? I'm a busy man, unlike some."

Kendrick grinned and passed across the message which had reached his desk an hour-and-ten-minutes earlier.

Jackson took it and quickly scanned the information. "How good is the stuff we're getting from these guys?"

Kendrick shrugged. "Who knows? Most of it's pretty low priority, like this. But I understood from the briefing last Monday that we'd opened up a little to the South Africans in line with the changes they're making internally and I thought this might be of interest to them."

"I guess it would be. Although they're on better terms with the Mozambicans these days. There probably isn't much in it." He rubbed a hand over his chin. "What are the chances of the Russkis zapping us on this one? It could work out real embarrassing."

Kendrick shook his head. "Disinformation? At this level? I don't think so. They've got nuthin' to gain, everything to lose. I reckon it's on the up and up."

"In that case we can send it across. Just copy me when you do 'cause I might be needing a little scratch on my back from the South Africans soon."

It was at 12.15 pm local time that the information went out on the air from Langley.

*

Roger and Michelle flew into Skukuza on the feeder airline and were met by a Kruger Park minibus. An hour later and they had checked in. The N'wanetsi camp would not be ready for them until the Tuesday morning. They were shown to the bungalow they were to use for not one, but the following two nights. Roger was glad. Mary-Ann was here in Skukuza. He might need all of that time convincing her to think about his idea.

While Michelle unpacked their suitcases, Roger used checking on their timetable and finding their hire car as an excuse to get out on his own. He wanted to locate Mary-Ann.

*

The National Intelligence Service, or NIS, headquarters in Pretoria, South Africa, received the information about the Mozambican troop movements at 7.15 pm local time. Despite it being Sunday, Dr Lukas Daniel 'Niel' Barnard – the 44 year-old, urbane head of the NIS – was, within three-and-a-half minutes, advised of the information by telephone.

The NIS fell directly under South Africa's State President, PW Botha. Dr Barnard, despite a relatively lacklustre academic background, had been appointed head of the NIS from the obscurity of one of the smaller Universities in the country. He was only thirty at the time. The service was in a mess. The State President who appointed him to the position must have known something few others did. In a short time Dr Barnard turned the service around. Now it was efficient. People were proud to be associated with it and he personally commanded a fierce loyalty from his staff.

Dr Barnard quickly apologised to his house guests, who understood he could not make mention of why he was leaving in such a hurry. Within minutes of the call he headed out of the door on his way to the State President's house. Half way there he was advised by car telephone that the State President had already left his house accompanied by his wife and their attendant security men. They were on their way to the evening service at the Dutch Reformed Church in Wonderboom, a suburb of Pretoria.

Again the car telephone did duty. It was soon arranged. While his wife attended the church service State President Botha would wait outside the church for Dr Barnard.

*

The pickup truck bounced, swerved and slid down the rutted rarely used track that led to the ford in the river. In the passenger seat Brian pulled a large white handkerchief out of his pocket and mopped at his face.

"Do you think you'll get permission?"

Jakes grey beard jutted aggressively. "The strain could've been here all the time."

"And that means you haven't asked for permission, right?"

The question hung in the air between them. They were both silent for a while.

Jakes jabbed the air with a gnarled forefinger. "To establish one male lion in the valley in the hope that he'll start a pride is not flying in the face of nature. The white lions in the Timbavati evolved quite naturally – they weren't specifically bred. Differing strains are a natural phenomena."

"Whoa there, Jakes, while white lion are quite common, and some also occur naturally here in Kruger, black lions are extremely rare. I just think you should try and get management to go along with this."

Jakes shrugged. He hadn't wanted anyone else to know. He would have preferred not enlisting Brian's aid. This was always meant to be between him, his guys, and the bush. But he was concerned his contract would eventually expire and he wouldn't be around to see his project through.

"Do *you* think they'd give me permission? I'll be gone one of these days. He must have time to form his own pride. Just keep an eye on him. For me."

"I can do that." Brian sighed. "But the whole thing smells like trouble – big trouble."

*

The South African State President, PW Botha, called the emergency mini-cabinet meeting to order. Only two others were present. After thanking them for coming along so quickly, he apologised for disturbing them on a Sunday. He briefly brought them up to date with what he had been told by Dr Barnard, the head of the NIS, forty minutes earlier.

He raised his eyebrows at the Deputy-Foreign Minister, Barend Louw, the Minister of Foreign Affairs, Pik Botha, was still overseas. "What's the likelihood this has anything to do with us?"

Louw shook his head decisively. "None. Relations between us are the best they've been since the Portuguese pulled out although they don't feel they can come out publicly and say so. We've also recently agreed to co-operate with Portugal and Mozambique in resurrecting the Cahora Bassa hydro-electric project. Economically the Mozambicans can't afford to have trouble with us. They need our money and technical expertise. They need us to buy their electricity. My opinion? There's nothing in it."

The State President nodded. "Have your people liaise directly with the Mozambicans. Ask them politely for an explanation. They know they're supposed to advise us of any military activity close to our borders."

He turned to Magnus Malan, the Minister of Defence. "We must move additional men and machines into Kruger, but keep it a small group. We only have a handful of military personnel stationed there to help the police with refugees trying to get through. We've also got a by-election coming up. The conservatives have accused us of being soft on security. Use this to show a little muscle –"

The Deputy-Foreign Minister interrupted. "When they interview you on TV remember to give a growl or two."

The other two men laughed. They all stood up, started to pack their briefcases.

*

Roger looked at the small map of the camp. Skukuza really wasn't a big place. Excluding the tourist accommodation there was only a small shopping and administrative area. Off to one side lay the staff accommodation area, to which public access was restricted.

He was desperate. His father's death made it imperative he do something immediately. He hurried off in the direction of the shopping area. As he approached it he saw Mary-Ann emerge from the small shop.

Roger called out her name. She stopped, turned around, frowned. Suddenly her eyes flew wide open. For a moment she looked like a startled buck about to be taken by a lion.

Roger walked up to her. "I guess you're surprised to see me."

"What do you want?"

"I accept I was wrong. Please just give me a chance to explain."

Roger was instantly annoyed with himself. That wasn't what he had intended saying. He wanted to keep it impersonal.

"You're wasting your time. You lied to me. That's totally unforgivable. Are you completely devoid of all decency?"

"I understand you won't listen to any personal stuff. Please try to put that aside. There's something else I need to discuss with you. It's important."

Mary-Ann shook her head in frustration, stamped her foot in the dirt, a small puff of dust drifted away low in the sultry evening air. "Get it through your thick head. I don't want to talk to you about anything. I want you out of my life."

"But these are two separate issues –"

"I don't care." She turned away from him.

Roger put out his hand, held her arm.

She pulled her arm free, rocked back onto her heels, sunk into the cat stance, poised, balanced. "I wouldn't do that if I was you."

He quickly let go, held his hands up, watched helplessly as she marched off with her head held high, arms swinging. He just stood there until she was long gone. There had to be some way of getting through to her.

"I wondered where you'd got to," Michelle said behind him. "You just disappeared."

Roger spun around on his heel. He had completely forgotten about his wife.

She stared at him. "You look as though you've seen a ghost."

Roger shrugged, shook his head wordlessly.

She pulled a face. "Why don't we take a drive, in the vicinity of the camp?"

"What?" Roger felt really stupid, it was as though she was using a foreign language.

She waved a brochure at him. "We've an hour before the camp gates are closed for the night. Let's go for a drive. That is why we're here, isn't it? To see the wild animals."

"Sure, whatever."

She stared at him for a while. "Apparently the Selati restaurant here is very good. I was reading all about it in this brochure. Could we eat there tonight?"

"Sure."

Michelle's eyes were round and bright and not a little desperate.

"The restaurant is made up of railway carriages. Listen to this," she read from the brochure, "The bodies of two Prime Ministers were transported by rail to their final resting places in the funeral carriage which had originally been a dining saloon, built in Belgium. The restaurant comprises two carriages: the former funeral carriage which today serves as a cocktail bar; and the Lundi a double-diner which was built in Durban in 1924."

Michelle looked up from the brochure.

"Isn't that interesting?" she asked, her eyes very bright now, squinting a little.

"Sure," Roger said, a blank expression on his face.

*

The mini-cabinet meeting ended at 8.13 pm on Sunday, 17 November.

By 9.37 pm the Chief of the South African Defence Force, General Johannes 'Jannie' Geldenhuys, entered the Union Buildings, seat of the government's administrative arm. He wasn't in uniform. He had just come in from a late afternoon round of golf.

He entered the offices of the Minister of Defence, Magnus Malan, an old warhorse who had himself once been the head of the Defence Force. With large ears giving him a slightly, and deceptive, comic look he was a man who smiled easily but always gave the impression that the smile could disappear as fast as it had arrived. The Minister stood up to greet the General, shook his hand. Without delay he related what had been decided at the mini-cabinet meeting.

"Thoughts?"

The General shrugged. "Solitary Alo's can drop off recces at regular intervals along the fence. It's not a complicated mission. We can have troops on standby in case they spot anything."

"There's a lot of tourists in the Park. Your people must keep a low profile."

"No problem," the General replied.

"I have maps of our border with Mozambique. Over here."

The Minister of Defence grinned happily: he loved this stuff. As usual a sense of power and authority coursed through him. The defence portfolio could have been purpose designed for him.

After studying the map for a while and discussing various options the Minister raised an eyebrow. "Any particular units? Besides the recces, that is."

Jannie Geldenhuys didn't hesitate. "The Buffalo Battalion."

"Reasons?" queried Malan.

"They're Angolan professionals who joined us during the Namibian campaigns, the officers are mostly South African.

They're very experienced in bush war and won't have local family connections. That could be important."

"How long to put all this together?"

The General shrugged. "We could be in there tonight, but that would cause a stir. It isn't urgent. Our people can drift in tomorrow. We'll be organised by tomorrow night."

The Defence Minister stood up. "Very well. Let's do it that way. And please keep me informed."

*

Jakes, Mary-Ann and Brian had eaten dinner together at Jakes' cottage. It was almost 11 pm on the Sunday night when Jakes decided to turn in. Afterwards Brian suggested Mary-Ann have a last cup of coffee with him outside on the stoep. He obviously had something on his mind.

Sitting out there, for a while, they were both silent.

A jackal howled somewhere in the dark and was answered by another yowl from a different direction. Far away a spotted hyaena gave the concept of a witch's cackle new meaning. Spread through the bush around Skukuza came the soft barking of impala, like distant dogs. Suddenly a booming roar echoed out of the night, followed immediately by a number of others.

Mary-Ann grinned. "That'll get the tourists going. They'll all think they heard lion tonight."

"Yeah. I've been fooled by ostriches before."

A short pause.

"Did you know Jakes is trying to breed black lion in that valley of his?"

Mary-Ann sat up straight. "I didn't know. You'd better tell me about it."

Brian told her what Jakes had told him earlier that day. "I don't think it's right," he concluded. "We're supposed to keep our interference to a minimum."

She shrugged awkwardly. "It's not as though he's poaching or something. There've been a few of those. What about that ranger who smuggled ivory?"

"That doesn't excuse what he's doing," Brian said softly.

Mary-Ann nodded, was quiet for a while, then spoke defiantly, "Look at the situation technically. He's moved one healthy young lion into a specific area hoping it'll form a pride and reproduce its very unusual genes. That shouldn't cause a major disruption. I wouldn't worry about it too much."

"I hear you. But I really believe in allowing the game to sort itself out. I've always admired the old man so much. I became a game ranger, not because of my own father, but because of your father." He suddenly broke off, then added, "You've never minded sharing Jakes with me, have you?"

Mary-Ann swooped on the change of subject. "Of course not, you idiot. It's a privilege to have such a nice brother. And what about your studies? Surely you want to work on a more technical level. You have to. The whole business is becoming more competitive every day."

"I haven't been able to raise the finance. Now this black lion business had got me so worried I'm incapable of thinking about anything else."

Again there was a long silence, punctuated only by the sounds of the African bush.

"What do you think's wrong with the old man? Do you think he's cracking?"

Mary-Ann looked sharply at Brian, but realised he was being neither insulting nor funny. He meant it when he said he regarded Jakes as a father. He was seriously concerned about the old man, just as a son would be.

"That's not a fair question. He's been lonely since my mom died. That's why he came to Africa. You know that. His research became a kind of surrogate wife. He's always related more to the wild than to people, not in a scientific way, but practically, as though he was part of it and it was part of him. After Mom died he just took it further. Now he feels rejected by the Trust and he's lonely and upset. I think he'll get over it and we'll all come through this with flying colours."

"But what about the black lion?"

"There's not much he's actually asked you to do, is there?"

"Just monitor its progress."

"Treat it as an interesting phenomenon you've just come across. The whole thing is in the lap of the gods anyway."

*

A jangling telephone pierced the darkness.

From under the bedcovers, a slender white arm stretched out towards the bedside table, found the corner, slowly crept in the direction of the pink telephone. It hadn't yet reached the half-way mark when a well-muscled, tanned and hairy arm also appeared. The hand on this arm fastened itself on the wrist of the first arm and firmly drew it away from the bedside table.

"Really, Paul! It might be my husband!"

The bedcovers slid to one side revealing one shoulder and beyond that a full, but well-shaped and very naked breast.

"Shush, wait a moment!"

After six rings the telephone fell silent. Then it started again. The telephone cut off by itself after the third ring. A thin frown marred the smooth alabaster of the attractive woman's forehead. She opened her mouth to speak and abruptly shut it when the telephone again started to ring. It was the third time. This time she didn't move. It rang six times and fell silent. She turned to stare wordlessly at the broad-shouldered young man who was now also sitting up in bed.

"I hate to say this," Paul Hammond said, "but I've got to go."

She sat up even straighter as he sprang lightly out of the bed and walked around to the other side, leaned over and kissed her on the nose.

"Don't look so sad – I must."

She cocked her head to one side as she looked up at him. "As handsome and desirable as I might think you are, right now I'm not sad because you're leaving. Who did you give the number to?"

"My flight engineer, but don't worry – to him it's just a number."

She nodded her head slowly, ran her tongue over her lips, sighed softly. "And just to think, here I've been waiting for you for ages while the beasts had you in the desert somewhere." Again her tongue flicked out over her lips. Suddenly her hand went out and grabbed him as he was about to put on his trousers.

"Hmmm – you're beautiful and big."

The bedcovers slid down to her waist as she leaned forward to take him in her mouth.

Six – three – six, not their most urgent signal, not the least urgent either. Perhaps just one more time.

Some time later Paul strolled into the ready room to be greeted with a fierce whisper.

"Where the hell have you been?"

Marty glanced over his shoulder at the closed door on the other side of the ready room, betraying his anxiety. He slid his boots off the table and stood digging his fists deep into the pockets of his flying overalls. He leaned forward confidentially.

"The old man's steaming. He started looking for you nearly an hour ago."

Paul shook his head sadly. "Do you know what she had the cheek to say?" His voice went up into a falsetto. "And to think I've been waiting for you for ages while you were stuck in that beastly desert."

"I don't believe it!" Marty growled. "The bloody woman gave me exactly the same line last week. I'm devastated."

"It's not my fault you hang around with married women, my friend. If you can't take the pace you should try keeping to singles and divorcees."

"You'd best go through. Our gallant Colonel has a job for us."

"Is he getting back at us because we wangled our way home?"

"It's something to do with something I didn't bother listening to. You're the officer here. You gotta earn that extra pay. And you have to find your way to wherever we're going. I just fix everything you keep breaking."

Paul chuckled.

"And Hammie, I told him you were feeling bilious and went for a long walk to try and clear your system in case you had to do any flying."

"It obviously worked. I feel fine."

Paul turned and walked across to the door bearing the name of Colonel Wallender. He smoothed down his overalls fractionally as he stood outside. He felt the old surge of excitement wash through him. He hoped this one was interesting. He hoped it turned out to be a real snorter. Unless something broke the monotony soon he was going to get into real trouble.

*

Early Monday and Roger was on his way back from the Skukuza administration buildings. He and Michelle had one more day there. They would be going through to the private camp, N'wanetsi, the next morning. Then he saw Mary-Ann crossing to the administration buildings from the staff accommodation area.

He watched her for a moment. She looked tired, unhappy. Roger ached for her. He wished he could undo all the things he had done, the hurt he had caused.

Roger called out. Mary-Ann turned to look. He hurried over to her.

"Still hanging around? Try chatting up your wife for a change."

"I need to talk to you," he said, disturbed by her proximity.

"When I say something I mean it. And it bloody well stays said."

"I understand that, but *you* don't seem to understand this is different. It's not personal. Don't let your feelings get in the way of what I want to tell you."

"I don't have any feelings for you," she said, suddenly very casual. "I'm just not interested in anything that you might have to say. You lied to me, that's unforgivable. Can't *you* get that through *your* thick skull!" She spun on her heel and marched off.

"No feelings?" he called out to her back. "S'funny you mentioned my wife. You took the trouble to find out whether I was alone here or not."

She didn't respond and he had no idea whether she had heard him.

Roger stood staring after her, totally dismayed, wondering what he had to do to get her to listen. Soon they would be after him from England and it would be decision time.

He had to get Mary-Ann to listen before that happened.

*

Michelle stood on the porch of their small bungalow waiting for Roger to return. The heat was already oppressive. A ranger had said the rains were due. Slowly the early morning sounds of the African bush crept up on her.

To hear them properly she'd had to learn to listen all over again. Like all city-dwellers she automatically tuned out extraneous noises, to avoid the constant auditory intrusions that formed the backdrop to city living. Now she had to be consciously still, to become aware of what were really quite small sounds. She found listening to the bush restful, it permeated deep into her psyche.

She relaxed, idly looked around. Saw two people talking. It was Roger and a woman wearing a khaki shirt tucked into khaki slacks. The woman turned her head slightly and Michelle recognised her.

It was that bloody Mary-Ann!

Michelle fumed, a one-person audience to the little drama being played out before her. She had all along known he had an ulterior motive for coming to Africa. This was just confirmation that suspicion had been justified. He was here to run after that bloody floozy! Michelle tried to be rational. The situation had to be handled carefully. She sensed he was on the edge. Lay into him now and he could be lost forever. And this was Mary-Ann's backyard.

Michelle watched.

Her rival spun on her heel, marched off. Roger called after her, but Mary-Ann ignored him. Roger stood there for a short while watching Mary-Ann go. Finally he turned away, started to walk back in the direction of their bungalow.

Michelle quickly re-entered the bungalow. Her time would come. She sat down in front of the rustic cane dressing-table and ran a comb through her already immaculate hair. Roger came in through the door she had left half-open.

"We leave for N'wanetsi in the morning," he said.

She turned around casually on the stool, lifted her eyebrows. "Sorry, what was that?"

"The N'wanetsi place will be ready in the morning."

"That's fine," she replied.

Was he sad? Had she already lost him? She couldn't be sure. There was so little she could be sure of these days. Her world had been perfect the way it was. Where had it gone wrong? What should she do? And if it didn't come right – what would happen to her? How could she know what Roger would do next?

She didn't feel like being rational. She felt like screaming and throwing things and running away and having him follow her – to make him show he really cared.

Michelle smiled pleasantly at Roger. "Shall we go for a morning game drive?"

*

The sound of a big truck grinding to a halt penetrated the administrative offices. Brian stood up from his desk, peered out through the window. He turned to look at Jakes. "The soldiers have arrived."

The two of them stepped out of the office and walked across to the khaki-green Bedford truck. The left-hand passenger door of the truck swung open. A man jumped out, landed on his feet like a cat. His shoulders were so broad and his frame so solid he seemed quite short.

But it was an illusion.

Brian smiled to himself. A serious mistake. He was at least three centimetres taller than Brian's one-point-nine metres. He wore the five pointed star – a representation of the Cape Town castle – on his shoulder epaulettes. The muscles under the shirt could have been added with weight workouts in a gymnasium, but looked far more as though they had been earned in a lifetime of continual strenuous physical activity.

"Anderson, Major, 32 Battalion," the soldier nodded brusquely.

Brian held out hand. "Brian Lombard and this is Jakes Webber."

Major Anderson automatically addressed the older man, "Are you the gentlemen we're meant to liaise with?"

"He is," Jakes replied, pointing at Brian. "But I've spent more time in the border region so he's asked me to help."

"Do you have somewhere for a tented camp?"

Brian nodded, pointed to a fence lined with vertically-fixed dry thatching grass.

"The other side of that. It's a dormant old vegetable patch. Help yourself."

The Major gave him a quick smile, turned to the burly black soldier who appeared from out of the back of the truck.

"Sergeant-Major. Make it a competition. They start from here on foot plus all their gear. The first team to get themselves completely set up gets an extra three days leave when we get back to base."

Big drops of water started striking the ground around them. Initially small puffs of dust kicked up as each raindrop hit the thirsty earth.

The Major turned back to Brian. "Rains started yet?"

He wore a well-tailored camouflage uniform, the creases immaculate despite having spent the better part of the day in a truck. His hair was close-cropped, a camouflage beret pulled down tightly over one ear, the steel-grey metal buffalo head insignia centred perfectly.

Brian nodded, looked up, studied the sky. "Yeah, up north. We had some yesterday and a few more drops last night, but the real stuff should get here any time now. Do you mind telling us what this is about?"

"Do you have an office for us?"

Brian nodded. "Mine. This way."

Seated inside the Major told them of the Mozambican troop movements. "Probably nothing will come of it. We're here just in case. And we're under strict instructions to avoid your tourists at all costs. Sorry to rush you, could we go over a few maps?"

"We got out those you'll need for this area," Brian replied.

He spread a map out on the desk, placed weights on the four corners to stop it from rolling up. The Major listened carefully as Jakes started to tell him about the terrain they could expect.

*

The flight engineer bent the stalk of the microphone until the mic touched his lips. "Despite the excellent game-viewing opportunities afforded by low-flying, we'd better climb soon. It's not far now."

Paul grinned across at Marty on his left. "Guess you're right."

He raised the collective, increasing the pitch on the blades, and with a short-lived clatter the Alouette III helicopter, powered by a Turbomeca Artouste IIIB turboshaft powerplant, and with only two on board, started to climb like a homesick angel.

"Flies well when you haven't being working on it, hey?"

"Hope we don't get reported by someone in those cars you buzzed."

"What on earth for?" Paul was clearly astonished.

"Law says you gotta stay 1500 feet agl over a game reserve."

"Good God, man, we're here to defend our country from invaders. Those rules don't apply to us. We're laying our lives on the line –"

"You mean I'm laying my life on the line flying with you … not to mention any hope of promotion."

"You don't want another promotion. The responsibility is murderous. We're talking ulcer country here."

"That must be Skukuza – over to the right a bit."

"I knew that," Paul retorted.

"You were looking at me," protested Marty. "And it's starting to rain."

Paul sighed heavily. "Helicopter pilots …" pausing for dramatic effect, "… can see out of the corners of their eyes. It's a well-known medical fact."

Paul landed the Alo about twenty metres away from the Bedford truck. He let the engine rundown for half-a-minute after pulling the fuel flow back and then switched off. He jumped out and, followed by Marty, shambled over to a group of three men who had emerged from a nearby building.

The army major – with uniform creases you could use instead of a steak knife – studied Paul with slightly raised eyebrows.

Paul understood the problem: fresh oil stains appeared here and there on his flying overalls from the morning's chopper pre-flight, not quite concealing the older oil stains that had not yet been washed out of the cloth despite many seasons of wear. His sleeves were rolled up to his forearms and he had again forgotten to brush his hair flat after having taken off his flying helmet. Not to mention the flying gloves which hung out of a leg pocket.

Finally the Major nodded and the five men introduced themselves.

Major Anderson pointed to a grass-covered fence. "Our camp's over there, just beyond that fence. Ask Sergeant-Major Keller for a couple of our lads to help you get organised."

Paul peered in that direction. Jesus! It looked like a bunch of giant mechanical ants trying to create a new nest in the small paddock. It began to rain even harder. He shuddered delicately.

All of a sudden he snapped his fingers, scowled at Marty. "Damn, I knew there was something we'd forgotten to load. Really Sergeant. I mean that's the sort of thing you're supposed to take charge of. You can't expect me to do everything."

"But you said –"

"But me not buts, Sergeant," Paul cut him off quickly, sorrowfully shaking his head. He turned to speak confidentially to Major Anderson. "Never mind, he's a fine flight engineer."

Marty opened his mouth to speak, abruptly shut it, eyes suddenly wide with understanding.

"I'm sure we can be of assistance." Major Anderson said smoothly. "We've got spare tents."

"You have!" Paul stared blankly at him for a moment. Then quickly caught himself. "No, no, Major, as much as we appreciate your splendid offer – as dearly as we would like to take advantage of it, we cannot." Sorrowfully he shrugged his shoulders. "Our Colonel has had a lifelong feud with the Army. It would be as much as our wings are worth for us to accept any help from you guys. Unfortunately there's nothing for it but for us to rely on these good gentlemen here to help us with accommodation."

He smiled at Brian and Jakes, white teeth glinting in his tanned face, eyes laughing, betraying the carefully creased forehead. "Perhaps you have a bungalow to spare – or two, because," he added hastily, "officers really shouldn't sleep in the same units as enlisted men."

Brian grinned. "Don't tell me. Your Colonel doesn't like it."

"Yes, indeed – quite correct. For myself I couldn't care less, I'm a man of the people but," a sad shrug of the shoulders, "what can I do …?"

"There's often cancellations and we have special transit accommodation, so I'm sure we can find you something, but not two. That won't be possible."

"That'll be fine. No problem I can assure you."

Later, relaxing on one of the two beds in the rondavel – a circular conical-roofed bungalow – Marty opened his eyes. "Man, oh man," he said, talking to the light fitting in the ceiling, "isn't he a genius? Isn't he a beauty? And to think I nearly blew it." He shook his head in frank admiration of Paul's more sterling qualities.

"Despite my natural modesty I have to agree. Now we're going to have to work out a set of signals. When we're free to enter and when not, that sort of thing. If the wire mesh door is tightly shut it means one of us is in here with a live one and is not to be disturbed, okay? Marty?"

Marty nodded his head dreamily.

"Right, so the signals are done. All military efforts have to have good signal systems. It lies at the heart of the whole thing. Now have you spotted anything interesting yet?"

"Jesus, Hammie, we've only just arrived. Gimme a break."

"Okay, well I've got one possibility so far, I glimpsed her through the doorway earlier. I think she was coming across to that office we were in. When she saw us there she changed her mind. Standard rules apply. I have a clear track for twenty-four hours before you get to try your hand."

"Fair enough. But you'd better come up with an accurate description because you'll just claim anything that comes along as being the one you saw first. And as the only real working man around here I want first shower."

"She was beautiful," Paul said dreamily. "Blonde hair to die for. Tall, about five-ten, dressed in khaki slacks and shirt and wearing a pair of those cute little brown ankle-high hiking boots. It could've been a uniform."

Marty opened another can of beer and shambled off to the shower. "Me for a clean up – I just hope to God you don't disturb me." Quickly he ducked through the doorway into the bathroom as a pillow hit the closed door.

"It was probably a uniform," Paul muttered to himself. "I've always been partial to women in uniform."

*

Joshua Manyoba was feeling his age. They had been marching through the bush since early Saturday morning. It was now late Monday afternoon. The three days were beginning to catch up with him. He glanced across at the two Europeans. The blonde one called Karl was doing fine, but the older one, Fitzsimmons, was obviously missing his bottle. He looked worse than Joshua felt.

Up ahead Abel Gamellah stopped, held up his hand. "Listen."

Not moving it was easier for them to hear the pop-pop-pop of distant gunfire.

Karl drew level with Joshua. "What the hell is that?"

"We always have two parties out – advance and rearguard," Joshua explained. "Stops us walking into ambushes and having Frelimo sneak up behind."

Fitzsimmons came up alongside Karl. He stared at Joshua. "Does that mean the rearguard party is fighting with someone?"

Abel joined the small group. He worried Joshua. The Butcher's time horizons had shrunk. He no longer seemed to care about the outcome of the war or the peace talks. His own devils, whatever they may be, were driving him now.

He was more gaunt than ever and at times even seemed unsteady on his feet.

Joshua shook his head. "The rearguard won't engage Frelimo. The advance scouts have the same instructions. They'll try to keep out of the way. We don't want to give our position away. If Frelimo have troops in an area we sneak out of there."

Understanding washed across Karl's face. "So the rearguard party has walked into an ambush. They're shooting because they have no choice ... but that means Frelimo knows –"

Joshua cut him off. "Listen. The firing has stopped."

"The rearguard party has scared them off?"

Joshua shook his head. "Our people have been wiped out."

"The Lord giveth and the Lord taketh away. Come, we must go."

The Butcher jogged away to the head of the column and then just kept on going.

Karl shivered. "I wish he wouldn't say things like that. It gives me the creeps."

"You and a few others," Joshua responded sourly.

"Are we still going to the coal fields? Or do we go back?"

"Forget the coal. That's over. And we can't go back, they're behind us. If we try to get out of the valley here they'll pick us off while we're on the slopes like swatting flies on a window-pane. We have to carry on and hope to find an easier place to climb out, to the north or south."

They began to jog as the column strung out behind Abel.

After a while Joshua's breath came in short hard bursts – in and out, in and out.

"What about Fitzsimmons?" Karl panted alongside him.

Joshua looked back. The run was taking its toll. Slowly the geologist fell further behind.

"We can't afford to slow down ..." Joshua paused in what he was saying to gasp for breath, "... if we do they'll catch us … have to keep going … maybe an easier place … to get out of the valley."

Karl matched Joshua stride for stride. "What will they do to Fitzsimmons?"

But Joshua knew Karl was actually asking what would happen to him if he also fell behind. So all he did was grunt and keep on running.

*

It was a disaster!

Jakes Webber squatted in the dirt alongside Lungile, his face chiselled from stone. The river was starting to run. Soon he would have been able to pull his men out. Then there would have been little chance of his black lion escaping the valley.

Now this – a disaster.

He looked into Lungile's expressionless face. "When did this thing happen?"

"Yesterday," replied the stoic old man, as he swept an arm around to point up the valley to the east. "It was Kambala's turn to look for spoor. We heard the lion, a few night's back, when he came down to the river after the sun had gone down. Then he disappeared. We've been taking turns to look for his spoor while the other stays here. As you instructed, *Mandevu*.

"Kambala left when the sun's first light was red upon the earth. Later, when the sun was directly overhead, I heard a male lion call. It was not the voice of a lion that could fight a buffalo. It was that of a lion whose heart is weak. Last night Kambala didn't return and I became concerned. But I stayed by the place where one can cross the river."

Jakes waited impatiently. But there was no point in rushing the old man.

"By sundown," Lungile continued, "I tracked the lion part way down the valley. He stopped plenty, walking softly on his right front foot. He twisted it as he walked, the way a man will do if he doesn't want to put weight on that leg. The leg is hurt, maybe high up. He stops a lot but not like a lion who has had enough to eat and is too lazy to move. Also he is not hunting. He passed within a twenty paces of impala. They didn't move, they also knew he was hurt. He didn't try. He's already learnt he can no longer charge properly."

Jakes mind wandered as he listened to Lungile. The injured lion must have been caught in a poacher's snare. Armed poachers would be after ivory or rhino horn, although the demand from Asia for lion bones was picking up, as well. Unarmed poachers would be after food and they used snares, but they had never come into this valley before.

Now this – a major disaster.

"He was looking for food under bushes and under logs," Lungile was saying, "like a jackal or hyaena. But he was also moving along behind Kambala, who had been searching for his spoor by cutting backwards and forwards across the valley. It was easy for me to stay in the middle, at the bottom of the valley. Kambala's spoor went from side to side and the lion's spoor followed Kambala. The lion killed Kambala when he came back to the main path."

"Jesus! Not Kambala!" Jakes stirred restlessly, set his face. "Was it my black lion?"

"You were sad the time Kambala said your lion was injured."

"I just said it's easy to make a mistake with a spoor." Jakes grunted irritably. "Did *my* lion kill Kambala?"

Lungile paused for a long while before answering, finally he shrugged his bony shoulders. "It was half light. But the spoor was that of a young male with only three good legs."

"Three good legs …" Jakes echoed for no good reason.

"Yes, *Nkosi*, where the front right touches the ground you can see it is badly hurt."

Jakes felt a surge of determination. A tribe of black lions in the game reserve where they would be safe would be his own personal link to the African bush. Except for Brian and his assistants no one would ever know. Now he would have to determine how badly the man-eater was hurt and if it was his black lion.

Neither Kambala nor Lungile had actually seen the lion. They could still be wrong about its identity. No one was perfect and least of all when it came to tracking. Even though the two men were amongst the best in the business. But this time they could be wrong! This time they had to be! Anyway they had both admitted they could be wrong. And a damaged paw didn't mean a lion couldn't breed. He could still start a pride.

"So, *Nkosi*, we hunt the man-eater at dawn?"

Jakes looked up in surprise at Lungile, realising how far along a different tangent his thoughts had already taken him. Of course, everyone would expect an injured man-eater to be shot immediately. A man-eater in Kruger wouldn't be – couldn't be – tolerated. Jesus! Tourists were all over the place.

"Of course we must hunt him. But we must keep this story to ourselves. And you have done good work for me. You must take a long holiday. In the morning I'll take you out to your village. Then I'll come back later – with some other trackers – we'll hunt the man-eater."

"*Mandevu*, I do not understand why this animal should be hunted without me. In twenty years I have always done the tracking for you."

"I'll be honest with you," Jakes said, but he couldn't meet Lungile's eyes. "I've been told to start with new people." He quickly went on before the other man had a chance to respond. "If we are too many we'll find it difficult to track this animal. You know that yourself."

"We could use the helicopter to find a man-eater. We could use a long line of beaters. That is plenty of people. We wouldn't hunt a man-eater with just two men on foot. This is not sport, *Mandevu*. This is serious."

"You're turning into a fusspot, Lungile. I'll sort it out. You've done well for me this season. You've spent many months here. You must have time with your family. You must have time in the sun, watch your grandchildren take the cattle, sheep and goats out each day. Maybe find yourself another wife, a new young wife that can keep you warm in the winter in the way that only a plump new young woman can do for a man."

"Kambala was a friend of mine. We came to you together. Before that we herded cattle, sheep and goats together," he held out his hand at thigh height, palm upwards in the African way, so as not to put a bad spell on growth, "when we were so small. Later we walked together to seek work."

Jakes held up his hand. "I know that, old friend. I am also upset about Kambala. His widow and children will be well-provided for. I will see to it myself. But now you must also retire. You will also be well-provided for."

"It's not about money, *Mandevu*. The lion has devoured Kambala's spirit and one of us who were his brothers must kill him to release that spirit, so he may rest easy."

Jakes squirmed a little on his haunches. Suddenly squatting became uncomfortable so he stood up and stamped his feet to get the circulation going again. "Sooner or later that spirit will be released. I promise that, Lungile."

"But I would –"

"Enough of this talk," Jakes cut him off. "You're becoming like an old woman the way you talk without stopping. What has happened to Lungile, the silent one?"

After a short silence Jakes turned to look at Lungile. "Surely you're happy that you'll be at your house for the rainy season. You can see for yourself that the planting is done right, that all your children are working properly for the family."

"Yes, I'll be happy to be with my family at this time of the year. But my heart is sore for Kambala."

Finally Jakes spoke with absolute sincerity. "Of course, so is mine."

*

Paul had already spent most of the evening sitting by himself in the old railway carriage cocktail bar. He had taken up residence there not long after arriving at Skukuza. He was on a mission. Mary-Ann had come in a little earlier but had gone into the restaurant when a much older man, with a small goatee beard, had arrived, presumably to have dinner. Beyond Paul learning her name, she had been icily indifferent to his attempt at chatting her up.

He grinned to himself. Very disappointing, he had been convinced his search for the perfect woman had come to an end. She was a splendid creature, long-legged and lithe, when she moved it was a leopard checking its territory. It was a pity she seemed to have the temperament of a shrew.

He shook his head sadly, what a waste.

Having spent the whole evening drinking Paul finally decided nothing was going to happen in the cocktail bar and he wandered out into the night. He strolled down to stand by a rail. The spot overlooked a bend in the Sabie River at least a hundred metres below. He leaned on the rail. The damp night air, soft from the rain, felt fresh after the heat of the sun during the day.

He wondered what adventures would befall him in Kruger – both flying and female – and in that order.

*

For some time now Roger hadn't heard a word Michelle had said.

"This restaurant caters for about 12,000 guests annually," Michelle added brightly, taking another deep draught from her glass of dry white wine, a fine Cape Chardonnay, which she drank as though it was water. "Oh, look at the menu. This is so exciting. They've got buffalo tongue with mustard sauce and marula jelly, crocodile mayonnaise, medallion of crocodile and catfish as starters. The main courses include grilled buffalo, kudu fillet and warthog Stroganoff. What are you going to have?"

"That's interesting," he said.

Mary-Ann sat on the other side of the restaurant. She shared a table with an older man, so even if he had wanted to try talking to her it would have been awkward. They seemed to be well-acquainted. Who was he?

Michelle refilled her own glass from the bottle in the ice bucket and then immediately drank most of that.

"There's some consolation for diners with less exotic palates," Michelle said, not altogether clearly. "They also serve the more usual sirloin, chicken, some sort of fish called a Kingklip and Karoo lamb cutlets. I'm going to be daring and have one of the exotic dishes. What are you going to have?"

Roger peered across the restaurant. She hadn't even acknowledged his presence. Her eyes had passed over him as though he were a complete stranger.

"What are you going to have?" Michelle slurred.

Roger glanced warningly at her. Michelle had been drinking much more than her usual one or two glasses of wine with a meal. And it was beginning to show. She was talking too much, her speech was thick, her eyes were red and a fine patina of moisture had formed on her upper lip.

"There's something for –"

Abruptly Michelle abruptly stopped talking. She stared at him. Then her eyes followed his. "That's the real problem, isn't it? That's really why you're here," she was having difficulty getting her tongue around the words. "You arranged to meet your floozy here."

He wanted to explain, someone to understand what he was thinking. He was tired of keeping it all to himself. He wanted to share his thoughts.

"You're right. I do want to talk to her. But it's not personal. Despite that she won't listen to me."

Michelle looked at him owlishly for a while, finished off what was left in her wine glass and helped herself to some more from the bottle, filling her glass to the brim.

Roger frowned. "Don't you think you've had enough?"

"What do you care?" Michelle spoke in a loud voice. "You're in love with her, aren't you? You're staring at her like a lovelorn puppy."

She picked up her glass, banged her elbow, spilled wine on the tablecloth. She drank half the glass in one long swallow, without pausing for breath.

"It's not personal," he whispered fiercely.

"Bullshit!" Michelle said loudly, turning a few nearby heads in the restaurant. "What you want is between her legs. That's what you want." Tears welled up and the mascara smudged beneath her eyes. She sniffed. "It's really all over for us, isn't it?"

Roger felt guilty. He hadn't been fair to her. In her own way and for her own reasons, she loved him. But the time wasn't right for the two of them to talk. She'd had too much to drink. They needed to be sober and alone somewhere.

Now, softly, he said, "I'm not the same man you married."

"You make me sick!" Michelle jumped up and ran out of the restaurant.

Concerned, he quickly settled the bill, walked out into the night, but it was too dark to see much and he had no idea where to start looking. She couldn't go far in the well-fenced camp. It was an old ploy of hers – go off in a huff and wait for him to come and fetch her. He wasn't in the mood for games and made his way back to their bungalow.

*

Paul stood in the shadows. Further along someone else came to lean on the rail. He kept quiet. He was enjoying it, being there alone, standing in the dark, high above the bend in the Sabie River which lay far below. He liked watching the animals come out to drink, as they warily looking around, tentatively drifted to the water's edge.

He felt at one with the night, fascinated with the bush life unfolding before him. Cicadas rasped for a mate while the occasional bat whirred by in search of an insect meal. Somewhere in the night a leopard coughed. There seemed

so few nights like this in his life and he sometimes
wondered why he was always running around so
frenetically.

He suddenly laughed quietly to himself, standing there in
the dark. He ran because he had legs. The thought tickled
him. Could the concept be stretched to cover flying? I fly
because I have wings. Yeah, but they're actually rotor
blades. He nodded his head sagely – at least that proved he
wasn't cut out to be a poet.

A new sound joined the rest of the night's sounds. The
person standing over there in the dark was crying. It was
the soft mewing of a kitten newly weaned. Oddly touched,
Paul hesitated, stepped forward.

"Are you all right?" he called out softly, into the night,
not wanting to intrude unnecessarily.

"Who's that?" The voice was small and frightened in the
dark.

The woman turned to face him. He could see the whites
of her eyes reflecting the moonlight.

"It's okay," he called out softly. "My name's Paul. I'm a
pilot. I brought in the helicopter today."

She suddenly giggled through the tears. "You're a
helicopter pilot – that's supposed to make me feel safer?"

He chuckled quietly. "I guess not," he hesitated and then
added, much more seriously, "If you want to be alone …"

"No," she replied. "I don't want to be alone. I've been
alone for far too long now. It seems as though I've been
alone all of my life."

"Yeah, you sure gotta be plensh lonely to accept a
strange helicopter pilot for company."

She laughed out aloud. For a while they stood there,
quietly, listening to the night, not saying anything. Paul felt
as though they were sharing the sounds and the dark and the
sliver of a moon that shone through the clouds.

"You're English, aren't you? Travelling alone?" he
asked, trying to be diplomatic.

"Can we pretend there's no such thing as a past or a future – just for a little while."

Paul shrugged. "Sure. Why not?"

He felt comfortable with this stranger in the night. For some reason he felt no need to get her into bed or to somehow win her favour. It was as though the dark that surrounded them was a shield against all the normal obsessions that drive people to behave towards each other with less than honesty. He felt drawn to her. He moved sideways, instinctively understanding he could move closer now, that she wouldn't mind. Their elbows almost touched. They both leaned on the rail, side by side, looking down on the Sabie River.

She stirred restlessly. "I've been drinking."

"So have I."

"Probably not as much as I have." She was silent for a while then glanced quickly at him. "I saw your helicopter come in today. Are you on a special mission? Or is it a military secret?"

He laughed. "Hey, hey, hey. What's this? No pasts and no futures, remember?"

He could feel her eyes on his face.

"Yes," she said carefully, as though it was a new and somehow shocking idea. "Of course – no pasts and no futures." The words seemed to hold a kind of magic for her.

They were out there in the night, standing against the rail, looking into the dark, for a long time and it became a game. They talked but didn't allow each other to say or ask anything that related to a past or a future. They talked about anything and everything else. The game released them from all the posturings and petty acts people everywhere put on to create their public faces. The game allowed them to be who they really were.

Later it became chilly. Paul, with all the innocence of a small child, suggested they go indoors. And it was absolutely natural and right they should do that together, as though no other possibility could have existed for them.

Paul went ahead to clear the bungalow and even that seemed right.

They wanted to be by themselves.

They made love and it was soft and gentle and natural and right and he had nothing to prove and she had nothing to hide. The dark and the game still held them in a time warp with no links to the world from which they had come.

Somewhere along the line she cried out, but it was happy sound.

Afterwards he said very deliberately, "I love you," and the wonder in his voice surprised even him. Could it really happen that quickly?

They slept then, each holding the other gently, the way a little girl sleeps innocently cuddling her favourite teddy bear.

*

A shell whistled overhead and Karl, still running, ducked instinctively, pulling his head well down into his shoulders.

"Jesus Christ!" he shouted.

A scream from behind pierced the air. He stopped to look back. There was enough moonlight filtering through the clouds for him to see that Fitzsimmons must have been hit, he was kneeling about 200 metres behind them.

"Get down!" Joshua yelled at Karl, pulling on his arm.

But a mesmerised Karl stood there, staring, eyes wide. Joshua followed his eyes. Fitzsimmons managed to get one foot underneath him, but he was still on one knee when the earth around him erupted into small spurts of dust. He jerked in a half-circle flipping like a fish out of water. He finally lurched to his feet, staggered three paces toward them before pitching forward to fall flat on his face.

"That machine-gun caught him fair and square," Joshua said flatly. "And you're going to be just as dead if you don't get down and follow me."

Joshua leopard crawled through the grass. He made his way around the clearing they had been skirting when they had heard the firing which brought down Fitzsimmons. On the other side, he swung his legs around, flopping onto his belly, facing back the way he had just come. He pushed the AK47 out in front of him, sprayed the bushes across the clearing. The Swiss crawled up nearby.

"What are you shooting at?" asked Karl nervously.

Joshua gave him a quick grin. "Nothing in particular. A lot of bush warfare is like this. Shooting at random. Hoping you hit something out there or scare them away or just make 'em keep their heads down."

Bullets hummed by overhead, like bees on steroids. Karl cowered behind a small shrub, his hands over the back of his head, his nose pressed into the dust. The Butcher appeared alongside him, leopard crawling. He laughed at the Swiss.

"You only start worrying when you stop hearing them." He crawled on to where Joshua lay.

Joshua gestured with the AK47. "We've got to break the trap."

"There's only one way out – and they won't dare follow us."

Joshua nodded. "You're right. But we need a diversion."

Abel grinned mirthlessly. "Some of my sad ones will volunteer for the privilege."

Joshua shivered. Abel was happy to allow those who had contracted the thin sickness – as HIV/Aids was commonly called in Africa – to tag along. At one time the Butcher had gone out of his way to recruit men kicked out by other commanders for having the thin sickness, provided them with a home, however temporary. It gave his men so afflicted a reckless disregard for their lives which went beyond anything a brave man might try. It explained Abel's seeming ability to fight his way out of any kind of situation, no matter how desperate. Send in the walking dead as a rearguard and they would stay until they died. Joshua figured the Butcher had brainwashed them somehow into doing it for him.

The Butcher grinned and jerked a thumb in Karl's direction. "Looks like the little china doll is scared."

Joshua just shrugged. He actually felt sorry for the Swiss youngster. "When do we make a break for it?"

The Butcher resembled a death's head. Gaunt cheeks and deep-set dark-hollowed eyes sunk into the skeleton behind the mask of his face.

"My sad ones will move up now. When they're in position we can start our withdrawal."

Joshua nodded. "I'll be ready."

Abel was still grinning. "Don't leave china doll behind."

"Don't worry, I'll see he comes along."

This time Abel nodded and said nothing. Quickly he squirmed backwards until he disappeared from sight in the low shrub behind them.

Joshua went back to hosing the bushes on the other side of the clearing with his AK47.

*

Paul woke up. A rose-coloured light stained the curtains. He turned his head on the pillow and Michelle woke up. They lay like that for a while, half asleep, feeling the warmth of each other, not stirring.

"I don't even know your name," he mumbled at length.

And the spell was broken.

"Oh my God ... I ... don't know what came over me ... I don't normally behave like this ... very embarrassing ..."

"Hey, relax. We're friends – remember?"

Michelle's face grew even redder. She desperately tried to cover herself with the corner of a blanket while at the same time trying to get dressed.

"Come on," he said. "What's the rush? Tell me –"

She rounded on him, cutting him off. "This is disgusting. Men are such pigs. You took advantage of me when I'd had too much to drink."

"We had something special going last night."

Michelle was almost finished dressing. "You took advantage of me."

"It takes two to tango," he growled, fiercely disappointed.

"I feel so dirty and ugly and unhappy. I wish I was dead." She rushed out of the bungalow.

Paul sat up, stared at the open doorway.

He lay down again, flat on his back, stared at the ceiling. He didn't understand what had happened this morning – but he sure as hell knew what had happened the night before. He had never told any woman that he loved her. And when he had said it the previous night he had meant it. Who was this woman with no name? He had never met anyone like her before and he knew that he never would again.

He heard the fly-screen bang closed and quickly sat up, hoping the woman with no name had relented and returned. Marty wandered in, leaned against the door-jamb. Paul flopped back on the bed again. He opened one eye to see Marty stretching.

"Man, you owe me big time. I'm sick of sleeping in choppers."

Paul said nothing for while.

"Sure," he said at length.

Marty wandered through to the bathroom, collecting his towel en route. A short while later he stuck his head through the doorway, sighing. "I've never seen you like this before. You'd better tell me all about it."

*

The sun had barely risen as Roger watched Michelle sidle into the bungalow, dishevelled and obviously hungover. He decided to postpone the talk they needed to have.

"I've nearly finished packing. We're going through to N'wanetsi this morning."

Michelle refused to meet his eyes. "I … I just want a quick shower."

Roger had no idea of where she had been the night before. But if she wasn't going to talk about it neither was he.

Carrying their suitcases to the hired Datsun, Roger had to scurry. A faint drizzle fell. In the car he took out a map and studied it. Michelle showed none of her usual impatience, made none of her customary demands. She seemed extraordinarily low-key.

Roger held up the map. "I want to take a specific route to N'wanetsi."

Michelle shrugged her shoulders.

Still in Skukuza, they drove past a parked helicopter.

She turned to look back. "What sort of helicopter is that?"

"I think the South Africans mostly use Aerospatiale machines, Alouettes and Pumas. That's probably an Alouette being the smaller of the two. Since when have you been interested in helicopters?"

She stared out of the side window. "Just curious."

After they had travelled some distance in silence, she spoke without looking at him. "You aren't trying to find animals. You're looking for something else."

It was Roger's turn to shrug. "Maybe."

After that they continued in silence.

Roger carefully followed their progress on the map he held in one hand. Would he be able to identify the little road which led into the western end of Hawke's valley? Eventually he stopped, peered at the scrub alongside the main road, reversed a short distance. This faint track lead to the valley. He was sure. It was only a few miles short of N'wanetsi and they were in no hurry. Roger killed the engine, stayed parked alongside the start of the track.

Still looking out of her side window Michelle said, "I guess you're still moping about your floozy? Is that your problem? Still lusting after a little more wildlife?"

He turned in his seat, stared at her. "You have no idea of what you started. When you got your father to have me thrown off the yachting project."

She shifted uncomfortably, she obviously hadn't realised he knew. "I don't see why that should've caused trouble."

"That's how it all began," he said.

Sitting at the side of the road, in the middle of nowhere, he told her word for word exactly what had happened. Osbourne-Kerr's suicide; how he had decided to have a go at Hawke; going through Hawke's papers; how that led him to Mary-Ann and the valley with the coal in it. Finally he pointed to the track next to the car.

"That's the track that leads to the valley I'm talking about."

He said it as though the existence of the road would prove what he was saying. Roger felt as though he had run a marathon – and the experience was strangely cathartic.

Michelle stared at him wide-eyed, her face the pale grey of a London smog.

"That's nonsense. How can you blame me? You're just like all the rest. You all think you're better than me because my father is Lebanese and changed his name to try and fit in." Softly she began to cry. "You're just a snob, like the rest of your family."

Roger stared at Michelle in astonishment. He had no idea she thought this way. He knew it wouldn't change anything now, but it meant he understood a lot more. His expression softened. There was the world of sympathy in his voice.

"That's why you didn't want me in the BOC, why the title was so important to you."

"It's not me, it's you. You're just saying that stuff because you feel guilty about this Mary-Ann woman and now you're trying to lay the blame on me. You're an adulterer and she's a dirty slut," she screamed wildly. "That's what the two of you are – an adulterer and a dirty slut."

They were both astonished by Michelle's violent outburst. After that there didn't seen anything else worth saying and Roger started the car. He drove on to the N'wanetsi camp. After they had arrived and unpacked, all in silence, Roger turned to Michelle.

"We need to talk seriously. This can't go on."

"You're saying I started it to make me feel small, to dominate me."

"Don't be ridiculous."

"You're ridiculous. What you want is an obedient little Japanese geisha girl for a wife, someone you can boss around all the time."

"I'll tell you what I don't want – a bloody fishwife."

"You just want a geisha girl who'd go into that valley with you and who'd crawl around on her hands and knees looking for coal or whatever. Instead of arguing with you the way I am."

"This is ridiculous. In any event there isn't a proper road into that place and it's off limits to the likes of us."

"Oh, it is, is it, Tarzan? And who told you that? Little jungle Jane?"

"All right, it *was* Mary-Ann who said the valley's off-limits to the public. But that's not the point. The point is that I don't want –"

"I've got news for you, Tarzan," she cut him off. "If I want to go in there I will and no floozy's going to tell me I can't."

"This argument is crazy. You're not allowed in that valley and that's the end of that. It doesn't matter who said it."

"We'll see about that. We'll see what terrible things happen if I do. Maybe they'll even send that helicopter to come and fetch me."

"What on earth are you babbling about? In any event, I forbid you to go into that valley."

She stood up and started towards the door. "You do, do you?"

"Don't be stupid, Michelle. Neither Mary-Ann nor I make the rules so it won't prove anything if you go in there. I'm ordering you to stay out."

"We'll see about that," she snarled, marching out the door.

"You come back here," Roger yelled after her.

"Go to hell," she yelled back.

Roger shook his head. Stubborn woman. She wanted him to come running outside to stop her. To hell with her. Roger stalked through to the bedroom, lay down on a bed. She wouldn't go through with her threat. Another infantile game. It was something she had often done before and he had always obliged her in order to keep the peace.

"But not this time," he muttered aloud. "Like last night she can bloody well sort herself out."

Roger lay on the bed, looking at nothing, listening to the soft sound of the water streaming from the swollen sky on to the thatch and the small wind soughing around the eaves of the bungalow. And then – much to his annoyance – he heard the engine of the Datsun turning over and cough as it took. He stood up, quickly walked across to a window in time to see the chocolate-brown car go past and out of the gateway.

"Stubborn bloody woman," he muttered under his breath. "She'll be back and she'll look the fool." Sooner or later she would realise he couldn't follow her because he didn't have any transport.

Abruptly he turned on his heel, marched back into the bungalow, lay down again. Eventually she would come back of her accord, probably with some cock-and-bull story of having been in the valley, after all. She had probably parked around the first corner waiting to see if he would come looking for her.

She wouldn't go off the beaten track by herself …

*

A tall, thin – almost emaciated – character appeared in the doorway to Brian's office. His weather-scored face carried a tan the colour of dark oak. No more than twenty-five or twenty-six years of age, the hand he had on the door-jamb was brown and mottled with dark liver spots from long hours of exposure to the sun. His face was curiously heavy for one so young with heavy eyelids which hung low over expressionless eyes.

Major Anderson gestured at the doorway. "Gentlemen, Lieutenant Luke Smith. He's brought four recces along to help us." The Major introduced the men to each other.

Jakes saw a flash of recognition between the helicopter pilot and the Lieutenant. He looked from one to the other. "You know each other?"

"We've met," grinned Paul.

The Lieutenant nodded. "I owe him a big one. From deep in Angola."

Paul laughed. "Now you're back on your feet you can buy me a beer – or two."

"Recces?" queried Brian Lombard.

"Reconnaissance Commandos," replied the Major shortly.

"Our version of the British SAS or the US seals," added Paul. "Crazy characters. Happy to spend months on end running around the bush in pairs, or even alone, eating worms and snakes and things – raw," he shuddered delicately, "no fires allowed, might give them away to the enemy."

There was a short silence, broken by Brian.

"What happens now? I mean how do we go about organising this thing?"

The Lieutenant stayed in the doorway, leaning against the doorjamb, absolutely without movement but not restfully, more like a cat belly-down in the grass, motionless, watching a bird hop closer. The other four men were scattered around Brian's office but there were insufficient chairs. Paul half-sat, half-lay on the floor, the tops of his shoulders resting against the wall. Major Anderson used a canvas folding camp stool he had brought in for himself.

The Major responded to Brian's questions. "If it's okay we use this office as our ops' room. Everything will be co-ordinated from here. Radio work and that sort of thing. We'll discuss the signals we'll be using in due course."

Paul raised his eyes to the ceiling. "Oh goody," he muttered under his breath.

Major Anderson gave Paul a cold stare. "You wanted to add something, Captain?"

"Who me?" Paul's eyes went wide, waved a hand casually in the air. "All military efforts have to have good signal systems," he explained to the two civilians. "It lies at the heart of the whole thing."

"Thank you for the contribution, Captain."

Paul smiled beatifically at the army officer. Brian looked across at the Lieutenant. Was there the faintest hint of amusement lurking behind those otherwise expressionless eyes?

"To continue," Major Anderson said pointedly, "First of all we don't expect anything to happen. But we have to prepare for the worst-case scenario. The Lieutenant and his men will be under my command in this sector. My troops – "

"Sorry, Major," interrupted Brian. "This sector?"

"We've divided the border fence into three sectors – north, central and south. We have an identical force operating in each sector. We're central. My troops, from the 32nd, are to be held here in Skukuza as a reserve force. Because of the considerable tourist activity in the area we want to keep as low a profile as possible. So only three choppers are to be used, one to each sector.

"Our chopper patrols the border fence with recces on board," the Major continued, "Anything suspicious and they drop off one or two recces at a time so they can investigate the situation on the ground. My buffalo soldiers will be here as backup should the recces find something."

Brian sucked in his cheeks. "Do you really have enough men to handle an invasion?"

Major Anderson laughed. "No way. We would just provide a holding action. That'll give time for the main defensive forces to be mobilised."

Jakes interrupted the Major by suddenly standing up and walking over to the large-scale map they had taped on a wall in his office. He ran his finger down the demarcated border. "It really wouldn't pay you to just fly up and down the fence."

Brian frowned at him but Jakes avoided meeting his eyes.

"Why not?" queried the Major.

"The border fence is too long to start at one end and just finish at the other end. I'm not a military man but it would probably be too predictable, as well. I think it would be better to do random checks on those stretches of the fence I can point out as being the most likely areas of infiltration."

Major Anderson nodded. "That makes sense. But we'll be relying heavily on local knowledge."

That suited Jakes. He didn't give a damn about the military types or what they needed. All he wanted was to keep them away from his valley. No one must disturb his black lion. The start of a new pride in the valley had already cost Kambala his life. Jakes wanted to make sure he hadn't lost it in vain.

Major Anderson turned to Paul. "Can we still fly?"

Paul sprang lithely to his feet and peered out of the rain-streaked window. "As long as it doesn't get any worse and the wind doesn't pick up." He suddenly sounded much more professional.

"All right, gentlemen. Let's pick a starting point."

The five men clustered around the map on the wall.

*

As the five men met in Jake's office on that Tuesday morning Michelle, still in a high dudgeon, reversed out of the carport and turned left and left again to follow the track that led past the front window and porch of their bungalow at N'wanetsi.

Michelle felt sick to her stomach with herself, Roger, Mary-Ann and the helicopter pilot – the whole damned mess. She had a horrible feeling Roger was right and that she was behaving very childishly indeed. She slowed right down while passing the bungalow. If Roger came out and called, she would stop immediately.

"If he spent as much time thinking about me as he did about that floozy," she told herself aloud, "he would have come out to stop me."

As the car passed the bungalow she glimpsed Roger standing at the window. Her heart lifted.

"He's not as disinterested as he makes out," Michelle muttered aloud. "He was at the window. I'm sure of it."

Then she was around the corner and she could no longer see the bungalow in her rear-view mirror.

Would they send the helicopter to fetch her if she did go into the valley? Her face suddenly felt warm. She quickly switched her thoughts back to Roger.

"I'll make the bastard sweat," she mumbled aloud.

Involuntarily her thoughts again turned to the pilot. Cautiously she explored her feelings about him. She had never experienced anything like the night before. Was it just the alcohol? She'd had a lot to drink. She was also embarrassed. Surely she wouldn't be able to look him in the eye if they were to meet again? He was so confident and she was so unsure of herself, the difference was so much so that in a funny way she also disliked him because she was scared of him.

The sandy bush track leading to the valley loomed up out of the rain.

Almost without thinking she turned the steering wheel and the Datsun lurched off the main tar road. Very slowly she drove down the small dirt track. Why hadn't Roger come out of the bungalow to stop her?

The car slithered along the wet track. What if it got stuck in one of muddier patches, where rainwater had collected in small puddles? That would serve him right. Imagine his embarrassment if he had to arrange for someone to come and dig her out. Quickly she floored the accelerator. The Datsun shot forward, sliding viciously from side to side, but the wheels held in the ruts, and it didn't get stuck. She slowed down again. The road sloped away from her now, heading downhill, making it less likely the car would get stuck.

A misty rain continued to fall. She drove on, slower and slower. Eventually she came to the bank of a swift-running stream, grey-brown from the storm water fed in from its catchment area up north. Giving herself no time to think she impetuously floored the accelerator again. The car hit a bump in the road, slithered to one side, wheels spinning uselessly on the muddy track.

But it was downhill, and the car had its own momentum, it slid forward, the wheels bit and she was into the stream. Terrified out of her wits Michelle kept her foot flat on the floor and with water streaming off the bonnet the car plunged forward, bucking into the river of brown water that slid past, going deeper and deeper.

*

The young male lion lay just inside the cave entrance, facing outwards. He had eaten recently and some of his strength had returned. But the fire raging in his system sapped him of the desire to search for conventional food. His instinct for survival only rose to the surface when stimulated by the close proximity of easy food. Then it coiled and uncoiled inside him like a python. He didn't have the will to go looking for food that could run fast or fight hard.

But he had also discovered humans were strangely vulnerable – considering the fear they normally evoked. He had been down to the river crossing again, but the second man-smell had gone.

A sound drifted up to him. It was from the river crossing. On an instinctive level he immediately associated it with the man-smell. The car engine revved high. The sound bounced back and forth, down the valley. The young lion was hungry and he was sick and he needed food. The coiled snake residing in all species stirred in him and saliva wet his dry gums and tongue and a low-pitched rumble sounded from deep in his belly.

Slowly the young lion, coiled instinct wrestling with weakness, drew himself to his feet. He tentatively took a step forward, swayed, took a second step. He moved one soft paw after another. Slowly he picked up speed as flexibility came back to his stiffened muscles, except those in his right front leg, which he now dragged along the ground.

*

Michelle was scared.

The water built up into a small tidal wave ahead of the Datsun's bonnet – and she knew real fear. The fear kept her right foot rigidly pressing the accelerator to the floor. At one stage the engine hesitated and coughed. She couldn't believe the situation she had got herself into. The car started to drift sideways as the deeper water lifted it off the sandy bottom of the river. Almost a metre sideways and then the wheels bit on a small sandbank. Again the car moved forward, slid sideways once more, and at last she was through the deepest part of the stream.

Holding her breath, foot still keeping the accelerator pedal on the floor, mesmerised by the swift muddy water around the car, Michelle sat as rigid as a jade Buddha behind the steering-wheel. The tyres bit deep into the river bed and the residual forward momentum of the car helped to keep it moving even as the brown fast-flowing water pushed at it from the side. The bottom began to shelve up towards the far bank, the rear wheels dug deep and the car surged forward, engine screaming.

The Datsun came out of the water on the far side of the river. It hit the rutted slope of the far bank with a bang that rattled Michelle's teeth. Water poured off it like a submarine surfacing at sea. She kept the accelerator pressed to the floor. The wheels spun in the heavier, clay soil that formed the banks of the stream and churned the sticky grey mud. Eventually the vehicle lurched over the top.

Michelle was relieved to be away from the rushing water. She took her foot off the accelerator altogether. The car slid off the track, buried its nose in the scrub and the engine stalled. Shaking as though with a fever Michelle, still gripping the steering-wheel, dropped her head onto the back of her hands. Tears ran freely, leaving dark mascara smeared down her cheeks.

After a while she looked up. Should she get out to inspect the car for damage? To hell with it. They had an accident clause. The insurance company could pay. She finally decided she was still too close to the stream. She wanted Roger to feel real shock and horror at her situation. He must pay a real price for upsetting her so much. It was his fault she was here in this godforsaken place. If he had just come outside, waved her down, she would have accepted the tacit apology and gone back into the bungalow.

But he hadn't …

She felt a hot surge of fury. She put out her hand to reach for the ignition key, it shook quite badly. The engine ground for a while and it took several attempts before she was able to get it properly started. Carefully she reversed the car, riding the clutch to avoid having the wheels spin on the slippery clay. Then she edged the Datsun forward, away from the river. She followed the faint tracks in the grass, winding through the mopane bush.

She would just go a little bit further into the valley so as not to be obvious from the stream. Then she would stop and wait for Roger to come and fetch her. He would be sorry and, like always, he would apologise for having made her feel bad.

Michelle only managed another twenty metres when the wheels again lost traction. The Datsun slid sideways and stopped half in the scrub. Michelle tried revving the engine high and then riding the clutch, but the Datsun's rear wheels spun uselessly in the mud. She slipped the gear into reverse and tried again, this time she saw the mud from the wheels spatter past the driver's window as once again the wheels spun uselessly. She turned to look out of the rear window. The stream was no longer visible.

It was far enough. Roger would panic when he saw what had happened. And all as a result of his intransigence. Michelle settled down in the front seat to wait. Within a few minutes she became restless and bored. She began to wonder how much damage she had done to the vehicle.

She slid across the seat – her driver's door was jammed against the bush – opened the passenger door of the car and slid out, just to have a quick look. Despite the drizzle, she wanted to know what Roger would see when he found her.

*

Roger looked at his watch – just past 2 pm. Michelle had already been gone for over five hours. What if she was lost in the bush somewhere? He felt responsible. He had been unfair by not being honest from the beginning. He had behaved unforgivably and she had every right to be seriously upset.

He walked out on to the porch of the bungalow to gaze in frustration down the road. There was no sign of her. She should have returned by now. Would she really be pig-headed enough to go into that goddam valley? He had to do something. He would talk to the elderly black caretaker at N'wanetsi. What was his name again? They had talked that morning – yes, he remembered now – Samuel Gondo.

Roger hurried outside, ignoring the rain in his haste. He found the old man sitting under a thatch shelter. An equally elderly rifle leaned against an upright. He stared with empty soft brown eyes at the rain that came slanting down across the yard in small squalls.

"Good afternoon. What's the chance of finding something to drive here? Like a car or small truck, anything will do."

Gondo shrugged. "Maybe in morning, if boss comes. You talk him."

Roger hesitated, but when Gondo remained silent, he asked, "Can we can go look for my wife? I'm worried about her."

Gondo shook his head. "You not walk one-one. Only with ranger."

"We must be able to do something."

"Is no problem. She be back – half-past seven. Close gates – quarter-to-eight."

Roger returned to the bungalow. He stood looking out of the window at the shelter where Samuel sat, and beyond him, to where the road left the camp through the gate.

Surely there must be something he could do? What happens if she doesn't get back by half past seven?

*

Colonel Domingo squatted tiredly on his haunches at the side of the clearing. He scratched in the waterproof tin. Carefully he extracted one of the sweet-tasting, black, cheroot-like cigarettes so popular in Mozambique. An old campaigner, he knew how to enhance his more precious moments in the field. The battered Zippo lighter, which worked off petroleum distillates of all kinds – depending on what he could get hold of – had also been a faithful companion on many an expedition, first against the Portuguese and now Renamo. He puffed smoke into the air as he watched the young Lieutenant angling towards him across the clearing.

The Lieutenant was in the army for the right reasons. So many of the fighters, on both sides, were there for the killing, the rape, for what they could steal or because they were desperate for work which was otherwise unobtainable. Or, worst of all, because they had been press-ganged.

"They lost twenty men, Colonel. And one of them's a foreigner, a European."

"A mercenary?" Colonel looked up quickly. This would be a new trend, a dangerous trend, an escalation.

"No, he's a civilian. I'm sure of it."

The Colonel frowned. "Why should they have a European with them? And how many did we lose?"

"Two wounded, neither serious."

The Colonel nodded, studied the end of his cigarette, squinted up at the young officer. "And the tracks?" he asked softly. "What of the tracks?"

The young Lieutenant shuffled his feet in the dust, looking everywhere except at the Colonel. "We still haven't found which way they went, Colonel."

The Colonel wasn't surprised, but he saw no need to ease the Lieutenant's discomfort, it could only do him good, make him realise he still had much to learn. So he said nothing.

After standing there awkwardly in front of the Colonel for a while the Lieutenant shuffled his feet in the dust once again. "They were very thin. As though they've been hard pressed for a long time, with very little food to eat."

"The Butcher always leaves those behind," the Colonel said cryptically. "The ones who have nothing to lose make the best rearguard fighters." He shrugged. "It's well-known."

The Lieutenant frowned. "I don't understand, Colonel."

"You've enough time, and this war will go on for long enough." Abruptly he stood up. "We need to make plans. The Butcher is good. We must give the devil his due. But we must be better. This is the best chance we've ever had of catching him. We can't afford to let him slip through our fingers."

The Lieutenant nodded but said nothing.

The Colonel squinted at him. He was a good boy, who knew when to keep quiet and when to talk. A man could go far with that knowledge alone.

"We need to decide what to do." The Colonel squatted down on his haunches again. He picked up a nearby twig and began to scratch in the dust, drawing in the two sides of a valley, and then pulling in a line across it.

"This is the border," he said, pointing with the twig at the line he had drawn at right angles to the outline of the valley. "And we're here now, about ten kilometres east of the border. We know they couldn't have bypassed us. We'd have seen them. So there are two possibilities: firstly, they're heading for the border or they've managed to find an easy way out of this valley up and over the mountains."

He looked up at the Lieutenant. "Have our scouts reported in?"

"Yes," replied the Lieutenant. "They've found no sign of tracks going off to the sides."

"We have to pick up a spoor. I know the rain doesn't help. Have the men fan out, half to the north and half to the south. They're to work in the usual groups of four – two tracking, two keeping a lookout and changing places every fifteen minutes." He was silent for a while studying the scratches he had made in the dirt.

"They're heading west –"

The Lieutenant cut him off. "But that's straight over the border … er, sir." He sounded surprised.

"That's the Butcher – always the unexpected."

*

The sound of a car was loud in the black lion's ears. It lifted his pace. The excited revving provoked a corresponding excitement in him. The man-smell associated with that sound would be back and the man-smell meant easy food – he knew that now – even if it still caused the hairs around his neck and half way down his back to prickle with an inherited fear.

The young lion wound his way through the bush, cutting down the slope of the southern mountain, towards the river crossing. The sound stopped altogether. His pace slackened almost as though the sound itself had been reeling him in. He carried on downhill. It was the easier course. He still had to eat and the engine sounds still echoed in his ears.

He heard the sound of a slamming door, a skirt brushing against branches, a low voice cursing. He went low until his belly almost touched the ground, his right foreleg quivering under the strain. Slowly he crept forward. The sound was just ahead of him, not ten metres away – and now the scent reached him, too. The survival snake in his belly uncoiled, even his right foreleg dragged less as he silently moved forward, belly to the ground, low through the bush.

Feet dragging at clay made small sucking sounds. The young male stopped just this side of the last thin screen of mopane bush, blended into the shadows. Slowly he pushed his head forward. The flash of a skirt, like an otherwise stationary impala twitching its tail.

The car door opened, the flashing skirt disappeared into the vehicle. The door slammed shut with the crack of a rifle shot. The lion crouched down into the earth as though he wanted it to swallow him whole. He trembled slightly and a rumble grew in the back of his throat, swelled for a second and then died away again.

He would have no access to the vehicle. The man-smell had to be taken in the open. After a short while he half rose up again. Unblinking he stared at the vehicle, then lay down under the very last bush in line, settling down to wait, with his nose pointed at the vehicle like a bird dog pointing up its quarry.

Maybe he couldn't run. But he could still ambush a single human. Especially when his instincts told him it was the more vulnerable of the species – a female.

*

By 5 pm Roger was more than just a little worried. Michelle had now been gone for over seven hours. He had no alternative but to go out himself to bring her back. The hell of it was, she could be waiting just around the first corner. She had done it before and she would no doubt do it again.

Clearly Samuel Gondo wasn't going to let him leave the camp on foot, even just to have a quick peak around the first corner. During the course of the day Roger had tested those waters to no avail.

Roger returned to the window at the front of the
bungalow and peered out. Gondo still sat on his carved
wooden stool under the small thatched shelter, right next to
the gated entrance. He sat placidly, unmoving. It was as
frustrating as hell. Roger couldn't even take the simplest of
walks through the front gate down to the corner for a quick
look down the tar road. So there had to be another way.

The drizzle had virtually stopped now with just the
occasional drop falling from the solid ceiling of dark grey
clouds that covered the sky. Although sunset was only due
at 7.45 pm the cloud cover made it seem darker and later
than it really was. The gloomy weather did nothing to
improve Roger's mood.

Roger made his way through the bungalow to the
bathroom, peered through the small window. The glass in
the rectangular frame was opaque and the window itself
was hinged at the top. He pushed the bottom outwards and
peered through the gap. There was a small gate in the
sturdy wire fence surrounding the camp. It probably led to
where Gondo and his family lived.

A woman, presumably Gondo's wife, with a small child
held against her back by a wrapped-around blanket, walked
along the far side of the fence, a bucket balanced on her
head as naturally as a top hat worn by a trouper. In her arms
she carried a few sticks of firewood. There was no going
out that way. He was bound to be seen. There would be no
second chance.

Roger walked back through the bungalow and out on to
the porch. He unobtrusively studied the grounds while
lounging on a comfortable folding chair with wooden arms
and a canvas seat. Birds sat and sang in a few trees on the
south side of the grounds. Michelle had driven off in that
direction so Roger wanted to go that way, too.

First he had to give Gondo something to think about
while he was away. It was essential that he allay any
suspicions before they arose. Roger wandered out of the
bungalow and loitered under the trees in front. A mighty

and ostentatious yawn overtook him, he stretched, gave Gondo a cheery wave of the hand, and disappeared back into the bungalow.

Roger allowed an impatient ten minutes to go by. Opening the back door only a crack he peered through the doorway. He could see no one. As unobtrusively as possible he slipped out of the back door of the bungalow and made his way quietly across the open ground, around the shed and over towards the fence on the southern side of the camp.

It was made of five strands of heavy-duty barbed-wire. It was the work of a moment for him to climb over near one of the uprights. Immediately he crouched down lower than the fence so that if anyone were to look in that direction he would not be easily seen, but the precaution was unnecessary. That side of the camp remained as deserted and as quiet as a country graveyard.

Was he doing the right thing?

But he had been unfair to Michelle. The least he could do was play her game and get her to come back. Although this would be the last time. After this – no more. Michelle would have to accept their marriage was over. He had lived too many lies – of which most had been to himself – for far too long.

Quickly he left the fence and, bent double at the waist, awkwardly jogged through the thin scrub surrounding the camp, wanting to get through to the first line of trees proper, albeit sparse even there, so he wouldn't easily be seen from N'wanetsi. After a few minutes he stopped, again crouching down on his haunches so as not to be too obvious to any casual observer.

He glanced back.

The camp was all but obscured by the scattered trees. No one followed. Quickly he ran through the trees at ninety degrees to his original direction of travel. He wanted to cut across to the main tar road. With a little bit of luck Michelle would have parked the car just around the first corner. They would be safely back at in the camp within ten minutes. Eventually he reached the tar road. He checked right and left. No traffic in sight. He stepped out into the road and looked in a northerly direction, to where the entrance to N'wanetsi fronted on the tar road about two hundred metres back. No car.

"Damn that bloody woman," he cursed aloud.

The drone of a car engine intruded on the quiet. Michelle or someone else? He quickly ducked back into the acacia trees beyond the verge. Crouching behind a slightly denser clump of bushes he saw a car, with what looked like a family of four inside, go slowly cruising by. After it was out of sight Roger walked back out on to the tar road and this time looked to the south. The road was empty. However, only a few hundred yards down the road it curved away to the east and disappeared behind trees.

Michelle could be just around the next corner. It was worth a quick look.

To avoid the embarrassment of being stopped by a passing Park employee, he stayed in the bush just out of sight of the tar road. He wouldn't get lost as long as he travelled parallel to the road. Doing it that way would make it possible for him to see if Michelle was there – without actually being seen himself by anyone else using the road. Once found she could give him a ride back to camp.

As he trudged along through the scattered acacia trees, it occurred to him Gondo would be absolutely astonished if Roger came back into the camp as a passenger in the car with Michelle. For a moment he rather hoped that Gondo would diligently stay at his post until they returned. But he knew he wouldn't let the old man see him. He would duck below the dashboard. The caretaker of N'wanetsi would never know Roger had been out.

"Michelle's probably sitting around the very next corner," he muttered to himself, as he jumped over an old dried-out tree trunk that lay across his path. He was convinced he wouldn't have far to go to find her.

*

By 6 pm Michelle was in a curious state composed of equal portions of terminal boredom, spluttering fury and unimaginable terror. When she at last calmed down from her initial anger it hadn't taken long for her to remember Roger had no transport available at N'wanetsi. If the Datsun hadn't been stuck in the mud she would have immediately returned to camp as though she had merely gone for a drive. Instead she had been sitting there for most of the day without a telephone to use or a shop to visit. She was convinced she was close to dying from boredom – literally. On the other hand, even an unfeeling callous idiot like Roger should have organised something by now. That he hadn't turned up to ask her to come back was further proof he was deliberately trying to get at her.

And – hardly wanting to think about it – she had earlier heard the most scary rumble emerge from a bush but a few metres away. The sound was so deep and powerful she had felt it as a vibration as much as heard it. She had immediately closed the windows and it was now stifling in the car. Oddly enough it was the exhaustion caused by fear of the sound she had heard that finally had her fall asleep curled up on the front seat.

She woke up from a fairly pleasant dream to a real life nightmare. Jabbering voices brought her to the edge of wakefulness, dreaming of being rescued by a handsome and daring helicopter pilot. The further rough intrusion of those same voices woke her up properly. Three dark faces leered at her through the car windows.

She sat up, knew immediately this was no rescue party.

All of the Park people she had seen had either been neatly dressed in khaki uniforms with green epaulettes on their shirts or wore green overalls. These three were dressed in dirty and torn khakis. Over their shoulders were slung some sort of rifle, but in such a way which, even she could tell, meant they would always be ready to hand. The rifles were stubby. The curved magazines sticking out below looked like flat, squared off metal bananas.

The eyes of the three men were an obscene red-streaked yellow-brown and they looked at her with half-lowered eyelids. One, who appeared to be the leader of the small group, had an old blood-stained cloth wound around his forehead. The other two wore dirty camouflage caps pushed back on their heads in a way that no organised military would have accepted.

Michelle waved her hands at them, showing they should go away. This afforded them great merriment. While they guffawed loudly Michelle quickly took the opportunity to lock the doors. The one with the headband – the one she thought of as the leader – took one pace back from the car, lifted his rifle and calmly smashed the butt through the side window, showering her with shattered glass. Michelle cowered away to the driver's side of the car. The leader put his hand through the broken window and pulled up the locking lever on the door, opened the door itself, leaned into the vehicle, grabbed her by the arm and summarily pulled her out.

"What do you want with me?" she asked tremulously, on the verge of tears.

The leader said something to her. She didn't understand the language, stared at him blankly. He studied her from top to bottom and said something to his companions in the same language. They all laughed. The younger one of the other two – probably no more than fifteen or sixteen – must have taken what was said as an invitation because he nodded eagerly, stepped forward, and with his free hand grabbed her painfully by the breast. When she tried to pull away he dropped his rifle and shoved his other hand up her skirt.

The leader banged the youngster on the side of his head with the butt of his rifle and he went down onto his knees like a half stunned ox. This really amused the third one – who wasn't much older than the youngster – and he capered around like a buffoon, hopping up and down first on one leg and then the other, guffawing loudly all the while.

The leader shouted something and the other two immediately joined him. He pushed Michelle in the small of her back, used his rifle to show her the path he wanted her to follow.

By now Michelle was crying. When she raised a hand to wipe her face, it shook uncontrollably. She tried to muster some dignity but with little success.

"What do you want with me?"

The leader again spoke in the strange language. The other two laughed but much more soberly. This time the leader's gesture for her to follow the path through the bush was more abrupt. Scared of offending the man she started to walk.

They walked through the bush for at least an hour, angling uphill all the while. When the sun was well down on the horizon they approached an encampment. There must have been twenty or thirty men lying around, all of whom seemed to be dressed more or less like her original captors, although some were a lot more ragged.

She was very close to being totally unnerved by the way all talking stopped as she and the leader worked their way through the camp. Those who were lying down sat up, those few bending over fires stood up straight and one or two even appeared out of the bush to stand and stare. Someone said something in the strange language and to a man they all burst out laughing.

It was an ugly sound.

On the far side of a fire, which burned in the centre of the camp, two men sat on a large rock. She was taken to them. The one spoke to her but used a language different to the others. This time – although it was equally unintelligible – she at least recognised it as being Portuguese.

"I only speak English," she said, trying to sound defiant. "And these men have no call pulling me around like piece of garbage."

The man who had spoken had a very lean face, gaunt even, with the cheek-bones sticking far out, stretching the skin across his face so that it looked as though it would soon tear and let the bones through. He spoke to the man next to him in the strange language, and laughed. The man next to him said nothing and didn't laugh. He was a bit older, not nearly as thin as the other man, with an altogether more pleasant mien.

She looked at this other man. "Can you help me? Do you speak English?"

He nodded gravely. "We both do."

She was astonished. His English was almost flawless with at most the hint of a Portuguese accent in the background. He sounded like an extremely cultured European of Mediterranean stock who spent a lot of time mixing with the very best people in London.

"Who are you people? What do you want with me?" she asked, not sure to whom she should direct her questions, but emboldened by being able to converse in a language she understood. "Are you poachers?"

"Only of souls." The gaunt-faced man stared at her. "Mens' souls. Now rejoiceth not in iniquity, but rejoiceth in truth. Who are you?"

For a moment Michelle stared at him and all pretence at defiance collapsed. She quickly told them she was just a tourist who – she said – had taken a wrong turning and got lost. She was sure her husband or a ranger would be organising a search party for her soon.

*

Joshua turned to Abel. "She's right. We don't have much time." He looked back at her. "You may call me Joshua and this is Abel. What do we call you?" he asked courteously.

"Michelle," she replied and, because he seemed to be the most sympathetic of the bunch, quickly asked, "Can't you let me go? I won't tell anyone you're here."

Abel sneered. "But the evil which I would not, that I do."

Joshua stood up. "You'd better come with me while we decide what's going to happen." He looked at Abel. "We can't go back now. Frelimo will be waiting."

"You, too, brother, rejoiceth in the truth," said Abel, seeming not to care one way or the other. "My men say this valley isn't set up for tourists. Only a ranger's going to find us. There are no villagers to report our presence. We've probably got a few days before we're discovered. The wicked flee when no man pursueth: but the righteous are bold as a lion. I say we rest until we're certain Frelimo has gone. Then we go back. Ye have heard of the patience of Job." The Butcher paused, "we'll decide what to do with the woman later," and he smiled.

It was not very pleasant.

*

The injured black lion had become aware of humans approaching. It meant his hunt would be disturbed. And he was hunting, albeit passively. He had spent most of his day focused on the car down by the river crossing. The man-smell inside represented easy food and all he needed was patience. Also, having used some of his dwindling resources to go down there to seek the easy food, the lion didn't now have the spare capacity to look for other food, which might or might not be available to him.

But the approaching humans constituted a problem. There were too many. His fear of humans overpowered his need for food. But they drove him off a potential kill. The rumble started down in his belly, built up into a throaty growl and died down again. The female in the car was his.

He stayed crouched behind a thick screen of scrub. The humans passed him by and stopped at the car. After a short while they all left again, filing along the game trail, past the scrub, behind which he pressed his belly to the ground. He crouched right down as the sounds came near. His stomach rumbled as the appetising smells of old blood came drifting across. His yellow eyes – startling against the black of his coat, despite being bloodshot – blinked in response.

His nostrils twitched and his tail flicked from side to side in sympathy with the rumble deep in his belly. Again his nostrils twitched. The cold eyes stared unblinkingly at the bush between them. Slowly the black lion rose to his feet and limped forward, holding his head down lower than his shoulders as he sought the scent. His mane, as dark as the rest of him and not yet properly grown, a black ruff around his neck, stirred in the light wind drifting through the trees.

Like a black ghost he suddenly appeared on the game trail. Slowly he limped along the faint path, moving at the same speed as the group of four he followed. The sound of the humans' progress drifted back to him, but it was the scent of the female human that pulled him along behind them.

*

The quick flat-edged chopping of three rotor blades and the contrapuntal high-pitched scream of the gas turbine – jet – engine – pushing out 570 horsepower – bounced off nearby rocky hillocks as the Alouette bucketed along ten foot above the trees. Without conscious thought Paul used small pressures on the cyclic, which he held lightly in his gloved right hand, to jink the helicopter left or right around the odd tall tree that stood higher than the rest – usually a marula or white seringa but occasionally a sneezewood or Cape ash.

"What's ETA at Skukuza?" asked Lieutenant Luke Smith over the intercom.

Paul's eyes flicked to the clock in the panel. "Zero two."

"Hmmm, two minutes past seven," muttered the Lieutenant. "Not bad. Early start tomorrow?"

"Before sunrise," came the curt reply.

There was a few moments of silence.

"You aren't singing," stated Marty Martins at length over the intercom.

Paul gave the flight engineer on his left a quick grin. "You're right," he announced over the intercom. "Gentlemen, I owe you all an apology. I haven't been my usual self today."

"Good God," Marty cut in hurriedly. "That doesn't mean you must start now. I was actually thinking about how lucky our guests were. When we're brushing tree tops our noble pilot thinks he's Pavarotti." He added moodily, "It's awful."

Paul smiled around his mic, mind elsewhere. The truth was he had never met anyone like the mystery woman before. And she had already managed to disappear from Skukuza before they had even taken off that morning.

Who was she? Where was she? Would he see her again?

*

Joshua sat in a cave entrance on a small rock, with Michelle deeper in behind him. The Butcher stood in front of Joshua staring down at him. The rest of Abel's fighters were scattered further down the hillside, most of them sleeping where they lay.

Joshua leaned forward, spoke in Shangaan. "Abel, why don't we trade this woman for money and a free pass to another country? Mugabe might help. Maybe even much further up north – what about Gaddafi? She's an English tourist, they wouldn't want any harm to come to her. I've a bad feeling about all of this. The talks between our people and Frelimo are starting to get somewhere. We should grab this chance. When the country's more settled we can return. Part of the deal will be an amnesty for all fighters. I'm sure of it."

Joshua glanced back into the cave. Michelle was sleeping now. She lay in the dirt with her head on a pillow Joshua had made for her by rolling up his jacket.

The Butcher shook his head, responded in English. "But when the Crier cried, 'O Yes!' the people cried, 'O No!'"

"Why not?"

"To every thing there is a season, and a time to every purpose under the heaven: A time to be born, and a time to die."

Joshua's eyes went very wide and instantly many things were explained for him. He was silent for a while.

"Aaah! Aids," he said at last. "I'm sorry."

Abel snorted. "Why should you be sorry? You never liked me anyway." He smiled again. "Let us eat and drink; for tomorrow we die." He limped off, angling down the hillside.

Joshua leaned against the wall of the cave and dozed off. Only to be awakened by a scream. He was on his belly and rolling away to the far wall of the cave with his AK47 ready before he was properly awake. The men scattered around the fire laughed among themselves. Joshua frowned. He looked at his watch – 7.10 pm. He looked around and his eye fell on the man who had found Michelle. Joshua didn't know his name. He beckoned the man over to the cave.

"What the hell's happening?"

The fighter with the bloodstained headband grinned. "General Gamellah is making a bride of the one he calls china doll."

Joshua sucked in his cheeks.

The fighter still grinned. "After that it is our turn."

As he turned to leave he nodded to the inert figure of Michelle. "And then it is her turn."

*

Roger stayed well back from the tar road. He wanted to do what he had to do, but he didn't want anyone else knowing about it. He had to get Michelle back without a fuss. He had caused her enough agony and there was nothing he could do about that or about their marriage being over, but he could at least save her this last embarrassment.

After twenty minutes of walking he crossed over to the eastern side of the tar road. She had said she was going to go into Hawke's valley. If he had to trek all the way to the small track to find her, he would, but he also didn't want to miss it. Not that he really thought she would have gone that far.

Each time a car came past he had to step closer to the tar road. Any one of them could be Michelle on her way back to N'wanetsi. It never was. But he kept hoping – either she had come back or she would be parked around the very next corner.

Roger hadn't realised how fast he had walked until he came across the track that led to Hawke's valley. He looked at his watch. He had covered about seven kilometres in an hour.

He checked the track. He didn't for one moment fool himself into thinking he was able to track a vehicle along a dirt road, but he was equally sure that when they had stopped there earlier in the day the sandy track had been smoothed by the rain. Now the mud carried deep scars. He knelt down to get a closer look. Tyres had squelched down into the muddy ground. It had to have been Michelle.

Roger's heart thudded in his chest. He had already gone much further on foot than he had ever intended. It was a ridiculous situation. He was half tempted to abandon Michelle to her fate.

"Hell," he muttered aloud. "At least she's in a car."

He had felt increasingly vulnerable as he walked through the bush, but had drawn at least a measure of comfort from the nearby tar road. If he followed the track he would be leaving that behind – and it was getting dark. He stayed there squatting on his heels, suddenly aware of the soft rain drifting down the back of his neck. Indeed his upper body was soaked. He dragged his arm across his forehead.

What to do?

It was a long way back on foot. If he found her it would mean a lift. And he would have dug her out without anyone else knowing. How far could she be? Just a few more minutes. He would follow the tracks for a short way. She was probably just around the next corner.

*

It was quite dark in the cave when Michelle woke up. Joshua sat near her in the entrance. She immediately felt comforted.

"Joshua, I had an awful dream. People were being tortured. They screamed a lot."

"Did you see the very big tree on the other side of the clearing?"

"Tree?"

"It's a baobab."

"Okay ..."

"My people call it the 'upside down' tree," he said. "They get *very* big. The largest recorded one is on Mount Kilimanjaro with a girth of more than 90 feet. I've even heard of one with a girth of 120 feet."

"But what was the screaming about?"

"They reckon the tree lives between 1,500 and 4,000 years."

She remembered the baobab now, Roger had mentioned the name. There had been none around Skukuza. The first to be seen was halfway to N'wanetsi. They had massive, squat trunks topped by heavy, mostly bare branches which appeared spindly in relation to the thick stem.

"Many old ones are hollow," he said. "David Livingstone saw one 'in which twenty or thirty men could lie down and sleep as in a hut'. These hollow trees can hold a lot of water. But the baobab's use to people does not end with its ability to store water."

"Joshua, the scream –"

"A baobab in Katima Mulilo has a flushing toilet, while in Zimbabwe one is used as a bus shelter for up to 40 people. A hollow one in Kasane was used as a temporary prison. And near the old gold-mining town of Leydsdorp a baobab with a hollow trunk was converted into a bar during the gold-rush –"

"And all of this," she interrupted firmly, "is, I assume, to take my mind off the situation I'm in?"

Joshua smiled at her. "It's not going to be easy pulling the wool over your eyes."

Michelle hesitated. "If you don't mind me saying so – you seem different to the others."

Joshua laughed. "I don't mind you saying so. I wish more people shared your view."

"Why then," she jerked a thumb in the direction of the rest of the band, "are you with them?"

Joshua told her how a hardline authoritarian socialist one-party system had methodically destroyed his country. "But it's not unique," he finished. "Every independence disaster in Africa can be laid at the door of the same economic policies. For some reason my fellow Africans never seem to learn. But tell me why you were wandering around alone so far off the beaten track?"

"You didn't believe my story?"

"Even game reserve roads are better signposted than that."

"And the other man, Abel. Didn't he believe it either?"

Joshua shook his head.

"Knowing you better now I can understand why you didn't say anything. But why didn't he say something?"

"He doesn't care anymore." Joshua paused. "You still haven't answered my question."

"I … I was betrayed by my husband with another woman. I was angry and deliberately went off the main road."

"I think we were betrayed, too. That's the only way Frelimo could have known where we were headed. It was either by a man called Hawke or a Frelimo politician called Dos Santos, who was supposed to be helping us – for a price, of course."

"What do you mean – by a man called Hawke?"

"Basil Hawke in London. He's the merchant we've been getting most of our arms from recently."

"I don't believe you!" Michelle almost shouted. "I don't know how it's possible, but Roger put you up to this."

"You know this man Hawke?"

She nodded, suddenly realised her danger if what he had just said about her father was true. "I've heard the name. I don't know if it's the same person."

"Would you recognise an employee of his?"

She shrugged. "I suppose so."

"Come and take a look."

Michelle followed Joshua down towards the fire, then stopped short. A naked Karl Hoeniger sat close to the fire hugging his knees – too close. Despite his proximity to the flames he was shaking and quivering as though suffering from St Vitus Dance. His face was red and puffy in the firelight. His eyes were hollow and deep and dark and stared at nothing as he shivered close to the heat. Michelle backed off quickly although she had a feeling he was no longer capable of recognising anyone.

Back in the relative safety of the cave she turned to Joshua. "What happened to him?"

Joshua shrugged uncomfortably. "I have to speak to some of the men. I have a plan to help you. Stay here. Don't go out. I'll be back soon."

Michelle nodded, frightened at the idea of being left alone. Later she noticed that Joshua was slowly moving amongst the fighters, talking to one and then to another.

Sitting in the cave entrance, watching him circulate, Michelle thought about her father. It all fitted. She couldn't go back, not to England. Not now.

She suddenly regretted not knowing Paul, the helicopter pilot, better. It was the first time she had ever let herself go like that. She felt her cheeks grow warm at the memory. But she also knew it couldn't work. A person like Paul could never need her in the way, she realised now, she had to be needed, to be secure in a relationship.

At least she understood that much about herself – and wondered if the self-knowledge had come too late.

*

The injured black lion lay downwind of the Renamo fighters who clustered around the entrance to his old cave. He had followed the group from the river crossing. But the man-smell was very strong, there were too many of them, and it scared him, so he laboriously climbed higher. Slowly the lion limped up the slope of the mountain until he reached a crevice, which opened up lower down to become the cave.

Here he lay down to await developments. He had all the time in the world. He wasn't going anywhere. But he wouldn't be deprived of his prey. The female human was still amongst the group – and she was still his.

*

Roger Denton followed the track, jogging now, worried about the gathering dusk. Eventually he came to a river. It was still light enough for him to see a car's wheels had spun and churned up the mud on the far bank.

"Fuck it!" Roger cursed aloud. "Just how stupid has the bloody woman been?"

He looked at his watch – 7.20 pm. The gates to N'wanetsi would close in another 25 minutes. They could just make it back by car if they left soon. But he would have to find Michelle first. He raised his arms and looked down at himself. His upper half was already soaked through from the rain.

"The stream can't be that deep," he muttered to himself, "otherwise the car wouldn't have got through."

Gingerly he put one foot into the water and tested the bottom. It felt sandy and seemed solid enough. He took another step forward. Now the water swirled around his ankles. He tentatively tried another step. The footing was still firm. He studied the water as it swirled past, brown and sullen and swollen from the rains that had fallen throughout the stream's catchment area.

He looked back. His footprint on the bank filled with water. The level visibly rose before his eyes. He really didn't have much time. How deep was it? Soon they might not be able to get the car back across. He tried to recall the map of the area. Were there any other exit roads from the valley? He didn't think so.

With Michelle the other side – did he have a choice?

Without further ado he started to wade across the stream,
holding his arms out sideways to help keep his balance.
Halfway across and the water swirled around his waist.
Roger hesitated. He took another step and it must have been
into a hole in the river bed. He instantly lost his footing,
was immediately swept off his feet by the rushing water.

Roger was a strong swimmer. He launched himself
horizontally, swimming hard. The rushing water swept him
sideways but with a few hard strokes he reached the far
bank.

He grabbed the trailing root of a small shrub on the side
of the stream and it tore loose from the soil. Roger was
swept another five metres downstream before he managed
to stop himself. This time by grabbing a trailing branch of a
lot more substance. He used that to haul himself out of the
water.

After shaking himself like a wet dog, Roger set off along
the river bank, heading upstream. He couldn't take a chance
by cutting across the bush at an angle, because he might
miss Michelle altogether. He had to go back upstream to
find the place where the car had emerged.

Roger Denton was a worried man.

Clambering along the river-bank wasn't easy. In a
usually parched subcontinent the thickest growth is
reserved for the few metres on either side of streams and
rivers. Roger pushed his way through the heavy
undergrowth, loathe to go far from the rushing stream
which, like the tar road earlier, provided him with a degree
of comfort in the fast-gathering gloom.

By the time he reached the ford where the car had gone
through, Roger had a terrible shock. Unlike Europe, there
had been no twilight. One moment the sun had been on the
horizon – and if asked he would have anticipated at least
another hour or two of light. Instead the next time he
looked around it was dark. He was committed for the night.

Roger stood by the track and listened, vulnerable.

The night sounds of the African bush drew in on him. He felt very alone out there. He decided to stop where he was, to hide himself in a thorn bush for the night. He found a suitable clump of bushes close to the river crossing. With some difficulty he forced the branches apart and wormed his way in. He didn't feel very much more secure. As he settled down in the thorn bush he shivered. He was soaked through.

A long, cold and scary night lay ahead of him – if he survived it.

*

Jakes smiled at Major Anderson. He had never done so much smiling in all his life. He felt like a politician. He had to do everything he could to make them trust him.

The Major returned the smile. "We really appreciate your help. Usually we're operating blind. Sometimes we go into areas which seem likely to us but – as we'd discover after many days – which turn out to be impossible for the opposition to get to from their side. We'd have spent ages chasing shadows." He laughed.

Jakes smiled again, before turning back to the map on the wall. "Tomorrow you'd better look at this section of fence here," he jabbed with a rigid forefinger, "and all along here." He turned to Paul who had just entered the office carrying an opened can of beer. "How much fence can you do in a day?"

The helicopter pilot shrugged. "It depends on how often the recces want to stop off and whether we wait for them or continue and come back later to pick them up. With refuelling stops and an eight-hour flying day – twenty clicks, maybe twenty-five."

"Clicks?" queried Brian Lombard, having just appeared in the doorway.

"Kilometres," replied Paul.

Jakes was surprised. "That's not much."

"We have two problems," Paul replied. "Firstly, we have ferry time from Skukuza to the border. Secondly, we're basically looking for holes in the fence. They may be small and they may have been closed up after use. We go slowly to try and spot 'em."

"We can easily cover our section in ten days," said Major Anderson. "Perhaps we shouldn't be skipping parts."

Jakes pursed his lips, eyes narrowed. "It's entirely up to you. But if there's no possibility of anyone getting through it does seem a waste of time. They could be coming across somewhere else while you're checking unlikely sections."

Major Anderson nodded. "You're right. And you know the terrain. It just makes a man nervous knowing there's unchecked fence out there."

Jakes nodded again. "I understand. But remember I don't want these people coming across any more than you do. Tomorrow I'd suggest you patrol this area." He ran a finger along the clearly demarcated border. He looked at Paul. "There's a couple of prominent landmarks you can use."

Paul nodded. He pulled a much folded aeronautical chart out of a pocket in his overalls. "I'll make a few notes."

Brian frowned, hesitated, started to say something and then didn't. But he wasn't happy: Jakes was keeping the military well away from the lion valley.

He saw Jakes looking at him over the shoulder of the pilot, his eyes and face calm. Damn it. Jakes was deliberately taking advantage of how he felt about his surrogate father.

Tight-lipped Brian nodded to the others. "If I'm not needed here I'll get going."

No one replied, so after a few moments Brian nodded again and left the room.

*

Roger woke up long before sunrise on the Wednesday morning. Actually it wasn't so much a waking up as a deciding to get out of the thorn bush. He had probably dozed off but felt as though he hadn't slept all night. There had been moments. The sounds of animals prowling in the dark. His neck was stiff, he had a bad taste in his mouth and he felt dirty – but alive. And he was cold – really, really cold. He had to keep moving.

He worked his way out of the thorn bushes. It was more painful getting out than it had been getting in. Fear is a wonderful anaesthetic. He went down to the river's edge. Despite the colour of the water, he splashed a few handfuls over his face. During the night his clothes had dried out leaving them corrugated with brown stains.

Feeling only mildly refreshed from his abbreviated ablutions he started to follow the tyre marks left in the mud. Much to his chagrin he discovered the car less than twenty metres from where he had spent the night. If only he had known. It would have been pure, unadulterated luxury. Company would have been welcome, too. He drew closer to the vehicle, started to run. It was empty, and the passenger window had been smashed in.

"Oh Jesus Christ!" he groaned aloud.

Roger scouted around as best he could. A bunch of people had come up to the car. They had found Michelle there. There seemed to be a much smaller shape in amongst the other, larger, footprints. Michelle had gone off with these other people. His heart lifted. She had been found. Which also meant there was a different way into and out of the valley. He was relieved it was all over. Suddenly the embarrassment of having the whole affair become public knowledge was a small price to pay, to know that everything was going to be all right.

He tried reversing the vehicle but the wheels were deep in the mud. He would need help to move it. He started following the footprints in the mud. His spirits were high. The car could be sorted out later. He hoped Michelle and her rescuers were not too far ahead. He no longer wanted to be wandering around the bush on his own. And he was utterly beat. He needed a long hot soak and twenty-fours sleep in a decent bed.

"Make that a week," he said aloud and grinned. He was feeling better already.

With a new lift in his step, Roger followed the footprints deeper into the valley.

*

Samuel Gondo woke up on the Wednesday morning at his usual hour – just after 6 am. He stared at the ceiling for a short while. He turned to look at the large blue alarm clock next to his bed. It was usually correct to about fifteen minutes and the alarm no longer worked but it was all he needed.

He was happy at N'wanetsi.

His two wives also worked there and they cultivated – unbeknown to the area ranger – a small vegetable patch just off a river bed nearby. His two older sons had gone to live in Soweto, the large dormitory township on the outskirts of Johannesburg. He wasn't sure what they did there, but they seemed to be all right. When he did see them, which was not too often these days, they always talked as though they were making money. Not that they sent him any of it, as was the custom when he was young.

His youngest, also a boy, was still at the school which the park provided for the offspring of their employees. He knew three sons wouldn't seem much to the rest of his family still living in Mozambique, but he was content. And the number of children he had was right – or so he understood from his younger wife, who attended the family planning clinics arranged by management. There wasn't much more he expected from life or wanted.

Samuel rolled out of bed and yawned widely.

He would take a stroll around the camp. The sunrise was a smear of red and yellow through the trees. There was no reason to doubt all was as it should be, indeed as it had been for over twenty years now.

The discovery – ten minutes later – that a tourist was missing, came as such a shock that it actually stopped him breathing for a half-a-minute or so. It took a while for him to recover.

As was his custom at 6.30 in the morning he had gone along to Mr Denton's bungalow to see if any firewood was required for that day. Most of the guests preferred to cook over wood coals rather than in the kitchen. It was part of the atmosphere of being in the African bush. When he received no reply to his energetic knocking his worst fears were confirmed. He had lost a tourist. He knew Mrs Denton hadn't returned the previous evening, but assumed she had stayed over at one of the other camps.

It was impossible for Mr Denton not to be at N'wanetsi – he had no transport.

In thirty years in the park, with twenty of those in charge of the N'wanetsi camp, Samuel had never before had such a problem. And he had thought he had seen it all.

Samuel hadn't run anywhere for a very long time, indeed hadn't moved at more than a crippled snail's pace for over a decade, so the jog he broke into as he cast around for signs of what had happened to the tourist provoked another fit of coughing, interwoven with a great deal of heavy breathing.

It didn't take long to confirm that his missing tourist was nowhere to be found within the confines of the camp. Samuel extended his search and eventually found where Roger had climbed the fence, although the rain had washed out a lot of the spoor.

Samuel had been raised in rural Mozambique, and except for a few years at a Roman Catholic mission school, had spent all his years in the bush. He could follow a track as though it was a white no-overtaking line painted along the centre of a highway. As quickly as his bulk would allow he followed the tracks left by Roger. He found where he had crossed over the tar road to the east side.

The footprints headed south.

Samuel found where Roger had turned off the road altogether and followed the path leading down to the river. Here tracking was even easier and he could read the tracks as easily as a university student could read from a textbook. Half way to the river he had to stop, his chest heaving with the strain of walking further than he had had to walk in many a long year.

Samuel arrived at the river crossing.

Roger's wife had not spent the night at one of the other camps. He hadn't only lost one tourist but two. The river was up and rising. He wouldn't be able to cross. He wasn't even going to try. He couldn't swim. He turned back to N'wanetsi. He would have to work out what to do next. He could radio through immediately to tell the area ranger, Brian Lombard, what had happened. But these were the first tourists he had lost. And it was guaranteed to get him into more trouble than he had ever had before.

But wasn't he the only one who knew the obviously mad tourists were missing? What if they were already on their way back? Perhaps he should wait. This would give the Dentons time to get back to N'wanetsi. Then they could all pretend nothing had happened. If the mad tourists didn't return, he could then say that it had only just happened and he would be in no more trouble than if he had reported it straight away.

By the time he had formulated his plan, Samuel was back at N'wanetsi.

When they returned he would extract payment for his worries by giving them a lecture on irresponsibility they wouldn't forget for the rest of their lives. After that he would very generously tell them he wouldn't report the infringement to his superiors.

Settling down on his carved chair, worn shiny over the years by the seat of his trousers, it occurred to him that he may even get a bigger tip than normal, as a result of his generosity.

*

Joshua felt Michelle's eyes on him. He knew she had been awake for a while, but his thoughts had him feeling old this morning and he really didn't want to talk. He kept his gaze on the scene before him. Abel's fighters were still rolled up

in their blankets like so many dead logs scattered around
the previous night's burnt-out fire.

"What were you trying to do last night?" she asked at
last.

"What do you mean?"

"You spent hours drifting around from one man to
another. And you were the one doing all the talking."

"I'm trying to get between Abel and his men."

Michelle shifted nervously from one buttock to the other
and back again. "Is that wise? Won't that just make him
mad?"

Joshua shrugged. He had already discounted that. He
didn't want to explain that any *extra* trouble for her could
hardly make matters worse.

"I'm trying to convince them a better future awaits in the
new Mozambique. I'm saying we should trade you for cash
and a free passage to Europe and then we all go back to
Mozambique when it's safe."

"Will it work?" Michelle sounded dubious.

"We can't just give up, can we? We have to try
something."

He looked across the camp. The Butcher was growing
bored with Karl Hoeniger. Soon the blonde Swiss would be
handed over to his men. He glanced at Michelle for the first
time that morning and away again.

*

Colonel Domingo stared at the ripped border fence. It had
been blown wide open. Three men could pass through
walking shoulder to shoulder. So the Butcher had done it
again. He turned to the tracker who had first directed their
attention to the hole.

"When did they go through?"

"Yesterday morning."

The Colonel nodded thoughtfully. "Thirty six hours ago.
Damn it! This time I thought I had him. I've been trying for
such a long time. It seems as though there's a cosmic plan
to protect him from me."

The young Lieutenant drew patterns in the dirt with the toe of a combat boot. He looked up at his commanding officer, frowned.

"This isn't a ploy, sir? To throw us off the scent."

The Colonel's expression was as sour as though he was having to suck on the bitterest of lemons. "The trackers say they all went through. The scouts have been out and back along the fence to see if they came back in. And they haven't. No, he's done it again."

The Lieutenant hesitated. "You said something ... about getting him ... it seemed personal ... the way you talked ..." his voice petered out.

The Colonel paused, shrugged. "You may as well know. You know how the Butcher got his name?"

"Yessir. He killed people in the streets of Beira – shot children, old people and even a pregnant woman. He gutted her with a machete before she died."

The Colonel's face aged as he stared off at something only he could see. "The pregnant woman was my wife. She was carrying our first child."

The Lieutenant stared at him for a while. He felt physically ill.

"Colonel," he said at length. "I'd like your unofficial permission to take some of the men and to follow the Butcher across the border. I'll get him for you, sir. If anything goes wrong I'll take the blame."

The Colonel's eyes went wide, then narrowed. It was a tempting idea. He shook his head as though to clear it of such thoughts. It wasn't worth it. It would be the end of the Lieutenant's army career. In a way he was the boy the Colonel had hoped his wife would one day have. It would also do his country more harm than good.

He looked at the Lieutenant, a hint of pride glinted in his eyes. "I thank you for the offer, Lieutenant," he said formally. "But we're professional soldiers, you and I. We fight for our country, not for ourselves." He was silent for a while.

"Send a message to Maputo that the Butcher has crossed the border," he said at last. "We recommend they advise the South Africans accordingly. We'll set up a blockade across the valley, just inside the border fence. If the Butcher tries to come back we'll be here."

The Lieutenant snapped to attention. He saluted crisply, as if on a parade ground, with much more formality than they normally used in the bush.

"It will be done at once, Colonel."

*

"What?" shouted Brian Lombard, not believing he had heard Samuel properly, but the radio reception was good enough to know what he had heard. He didn't want it to be true. It couldn't be true. "Are you absolutely sure?"

"Yessir," Samuel replied, his voice muffled by the radio waves.

"Samuel," he forced his voice to be calm. "When did you discover this?"

There was a long hesitation.

Samuel sighed. "This morning," he replied eventually, then added, more firmly, committed to telling the truth now. "Yes, it was this morning."

"Why didn't you radio me at once?"

Again there was a very long silence.

Eventually Samuel responded. "I was hoping they'd come back."

"And you don't know where they are?"

Again the long hesitation.

"They went off the road south of here," Samuel said, and then added, "And then headed east ... and crossed a river which is very full ... perhaps they can't get back."

"And how do you know this?"

"Well," Samuel muttered over the air. "I ... followed their tracks ..."

"Samuel, if you don't tell me everything right now you're dead. I will personally come there and kill you. Do you hear me?"

Quickly then, as though to rid himself of a burden he had been carrying for far too long, Samuel told Brian everything he knew.

"And the river – how does that look?"

"It's very high," Samuel replied. "That river is already up and still rising," he hesitated, "even a four-wheel drive won't get through now."

"And people swimming?"

"Perhaps young people," Samuel replied hesitantly. "Now I'm too old."

"Samuel," Brian responded, "you couldn't cross that river in the dry season when you were only fifteen years old."

But his racing mind was already miles away – what the hell happened now?

*

The black lion lay slumped on his left side, like an old bag of bones. This put his head flat on the ground and next to the crevice, which brought the sounds and the smell of the female human to him. His right front leg stuck out straight.

The fire that raged in his system had reached such a heat his breath was raggedly uneven. The stiffness in the front leg had spread throughout his shoulder and into his chest and his flanks heaved spasmodically with every breath. And yet the magnificent spirit, driven on by the all-powerful instinct for survival, had kept him on the trail of the weakest of the humans that invaded the valley. His best chance for food lay with the female human. And lying next to the crevice his nostrils filled with the smell of her.

Eventually he would catch her alone – then he would feed.

*

Mary-Ann listened to Brian with growing dismay. Sitting there on a stoep framed in bright red bougainvillaea, it all seemed totally unreal.

"Jakes has also taken liberties with the army," Brian added, "he's deliberately being keeping them away from that valley. Which doesn't help with the N'wanetsi problem."

"Who are the tourists?" she asked, but already knew the answer.

"The Dentons. Mary-Ann, we've got to go and look for them. The army should be checking the border fence at the eastern end of that valley anyway. But what about Jakes?"

Her voice softened. "You don't owe him anything," and hardened again, "you've already gone out on a limb. He should never have asked. He knows the rules. It could ruin you for life. To hell with him."

"Are you sure?" he asked miserably.

"Hey! Stop worrying! We just do the right thing." She stuck her chin out. "I'll deal with Jakes."

Brian looked at her, the relief obvious in his face, he spoke quietly, "Thanks Mary-Ann."

"If the ford's closed, use the JetRanger."

"It's up north – rhino darting. It won't be back until tomorrow."

She stood up.

"Where are you going?"

"The army must help," she said decisively. "They should be checking the area anyway. What else is there to do?"

With Brian on her heels, Mary-Ann jogged across to his office. Was any of this her fault? She had deliberately avoided thinking about Roger. Was that the right decision? He had come all the way to Africa, not for himself, but with an idea which would help her – or so he had said. Had she been uncharitable in not giving him the opportunity to explain?

No! He had lied to her – that was unforgivable!

Outside the office, Brian put his hand on her arm. "Mary-Ann …"

"Leave it to me," she said calmly. "I know how you feel about Jakes."

Mary-Ann marched into the office-cum-ops' room. "We need your help," she announced loudly.

All chatter ceased. Everyone turned to stare.

"Some tourists are lost in a valley south-east of here. The Park's JetRanger can't get back here until tomorrow. Will you help?"

Jakes frowned at her.

"With pleasure, ma'am," responded Major Anderson with alacrity. "Show us on the map. The chopper can go out there at once. Jakes can help us search."

"I don't think so," she said deliberately.

Major Anderson frowned.

Jakes pushed his way forward. "Mary-Ann! How dare you!"

Major Anderson sat down on the corner of the desk. "You'd better explain yourself, young lady."

Instead Mary-Ann turned to her father. "Dad, you're taking the project too far. It's become an unhealthy obsession. You can't keep them away from the valley."

Jakes stared at her with narrowed eyes. "You also," he growled, he turned to face Major Anderson. "She no longer works here – they fired her."

Mary-Ann felt the stinging in her eyes. "I'm not getting into a fight with you. But we've got to do the right thing."

"Don't listen to her," Jakes raged.

Major Anderson gestured at him, the threat unmistakable. "Please, sir. Let the lady speak her piece."

Mary-Ann walked over to the map on the wall. She pointed to the valley. "My father's kept you away from here. And there's a perfectly easy place for people to cross the fence." She glanced at her father. He just stood and stared at her. His face carved from granite. "And now two tourists have managed to lose themselves in there. Someone has to look for them."

Major Anderson looked at Jakes. "Is that true, sir?"

Jakes just stared at him.

Major Anderson shrugged and turned to Brian. "And you, sir. Do you know anything about this?"

Brian glanced at Jakes who stared at him. His eyes went to Mary-Ann. She gave him the slightest of nods, just an inclination of the head. Brian turned back to the Major.

"Yes," he said reluctantly. "She's telling you the truth."

"Right," Major Anderson swung into action. "Kellerman," he bellowed, and almost immediately the Sergeant-Major appeared in the office doorway. "That chopper has to lift off within the next five minutes. Tell Lieutenant Smith he and his men are to be on board. The pilot's to report here in one minute for a briefing." He turned back to Brian. "Do you know this valley, sir?"

Brian shook his head. "No," he nodded in Mary-Ann's direction, "but she does. She's been there many times with her father."

Major Anderson inclined his head. "Will you accompany our men, ma'am? It could help a –"

Jakes cut him off. "I know that valley better than anyone else. There are places and things about it my … Mary-Ann doesn't know about. I must be the one to go."

Major Anderson stared at him coldly. "I don't think so, sir. You've done quite enough as it is."

Jakes turned to Mary-Ann. "Thank you very much," he said bitterly. "An excellent example of filial loyalty."

"That's not fair," Mary-Ann responded quietly. "I'm just trying to live according to the principles you taught me in the first place. The one's you always said came from mom."

Jakes' face went red. "How dare you bring her into this? You have no respect."

"I'm sorry, dad, but I think you're wrong. You've become blinded to everything decent. I agree you haven't been treated fairly, just as some folk haven't been fair to me, but that doesn't mean we have a licence to stop behaving in a civilised way."

Jakes pushed his chair backwards so hard it fell over and stomped out of the office.

*

It was now the middle of the afternoon. Roger had been stumbling through the bush for most of the day. He hadn't realised how inadequate he could be made to feel over something as simple as a few footprints. He was also very hungry.

He kept losing the tracks when they crossed grassy areas. This meant he had a fifty percent chance of going off in the wrong direction at each game trail crossing – of which there was one every five metres or so. To his chagrin he would only discover his mistake when he got to the next sandy patch. He would then have to backtrack to the last game trail intersection to try and work out which way he should have gone.

After a while he started to break small twigs as markers whenever he changed trails. This helped speed up the process. The realisation that the direction of the tracks slanted uphill also helped. After that he disregarded game trails meandering off downhill. But he had lost his earlier high spirits.

Eventually Roger heard voices. The sound served to lift him and he eagerly pressed on. He covered the ground much faster. Homing in on the voices was much easier than following footprints. Soon the sounds grew much closer. Roger correspondingly walked a lot faster, forgetting even his hunger in his excitement.

He was almost jogging when, without warning, a terrible blow struck his shoulder. It was as if he had been hit by a giant's fist. Roger was slammed around – almost going full circle like a top – before he crashed backwards into a low shrub. He just lay there, out of breath, semi–stunned from shock, unable to understand what was going on. When he saw the slow spreading red stain on his left shoulder he realised for the first time he had been shot, but he still felt nothing, his shoulder was numb.

Roger made a half–hearted attempt to sit up, stopped. Three dark-skinned men stared down at him. One prodded him in the cheek with the toe of a worn combat boot. They were unkempt, wore dirty khakis.

Were these poachers? His stomach churned. Was Michelle okay?

"Who the hell are you people?" Roger ground out between gritted teeth. The steel poker in the bullet wound started to warm up, turned a dull black-red in his shoulder.

The three men gesticulated wildly, talked to him in a language he didn't understand. Roger shrugged his shoulders at them. That proved to be a mistake. The hot poker turned a cherry-red. Finally the waves of pain receded. He could see again. One of the three men had disappeared.

The other two shouted at him now. One waved a stubby rifle in Roger's face, jabbed him in the belly with the barrel. Roger recognised the weapon from TV – an AK47. They tried a different language, now it was European, possibly Portuguese. Not that he understood a word of it.

The third man reappeared. A fourth striding along behind. Roger had never seen a face as haunted. It was truly skeletal. This new person stood over Roger for a moment. Without saying a word he took a pace forward and stood on Roger's wounded shoulder. Roger screamed, writhed in the sand.

The pressure from the boot eased up. After a while his eyes cleared enough for him to again see. A mirthless grin twisted the lips of the gaunt–faced man.

"My men tell me you don't respond to Portuguese. Do you understand English?"

Roger, gritting his teeth against the waves of pain threatening to engulf him, nodded his head.

"Who are you? Where do you come from? Why are you here, in this valley, at this time?" The questions were hurled at him in rapid order.

Grunting with the effort Roger sat up. "Who are you people? And who the hell do you think you are shooting people for no reason?"

The gaunt–faced man smiled at Roger. Without any
warning, he kicked the wounded shoulder. Roger went over
backwards as though struck across the forehead by a
baseball bat, his spine arched with the pain. The poker had
just turned white-hot.

The gaunt–faced man still grinned. "I ask the questions,"
he said mildly.

"I'm looking for my wife," Roger managed.

"Ah, the fair Michelle. All right." He turned to the other
three men, barked out commands unintelligible to Roger,
and turned away.

The gestures with the AK47 were unmistakable. Roger
looked around to see whether he couldn't appeal to the
gaunt-faced man for help, as he was the only one who
seemed to understand English, but he was already striding
off without so much as a backward glance.

Finally Roger, having been pushed from behind most of
the way, arrived at the cave and saw Michelle. After she got
over her astonishment she introduced him to Joshua. The
latter organised bandages and pain relieving tablets –
earning a caustic comment from Abel. After removing his
shirt Michelle tied up Roger's shoulder as best she could.

Joshua told Roger the bullet had gone right through,
apparently without hitting any bones. It was a clean wound.
Was he meant to feel grateful?

Slowly his shoulder did indeed feel better as the tablets
took effect, becoming more of a constant nagging ache than
the earlier sharp pain. Joshua and Michelle together
convinced him to lie down and rest, deeper in the cave
where it was cooler.

Not long after he had got his head down, a muted – but
growing – quick hard chopping underpinned by the thin
scream of a jet engine shredded the air along the valley.

"Chopper coming," Joshua said laconically.

Roger crawled to the front of the cave. He was just in
time to see the last few men from around the fire
disappearing into the bush. Further down the hillside some

of the men were caught in the open still scurrying for cover. Guns popped off against the flat clatter of turning rotor blades with the whine of a jet engine in the background.

"C'mon, both of you, get back, deeper in." Joshua squirmed backwards into the cave. He shook his head. "I warned Abel. Sooner or later they'd find out we'd crossed the border."

Deeper in the cave Roger touched Joshua's arm. "Who would it be?"

"That's an Alo – military – South African," Joshua replied calmly. "There's no mistaking the sound. And they'll be back." He squinted at the sun which was already low in the west. "Maybe not tonight, but in the morning they'll be back for sure." Suddenly he stopped. He shook his head. "They're landing down below. They're dropping off troops."

"Are you going to make a run for it?" Roger asked. "Will you leave us behind?"

"It's too late to run now. If we were going to do something, we should've done it earlier." Joshua shook his head slowly from side to side. "No, this is it. This is the end of the line. We either try to do a deal or fight."

"Deal? Fight?" Roger turned to Michelle. "Please tell me what's going on."

*

The young lion shifted his position, but it didn't help, the inner fire still raged and his whole chest was stiff now, down to his belly. Flies clustered everywhere: around the stiffened black wound in his shoulder, in his mouth and on his eyes.

But the scent of a female human still drifted up to him. He had no option but to remain focused on the weakest of the species. He had to somehow cut her out from the rest of the humans as he would cut a female impala from a breeding herd.

Except for the heaving of his flanks the lion hardly moved at all now, lying alongside the crevice which formed the cave's outlet to the sky. When the female human started to move so would he.

High up above tiny black dots had just begun to sketch wide circles in the sky.

*

Major Anderson stood with his back to the map on the wall, legs spread wide, as he called the meeting to order. Mary-Ann watched quietly from the back of Brian's office.

"Attention, please," the Major called out. "There have been a number of developments."

Mary-Ann got the distinct impression the Major avoided looking at Jakes, who sat off to one side. There was an atmosphere of distrust in the air which she felt particularly keenly and which disturbed her greatly.

The hubbub in the office quietened down and everyone turned their attention towards the Major.

"Thank you," he said. "First a quick debrief on the encounter in the valley. Captain, if you don't mind." He glanced disapprovingly at the can of beer in Paul's fist.

Paul smiled sweetly and stayed sitting on the floor. "The valley's lousy with bad guys. Who else would take pot-shots? Between twenty and forty of 'em. We didn't see any sign of the missing tourists. We dropped off Luke and some of his boys to keep tabs on the bad guys. Then we came scooting back here."

Major Anderson frowned, didn't comment on Paul's style or delivery, although he clearly disapproved. "From a military point of view we obviously don't know whether this is a serious invasion by the Mozambicans, although that's unlikely. It could equally be an armed band of poachers. But there seems to be too many for that. For the sake of planning we'll have to assume they've got the missing tourists. Any questions or ideas so far?"

Mary-Ann felt like holding up her hand but restrained herself. For some reason the Major made her feel as though she was back in school. She cleared her throat instead. "The river's up. You're not going cross that easily."

Major Anderson nodded his head in her direction. "Thank you, ma'am."

"If you want to go in by helicopter the best place would be pretty close to the river. There's a place to land there."

Major Anderson nodded briskly. "Then the answer's straightforward. In case this is a feint we won't ask the north and south sectors for help, and they can go on monitoring their own areas. We shouldn't need help anyway. My troops will handle the situation. There's nothing we can specifically do about the tourists. We don't even know if the bandits have them or not. We'll just have to see what happens when we go in."

"My helo?" Paul asked.

"It's our best bet for getting in. Unfortunately we'll lose the element of surprise." He looked at the others. "The Captain will drop us off across the river. Five at a time. We'll then regroup and sweep the valley." He nodded in Paul's direction. "You'll also give us an eye in the sky. But we can't do this at night. My men, together with their equipment, will go out tonight by truck to the river crossing. They'll be ready for the air-lift at first light."

Brian shifted on the edge of the desk. "Anything we can do?"

The Major nodded. "If you could join us at the river crossing, in the morning. We might need your input."

Jakes pushed his chair back and stood up. "I should be the one there. I know that valley. He doesn't."

The Major stared at him now with unabashed hostility. "That brings us to a last unpleasant piece of business. You have consistently lied to us, deliberately kept us out of that valley. The bandits crossed the border with impunity because of you. We're not sure you should be allowed to attend these planning sessions." And then deliberately added, "You're American – a foreigner." Unspoken implications polluted the air.

Mary-Ann hurriedly chipped in, before Jakes could respond and maybe make matters worse, "My dad was wrong because of the black lion, nothing more. To suggest anything else is crazy."

Brian stood up. "I agree with Mary-Ann. I knew what he was doing. But it was just the black lion."

Major Anderson shrugged. "That's not what we've heard. There have been other rumours."

Mary-Ann's stomach did a somersault. With so many things happening she had forgotten about her old enemy. Prins was still out there, keeping his evil promise.

"And it would be better that you, Jakes Webber, leave this meeting," the Major said stiffly. "before you hear anything more of significance."

Jakes stared at the Major for what seemed like a lifetime. Mary-Ann knew her father to be essentially a non-violent man, a research scientist, albeit heavily field orientated, and of the old school, for instance he still enjoyed hunting for the pot. Nonetheless he was a non-violent man. Now it seemed as though he was going to launch himself at the Major.

With an enormous effort he brought himself under control. He pointed at Mary-Ann and then Brian. "It's a fine time for the two of you to come to my defence. If you'd supported me and shown me loyalty in the first place this wouldn't have happened." He stormed out of the office.

Brian looked distraught. Mary-Ann walked over to stand alongside him. She put her mouth close to his ear. "You didn't do anything wrong," she murmured quietly. "And I'll keep an eye on Jakes."

Brian nodded, seemed relieved. "Thanks Mary-Ann. I don't have much choice but to hang in here with these guys."

Mary-Ann looked out of the window, stood there, thoughtfully watching her father march away with long purposeful strides. She could read his body language. He was up to something. She hurried out of the room, started to follow him.

As she dogged Jakes' steps, Mary-Ann thought about Roger and the trouble he was in, and how much he really meant to her. But what could she do? What could she have done differently? There were no easy answers.

And he had lied to her. How can you lie to someone you love? Lying was unforgivable!

For the first time in a long while Mary-Ann suddenly felt sorry for herself. Mom, where are you? What must I do?

Then she told herself to straighten up and get on with it, because if she was alone, her father was equally alone. No one else was going to help a lonely old man. And where the hell was he going anyway? This didn't make sense. This was Jakes with a definite destination and – as far as she knew – he had nowhere to go.

*

That Wednesday night Roger and Michelle sat near the cave mouth in front of their own small heap of coals. They covertly watched Joshua and Abel arguing near the main fire. The two men indulged in a great deal of gesticulating and arm waving and both were clearly very tense.

At last Joshua threw his arms into the air and came stomping back to the cave. He seemed extremely dispirited.

"Problems?" queried Michelle.

Joshua nodded his head. "I can't get the men to agree to exchange you two for a free passage to Europe. They're Abel's fighters. They're going to do what he tells them to do. The bond they share is unbreakable."

Roger frowned. "That doesn't make sense. Surely it's a damn good way of getting out of an awkward situation?"

"If they weren't all doomed anyway," Joshua said hopelessly.

"What do you mean by that?" inquired Roger.

"He – and most of his men – have full-blown Aids. That's why they don't care anymore. None of it means anything."

"Oh my God," exclaimed Michelle. "The poor bastards!"

Joshua gave her a sour look. "Considering their attitude towards you, that's extremely charitable."

All three jerked around as a terrible screaming echoed around the valley. Karl Hoeniger, as naked as the day he was born, ran past the main fire, still screaming. Roger felt his skin prickle, contract, hairs rising. The sound was unequivocally the scream of a madman. The fighters at the main fire rolled around with laughter, holding their sides at the pain of their amusement.

Karl came running towards the cave, still screaming, eyes wide and staring at nothing. It wouldn't have been visible from the main fire but Roger saw Joshua beckon, hold out his AK47. Karl grabbed the rifle, stuck it in his mouth, pulled the trigger. The back of his head blew off in a fine red spray, his back arched in a taut bow, he fell backwards. His feet kicked once or twice and then he was still.

A frightening growl erupted from the men clustered around the main fire. They had only just started playing with their new toy. The Butcher strode across to stand over Joshua. A flood of words washed over the latter. Joshua put his hands up and shrugged his shoulders. The gesture was unmistakable –

don't blame me, the man was crazy, he just grabbed my rifle and shot himself before I could do anything.

After a few more shouts and a gesture in Michelle's direction the Butcher stalked off.

"You took a chance there, didn't you?"

Joshua shrugged. "He wasn't going to use it on anyone else. He just wanted the torment to end."

Roger pulled a face. "Maybe …. What was said about us in that little tirade?"

Joshua glanced quickly across at Michelle, shrugged. "Nothing really," he replied, biting his lip, not meeting her eyes.

"That's not true," Michelle said suddenly in a calm firm voice.

Her manner surprised Roger.

"He repeated something he said earlier, didn't he?" She was looking at Joshua.

Roger looked from one to the other. "What are you talking about?"

Joshua remained impassive, staring at the small flame that flickered in the small fire before the cave entrance.

Michelle spoke very calmly. "I won't let him touch me, you know that, don't you? I'd rather die first."

Roger's frustration boiled over, almost shouting. "What are you talking about?"

"Abel," she replied. "He wants me … you know … for sex." After a short pause she added, "he has full-blown Aids and I won't let him touch me. I'd rather die first."

Roger stared at her: Jesus, what next?

"We have to try something," he said. "We can't just sit around here waiting for him to come for you."

Joshua just looked at him. "Why do you think he hasn't taken away these," he gestured at the AK47, ran his other hand over the hand-grenades on his belt. "He knows there's nothing we can do against the rest of them."

Roger looked around in frustration. "There must be something we can do."

Michelle frowned in his direction. "It's not really your problem, is it? You'll probably be okay. And you've made it clear we're … we're finished. I know that now."

"Jesus, Michelle, gimme a break. I wouldn't sit by and let him do anything to you. You should know me better than that."

"It's not going to help much," Joshua cut in. "What can you do?"

"I don't bloody know," Roger growled. "But I'm as sure as shit not going to sit around studying my navel. Have you explored the back of the cave? It's more like a giant crack that broadens out at the bottom than a real cave. Maybe we can climb out the top."

Joshua looked at him for a moment, shook his head. "Not with an injury you won't."

"Then we can stay here and bloody well fight them off with that thing," he pointed at the rifle that leant against the rock, "while Michelle makes a run for it."

"One AK between the two of us? Why do you think Abel hasn't bothered to take it away from me?"

Michelle had a strange look on her face. "You'd do that for me?"

"Of course I would, Michelle!" Roger replied irritably. "Have either one of you explored deeper into this cave or whatever the hell it is?"

Michelle and Joshua both looked at him. They didn't reply, shook their heads.

"Technically you're still with them," Roger stated deliberately, hooking a thumb at the men around the main fire. "Are you going to help me – or stop me – if I go and explore the cave?"

Joshua dug a small torch out of one pocket and threw it to Roger. "The batteries are nearly flat but it's better than nothing."

"Thanks, pal."

"I don't stand a chance whatever happens," Joshua said sourly. "Hell, maybe I can rack up some brownie points with the folks who run things in the afterlife. I'm going to need them." There was a long pause.

Then he added, "I'll keep watch and Michelle can sit and talk to me while you explore the cave, then no one should become suspicious. Try not to stay away for too long."

Roger made rather a production out of picking up a blanket, yawned widely, casually ambling deeper into the cave. He grimaced. An actor he was not. He flicked on the torch. Joshua was right. A pale yellow cone barely extended a few feet from his hand, but it was better than nothing. He swallowed two more of Joshua's tablets and worked his way deeper into the cave.

Soon he found a hole and crawled through it into a secondary chamber, slightly larger than the broom cupboard you would expect to find under a staircase in a two-storey house. In the left wall of this chamber Roger found another hole. This proved to be a particularly tight wriggle. With a mild attack of claustrophobia he made it through and afterwards the cave seemed to open up again.

Roger hesitated. He had no idea how long he had been away, no idea how long it would be before the Butcher decided he wanted Michelle. And he still had no idea of how far the fault in the rock extended. They would just have to take their chances.

He scurried back to where he had left the other two, hoping the Butcher hadn't yet sent for Michelle.

*

Jakes marched arrow-straight to his bougainvillaea-covered cottage.

Mary-Ann slipped along in his wake.

He veered off at the last minute, strode purposefully to the garage, opened the doors wide. He slung a coil of rope into the back of the pickup, reversed it out, drove the vehicle around to the front door of the cottage. He moved fast, a short man with a short fuse and a short goatee beard, grey now, but still jutting out like the bowsprit on a fighting galleon. He disappeared inside the cottage.

Mary-Ann stayed in the tree shadows until she saw a light come on in his study window. She hesitated. Was she really going to spy on her own father? But she had to know what he planned. She slipped around the side of the cottage. Pressed against the wall she peered through the window.

Jakes stood in front of his gun safe, the doors swung wide open. This was not in itself unusual. He regularly spent many an evening cleaning those gleaming rifles and shotguns, keeping them in a well-oiled working condition. But tonight was not normal. He stood there for a while, staring into the safe.

His choice would be a sure indication of what he intended.

After a few minutes he took out a rifle. She saw the telescopic sight first and then the dark brown wood of the butt. She recognised it – the .30-06 calibre Ruger. He held the weapon for a short while, replaced it in the rack. He took out a rifle which bore no telescopic sight at all. He fondled the .458 Winchester Magnum.

So it was more serious game.

Again he shook his head. Now he moved with purpose. He racked the .458 and took out a third rifle. Like the .30-06 this one carried a telescopic sight. He slung the rifle over his shoulder, took out a box of ammunition and carefully locked the safe. She didn't really need to see the two centimetres wide plaited rifle sling she had once given to him as a birthday present to know which weapon he had finally chosen.

He had settled for his pre-64 Winchester .375 H & H. So what was he up to? It had a quick-detachable telescopic sight. A useful accessory if he had to go after wounded game in thick bush. It didn't have the knock-down effect of his .458 but it was the closest he would come to an all-round hunting rifle for Africa.

It was the one choice which gave her no clue as to what he was planning.

As Jakes left his study, Mary-Ann stepped back into the shadows, against the bougainvillaea. Her father came out of the bungalow, leaned in through the driver's door and slotted the rifle into the rifle rack behind his seat. He climbed into the vehicle and drove carefully and methodically out of the yard.

Mary-Ann made her decision in an instant. She noted the direction in which he had turned, flew into the house, grabbed a warm anorak off the coat rack in the small hall and slammed her way out of the back door. She flung open the door of her own small Toyota and had it started in an instant. She left her headlights turned off. She drove along a road dimly lit by the partly obscured quarter-moon, relying more on instinct and familiarity than being able to see properly.

She turned on to the road Jakes had taken.

*

Roger hurried to within whispering distance of the cave mouth. He sighed with relief. Joshua and Michelle still sat just inside the entrance.

"Everything all right?" he asked softly.

Joshua nodded.

There was no time to waste.

"There may be a way out the back." He tried to sound more confident than he felt. "It's worth a try. But we'd better go now."

Joshua shook his head. "I'll stay here."

Roger shook his head vehemently. "No way! You said you wanted to trade us for a passage to Europe. You can still do that. If … when … we get out we can say that's the deal. That's why you saved us. You're not doomed like the rest of them. So why die with them?"

"Thanks. But if they don't see anyone out here, how long will it be before they investigate. If I'm here it'll give them comfort. You carry on."

Roger hesitated. They shouldn't leave Joshua behind. It would be a death sentence. But they had a problem. Joshua was right. Roger really didn't have an alternative to offer. He still didn't like the idea.

"What do we have that could be useful?"

"Not a hell of a lot," Joshua replied. "There's my AK, the torch you've just used and two hand-grenades. Nothing more, I'm afraid."

Michelle stared gloomily at Roger. "Do you think we can make it?"

"Damn right I do," Roger replied, but he couldn't meet her eyes. "Okay, let's make plans. I'll lead the way back through the cave. So I'll keep the torch. Michelle, you hang onto my belt. I'll take it off, attach it to a loop on my trousers so that you have a decent length to hang onto." He suddenly wagged a finger at her. "And I don't want you trying to take my trousers off while we're in the dark."

She giggled.

Thank God for that, he thought, she loathed the dark.

He turned to Joshua. "I still think you should come along, even if only a short while later."

Michelle murmured her agreement.

Joshua nodded. "I'll give you a small head start and then follow. I'll keep the rifle and the two hand-grenades with me."

Roger eyed him dubiously. Was Joshua up to something?

"Before you leave make up a sleeping figure out of two rolled-up blankets and throw a third blanket over it." Joshua added, "I'll lay that across the entrance just before I go, it might give us a bit more time."

Reluctantly Roger nodded. "How do you think Abel will react when he finds out? Maybe he'll just let us go. They've got a fight coming in the morning."

Joshua shrugged. "Maybe." He didn't sound too enthusiastic.

Roger and Michelle quickly rolled up the two blankets. They pushed and prodded until it resembled a sleeping figure. They placed the mock-up just behind Joshua, threw the third blanket over it.

"There's no time like the present," Roger said awkwardly to Joshua. "We don't know when Abel might send for Michelle. I really ought to get her outta here."

Joshua gave him a crooked grin, eyes and teeth white in the dark face. "Just go."

"Yes, but –"

"Just go. Now. Before it's too late."

Roger and Michelle crawled backwards, deeper into the cave, where they couldn't be seen from outside. Roger took off his belt, threaded it through a loop, back through the buckle and gave the long end to Michelle.

They worked their way deeper into the cave. Saving the torch for the first twenty metres, Roger stumbled over the uneven floor of the cave. He could hear Michelle experiencing the same difficulties.

At the first bend Roger looked backwards. Joshua leaned against the rock in the mouth of the cave, the AK47 prominently propped up between his legs. They stumbled around the corner and Joshua was no longer visible.

Roger felt uncomfortable. Did the Mozambican have his own agenda?

*

Still lying on his side, head close to the crevice, the lion heard the small scraping sounds of leather against rock as Michelle dragged her feet over the uneven floor of the cave.

The lion came up off the sand, crouched belly down, directly over the crevice. He lowered his head, almost to the ground, flattened himself against the earth, just the very tip of his black tail flicking from side to side, listened to the sounds and smelled the scent that came up to him from the earth beneath.

Slowly the delicate sounds of leather on rock, a soft whisper, the breathing of two persons moving drifted up to him and, still semi-crouched, he began to follow those sounds, moving at precisely the same speed as his prey.

*

Jakes drove in a north-easterly direction from Skukuza, taking the road that led to N'wanetsi – and his valley. Mary-Ann wasn't surprised. Where else would he go? She stayed a few car lengths behind him, headlights still off.

When he slowed down he caught her by surprise. She was almost too close. They were still well short of the entrance to the valley. Jakes turned off the tarred road onto a rutted sandy track that wound its way, almost invisibly, through the low shrub and bush in an easterly direction. Mary-Ann followed.

She could hardly see the track in the darkness, kept running her small car onto the mound between the two tracks where it was higher than the differential. The car hadn't been designed for that kind of bush path. Fortunately the sump didn't hit any rocks. She bounced up and down, was thrown from side to side, as the Toyota jolted along. Eventually she found giving the car a minimum of guidance seemed to work best. The wheels tended to stay in the ruts by themselves. Only occasionally would the front wheels start to climb out. She would sense it happening – rather than see or feel anything – and then it took only the faintest of tweaks on the steering-wheel to line them up with the ruts once again.

After that discovery Mary-Ann found it much easier staying behind Jakes. She had virtually nothing to do. The whine of the gearbox in low had a soporific effect. She was on the verge of drifting off. She had little fear of losing her father. There would be few, if any, other tracks that led away from the one they were on. She half slept as her car bounced along.

So it came as a great shock when she rounded a corner and directly in front of her, in the middle of the track, two dazzling headlights sprang into life, main beams on. The sudden brilliance blinded her. Mary-Ann jammed on her brakes and her car slid quickly to a halt. She hadn't been going fast.

She shaded her eyes from the headlights, trying to see though the light. She was shocked to make out the figure of her father standing next to the door of his pickup with a rifle at his shoulder, aimed in her direction. Instinctively she pulled her head down into her neck as though to ward off a blow.

She quickly wound down her side window. "It's me, Mary-Ann," she called out loudly.

With a sigh of relief she saw him lower the rifle. He strode forward to stop next to her window.

"Go back," he growled. "I don't want anyone with me."

She shook her head and almost immediately realised he probably couldn't see the movement. She felt intimidated with him standing there like that, leaning over her, a black figure in the black night. He was a stranger. Mary-Ann twisted the ignition key to kill the engine and opened her door. At first she thought Jakes was going to prevent her from climbing out by holding the door closed. She prepared herself to push against the anticipated resistance, but it was as though he had read her mind. He suddenly stepped back from the door and it swung open easily.

To her surprise she heard him chuckle quietly in the darkness.

She stood tall next to the car, taller than he was by at least five centimetres. "What's so funny?" she hissed, suddenly furious that he should be so happy while she was scared, upset and worried, about him, about Roger and about herself.

"It's all right, Little Cat," he said. "With me you can always keep your claws sheathed."

It had been more years than she could remember since he had last called her Little Cat. It had begun when, at age five, she had turned on a wild dog, that had found its way into their garden and was threatening her pet kitten. She had shown such ferocity, hands up, fingers extended into tiny claws, that it ran back into the bush. She couldn't remember the incident but having heard it re-told many times it was as though she could.

"Where are we going?" she asked more calmly than she felt.

He chuckled again and quickly grew serious. "There's something I need to do by myself, Little Cat," he said, sliding the rifle back onto his shoulder so that it hung from the sling. He put his hands on her shoulders.

They stood there in silence for a while as she tried to find the right words. She took after her father and she hated being pushed into things, much preferring to be asked, allowed to make up her own mind.

"But it's not essential for you to be alone, is it?"

She knew he wouldn't lie to her. He, like her and her mom before her, couldn't stand lies.

"No."

She could just make out his head shaking in the dark. Her night vision was returning. She had a feeling she was going to need it, so she kept her eyes lowered, making sure she didn't look directly into the bright headlights of his pickup.

It was as though he had again read her mind. "I'll turn them off."

"I'd like to come along."

"And I'd prefer to do it alone," he said mildly.

"Do you understand why I have to go along?" she insisted.

"Of course," he said, hands still on her shoulders and she found it strangely reassuring. She couldn't remember him ever deliberately reaching out to touch her before. He added, "You think I'm too old and too stupid to look after myself in the bush."

"It's not that at –" she started to respond heatedly and cut herself off. He was teasing her. Wonder of wonders. Tonight was indeed a strange night, he had never done that before either.

"Come," he said, turning to walk back to his pickup. "We haven't any time to waste."

Obediently she followed him. "Where are we going?"

He grunted.

Back to normal, she thought.

"Where are we going?" she asked again, sighing.

"My valley."

"Any particular route?"

He turned around to peer at her. "Here, carry this." He tossed the coiled rope in her direction.

She caught it expertly, pleased that it had not fallen at her feet in a tangle. She slung the coil over her shoulder and hurried back to her car where she collected her anorak. By the time she returned to the pickup truck, Jakes had switched off its lights and was already twenty metres away, striding out through the bush with all the confidence of a city-dweller walking along the well-known pavements of his home town. Mary-Ann had to jog for a while to catch up.

She hoped he knew where he was going, because she was already lost.

As though in answer he looked over his shoulder as she caught up with him. "There's a small riverbed. There's only water when it's actually raining." He looked ahead again as he continued to speak, striding out as though they were in a long-distance walking race. "It starts right near the top of the mountain in front of us. It's a wonderful sight. The water shoots out of a big crevice that runs across the mountain. Then it falls straight down for fifty – sixty metres before hitting the side of the mountain again. It's dug itself a big hole there."

"I thought there was really only one easy way into the valley."

"There are a few," he said. "But at night this riverbed is the best of them, it'll be like a staircase. And the big crevice leads all the way across the mountain and then down into a natural funnel point in the valley. The only place we'll need that," and he pointed at the rope she was carrying coiled over her shoulder, "will be at the vertical face the waterfall has cut into the side of the mountain."

"Now I know where," she said mildly, "is there any chance of my finding out why?"

After a long while – although she wasn't consciously aware of walking uphill - Mary-Ann could feel her thigh muscles pulling and she knew it was going to be a long hard night.

And Jakes still hadn't answered her question.

*

Slowly Roger felt his way through the dark. Michelle hung onto his belt from behind. He had been along this first part earlier and was fairly confident the surface underfoot wouldn't just disappear. So he didn't use the torch, wanting to conserve the already weak batteries. They covered the first twenty metres at an incredibly slow pace. Roger being held back by a hesitant Michelle.

That twenty metres saw them reach the first small tunnel through which they would have to crawl.

"I've been through here," Roger murmured. "There's a small chamber on the other side and then another tunnel. Do you want to go first?"

"Thanks – but no thanks."

Roger grinned in the dark. Michelle was doing good.

"Then you keep the torch and use it when you crawl through."

"All right."

Roger handed her the torch. He crawled along the tunnel which was about a metre long. He felt a great sense of relief when he slid into the small chamber.

He stuck his head into the tunnel. "Your turn."

Michelle came scuttling along. She was able to move much faster because she was small enough to travel on her hands and knees whereas he had had to crawl through on his belly.

In the chamber she waved the torch around. "It's lovely. Just like a Wendy house."

"Over there on the left is another tunnel and beyond it the cave seems to open out pretty wide. From here it's new territory."

"That tunnel doesn't seem very big."

"We've got to go through," he whispered. "We really don't have a choice."

"I know," she whispered, sounding quite confident. To his surprise, she added, "I'll go first. I'm smaller than you."

Holding the torch extended in front of her Michelle pushed her way into the tunnel. This time she couldn't do it on her hands and knees and went in flat on her stomach. Roger saw her wriggle her way deeper into the tunnel until her feet disappeared from view.

He heard her calling.

Roger stuck his head into the tunnel and wriggled forward. The rock was tight and he had to hunch his shoulders inwards to make sure they fit. His shoulder, neutralized by the tablets Joshua had given him, came alive but more as a dull ache than a sharp pain. Tolerable, he thought.

He could hardly move his arms in the confined space. He made very slow progress towards the pin-point of light he could see further on. By the time Roger was three-quarters of the way along the three metre long tunnel his breathing had become ragged, on the verge of being out of control.

From young he had hated confined spaces. He could feel himself choking in there, the dust clogged his nostrils and filled the back of his throat, as though it would soon stop all air getting through. The tons of rock pressed in on him. It was a sensation he could have done without.

The seeming inability to breathe, combined with the sore shoulder, brought him suddenly and unexpectedly to the brink of panic. He was within a half-metre of the end when he could no longer hold his shoulders all hunched up. He relaxed and was immediately stuck, unable to move further forward. He felt a small hand take his hand and gently tug at it.

"It's okay," Michelle said gently. "Not far to go now."

Roger raised his head, looked up. She was right. Slowly he inched forward and finally popped out like a cork from a champagne bottle. Roger immediately sat down with his back against the rock as he gradually brought his breathing under control. Michelle sat down beside him.

"You poor man. You lost most of your shirt getting through there."

He squeezed her hand. She leaned against him and put her mouth close to his ear. "It's not often I'm grateful for being so damned small."

"You're not all bad, you know."

"Gee, thanks," she said, a smile behind her words.

He gave her hand another squeeze. "Come on, let's go."
He felt more at ease with Michelle now than ever before.

He helped her to her feet. She again grabbed hold of his
belt. He set off along the cave. The torchlight was a pale
yellow. Roger turned it off to conserve the batteries and
they made very slow progress in the dark. He had to feel
ahead carefully before taking each step to make sure the
ground didn't simply drop away beneath his feet.
Occasionally, when not sure, he would flick the torch on.
And quickly off again as soon as he had regained his
bearings. On one such occasion Roger suddenly stopped.

"What's wrong," she whispered.

"Look there."

He knew he sounded like a child in a toy store, he didn't
care.

Roger slowly ran the torch around the walls of rock that
surrounded them. They were covered in red ochre
drawings. Stick-like men with spears at the ready, thin
long-necked giraffe captured in simple lines yet showing an
amazing grace, powerful buffalo, cautious kudu, gentle
impala and skittish wildebeest adorned the walls. It was an
Aladdin's cave of Bushman rock art.

Roger knew that very few – if any, other than the original
artists – would have seen those drawings and he knew it
was a privilege. They transported him back through time. A
million years could have passed since the first of the
drawings had been made. He had a sudden fierce desire to
know when they had been painted, to learn more about this
race of men that had so long ago disappeared.

To grow, through that learning, closer to this part of the
planet called Africa. An enigmatic and contradictory place.
It was typical that a savage situation building to a climax
behind them should immediately be balanced by the
timeless beauty of Bushmen drawings.

Africa made it all seem so right; it was all part of a
cosmic plan that had, just for an instant, been sensed. He
had felt some of this in Mary-Ann, and she was inextricably

mixed up in what he now understood. He had a sudden fierce need to tell her about his idea, more convinced than ever that she would like it, that its inevitable rightness would make it acceptable to her, despite the mistakes he had made in the past.

"Come on, let's keep moving."

The urgency in Michelle's voice whipped him back from the past, through time and space, and into the present.

"Yes," he said. "Let's go on."

*

Brian left the office-cum-ops' room and hurried across to Jakes' cottage. Mary-Ann would tell him how Jakes was coping. His first reaction had been to walk out in support of Jakes, but that would have achieved little. Yet the seemingly endless discussions of troops and other preparations for the attack in the morning had nothing to do with him.

He had been bored with the whole thing by 9.30 pm and it was now, he glanced at his watch, past 11.00. Unfortunately he was the designated Park representative and he had felt he couldn't leave.

Brian was very surprised, and disturbed, to find the cottage empty. He had expected both Mary-Ann and Jakes to be there. He went out to the back of the cottage and checked the garage. Both Mary-Ann's Toyota and Jakes' pickup truck were missing.

Had Jakes gone off in a huff? Had Mary-Ann followed him? He wished he knew. Perhaps it was as simple as that. On the other hand it wouldn't do for the suspicious Major Anderson to find out Jakes was gone.

Finally he decided he would try again in the morning – surely they would have returned by then.

*

Just before sunrise on the Thursday morning one of the Butcher's men approached Joshua. He was asleep – mostly. As soon as Roger and Michelle were well on their way Joshua pulled the blanket off the mock-up sleeper and wrapped it around his own shoulders. He tried to stay on guard the whole night, but it proved impossible. Every so often he dozed off.

Half asleep now he watched the young fighter approach the cave mouth. Without saying a word he made to enter the cave by passing around Joshua. The latter remained seated and, although it wasn't an obvious movement, adjusted the AK47 on his lap in such a way that it pointed directly at the youngster.

The significance of the rifle wasn't lost on Abel's man. "You must give me the woman."

"Why?" enquired Joshua mildly.

"General Gamellah wants her now. He wishes to prepare himself for battle. She will be his *muti* – medicine – against bullets. Then she can be *muti* for all of us." The youngster shrugged. "It is my duty to take her to him."

Joshua stared at the bush fighter. So this was how it all ended, on the dirty floor of a dirty cave, killed by dirty people. At least, at the end, he was trying to do something clean.

Joshua shook his head. "No."

"No?" The fighter sounded shocked.

"No!" repeated Joshua firmly.

The youngster nervously shifted his weight from one foot to the other. "But I must take her to him. He said I must."

"You can go and tell him that I would not allow it."

"You will not allow it," repeated Abel's fighter stupidly.

"That is correct," Joshua said slowly. "You can tell him that I will not allow it."

With obvious reluctance the young soldier turned away. Joshua watched him walk away very slowly, muttering to himself as he went.

Joshua smiled. The longer it takes him to get there, the longer it would take before the Butcher used force to get what he wanted. He looked around. It would be folly to stay where he was. Even that ignorant callow youth who had just been there would be able to shoot Joshua from a distance. Not that he cared much anymore. But he had promised himself he would give the other two as much time as possible to find a way out.

Almost lethargically he shifted across, without standing up, until he was inside the cave, then he lay down and rolled over so that he was belly down and facing out of the cave mouth. He pushed the AK47 forward so that it fitted snugly against his right shoulder when he rested the front part of the stock neatly in his left hand.

Happy with the rifle's position he allowed his left hand to sink down onto the rock floor of the cave mouth, carrying the muzzle of the AK47 with it. The rock felt painfully rough against the back of his hand and he enjoyed the small hurt, it meant he was still alive. He closed his eyes and lay there enjoying the sensation of being half asleep.

After about ten minutes the scraping of boots on rock brought him back to full wakefulness. The sound stopped not too far from the entrance to the cave.

"General Manyoba?" The young fighter was back. "General Manyoba?"

Behind the young fighter Joshua could just make out the shapes of two or three others. They held a whispered conversation. Suddenly one of the others thrust the youth to one side and stood four-square in front of the cave mouth.

"General Gamellah said we are to –"

Joshua anticipated what the bush fighter had been told to do by the Butcher with a fraction of a second to spare. He opened fire with the AK47 just before the other man started to shoot. Lying down he was by far the more accurate and as his bullets tore into the man's chest. The stream of bullets from the dead man's AK47 ricocheted off the cave roof as he was blown backwards to land crumpled two metres further down the slope.

It was as though Joshua had turned an active beehive upside down.

A number of rifles opened fire and the bullets sang as they whipped through the cave mouth to splatter themselves against the wall of rock behind him. A few of them danced away from the first wall they struck, groaning like angry wasps, to end as a splashes of lead against an opposite wall.

Realising his danger Joshua pushed himself backwards with his elbows until he was much deeper into the cave and below the lip of the entrance. He didn't like the dark and the claustrophobia – which he had somehow neglected to mention to Roger – encircled his throat and chest with steel fingers. Trying to ignore the sensation of being strangled Joshua raised himself onto his knees and half crawled and half scuttled backwards ever deeper into the cave. Around the first corner he stopped, loosed off a few random shots back towards the entrance, and ran deeper into the cave.

He could have done with the small torch he had given Roger. Two paces further on and he ran full tilt into a rock wall. Half stunned he sat backwards as though onto a chair, his backside hitting the rock floor of the cave with a force that made it feel as though his spine was being pushed up through the back of his skull. Joshua had no idea how long he sat there, but that was exactly what he did. Then the humming like thousands of bees found him deep in that cave and galvanised him into action.

He grimaced. Jesus, there just had to be a way of getting further into the cave. Roger and Michelle had obviously found it. He was fighting hard against the panic caused by the proximity of the rock all around him.

He stood up again, trying to ignore the sound of leaden bees that filled the cave with vicious rumours. He felt the wall in front of him. It was solid rock. There just had to be some way through. Both Roger and Michelle were patently gone. He had to find it, despite the dark. He tried lower down. Yes, there it was, a tiny, suffocating, airless bloody hole in the wall. He felt around the circumference of the hole and then inside as far as he could and groaned. It was not a hole in the wall. It was actually a bloody tunnel.

He leaned against the rock. He was a damn sight fatter than the other two and he wasn't sure he would fit, but a new swarm of metallic bees made their presence known and spurred him on. He wedged himself into the tunnel. As he did so he felt a great blow on the back of one thigh as though he had just been struck by a club. He thought no more of it until he had finally – desperately – squeezed through the gap in the rock face and into the chamber beyond.

He tried to stand up but his right leg gave way beneath him. He couldn't figure it out. He felt around the back of his leg. It came away sticky in the dark and he knew then he had been shot. Joshua crawled forward until he came to another rock wall. Still in the dark and with his leg just beginning to throb he began to feel his way diagonally across that, anticipating now that this rock wall might also have a tunnel through which he would have to crawl.

Almost immediately he found the tunnel and he quickly ran his hands all over it.

And then he knew he wasn't going anywhere. There was no way he could get out of that chamber. The tunnel was physically too small even if his claustrophobia would have allowed it. And he wasn't going out the front – the Butcher would see to that.

Joshua had always hated confined spaces and the dark. And it didn't seem right somehow that a man who felt the way he did should have to end his days like a poisoned rat down a hole.

He could think of only one way to end it with some sort of dignity and control.

*

"Shhh!" Roger held up a hand to Michelle's mouth as she came up alongside him. "Did you hear that?"

"I thought I heard something above us."

"I meant back along the cave."

"I think there's something above us."

"The sounds I heard came from behind. And by now I would have expected to hear Joshua coming along to join us."

Roger switched off the torch to conserve the batteries. He didn't want to risk being stuck in the cave without any light at all. Not only was it comforting, but it also meant that they could still move at a reasonable pace. The darkness rushed in on them like a black wave. They were both quiet for a short while. Slowly the silence moved in as well and Roger felt Michelle stir restlessly next to him.

"We can't just sit here," she said. "Let's carry on."

"No, I'm going back."

A short silence ensued. "Are you going to take the torch?"

"I have to. You know that. Just wait here for me."

Roger heard a deep sigh. "Don't worry. I'm curling myself into a tight ball and I'm not going to budge until you get back."

Roger found that going back along the cave was very much quicker than when they had come along it in the other direction. Now he knew there were no holes lying in wait and Michelle wasn't hanging onto his belt.

Walking quickly along in the dark Roger again heard it – the pop-pop pop of gunfire. He broke into a jog. He started to sweat. It was hot down there and dank and humid and his shoulder hurt. Quite soon he reached the rock wall and found the tunnel he had battled to wriggle through earlier. He flicked the torch on to find the entrance.

A fierce whisper echoed along the tunnel. "Turn that off!"

Roger flattened himself against a side wall. After a short pause, he realised it was Joshua. He was at the other end of the tunnel, in the small rock chamber. The gunfire had stopped now. Roger squeezed his way into the tunnel until almost his whole length was in there. He wanted to talk without making too much noise.

"Are you all right?" Roger whispered.

"Yes, but be careful. They're already in the outer chamber," Joshua cautioned. "What are you doing here?"

"I thought you were going to follow us. I heard shooting."

"Yes, there's been a bit of that," came the dry reply. "But very little from my side."

Roger thought he heard a groan, quickly stifled. "Are you okay? Come through now and then we can get the hell out of here. Before they have another crack at you."

"No," Joshua said. "I won't get through there. And … and … I suffer from claustrophobia. You just carry on. I'll buy you as much time as I can."

Roger's frustration welled up, making his voice thick. "Isn't there anything I can do to help?"

"Nothing."

Roger needed to see Joshua one more time. He didn't question the feeling. He had never before left someone behind to die. It made him feel not part of this world but like a cinema-goer watching a film.

"Can I turn on the light for a moment?" he whispered.

A slight pause. "Yes, but just for a moment. I've no idea how much of it will show."

The tunnel through the rock wall was about three metres long. Roger was already half way there. He wriggled on some more, until he felt his head was very close to the chamber. He switched on the torch. He could see Joshua's face at the other end of the tunnel. It was grey, the sweat pearling on his upper lip, but already running down the sides of his face. His eyes were glazed and bloodshot.

"Are you sure there's nothing I can do." Roger's voice was thick again.

"Absolutely sure," came the quick reply. "Now go!"

Roger hesitated. There really wasn't anything he could usefully do. He stuck out his hand. "Goodbye," he said simply.

Joshua took Roger's hand. At first Roger thought that their hands were slippery with sweat. He looked down. In the torchlight he could see they were covered in blood.

"Jesus, you've been hit," he rasped.

Joshua took back his hand. "Turn off the light now. Someone's found the other entrance. Go! Now!"

Roger turned off the light. He too heard it. Voices in the dark, talking softly, on the other side of the chamber, beyond Joshua's position. He realised it would be churlish to waste the gift Joshua was giving them. Without another word he wriggled backwards until he was out of the tunnel, turned on his heel and began to make his way back down the cave, back to where Michelle waited for him.

After fifteen paces he turned the torch on again and began to jog. Gunfire crackled loudly behind him. It had a curious echo to it and he wondered if that was Joshua shooting from the chamber. He flinched at the thought. It must be like sitting in the kettle drum of a rock band in mid-song. The firing stopped.

Roger kept on going and almost ran over Michelle in his haste. Now it seemed to him as though they had covered too little ground. They were too close to the cavern where Joshua had decided to make his stand.

"Are you all right?" Roger asked.

"Boy, am I glad you're back!"

He held out his hands to help her to his feet. She was shaking as though with a malarial fever.

"What is it? What happened?"

She buried her face in his chest, sobbing quietly.

"I'm sorry, " he said, meaning it. "I really had no idea you would be so scared all alone. It must've been awful."

"It's not just that. There's something up there."

"Up where?" He wondered if she was losing control through fear of the dark.

"Shhh, just listen for a moment."

They stood there for a few seconds, Roger again heard the popping sound of firing. "Come on, we've got to keep moving."

He felt her head moving against his chest and assumed that meant agreement. She moved around behind him and he felt her grab his belt. He started to walk along the cave. The floor had a perceptible downwards slope now. Roger had visions of them running out of a surface to walk on, but he said nothing of that to Michelle.

*

The insistent ringing of the telephone beside his bed woke up Magnus Malan, the South African Minister of Defence. As he groped for the instrument he checked the radio clock on the bedside table - 2.38 am. He groaned to himself. She wouldn't say anything now, but he was going to hear all about it from his wife at the breakfast table. She hated being disturbed before 8.00 am on a Thursday. Wednesday was bridge night and she invariably came in late.

As quietly as possible he lifted the handset and muttered, "Ja?" He was still half asleep.

It was PW Botha, the State President, on the line. The Minister of Defence was instantly awake. "I've just heard from Louw," the State President said. "He's just received an interesting communication from his Frelimo counterpart in Mozambique. As you know we've had a credibility problem because of our earlier support for Renamo. This new development gives us the perfect opportunity to demonstrate our commitment to friendly relationships with Mozambique. It'll also prove we're not providing Renamo with covert support. You are to see that his suggestions are carried out."

"What would you like me to do, sir?"

The instructions passed on to him by the State President left the Minister of Defence smiling.

This was more like the old days.

*

They had been hiking upwards for a hour-and-a-half when
Jakes called a halt. Gratefully Mary-Ann sank to the
ground, lying stretched out, staring up at the few stars that
could be seen through the clouds, but not really seeing
them.

"How long do you think it will take?" she asked.

"Three, maybe four hours."

She wondered if the loss of Kathy, her mother, hadn't
finally caught up with him. People said he talked little and
she knew that to be true. But perhaps he had talked to
Kathy and missed that?

He started reading her mind again.

"I came over on the Trust's work in the seventies. That's
nearly twenty years ago. It feels like I've spent my whole
life here in Africa." He fell silent again.

Mary-Ann wondered if he was trying to give her more
time to rest.

They were both silent for a long while.

"I miss Kathy," Jakes said at last.

"I would have liked a mother," she said.

After a while he stirred. "I was very hurt by what the
Trustees did. And I didn't have Kathy to talk to. That made
it … difficult."

Mary-Ann moved restlessly, hesitated, finally decided it
was that sort of night. "That was probably my fault. That
had nothing to do with you."

"How can it be your fault?"

She told him about Professor Prins and Buenos Aires and
everything that had happened afterwards. Jakes was silent
for a long while after she had finished talking.

"Perhaps it's a good thing I didn't know about this
sooner. I would have done something foolish."

He paused.

"I know the man well. We've worked together for years.
He's arrogant but at the same time his knowledge of
wildlife is encyclopaedic. He's probably the best of all the

conservationists on this continent. We still have to respect him for that, even if we don't respect him as a person."

"I thought you found everyone in the city arrogant?"

Jakes chuckled. "I suppose so."

He talked about Kambala's family and how he had promised to look after them. "Little Cat, when I'm gone will you make sure they're all right? It's my fault Kambala was killed by a lion. The Trust won't dare back down from their responsibilities if they know someone's watching."

Jakes told her what he was trying to do with the black lion and how and why it had become so important to him. "But doing this thing," he finished sadly, "exposed Kambala to danger and then some other lion turned man-eater …"

"Is that where we're going now?"

"Yes. Lungile was right. Kambala's spirit must be released so that my old friend may sleep soundly in the shadow of his ancestors."

Mary-Ann realised to what extent her father had become a child of Africa. On the surface he still seemed American, but underneath flowed the strong raw currents of the dark continent. Had she too become infected?

"But in one way Lungile was wrong," Jakes added with conviction. "He was wrong about which lion it was that turned man-eater. It's not my black lion. It's some other lion."

Mary-Ann had known and respected Lungile and his understanding of game and tracking since she was a child. She also knew that his knowledge on those subjects was probably only rivalled by the legendary Bushmen of the Kalahari. Now she said nothing. This wasn't a subject on which she was prepared to play Devil's Advocate.

"Well," Jakes said after another short silence. "We'd better get on if we want to make the crest before sunrise."

*

Major Anderson beckoned to Sergeant-Major Kellerman. "It seems that our Minister of Defence is feeling his oats again."

"What's happened, Major?"

"I've just received the following message:

```
YOU'RE UP AGAINST A BAND OF RENAMO
REBELS STOP THIS IS OUR CHANCE TO SHOW
THE FRELIMO GOVERNMENT WHERE OUR
SYMPATHIES LIE STOP NO REBELS ARE TO
ESCAPE BACK TO MOZAMBIQUE STOP TAKE NO
PRISONERS.
```

The Sergeant-Major grinned. "We can go in boots and all, sir. The boys will like that. I'll tell them now. We're almost ready for dawn." He saluted.

The Major returned the salute. "Carry on, Sergeant-Major."

*

The lion limped along slowly, large head down, bloodshot yellow eyes fixed on the crevice. He was still following the scent and the sounds of the woman on the move as they drifted up from the cave below. The depth of the crevice shelved rapidly here and his prey was now only a few feet below him. The lion's instincts told him that such proximity was good as was his positioning for whatever charge he could manage. When he made his move he wouldn't have far to go on his lame leg. Also he was already above his prey so that his charge would be downwards making it more difficult for his prey to take evasive action.

The lion limped slowly along above the woman.

*

Brian Lombard hurried across to Jakes' bungalow. It was 5.00 a.m. The army would be waiting for him to accompany them to the river ford. It didn't take him long to discover the cottage was still empty, the vehicles still gone.

"Damn it," he cursed aloud, having a good idea of where they would be.

He would have to tell Major Anderson. The army had to know before they launched their attack into the valley. Brian hurried across to where he had last seen the Major outside his ops room.

"Right," the Major called out as Brian came around the corner, "we've been waiting for you. Now we can go. No time to waste. Sunrise in forty minutes." He turned to Marty Martins. "Could you please tell your Captain we're all here now. We can go any time he's ready."

"Sure thing. Hey, Hammie," he yelled across the intervening space between the buildings and the helicopter.

Paul stuck his head out of the cockpit of the Alouette.

Marty cupped his hands around his mouth. "You can kick the tyres and light the fire."

The Major shook his head. "What I meant, Sergeant, was that you could walk across to the helicopter like a civilised human being and quietly inform your Captain of the situation. If it was simply a case of screaming I could've done that myself."

"Major," Brian reluctantly interrupted, "there's something you need to know. The Webber's are missing – both of them."

The Major raised his eyebrows. "And the significance of this?"

"I'm think they're on their way to the valley."

Major Anderson's jaw muscles twitched. "I thought there was only one way in?"

"Jakes will know of others. Probably up and over a mountain. I think I've heard him say something about that."

Major Anderson slammed his fist into the palm of his other hand. "They've got to be stopped. Now that we know we're not dealing with an invasion the southern sector can lend us their chopper." He turned to the Sergeant-Major. "Radio for an additional helicopter from the south sector to search for them." He swung back to Brian. "Was that the Park's JetRanger coming in last night?"

"Yes, it was."

"All right then," Major Anderson barked. "Have the JetRanger search along the northern mountain range while the south sector Alo can search along the southern range. Come on, gentlemen, let's move. We want to be in the valley as early as possible."

*

Mary-Ann Webber needed something else to think about. It could be anything. She didn't care. Anything to take her mind off her legs. And particularly her thighs. They were beyond the tired stage and had now become simply numb – lumps of lead she had to pick up and put down – endlessly. So she had to think of something else.

Dawn in the bush was a good subject. How did a person know it would soon be time for the sun to put in its appearance, before any change in the east? It was a question of sounds. The night sounds slowly gave way to the day sounds. And that process of change started before the night sky had been affected. Unfortunately that exhausted the subject and Mary-Ann went back to thinking about her legs.

It was hard work walking behind Jakes. The slightest slacking off meant being left behind. Then it took an extra effort to catch up again. It was better to stay close all the time. And she suspected him of having already slowed his pace to accommodate her. Mary-Ann shook her head, wondered about this bandy-legged old father of hers that bounced along in front of her.

"The man's indestructible," she muttered to herself as she washed along in his wake.

Jakes stopped immediately and eyed her. He nodded. "Do you mind if we stop a moment, Little Cat. These old legs of mine can't take it anymore."

It was equally annoying that he should also have the hearing of a bat, no normal person would have heard her complaint. But Mary-Ann didn't argue. She was too tired.

With a huge sigh of relief she flopped bonelessly down onto the ground. Jakes handed her his canteen. She waved it away. She felt too tired to drink.

"Drink, Little Cat. You must take in water."

He was right. She raised herself onto one elbow and drank from the canteen. It really was refreshing. She looked at her father.

"I know it's different to the way you feel but I'm as committed to conservation," Mary-Ann said. "It's just that I have my own ideas as to how we're going to ensure that wildlife survives into the future."

"I've read your book. Your ideas seem sound."

Mary-Ann was astonished, he had never mentioned opening it.

"It's time for a new generation. I like your ideas. The biggest threat is not a lack of knowledge. We've gained a lot of that over the last fifty or sixty years on both the practical and scientific fronts. We need to ensure a macro environment that'll give people the time, space and money to actually get on with the job. In most cases nowadays we know what has to be done."

Mary-Ann stared at him. Why hadn't they had this conversation before?

"I don't give a damn what Professor Prins does, he's not going to force me out of conservation." She added, "It's seems such a pity he should waste his time attacking me."

"I agree and I think you're right to stay in conservation. It's where your heart has always been. Just be careful when the day comes and you start thinking of marriage. You'd better find a husband that understands your passion."

Mary-Ann didn't respond immediately. She lay there and thought long and hard about what he had said. Finally, hesitantly, she began to talk about Roger.

Floodgates.

It all came out in one great torrent of emotion. She told Jakes all about the man she loved. She also told him about the problem she'd had with Roger. That he was married and he had lied to her. Now she found herself unable to trust him.

Jakes stroked his goatee beard. "These are noble sentiments, Little Cat. But tell me - do you know why he lied?"

"Yes," she said, so annoyed she didn't have time to feel embarrassed discussing these things with her father, "so that he could go to bed with me."

"Do you think he loves you?"

"Yes," she said slowly. "Yes, I think he does."

"It sounds to me like the two of you should be talking. I think you should be trying to work through all these things. When you have finality – one way or the other – you will be able to get on with your life, with or without him, whichever way it works out. As long as this situation remains unresolved it's going to stand in your way."

"But he lied to me."

"I agree lies are unacceptable. And you have never told a lie?"

"No, Pa. Not in that way. Not to someone I love. Nothing can justify that. You cannot lie to people you love. I feel very very strongly about that. I would never ever lie to someone I love."

Jakes shrugged. "If that's how you feel then you must carry on without him." He stood up and brushed himself off.

"Come," he said then, "we must go. Soon the sun will rise and we want to be on the crest by then."

*

Joshua Manyoba listened to the crunch of Roger's departing footsteps until he was absolutely sure he could hear them no more. He crawled to the other side of the small rock chamber. He was back in the dark, all by himself. He smiled grimly to himself as he stuck the barrel of the AK47 into the tunnel that led to the cave entrance. He pulled the trigger without bothering to aim.

Joshua could barely hear the screams emanating from the front of the cave and the rantings that followed hot on their heels. His ears throbbed painfully after having fired the AK47 in the confined space. For a moment he worried about possible damage to his eardrums. He soon remembered his present circumstances and laughed at himself. The status of his hearing had to be the least of his concerns.

Joshua rolled over to lie on his stomach facing the tunnel which led to the front of the cave and as he did so felt the lumps on his belt. Of course, he still had his two hand-grenades. Then he remembered his idea from earlier. He only wished he could guarantee the presence of Abel Gamellah when it happened. But that was also a bit like worrying about his hearing. The Butcher had very little time remaining, even if he escaped again. It was the end of the road for both of them.

Joshua slotted his last magazine into the AK47 and stuck the barrel of the rifle into the tunnel. He fired blindly until the magazine was empty. He lay the weapon down on the floor of the cave. He crawled around to one side of the chamber and lay there with his back resting against the rock wall. He wondered if he would have the courage to go through with his plan.

There was only one way to find out.

Joshua unclipped the two hand-grenades from his belt and lay them down alongside his leg so that he would be able to find them again easily in the dark. He could feel them nestling there like two small puppies seeking comfort from the warmth of his body. He picked up one of the grenades and pulled out the pin. He slipped the grenade under his leg so that the weight would keep the lever in place. He picked up the second hand-grenade and also removed its pin. He held that in his left hand. He felt under his leg with his right hand until he was certain he had the lever of the second grenade under his palm and slipped it out from under his leg.

Joshua sat like that for a while.

He wondered what was happening in the front of the cave, but he was still deaf from firing off the last cartridges he'd had for the AK47. All he could hear was the ringing in his ears. Soon he developed an itch on the back of his neck. He tried to reach back with the grenade to scratch it with that, but it was not very efficient. So he consigned the itch to the same place he had consigned his concern about his hearing.

He had no idea how long he had been sitting there when suddenly somebody fired an AK47 through the tunnel. He felt something tear across his stomach as bullets ricocheted around the small chamber. Joshua felt a blow to the side of his head and then something slammed into his right shoulder. He could no longer feel his hands at the ends of his arms and knew that it was all over.

As the hand-grenades rolled out of his involuntarily unclasped hands, his last thought was a vague regret that the Butcher was not there, in that small chamber, with him at the end.

Joshua would have liked that.

*

The cave had really become just a fissure in the rock, but it still narrowed somewhat above Roger and Mary-Ann so they weren't able to climb out. But the fissure was cramped, a lot less like a cave along there, with the night sky and the stars clearly visible through the narrow gap above their heads.

The hollow boom of a giant bass drum sounded in the distance. Roger and Michelle jerked to a stop. As soon as they thought it was over, it was followed by the sound of nearby thunder as intimidating as the after-shock of an earthquake.

"Oh, my God!" exclaimed Michelle. "What was that?"

Before Roger could answer an instant squall from behind overtook them, carrying with it the smell and taste of a dust-storm. The swirling wind was gone as quickly as it had arrived. Roger sighed and said a silent 'thank you' to Joshua.

"What on earth was that?"

Roger shrugged. "At a guess I'd say Joshua let off a hand-grenade in the small chamber."

"But there seemed to be two noises."

"The grenade must have caused the roof of the chamber to cave in."

Michelle buried her face in his chest. "That's awful. This is a nightmare. That poor man."

Roger shrugged again. "It means we're probably safe from those characters back there."

Just then they both heard a soft sound from above, where the fissure in rock opened to the night sky.

"What was that?" Michelle whispered nervously.

"I have no idea," he replied. "Maybe just the wind." But he knew there was no wind. "We don't know for sure what happened back there. We might not necessarily be in the clear."

"Do you think some of ... those people ... are up there, too?"

"It could be them. I honestly don't know."

"What are we going to do, Roger?"

He held a finger to his lips. "Be very quiet," he whispered close to her ear. He pointed ahead of them. "There's the exit. We must wait in here," he looked around, "behind that rock there. No one will be able to see us if they just take a quick look inside. We're not leaving this place until the sun is up and we're sure it's clear."

Quietly, with his arm around her shoulders, Roger led Michelle across to the huge boulder he had just pointed out. She shivered uncontrollably.

*

The sound of the woman breathing and her smell were only a few feet below the lion now and they came from just one place. His prey had stopped moving. The black lion edged forward slowly, belly to the ground, the end of his tail

flicking from side to side. He came to the brink of the rock.
Here the upper surface – which had cracked to allow the
formation of the crevice – ended and there was a drop of
three metres down to a ledge which was on the same level
as the cave floor.

There were two possibilities. The lion could either go
down to the ledge and make its way into the cave to seek
out its prey or it could lie in wait for its prey to emerge.
Generally a male lion's instincts will have it wait in
concealment while the lionesses from the pride go upwind
of the prey, using their presence to drive the scared quarry
downwind to where the lions of the pride can launch an
attack from ambush.

Now the lion backed off a few feet from the lip above the
cave entrance proper. This close to the edge it was
particularly bare of any vegetation. He settled down low
amongst the stunted bush that grew further back on the
rocky upper surface. The lion's muscles quivered under his
skin.

The toll taken by the poisons spewing out from the
gangrenous wound in his shoulder had already severely
reduced his reserves of energy. The tension and effort of the
slow night-long stalk across the mountain top had almost
exhausted them altogether.

Almost.

But not quite.

Driven sufficiently hard by an instinct itself prodded by
the proximity of life-giving food the black lion would still
be able to manage one last desperate charge.

*

Major Anderson spoke into the radio. "Where are you
now?"

Lieutenant Luke Smith's whisper over the air barely
reached their ears. Instinctively Paul leaned forward so that
he could hear better.

"In case they moved we spent the night strung out to the
east, west and below their position on the hillside. Now

we've pulled back so that we can talk to you. There'll be no surprise attack. They're waiting. They've also got men down at the river. They saw the truck come in last night."

"We can't afford to wait then. The sooner we move the better. Lieutenant, I want you to pull back to the river and make sure the LZ is clear. The chopper's going to start ferrying my men across now."

"I'd like our landing zone to be clear, too," muttered Marty under his breath.

"Roger," replied Luke. "We're not far from there now. We should be in position within ten minutes." Major Anderson turned to Paul, but he had already climbed into the Alouette and was busy tightening his helmet strap.

Paul glanced across at Marty who gave him the thumbs-up. Paul rolled the throttle open to the indent starting position and squeezed the trigger switch. The electric starter motor whined shrilly. The rotors accelerated slowly. The turbine powered up. Throttle wide open he scanned all the gauges. Everything green. He gave Major Anderson the thumbs-up.

Four 32nd Battalion troopers and the Sergeant-Major clambered on board. They wore camouflage and bristled with bandoleers of ammunition, R4 rifles, grenade launchers, hand-grenades and canteens. With the two crew the Alouette could take 5 pax and their equipment, but then it was pretty full in there at the helicopters maximum all up weight – or MAUW – of 2,200 kg . Paul pulled up on the collective and could feel the weight but they were only going a short distance and weren't carrying much fuel so that made it easier.

The clothes of the circle of troopers – who would be on the next flight – flapped ferociously in the Alouette's gale and a small dust-storm built up around them as he took off.

The recces were meant to secure the LZ.

Maybe they had.

And maybe they hadn't.

Whatever.

Paul wasn't going to make it easy for the bad guys. He swung out wide across the valley climbing to get a fix on his LZ. From 100 feet agl he could see it, a small hole down among the trees alongside the river. He nosed the ship over in a steep dive.

The Alouette was really moving. Using the speed gained in the dive the helicopter flashed across the treetops at more than 200 kilometres per hour. When he judged the moment right, he pulled back on the cyclic and reduced collective to flare, looking frantically ahead, trying to see over the almost vertical nose of the Alouette to get his first glimpse of the LZ since he had started to dive. His tail rotor spun just a few feet above the trees. The LZ was dead ahead. Steeply, nose high, the helicopter rapidly decelerated for the landing. He saw some bushes ahead, and pushed the right pedal to swing the tail rotor away from them.

"Clear behind!" yelled Marty as he checked that their tail rotor wouldn't foul any bushes.

Halfway down the narrow funnel of trees surrounding the small LZ the rotor wash stirred up the surface and everything vanished in the dust storm. As the wheels hit the ground the buffalo soldiers started jumping out and bounding off towards the edge of the clearing, firing as they went.

From at least three different directions, the Renamo fighters opened up on the Alouette and the off-loading troopers with machine-gun crossfire. The LZ was suddenly alive with their screaming bullets. Paul tensed on the controls, involuntarily leaning forward, ready to take-off. He had to fight the logical reaction.

Marty watched the troopers disembark.

"Go! Go! Go!" He yelled over the intercom.

Paul hauled up on the collective and the now-light helicopter shot up into the air as though fired from a cannon.

Fifty-calibre tracers as big as tennis balls came in at them from up ahead. They sliced across the trees in flattened lazy-looking arcs. In between each tracer were four more bullets. A fifty-calibre machine gun spits out bullets a centimetre in diameter and two-and-a-half centimetres long.

Tick-tick-tick - bullet holes appeared in the Plexiglas over his head.

Tick – somewhere in the airframe.

He was up and out of the trees. Pedal-turn. Nose down. Tick. Go. Tick. Climb.

The heavy-calibre machine-gun raked the Alouette along its belly.

Paul shook his head. "These guys are on the ball," he drawled into his stalk microphone. "They knew which way we'd come in and go out. And they've set up machine-guns along our flight path." He paused.

"The next run's gonna be interesting," he added, "We gotta use the same route again."

*

Jakes stood with his toes stuck into a crack which ran across the width of the rock-face. The bottom half stuck out further than the top half and made it a very easy place to maintain his balance. Mary-Ann stopped alongside Jakes to give her arms a rest. They were a metre short of the ledge. She shook her head dubiously. "I don't know if I'd like to do this every day. Even with these ring things you've put in."

Jakes smiled at her.

After a few seconds she asked: "Do you want to go first?"

Jakes shook his head and gestured for her to go ahead.

Mary-Ann took a deep breath and then let it out slowly. The climb was well marked with plenty of handholds and small ledges for a climber to use. Over time Jakes had driven old-fashioned pitons into the rock face all the way from the bottom to the top.

Still, she didn't like heights and just making the climb easy was not going to change that. Mary-Ann clambered up the last metre and with a sigh of relief crawled out onto the top level. She immediately turned around to help her father over the edge.

Not that he seemed to need much help. He had climbed the rock-face like a dassie.

She looked over his shoulder, clapped her hands to her mouth.

"Dad! Just look at it."

She stood there absolutely enthralled.

This was one of the high points in the Lebombo mountain range giving an uninterrupted view to the far horizon. To the south the bushveld, ridged by rocky hillocks and the odd isolated small mountain, stretched out endlessly as far as the eye could see. The cloud build-up from the afternoon before had dissipated during the night. The brightest stars could still just be seen overhead in the dark blue night-sky. Yet smeared on the rim of the world, right around the horizon, were the reds and oranges of the sunrise.

She swung around. "And there's the sun now. It's magnificent."

The upper edge of the brilliant red-orange orb peeked above the eastern horizon. The coolth of the night dissipated. The day was going to be a scorcher.

Jakes smiled easily at Mary-Ann. Her enthusiasm was infectious.

"Come," he said. "there's a cave just across there. We can use that to get into the valley."

Mary-Ann nodded, still enthralled by the sunrise.

*

Just as dawn was breaking, with the dark shadows still long across the cave mouth, both Roger and Michelle heard a voice calling out. They crouched deeper into the dark behind the boulder just inside the cave entrance, glanced at each other. Roger put his arm around her shoulders. For the fraction of a second she gratefully rested her head on his shoulder.

Again the voice.

"That's a woman," whispered Michelle.

Roger started. Good God! So it was – and very familiar.

Michelle stirred restlessly against him. "Those other people didn't have a woman with them."

"That's Mary-Ann," Roger replied.

"Are you sure?"

"Yep," he replied. "I wonder if they're looking for us."

Michelle smiled wryly. "I never thought I'd be glad to hear *her* voice."

Roger helped her to her feet. "Let's get outta here."

Four paces and they were at the entrance to the cave. Roger peered out cautiously, just in case. Mary-Ann stood with her back to them staring out over the valleys and foothills that rolled away to the south. Even from the back Roger recognised her at once. A smallish man stood next to her.

"It's okay," Roger said. "It's Mary-Ann all right." Roger had his arm around Michelle's shoulder as he guided her out into the dawn light.

Emerging from the cave they suddenly heard the most terrifying and horrific of sounds, an earth-shattering, ground-shaking roar that made it seem as though the end of the world had come. The loud roar was so menacing and so powerful it disorientated Roger. Michelle shook uncontrollably under his arm.

Roger spun around wildly.

The roaring surrounded them, filled the whole world. In his peripheral vision a movement caught his eye. It was off to his left on the plateau above the cave. From that angle all he could see was the low scrub shaking violently as something charged through it. Roger grabbed Michelle's arm, pulled her back towards the relative safety of the cave. She was too shocked to respond. She pulled away from him, eyes blank.

Roger heard a man shout off to his right. It was so fierce it drew his attention despite the roaring. The bandy-legged man stood next to Mary-Ann, hands cupped to his mouth like a megaphone. The small man shouted again and darted off to one side. He ran along the ledge, waving his arms wildly, rifle in one hand.

Immediately, like a kitten drawn to a clockwork mouse, the dark shape that came hurtling through the scrub and off the plateau above the cave, effortlessly switched direction in one fluid movement.

*

Mary-Ann froze as she swung around to see her father run along the ledge to their right, waving his arms wildly. The dark shape from above the cave closed the gap with long-reaching strides.

"Dad!" Mary-Ann yelled.

But there was nothing she could do. A lion is capable of speeds up to 60 kilometres an hour in short bursts.

The lion easily overtook the running Jakes, reeling him in like a fish on the end of a line. Four giant strides and the lion launched itself into the air and landed on Jakes' back.

One giant paw, claws fully extended, passed over Jakes' right shoulder and covered his face. One hundred-and-fifty kilograms of lion drove Jakes into the ground. As he went down he contrived to roll onto his back.

Rooted to the spot, Mary-Ann could see little of the lion. Half of the sun was above the horizon and the bright ball was directly behind where the man and the lion wrestled on the ground. She heard the hollow boom of Jakes' .375 – and again – and again.

The lion roared some more, but the sound faded quickly.

The rifle's crack set Mary-Ann running. As she drew nearer the big cat reared up and backwards, before collapsing sideways. Still on his back Jakes tried to work the bolt of his rifle, but dropped it. The lion had fallen alongside him. When she got there she saw Jakes' bullets had all gone up into the lion's chest and straight out of its back, shattering the spine en route. Little wonder it had collapsed so quickly.

Mary-Ann fell to her knees beside her father. She stared in horror. Instead of a face all Jakes had was a bloody mask. His eyes, nose and his lips had been shredded away by the lion's claws. White bone gleamed for an instant as Jakes coughed up blood, then was hidden again in the red mask he wore.

"Dad! Dad!" Mary-Ann screamed. Then abruptly calmed down. There had to be something she could do. Mary-Ann quickly ripped the buttons off her khaki shirt and shrugged her way out of it. Using the ivory-handled knife from the sheath on his belt she cut off a sleeve. Roger reached her side. He silently stretched the material out as she hacked at it with the knife and tore it into strips.

"Mary-Ann? Little Cat?" Jakes gurgled as air forced its way through the blood in his throat.

She knelt down beside him. "Yes, Dad. it's me. Mary-Ann."

Jakes half lifted one arm, feeling blindly with his hand.

"Here, Dad, here I am." Mary-Ann took his hand in both of hers and clasped it tightly.

He turned his head in her direction as though he could see her. For a moment white gleamed where his lips had been. As before, the white was soon covered by the blood oozing from his face.

"It's … not … my lion, is it?" Jakes croaked.

Mary-Ann looked at the black male which lay alongside Jakes.

She had never seen a properly black lion before – unlike white lions, of which there were always a few around – black lions were extremely rare. The lion's coat was not altogether pitch black. She could just make out the normal dark lion markings faintly visible in the background. On the other hand the immature mane was of the blackest she had ever seen. Each hair in it gleamed like thin slivers of polished ebony.

She didn't hesitate.

"No," she replied softly, gently, but firmly, so there could be no doubt. "It's yellow."

The blood bubbled in the centre of what had been his face as he breathed in and out, the sound harsh in her ears. Momentarily he gripped her hand a little tighter.

"In twenty years," he said slowly and with obvious difficulty. So much so she was convinced he was never going to finish the sentence, "it's the first time I've known Lungile to be wrong about a spoor." His grip tightened again for just a moment. "You must never let him know he was wrong."

"I won't, Dad," was all she could say.

"But tell him Kambala's spirit is free to join his ancestors. You fix that."

"Yes, Dad."

"What do you want to do with this?" Roger asked helplessly, holding out the torn strips of shirt sleeve.

Mary-Ann's eyes were big and round and red as she turned to look at him. She started to shrug and instead said, "We should try to stop the bleeding."

Roger looked at her and she could see in his eyes the sympathy and raw emotion he felt, but right then she couldn't cope with that as well. "Let's just pack the cloth on ... his ... wounds. There's nothing else we can do."

As they worked all she could hear was the soft bubbling of the air through the rapidly thickening blood.

Roger knelt silently by her side.

"I don't know what to do," Mary-Ann said hopelessly, still on her knees by her father's side, clutching his hand. "There's nothing we can do. I can't help him."

"Can I get you anything? Is there any way I can help?"

Mary-Ann glanced up. Michelle had appeared at her shoulder. "Yes," she said, giving the dark-haired woman a small smile. "On my belt, there's a water bottle. Could you take it off for me?" She nodded to where she held her father's hand clasped in both of hers.

"Of course," Michelle replied, sliding the white plastic water bottle out of the webbing pouch which hung from Mary-Ann's belt. She unscrewed the lid. "Here." She held the water bottle to Mary-Ann's lips.

Mary-Ann drank deeply and gratefully. She was suddenly, desperately thirsty. "Thanks."

Michelle nodded in Jakes' direction. "Do you think …"

Mary-Ann shook her head. "No."

Mary-Ann sat there like that for forty minutes. No one said anything to her and she vaguely heard Michelle murmuring something to Roger, but she really wasn't paying attention. She remembered a whole lifetime in which so little was ever said between her and her father – until the long climb during the night.

Yet it had been all right, she decided finally. She had never felt deprived.

The high-pitched scream of an Alouette's jet turbine and hard chopping of its blades had her whipping around. A giant dirty-green hunchbacked dragon-fly appeared above the ridge, hovering just off the cliff face, the orange sun reflected in the silver windscreen.

The helicopter swung to hang in the air parallel to the ridge. In a blast of wind the ship slid sideways to hover in over the ledge and then landed. With the rotor blades still spinning wickedly, a man wearing khaki flying overalls jumped down and ran across to them.

He looked down at Mary-Ann and Jakes, turned his attention to Roger. "Are you Webber?" he asked. His voice was slightly muffled because he still wore his white flying helmet, the headset cable dangling down his back, swinging as he turned his head.

"No." Roger shook his head. He pointed to where Mary-Ann still kneeled beside her father. "They're the Webber's."

Mary-Ann looked up at the khaki-clad figure. He was so young, couldn't be more than twenty-one or twenty-two years old. What could he do to help?

"What happened?" The youngster was still looking at Roger.

Roger waved a hand in the air. "It was the lion. He took the charge. He saved our lives."

"C'mon, let's move," the youngster said quickly. "Let's get him to a medic."

Mary-Ann looked down at the man whose hand she still held in both of hers.

"No," she said. "There's no rush now."

She knew she sounded surprised. She hadn't noticed when he had stopped breathing – now there was no more need to hurry.

Roger picked up Mary-Ann's sleeveless shirt and she stood up to slip it on. No buttons – she couldn't remember how that had happened. She tied it in a knot at her waist.

Roger and the young flight engineer carried Jakes' body across to the Alouette. Mary-Ann and Michelle climbed inside. Because they were unable to hear with the noise of the blades and the jet engine the youngster pointed them to headsets they could wear. Mary-Ann put hers on numbly, trying to come to terms with a world in which her father no longer existed. She desperately wanted to turn to Roger, to bury her head in his chest, but felt awkward with Michelle there. The memory of the confrontation in London clear.

With a quick glance at Mary-Ann, Roger started to cover up the body on the floor of the helicopter. Mary-Ann caught his eye and shook her head, shrugged. It wasn't necessary. That wasn't her father. He was in her head, goatee beard jutting out, standing with arms aggressively akimbo. As long she remembered him like that, he would be alive for her – and she felt a little better.

The ledge fell away beneath them as the pilot took the Alouette up into a hover. Slowly they drifted sideways. Abruptly the ground disappeared as they swung away from the ridge.

Mary-Ann heard Roger's voice in her earphones. "Does it always shake like this?"

The pilot glanced back at Roger. He grinned behind his microphone. "That's how helos fly. They vibrate so much the earth rejects them."

He put the nose down and they rapidly built up forward speed. "We'll go to Skukuza. I've already radioed in."

For a few minutes they were all silent. The helicopter hustled along five hundred feet above the trees.

A voice came on the air and their pilot responded. A helicopter was in trouble, it said. He was ordered to turn back to the river where some of their troops were on the other side and under heavy fire, while the rest were unable to help being on the wrong side of the river.

"And the civilians?" the pilot asked curtly.

"Come in low and land where you see the truck. On the western bank of the river. They'll be all right there."

"Roger and out."

The pilot executed a steep turn to the right, rapidly going through 120 degrees before settling on a new heading. Five minutes later the Alouette seemed to swing on its own axis as it whipped around, skidding sideways with the abrupt but balanced movements of cyclic, pedals and collective. It floated down in a shallow dive until it seemed as though the wheels of the aircraft must be scraping the tops of the taller trees. And then, after a nose-up flare, they were on the ground.

Mary-Ann felt Michelle squirm on the seat next to her. She glanced at her, surprised to see the other woman white-faced. Michelle fidgeted again.

"The helicopter in trouble – is the pilot called Paul?"

The pilot glanced back over his shoulder. "Yes," he said into his mic. "Yes, he is." He sounded surprised, but didn't comment.

*

It was on their second run that the fifty-calibre machine-gun had really taken its toll. But that was later when they took off again.

As the helicopter neared the LZ Paul felt a ripple run through the ship's hull as lighter machine-gun fire hosed along her side. He 'bucked the horse' by pushing the helicopter's nose down with the cyclic and hauling up on the collective. The machine-gun fire fell away behind them as they accelerated. He pulled back on the cyclic allowing the ship to rise as her nose came up and banged down the collective and dropped her into the LZ, catching her again with the collective at the last moment, the wheels just kissing the ground as the rotors caught the falling chopper.

"Beautiful," Paul muttered to himself. "Just too goddam beautiful for words."

Within seconds the troops on board had disembarked.

"Go! Go! Go!" yelled Marty.

Paul raised the collective, demanded from the Alouette's jet engine the full 570 horses. With just the two of them on board and light on fuel the chopper came unstuck and climbed vertically like an express lift in a tall building.

They popped out of the hole in the trees. Paul pressed the cyclic forward and hauled up the collective as he bucked the horse out of there, but not before the fifty-calibre picked him up.

Tick-tick.

"Shit!" Paul yelled. "Those bastards have got us taped."

Tick-tick-tick.

As the bullets worked their way back along the ship's belly Paul felt the helicopter lurch uncomfortably. Tick-tick. Something had happened. Tick. But if they were going to go down it had to be on the other side of the river, otherwise they were dead meat. Everybody on the ground hates an enemy pilot.

Paul swung the cyclic left and kicked left rudder to enhance the movement. He felt the helicopter start to turn. He straightened the cyclic and centred the pedals in automatic anticipation of the helicopter reaching the right heading. But she kept on turning and he knew they had taken out the tail rotor. He slammed the collective down and closed the throttle to reduce the torque that the tail rotor normally countered but she kept on going and he was over the river and into the trees on the other bank.

The chopper hit as a grinding, crunching, screeching mass of metal and Perspex. The main rotor blades hacked at the trees doing close to five hundred miles an hour at the tips – and exploded into pieces. The mast snapped off. Broken parts flew everywhere. The gas turbine jet engine took on a life of its own and hit a high note that tore at his eardrums. A branch as thick as his thigh lanced through the Perspex windscreen and bounced off his flying helmet.

"Good things, bone-domes," he muttered as the helicopter ground its way through the trees towards the ground.

Halfway down the ship rolled onto its back, and rolled again before it smashed into the ground. Paul felt hot metal wrapping itself around his legs, but it didn't hurt – then.

As suddenly as it had started, it ended – an eerie silence after the terrible noises made by a dying helicopter.

"Marty! Are you okay?"

But there was no reply.

"Just don't burn, baby," Paul muttered aloud, hoping Marty was all right. "Just don't burn."

It seemed ages before he heard voices, but it was probably only a few seconds.

"Hey!" he shouted. "Hey! We're in here!"

Paul heard the voices say he was alive and he was glad they knew about that. But he heard them say the only way to reach him was to roll the chopper over onto her belly so they could get in through his door. A crack in the ship's airframe caught his eye and he traced it downwards. For the first time he was scared. He tried to scream 'No, don't do that', but all he could do was croak.

The helicopter began to tilt, but only the part around his upper body moved. The nose cone and the lower part of the fuselage – where his feet were all tangled up in the pedals – stayed where it was.

Paul was sure he had screamed or tried to, anyway. After that he must have blacked out, because he thought he had been having a nightmare.

Then he became aware of the mystery-lady-in-the-night looking down at where a medic was cutting away the trouser legs of his flying overalls. He was amazed the cloth was so dark and wet looking instead of its more usual khaki. His mystery-lady's eyes were big and round as she stared down at him.

"Both," the one medic said to the other. "Just below the knee."

"No!" he screamed at them.

"Hold him still – quickly now! Is the blood ready?"

"Yes," replied a voice from behind the medic.

Paul felt his sleeve being cut away from his arm. A needle slid in and he started to slip away. The last thing he saw was his mystery-lady staring down at him.

He wondered how it was all going to end.

*

While the army mopped up in the valley – after the rest of the troops were ferried across the river by the second Alouette – the JetRanger flew Roger and Mary-Ann back to Skukuza. Michelle stayed with Paul. The army medics wanted to stabilise him before having him flown out in the second Alouette directly to a military hospital.

Sitting in her father's cottage Roger talked to Mary-Ann for a long time. She couldn't sleep and didn't want to be left alone with her thoughts. As the hours slipped by and that Thursday disappeared forever, Roger convinced Mary-Ann of his sincerity and his love for her. He also explained his idea to her. He hardly dared breathe while he told her about it, but after a while she started to ask questions and he knew it was going to be all right.

Finally, at 3.00 am on the Friday morning she looked at him, nodding thoughtfully to herself. "You're pretty set on this, aren't you?

"Yes."

"And if I wasn't interested, you'd do it anyway?"

"Yes," he replied firmly. He had made that decision after seeing those Bushmen paintings on the rock wall in the cave. It wouldn't be easy without her, but he was prepared to give it his best shot.

She took his hand in hers. "That's what I like. A strong man who knows what he wants; who knows how he's going to go about getting it; and most important of all – what he wants is good!"

"I'm not as strong as you," he said quietly, "but I will do my best."

"You're stronger than you realise and your best will be fine."

After that they were both silent for a long time, wrapped in their own thoughts.

"Will *he* go for it?" Mary-Ann asked at length.

Roger shrugged. "All we can do is ask."

"What if he subsequently wants to renege on the deal?"

Roger snorted. "We'll get a signed document which would destroy him if he reneged and it was made public!"

*

It was 11.30 am on the Friday in London when Ms Mary Partridge breathlessly squawked at Basil Hawke over the intercom. "I've finally managed to get hold of the party in Mozambique. He's on line three, sir."

Hawke picked up the handset and immediately his sweaty palms made it wet. He pressed the button for line three.

"Minister dos Santos," Hawke was at his most unctuous. "I'm so pleased you could find the time to talk to me."

"*Senhor* Hawke. You must stop pestering me."

"I … I … don't understand. We have an agree–"

"We have nothing, *Senhor* Hawke. Absolutely nothing. We may have contemplated a possible issuing of mining licences, but that is all."

"But money was put into an account for –"

"*Senhor* Hawke! I've never touched any money you may've put into an account. We have a very fluid political situation here. What may have been possible yesterday will not always be possible today. I'd thank you not to contact me again."

The line went dead.

This time Hawke didn't ask Ms Partridge to put the call through for him. He made sure he had an outside line and began to dial. When his party came on the line he reminded them that when the money had been deposited provision had been made, as was his usual habit in this type of thing, for any one of two code names, together with the secret account number, to make withdrawals. They confirmed the balance was as yet untouched.

Hawke hesitated, but he had no choice really. Carefully he gave them instructions on what they were to do with the money.

*

Mary-Ann stuck her head through the doorway of the small office. "I'm all packed and ready. I've come to say goodbye."

Brian pulled a face. "I'm sorry to see you go. What are your plans?"

Mary-Ann shrugged, unfortunately she couldn't tell him yet, just in case something went wrong, it was all up to Roger.

"Not too sure. How are things with you?"

Brian looked extremely gloomy. "Management has it in for me. Because of this black lion story, helping to keep it a secret and it's against policy."

"I'm sorry, Brian. And it was all my father's fault, too."

"They've taken my area away from me. That's why I'm here in Jakes' old office."

Mary-Ann stared at Brian. Should she tell him about Roger's idea? Better not. It would only get his hopes up – maybe for nothing.

.

PART FIVE
Later ...

.

Raul de Rivera slouched in a deep cowhide-covered armchair. As head of the Darien Cartel he held court in the sitting-room of his sprawling ranch house. He turned to his brother Simon.

"Now for the last item of the day. I want a progress report."

"*No hay problema.*"

Simon walked across the sitting room and opened the door to the passageway.

It was a spacious spread-out room, colourful with antique hand woven South American alpaca wool carpets strewn over the polished red-tiled floor. The fierce Colombian heat was largely kept out by extra thick adobe walls and finally tempered by the natural air-conditioning provided by the cool sea breeze off the Gulf of Darien, which flowed through the house. Simon stuck his head out of the doorway.

"Enrique, *te toca a ti.*"

He walked back to the other end of the room followed by a tall slender man wearing a white open-necked shirt and pale cream slacks under a blue blazer.

"*Buenas tardes, Señor* de Rivera."

Raul leapt to his feet.

"Enrique Belmonte!"

He threw his arms around the tall man and patted him on the back. Being unacceptable in that South American community there was no cheek kissing. He held him at arm's length.

"You are looking well. Simon didn't tell me he was using you for this job."

Enrique waved his arms in the air. "Little brothers! What can you expect?"

Raul sat down in his armchair in the corner of the cool room and waved Enrique across to the sofa. "What news do you have for us?"

"The man you're looking for, he now calls himself Bashir Harik and is living in Beirut."

Raul smiled. "Well done, Enrique, *muchas gracias*. You're a miracle worker, as always. You know what to do?"

Enrique nodded, *"Si, Señor* de Rivera. It will be taken care of within forty-eight hours."

*

Colonel Wallender was apprehensive over the interview. What should he say? How should he handle the man? So much had changed from the last time they had met. Reluctantly he pressed the button on his intercom. "All right, Corporal, ask Captain Hammond to come in."

The door swung open and Paul rolled his wheelchair in fast, having to skid a little to avoid running into the Colonel's desk. The Colonel eyed him and gave a sigh of relief.

Following the wheelchair in was one of the most elegant women the Colonel had ever come across. Dark hair, carefully groomed, framed a beautiful face with high cheekbones and the most delightful sloe eyes. The pale blue linen suit she wore was devastatingly casual.

The Colonel stood up, inclined his head. He offered her his hand.

"You must be Mrs Hammond. I'm Brett Wallender. Please sit down."

"How do you do, Colonel," Michelle replied, smiling as she gracefully sat down in the chair in front of his desk.

She could have made a *Vogue* cover right there, he thought.

The Colonel sat down again. He felt like apologising for not having a better chair for her to use. Instead he looked at Paul. "I'm sorry about Marty – I know how close you were."

Paul winced and a short, awkward silence ensued.

The Colonel tried again. "How are you, Paul?"

Paul frowned. "Very upset, Colonel."

The Colonel rolled his eyes upwards and sighed, but couldn't resist the bait. "Why?"

"They don't want to give me a conversion on to the faster sporting model wheelchair – just in case you're not up on your wheelchairs, that's the Mark IV. The manoeuvrability on this old Mark III is terrible. The technology is outdated. Did you see my quick stop? I nearly hit your desk." He shook his head slowly from side to side. "The doc is already briefing me for my new feet. So he says there's no point in doing the conversion. I'm very unhappy, sir."

The Colonel and Michelle exchanged old-fashioned looks.

The Colonel straightened some papers on his desk. "Paul, you know you can't fly with us any–"

"And very glad I am, too," interrupted Paul, pulling a face. "Dangerous things helicopters. Ten thousand spare parts looking for a place to have an accident." After a beat he added sadly, "and they're very noisy."

The Colonel ignored him. "But we'd like you to be chief instructor on our new three million dollar helicopter simulator. It's a remarkable piece of –"

Paul eyes went wide open. He swallowed once and took a deep breath. Then he waved a casual hand in the air. "Read about it somewhere. Computer controlled, full three-axis movement, complete control of wind speeds and direction, weather as required, independent systems control to simulate any kind of emergency."

He turned to look at Michelle. "I knew they'd ask me. I knew that."

Michelle raised her eyebrows. "Sure you did."

Colonel looked from one to the other. "I must say you seem very happy together."

Paul and Michelle just smiled at each other.

*

Brian sat in Jakes' old office, behind Jakes' old desk. He was watching a sunbeam move across the scarred wooden surface, wondering why that gave him a sense of déjà vu. Either he had done it before or he had watched someone else doing it. A convenient way to pass the time – but only if you had absolutely nothing else to do.

Ah well, there was always his mail. The highlight of the day.

He quickly flicked through the pile. Nothing from a university but that was to be expected. They had all turned him down for a bursary already. Why should they change their minds now? Two or three bills. He could look at those later when he felt stronger. And a letter from England. Brian frowned.

He stuck his finger under the flap, tore the envelope open and extracted the letter from inside. It was brief – only one page – and to the point.

Brian let out a whoop that echoed through the administration block. He stared at the piece of paper in his hand. He reached for the telephone.

*

Mary-Ann frowned at the receptionist. "Long distance, you say," she sighed, looked at her watch. "All right, I'll take the call."

"Mary-Ann, Mary-Ann, are you there?"

"You're going to wreck my eardrum, Brian. Other than that it's always good to hear from you. Any special reason for the call?"

Brian's voice echoed hollowly in her ear. "I've just received your letter. Is this serious? I mean is this really going to happen?"

Mary-Ann smiled. "It's serious. You have a bursary from International Wildlife Limited. It'll cover five years of study at the university of your choice."

"Thank you very much, Mary-Ann. But how did you manage it? And what are you doing?"

Mary-Ann gave her wrist-watch another quick glance. "Brian, I'm sorry, but I just don't have time to chat now. I was due in a meeting two minutes ago. Can I call you back later? And will you be in the office?"

As soon as she heard his reluctant acceptance Mary-Ann rang off and hurried into the boardroom.

*

Roger looked up as the boardroom door opened. He rose to his feet and the rest of the men present did the same. "Gentlemen, you all know Mary-Ann."

She hurried across to him. "Have you started?" she asked quietly.

Roger shook his head. "Patrick hasn't arrived yet."

"It's all going according to plan?"

"Yes," Roger said, leaning close, so that he could speak softly into her ear. "Based on my rejection of the title and inability to father children, Patrick is now the Earl of Watbridge. So he controls the family's shares in the bank. In view of the large shareholding his fellow directors wisely– and unanimously – voted him in as the bank's new –. Ah ha," he said, interrupting himself. "Here's the man in person."

Patrick looked splendidly self-important in his dark blue suit with the appropriate broad stripe. He hurried around to the head of the boardroom table, placed his briefcase on top of it, neatly stacked his bowler hat on that. He inclined his head. "Good day, one and all."

A murmur sounded from around the boardroom table.

Roger whispered to Mary-Ann. "Sounds pretty chipper."

Mary-Ann nodded her agreement.

Patrick coughed into his fist. "Ladies and gentlemen, before we start I'd like to apologise for being a few minutes late."

Again a murmur sounded from around the table.

Patrick smiled his thanks. "I take great pleasure in opening the first official board meeting of International Wildlife Limited. If you'll bear with me I'd like to sum up the organisation for the record and the first entry in the company's minute book." He nodded in the direction of the secretary who sat with a pencil poised over the stenographer's pad on her lap.

"First, the core board members," he said. "As you know I have the honour to be patron and non-executive chairman. Dr Mary-Ann Denton is our managing director and CEO, while my brother, Roger, is our marketing director. The company's mission statement is incorporated in the best-seller authored by our very own MD." He coughed into his fist and had a sip of water from the glass in front of him.

"Because of my recent appointment as the bank's Executive Chairman I've been able to put together a consortium of associated merchant banks, that is, my bank here in the City, and our associates in Paris, Rome, New York and Tokyo. Together we'll underwrite the company's initial $50 million funding which is to be placed with bank clients.

"I would like it recorded in the minutes that the popularity of Mary-Ann's book, its concerns with ecology and the fact that she's made over all the rights to the company played a major role in convincing the banks that this was a worthwhile project in which to be involved."

"Hear, hear," Roger called out. He started to clap and was soon joined by the rest of those present. Even the secretary put down her pad and joined in.

Roger laughed at the red-faced Mary-Ann.

He leaned over to whisper in her ear: "I'm so glad their bankers' hearts are in the right place on the issue of conservation. Of course, it just happens to be bloody good advertising for them, too. Not to mention that they'll make a fat profit when placing the shares with their clients."

Patrick held up a hand. "Thank you." He gestured to Mary-Ann. "Before I ask Mary-Ann to say a few words I have really exciting news. A word of caution. This must for the next while remain confidential amongst those present. I have it on excellent authority that in the very near future Nelson Mandela is to be released from prison as part of the on-going talks between the South African Government and the African National Congress. I can't begin tell you what good news this is for our mission. It will be so much easier to promote inter-governmental cooperation between Southern African countries."

He again gestured to Mary-Ann. "A few words, perhaps?"

Mary-Ann rose to her feet. Roger thought she still looked slightly flustered from the applause. He saw her chin lift. He smiled to himself.

"Thank you for the laudatory remarks," she started. "Simply put, we're not waiting for governments to get their acts together. This company represents a private initiative to create one huge sanctuary for wild animals from South Africa to Kenya. A sanctuary that not only preserves those animals for future generations but makes a profit doing it.

"And the news about Nelson Mandela is indeed wonderful. The other African Governments will feel much less constrained about dealing openly with the South African Government. The support of those governments will make our goals much more attainable.

"In that regard then," she continued, "I'd like to introduce you to a gentleman who represents our first successful step." Mary-Ann gestured towards someone on the other side of the boardroom table. "I give you the vice-president of Mozambique, the right honourable Minister Juan Batero Dos Santos." She sat down.

Dos Santos stood up and bowed politely from the waist. "We, the Frelimo Government in Mozambique, have always been at the cutting edge of green issues. We believe in the advancement of animal life and we must stop poaching and the misuse of animals, too. This is why it gave me great pleasure to sign, on behalf of my government, the commitment to make land available for your most noble mission." He sat down again.

As chairman, Patrick took over again and they quickly worked their way through the rest of the agenda. Roger and Mary-Ann stayed behind as everyone else filed out.

Mary-Ann grinned at Roger. "Heaven forbid our Mozambican politician's new-found enthusiasm should make him go further and become an animal rights activist!"

Before Roger could reply the secretary stuck her head through the doorway. She looked at Mary-Ann. "There's another call for you. Will you take it in here?"

Mary-Ann nodded. "Sure."

The telephone gave a discreet beep and Mary-Ann picked up the handset. "Hullo," she said, and then almost immediately pulled the sides of her mouth down.

Roger raised his eyebrows.

Mary-Ann gave him a small smile, leaned forward to switch on the speaker-phone.

"Professor Prins, it's Mary-Ann here. What can I do for you?"

Roger's eyebrows crept even higher up his forehead.

"Mary-Ann?" A short silence ensued. "Is that you? I was told to phone the CEO of International Wildlife Limited." His voice sounded hollow over the speaker-phone.

"That's me, Professor," she replied. "Your application to act as a formally-appointed consultant to the company has been agreed to by the board, at the retainer you asked for. That decision, however, is subject to my final approval. Do you still want the position?"

Again a short silence. Roger wondered if he had just heard a soft sigh come over the speaker-phone.

"Yes, Mary-Ann," the Professor said heavily. "It's the most exciting project I've ever come across. I must have that position."

"Excellent! Then I approve it now. Welcome aboard. Your knowledge of wildlife will be invaluable to us. Oh, and there's one other thing."

"Yes?" the Professor said cautiously.

"My South African publisher, Monty Cohen, spoke to me. I believe you got your guarantee money back. I've been meaning to thank you for getting my book published. Because it was such a runaway success the British publishers want another – in a sense, a sequel. I don't have the time, but I recommended you to them."

"Why me?"

"Because you're the best man for the job."

"What did they say?"

"They agreed, but they've set a few conditions."

This time Roger *knew* he had heard a sigh come over the speaker-phone.

"What are these conditions, Mary-Ann?"

"Professor," she said deliberately. "The job is to be done under my supervision. Both our names are to appear as the authors of the work. And mine has to come first because it's the name the public will recognise."

This time the silence seemed to stretch forever and after a while Roger began to wonder if the connection had been broken. Then another sigh sounded over the air.

"Yes," the Professor said at last. "I will do it."

*

Deep in the valley, formed when a mountain range had been ripped asunder by gigantic forces aeons ago, a lioness, bearing a deep and vicious scar that ran from shoulder to flank on her right side, stretched her neck and yawned a cavernous pink-throated gape.

Shaded from the dry heat of the African sun by an acacia knobthorn tree, she watched lazily as the very dark shape of the young male cub, in a mopane bush nearby, backed into ever-deeper shadow. This one wasn't like its brothers and sisters who instinctively would have chosen a yellower, dappled shadow for camouflage.

Trial and error had been a demanding teacher but had had a willing pupil.

The young male cub was trembling with anticipation as its prey stepped out of the mopane scrub on the far side of the small clearing. The small very dark shape crouched down, making itself even smaller and even less obvious, and then invisible as it became part of the black shadows. The dappled yellow prey, equally small, poised, one soft paw raised, swinging its head from side to side, suspecting something. After a while, it relaxed and trotted forward across the clearing toward the lioness.

Suddenly, and without warning, the black cub launched itself out of the mopane bush, hurtled forward to land crashing on the yellow cub's back, a front paw wrapped around the yellow cub's muzzle. Tumbling down the gentle grass-covered slope the two cubs growled ferociously at each other as they practised that which they would have to one day do in deadly earnest as part of an irresistible instinct to survive.

THE END

AFTERWORD

A start has been made towards Mary-Ann's dream.

Progress has been slow but on 9 December 2002 in Xai-Xai, Mozambique, the Presidents of South Africa, Zimbabwe and Mozambique signed the Great Limpopo Transfrontier Park agreement with to view to joining the Kruger (South Africa), Gaza (Mozambique) and Gonarezhou (Zimbabwe) game reserves into one giant transnational park. The cost of creating the over 35,000 sq km park (almost the size of Switzerland) was estimated at (USA dollars) $43 million.

A meeting between two men, concerning the development of transfrontier parks, helped put flesh on the bones of the idea. They were former, and first democratically-elected, South African President, and Nobel Peace Prize winner, Nelson Mandela, and Anton Rupert, the billionaire founder of both the Rembrandt Group and Peace Parks, an organisation set up to promote cross border parks.

"Enlarged parks allow a more natural pattern of migration," said Irma Engelbrecht, spokesperson for Peace Parks. While Stefan Coetzee, a director of Peace Parks said, "If the elephant walking in the veld (bush) can't pay for itself, in 10 years it won't be there."

Keith Cooper, the conservation director of the Wildlife and Environment Society of SA. added, "All conservation institutions are experiencing funding problems and have to find innovative ways to ensure sustainable development and ways to remain in business."

Clearly the new management of the National Parks Board which controls Kruger agreed. Sites were allocated to private investors for the building of luxury accommodation as well as the outsourcing of restaurants, retail shops and picnic sites.

Helping to avoid a cull, at least 1,000 elephants were shipped from Kruger in South Africa to Gaza in Mozambique.

Mary-Ann would have been proud to have been part of all this.

AUTHOR'S NOTE

In order to simplify the narrative flow some liberties have been taken with the way discipline was maintained in the South African Defence Force, and, indirectly, with command structures, in both the South African Defence Force and the Mozambican Military; but they were there at the time and they operated largely as depicted and their ranks and equipment were as described. The actual soldiers and airmen are, however, entirely a product of my imagination.

The historical context is correct as best my research can make it and that includes the major political figures who were in situ at that time. Where the – very few – players who are still alive may have objected to the words put into their mouths fictional characters have been substituted in their places.

None of this makes the politics of the day, whether with respect to Russia, USA, Mozambique, Zimbabwe, UK and South Africa, any less accurate, again as best my research can make it.

In the early 1980's the Bank of Credit and Commerce International – or BCCI – was already under suspicion as having being expressly set up to facilitate, inter alia, money laundering. By the mid 1980's an undercover agent from the United States Treasury Department had already infiltrated, and was operating, at the highest levels of the bank.

BCCI did, illegally, take over an American Bank allegedly for the purpose of laundering drug money.

Whether rumours had started to float around the banking halls of Zurich by the mid 1980's is open to conjecture. What is without question is that all branches of the bank around the world were finally closed down in the early 1990's, but by then individual sovereign banking jurisdictions had already put in place their own measures to try and contain the fallout of the world's biggest banking scandal.

For the sake of fictional continuity certain CITES decisions have been allocated to the 5th COP meeting of CITES held in Argentina, instead of the 6th COP meeting held in Switzerland.

There *are* major coal reserves in the Kruger National Park but the environment is protected from exploitation of those coal fields by national legislation. In any event, it would now appear as though fracking, much further south, supplemented by sustainable green energy initiatives, is more likely to take centre stage as regards South Africa's future energy needs.

So the game reserve should be safe.

Did you enjoy this book?

Then you might enjoy the author's *A Shadow On The Sea*.

"Red on the surface changes colour at depth and thin green streamers wavered away from where the spear had entered his side. Small fish darted in to nose at the rapidly diffusing blood. Then he almost stopped moving altogether, floating up against the ripped steel, his fins twitching nervously …"

Murder, kidnap, rape, theft …

How much will Nigel Ryan and his friends have to endure because he stumbled across a secret he wasn't meant to have?

Who among them will end up paying the ultimate price?

When does he start to fight back?

But identifying the real enemy to go up against turns out to be the biggest problem of all …

A Shadow On The Sea is available as an ebook and in paperback through many fine stores, including Amazon and Barnes & Noble.